Praise for the novels of #1 *New York Times* bestselling author Debbie Macomber

"Macomber's assured storytelling and affirming narrative is as welcoming as your favorite easy chair."
—*Publishers Weekly* on *Twenty Wishes*

"Macomber's endearing characters offer courage and support to one another and find hope and love in the most unexpected places."
—*Booklist* on *204 Rosewood Lane*

"It's clear that Debbie Macomber cares deeply about her fully realized characters and their family, friends and loves, along with their hopes and dreams. She also makes her readers care about them."
—*Bookreporter.com* on *Susannah's Garden*

"Macomber is a master storyteller."
—*RT Book Reviews*

"Macomber spins another pure-from-the-heart romance giddy with love and warm laughter."
—*Bookpage* on *The Snow Bride*

"Popular romance author Debbie Macomber has a gift for evoking the emotions that are at the heart of the genre's popularity."
—*Publishers Weekly*

"Debbie Macomber writes characters who are as warm and funny as your best friends."
—*New York Times* bestselling author Susan Wiggs

Dear Friends,

Early in my writing career, I met a reader named Ginny Manning. She was a special woman, raised in (believe it or not) a jailhouse in eastern Washington, not far from my hometown of Yakima. She liked my books and encouraged me as a writer. I occasionally met with her over the next few years, and when I decided to write a series of books revolving around a large family, I called that family Manning, after my friend Ginny. The Manning Family series, five books in all, together with a sixth connected story, delighted my friend, who took great pride in the fact that I'd chosen her name.

Ginny came to visit me about eight years ago, and she was as spirited as I remembered. She was a bit slower—she was in her eighties, after all—but it was the same wonderful Ginny. Just a couple of weeks later, one of her sons wrote to tell me his mother had been diagnosed with cancer. She died shortly thereafter, and I realized she'd come to tell me goodbye.

It gives me great pleasure to see the Manning Family books reissued again. These first two, *The Cowboy's Lady* and *The Sheriff Takes a Wife*, feature the Manning sisters. The books, originally published in 1990, were refreshed and updated several years ago—but Russ Palmer and his friend Sheriff Cody Franklin are still as opinionated (and traditional!) as ever in their views. It takes two Manning women to show these cowboys the light. Watch for the next two volumes, *The Manning Brides* and *The Manning Grooms*, which will be coming soon. I know my friend Ginny would be pleased to see new readers discovering "her" stories.

I invite you to enter the world of Montana men and Manning women!

Debbie Macomber

PS: I love to hear from readers! You can reach me at debbiemacomber.com, via Facebook or P.O. Box 1458, Port Orchard, WA 98366.

DEBBIE MACOMBER

The Manning Sisters

MIRA

ISBN-13: 978-0-7783-1838-5

The Manning Sisters

Copyright © 2015 by Harlequin Books S.A.

The publisher acknowledges the copyright holder of the individual works as follows:

The Cowboy's Lady
Copyright © 1990 by Debbie Macomber

The Sheriff Takes a Wife
Copyright © 1990 by Debbie Macomber

Recycling programs for this product may not exist in your area.

For questions and comments about the quality of this book, please contact us at CustomerService@Harlequin.com.

www.MIRABooks.com

Printed in U.S.A.

Also by Debbie Macomber

Blossom Street Books

The Shop on Blossom Street
A Good Yarn
Susannah's Garden
Back on Blossom Street
Twenty Wishes
Summer on Blossom Street
Hannah's List
The Knitting Diaries
   "The Twenty-First Wish"
A Turn in the Road

Cedar Cove Books

16 Lighthouse Road
204 Rosewood Lane
311 Pelican Court
44 Cranberry Point
50 Harbor Street
6 Rainier Drive
74 Seaside Avenue
8 Sandpiper Way
92 Pacific Boulevard
1022 Evergreen Place
Christmas in Cedar Cove
   (*5-B Poppy Lane* and
   A Cedar Cove Christmas)
1105 Yakima Street
1225 Christmas Tree Lane

Dakota Series

Dakota Born
Dakota Home
Always Dakota
Buffalo Valley

The Manning Family

The Manning Sisters
The Manning Brides
The Manning Grooms

Christmas Books

A Gift to Last
On a Snowy Night
Home for the Holidays
Glad Tidings
Christmas Wishes
Small Town Christmas
When Christmas Comes
   (now retitled *Trading*
   Christmas)
There's Something About
   Christmas
Christmas Letters
The Perfect Christmas
Choir of Angels
   (*Shirley, Goodness and Mercy,*
   Those Christmas Angels and
   Where Angels Go)
Call Me Mrs. Miracle

Heart of Texas Series

VOLUME 1
   (*Lonesome Cowboy* and
   Texas Two-Step)
VOLUME 2
   (*Caroline's Child* and
   Dr. Texas)
VOLUME 3
   (*Nell's Cowboy* and
   Lone Star Baby)
Promise, Texas
Return to Promise

Midnight Sons

VOLUME 1
  (*Brides for Brothers* and
  The Marriage Risk)
VOLUME 2
  (*Daddy's Little Helper* and
  Because of the Baby)
VOLUME 3
  (*Falling for Him*,
  Ending in Marriage and
  Midnight Sons and Daughters)

This Matter of Marriage
Montana
Thursdays at Eight
Between Friends
Changing Habits
Married in Seattle
  (*First Comes Marriage* and
  Wanted: Perfect Partner)
Right Next Door
  (*Father's Day* and
  The Courtship of Carol Sommars)
Wyoming Brides
  (*Denim and Diamonds* and
  The Wyoming Kid)
Fairy Tale Weddings
  (*Cindy and the Prince* and
  Some Kind of Wonderful)
The Man You'll Marry
  (*The First Man You Meet* and
  The Man You'll Marry)
Orchard Valley Grooms
  (*Valerie* and *Stephanie*)
Orchard Valley Brides
  (*Norah* and *Lone Star Lovin'*)
The Sooner the Better
An Engagement in Seattle
  (*Groom Wanted* and
  Bride Wanted)
Out of the Rain
  (*Marriage Wanted* and
  Laughter in the Rain)
Learning to Love
  (*Sugar and Spice* and *Love by Degree*)

You...Again
  (*Baby Blessed* and
  Yesterday Once More)
The Unexpected Husband
  (*Jury of His Peers* and
  Any Sunday)
Three Brides, No Groom
Love in Plain Sight
  (*Love 'n' Marriage* and
  Almost an Angel)
I Left My Heart
  (*A Friend or Two* and
  No Competition)
Marriage Between Friends
  (*White Lace and Promises* and
  Friends—And Then Some)
A Man's Heart
  (*The Way to a Man's Heart*
  and *Hasty Wedding*)
North to Alaska
  (*That Wintry Feeling* and
  Borrowed Dreams)
On a Clear Day
  (*Starlight* and
  Promise Me Forever)
To Love and Protect
  (*Shadow Chasing* and
  For All My Tomorrows)
Home in Seattle
  (*The Playboy and the Widow*
  and *Fallen Angel*)
Together Again
  (*The Trouble with Caasi* and
  Reflections of Yesterday)
The Reluctant Groom
  (*All Things Considered*
  and *Almost Paradise*)
A Real Prince
  (*The Bachelor Prince*
  and *Yesterday's Hero*)
Private Paradise
  (in *That Summer Place*)

Debbie Macomber's
  Cedar Cove Cookbook
Debbie Macomber's
  Christmas Cookbook

CONTENTS

THE COWBOY'S LADY

To Merrily Boone
Friend
Title Finder
Speller of Impossible Words
Discoverer of Great Restaurants

One

Everyone in Cougar Point, Montana, knew the bowling alley had the best breakfast in town. For a buck ninety-five they served up eggs, sausage, hash browns and toast, plus all the coffee a body could drink. Russ Palmer was hungrier than a bear in springtime, but food wasn't the only thing on his mind.

He wanted company—of the female variety.

"Mornin', Russ," Mary Andrews, the lone waitress, called out when he walked into the restaurant. Her greeting was followed by a chorus from several other ranchers.

Russ removed his black Stetson and hooked it on the peg by the door. Although it was only a few days into September, the air was decidedly cool and he'd worn his blanket-lined denim jacket.

Sliding into the booth with a couple of friends, Russ picked up the tail end of what Bill Shepherd was saying.

"Pretty as a picture."

Russ's interest was instantly piqued. "Who?"

"The new schoolteacher, Taylor Manning," Harry Donovan answered eagerly. At twenty-three Harry still had the peach-faced immaturity of youth and fine, blond hair he couldn't seem to control.

A schoolteacher. Russ's curiosity level fell several notches. "Taylor's a funny name for a woman," he muttered, reaching for the menu, which was tucked between the sugar container and the salt and pepper shakers.

"The missus and I met her yesterday," Bill went on to say. "She rented old man Halloran's place on the edge of town."

Russ nodded as he scanned the menu. He ordered the "special" every Saturday morning, but he liked to see what was offered in case something else struck his fancy.

"She moved here from Seattle," Harry informed Russ enthusiastically.

"Then she's a city girl," Russ said, and a hint of sarcasm slipped into his voice. The kid had it bad. Personally Russ didn't hold out much hope of the new teacher sticking it out past Christmas. Seattle was known for its mild climate. At best Taylor Manning could deal with four or five days of drizzle, but he'd bet his ranch and five hundred head of cattle that she had no idea what a Montana winter could be like.

"Whether she's a city slicker or not, I couldn't rightly say," Harry said with no lack of fervor, "but I can tell you one thing. She's real pretty. I swear she's got the bluest eyes I've ever seen and dark, silky hair that falls to about here." He gestured with his hand to a point well below his shoulder blades. "A man could see himself running his fingers through hair that soft," he said dreamily. Pink tinged Harry's cheeks as he stopped abruptly and cast a self-conscious look at his two friends.

Russ laughed outright. "Hell, Harry, she hasn't even been in town a week and already you're sweet on her."

"I can't help myself." Harry grabbed his mug so fast he nearly spilled his coffee. "Wait until you meet her yourself, then you'll know what I mean."

"I'm not going to be mooning over any schoolmarm," Russ told the two men. He hadn't gotten to the age of thirty-four safely unmarried only to be taken in by the charms of a citified schoolteacher. Especially one Harry Donovan would fantasize about.

Bill and Harry exchanged glances, then Harry snickered loudly, apparently amused by Russ's attitude. "You just wait till you see her yourself," he said again.

"What do you mean I can't use my American Express card here?" Taylor Manning demanded of the clerk at the small store. "I could use this card in Kodiak, Alaska!"

"I'm really sorry," the older woman said, "but as far as I know, no one in town takes American Express."

Shaking her head, Taylor pulled her Visa card from her wallet and set it on the counter. "I'll use this one instead." She pushed her chocolate-brown hair over her shoulder and looked around. This situation was becoming embarrassing. Taylor had used her meager savings to rent the house. She'd gone shopping for some kitchen things she was going to need, thinking she could use her credit card and pay for them when it was more convenient.

She was grateful there were only two other people in the store. A cowboy and his daughter. No, Taylor decided on second thought. The teenage girl was too old to be his daughter, but too young to be his girlfriend.

"I'm very sorry, but we don't take Visa, either."

"You don't take Visa," Taylor echoed in shocked disbelief. "*Everyone* takes Visa."

"No one in Cougar Point," the woman said apologetically.

Taylor smiled blandly. "Then what *do* you take?"

"Cash would work."

Taylor rummaged through her purse, drawing out a

checkbook. She studied the meager balance and sighed inwardly. "I don't suppose you take out-of-state checks, do you? Don't answer that," she said quickly. "Anyone who doesn't honor American Express or Visa isn't going to take a check from a Seattle bank." She stared down at the few items longingly and made her decision. "I'll simply put everything back and wait until the checks come through from my new account." She'd also have to wait until she'd deposited her first pay two weeks from now, but she didn't feel announcing that was necessary.

"I'm really sorry, miss."

Taylor nodded. "No problem," she murmured, and even managed a respectable smile. She turned, nearly colliding with the cowboy she'd noticed earlier.

"Oh, sorry," she said, slipping past him.

"Just a minute. Did I hear you mention Seattle?" His voice was deep and masculine. Without giving her a chance to respond, he added, "You wouldn't happen to be Taylor Manning, would you?"

"Yes. How'd you know?" Not that she should be surprised. Folks had been introducing themselves all week, telling her how pleased they were that she'd accepted the teaching assignment in their town.

Setting his black Stetson farther back on his head, the rancher explained. "The kid mentioned something about you this morning over breakfast."

"The kid?"

"Harry Donovan."

Taylor didn't recall meeting any youngster by that name, but there'd been so many names and so many faces that she'd long since lost track.

The cowboy smiled, and their eyes held for a moment. His reaction hinted at curiosity, but for her part, Taylor had no feelings one way or the other. Oh, he was good-looking enough. His head was covered with a crisp black Stetson; all the men in town seemed to wear them. His dark hair curled along the nape of his sun-bronzed neck as if he'd delayed getting a haircut a couple of weeks too long. He was tall, easily six-three, and he wore tight-fitting blue jeans and a plaid shirt beneath a thick denim jacket.

"Mabel," the rancher said, looking past Taylor. "This is the new schoolteacher."

"Well, for goodness' sake, miss, why didn't you come right out and say so?" Without a second's delay the clerk reached beneath the counter and brought out a tablet and started listing the items Taylor had wanted to purchase.

"Does this mean you'll accept my American Express? My Visa? My check?"

"No, I feel bad about that, but most of the commercial people in these parts don't do credit card business with those big banks. I'll just write down these items here and send you a bill at the end of the month the way I do with most folks."

"But...you don't know me." The woman hadn't so much as requested identification.

Mabel waved her hand, dismissing Taylor's concern. "I feel terrible about this."

Taylor turned her gaze to the cowboy once more. "Thank you."

He touched the brim of his hat in a quick salute and started down the aisle toward the younger girl.

While Mabel was writing up the sale, Taylor watched the exchange at the rear of the store. The teenager was standing beside a cosmetic display, gesturing wildly.

"If you could just sign here," Mabel instructed, turning the tablet around for Taylor. "I can't tell you how pleased we are that you've come to Cougar Point. There won't be much of a social life for you, but we have our moments."

"Yes, I know," Taylor murmured. She hadn't accepted this teaching assignment because of the potential night-life. She'd specifically chosen the backwoods of Montana in an effort to give herself the necessary time to heal after her disastrous affair with Mark Brooks. She'd moved to Cougar Point so she could immerse herself in her chosen profession—and deal with the bitterness of losing Mark. Next year she'd leave Cougar Point again, rejuvenated and whole. Her family, especially her father, had assumed she'd taken this job on impulse, and although her actions were often spontaneous, for once her father was wrong. The decision to spend a year in Montana had been well thought out, the pros and cons carefully weighed. She was taking this time to mend a badly broken heart, hoping twelve months in the country would do what six months in the city hadn't.

"I want a second opinion," the teenager cried as she rushed toward the front of the store. "Excuse me," she said brightly, holding out her hand. "I'm Mandy Palmer and this is my brother, Russ, who happens to be obstinate and stubborn and completely unreasonable and—"

"Mandy," Russ threatened in a voice few would challenge, "I said no."

"That's just too bad," the girl returned. Tears glistened in her green eyes. She was petite and very pretty, and wore her thick blond hair in a long French braid. It swayed when she jerked her head toward her brother.

"Mandy," Russ threatened again.

The girl ignored him with a defiant tilt of her chin and looked at Taylor. "When a girl's fourteen years old and going into her first year of high school, she's old enough to wear a little makeup, isn't she?"

"Uh…" Taylor hesitated. Mandy was staring at her with imploring eyes while her brother glared heatedly, silently demanding that Taylor mind her own business. "What does your mother say?"

"Our parents are dead," Russ said gruffly. "I'm Mandy's legal guardian and I say she's too young to be painting her face with all that garbage. She's only fourteen!"

"Were you wearing makeup when *you* were my age?" Mandy asked Taylor, the appeal in her eyes desperate.

"A little," Taylor admitted reluctantly. She clutched her purchases tightly, not wanting to get caught in the middle of this family fight.

"Mascara?"

"Yes," Taylor confessed.

"Blush?"

Taylor nodded, ignoring the fierce scowl being directed at her by the girl's brother.

"How about lip gloss?"

"I was wearing that in junior high," Taylor said, gaining a bit more confidence. In Taylor's opinion—although it clearly wasn't wanted or appreciated by the male faction here—Mandy should be allowed to experiment with a little makeup.

"See," the girl said enthusiastically. "And you turned out to be a fine, upstanding citizen, didn't you? I mean a little lip gloss at fourteen didn't automatically turn you into a…a lady of the night, did it?"

Taylor couldn't help laughing; that was the most ridiculous thing she'd ever heard. "No. But it was close. It all started with too much mascara, followed by blue eye shadow. Before I realized what I was doing, I was into perfumes." She hesitated and lowered her voice to a whisper. "The French kind."

Mandy gasped for effect.

Taylor didn't hide a smug smile as she continued. "From there it was a natural descent. I found myself standing on street corners…"

"It's time to go," Russ ordered. He gave Taylor a look that could have curdled milk. "We've heard more than enough."

Still amused, Taylor left the store. She sure hadn't made a friend of the rancher, but Russ was being too strict with his younger sister. It wasn't like her to take sides in something that didn't involve her, but his attitude had struck a familiar chord. Taylor's own father was often hard-nosed and outdated in his views. More than once the two of them had fought over the most ridiculous issues. If her mother hadn't been there to run interference, Taylor didn't know what would have happened. The crazy part was, she thought the world of her father. They could argue until the cows came home, but that never dampened the deep affection they shared.

Till the cows came home! Taylor paused midstep. Good grief, she was already beginning to think like a cowgirl. If this was the way she sounded after ten days, heaven only knew what she'd be like in a year's time.

Taylor was walking to her car when she ran into Mary Beth Morgan, another teacher. They'd met earlier in the week during a staff meeting. Mary Beth was in her mid-fifties, friendly and a country girl through and through. She was the type of woman who personified everything good about small towns.

"You're looking pleased about something."

Taylor nodded. "I just met Russ and Mandy Palmer. They were debating whether Mandy's old enough to wear makeup and somehow I got stuck in the middle. That man is certainly opinionated."

"Mandy can give as good as she gets. I once heard

Russ say that even Napoleon couldn't stand up to Mandy when she truly wanted something."

That seemed like a comment the cowboy would make and, despite herself, Taylor discovered she was smiling.

"Russ has a good heart, so don't judge him too harshly," Mary Beth said as they strolled down the sidewalk together. "He's raising Mandy on his own and genuinely cares about her. His views may be kind of outdated, but he tries hard to be fair."

"What happened to their parents?"

"Actually Mandy's his half sister. Russ's mother ran off when he was a toddler. I doubt Russ even remembers her. Fred Palmer took his wife's leaving really hard. I'm sure there are two sides to that story, though. Fred could be ornery and was as pigheaded as they come."

"Russ must take after his father then."

"He does," Mary Beth said, missing Taylor's joke. "Most folks around here would rather tangle with a grizzly bear than mess with Russ when he's in one of his moods. I suppose that has a lot to do with his living all these years without a woman's influence. Once Betty died…"

"Betty must be Mandy's mother?"

"Right. To everyone's surprise, Fred up and married again. Betty was the sweetest thing, and just the right kind of woman for someone like Fred. She was sweet and kindhearted and as good as the day is long. Mandy arrived a year later.

"Fred and Betty were happy. I don't think there was a dry eye in town when she died. Not long afterward Fred died, too. The doctors may have a complicated name for what killed him, but I'll tell you right now, Fred Palmer died of a broken heart."

"How sad." The humor drained from Taylor. No one could be unaffected by that story.

"Russ reminds me of his father when Fred was around that age. What Russ needs is a wife—someone like Betty who'll cater to his whims and pamper him and let him have his way."

That left her out. The thought startled her. She would no more consider marrying a rancher than she'd entertain the idea of riding a horse. As far as she was concerned, cows smelled, hay made her sneeze, and the sight of a horse sent her scurrying in the opposite direction.

"I'm sure if Russ said anything offensive…"

"He didn't," Taylor was quick to assure the other woman. But not because he didn't want to, judging by the look in his eyes. If ever there was a man who longed to put her in her place, it was this formidable rancher. Unfortunately, or fortunately as the case might be, it would take a lot more than one cowpoke to do it.

Mary Beth and Taylor said goodbye at the corner, and Taylor went to the grocery store. With a limited budget and a distinct lack of imagination when it came to cooking, she headed for the frozen food section.

Without much enthusiasm she tossed a frozen entrée into her grocery cart. The local supermarket didn't carry a large selection, and it was either the salisbury steak or the country fried chicken.

"Was that really necessary?" a gruff male voice asked from behind her.

"The country fried chicken?" she asked, turning to face the very man she and Mary Beth had been discussing.

"I'm not talking about your pathetic choice for dinner. I'm referring to my sister. She's going through a rebellious stage, and I don't appreciate your taking her side on an issue. We can settle our differences without any help from you."

Taylor was about to argue when she noticed the teenager coming down the aisle.

"Oh, hi," Mandy greeted her, brightening. She hurried to Taylor and her brother. "You're not eating that for dinner, are you?" the girl asked, eyeing the frozen meal in Taylor's cart. A horrified look spread across her face.

"It seemed the least amount of trouble," Taylor admitted. She'd spent a full day unpacking and cleaning, and even a frozen dinner was more appealing than being forced to cook for herself. As far as she could see, there wasn't a single fast-food place in town. The nearest McDonald's was a hundred miles from Cougar Point.

"I've got a big pot of stew simmering at home," Mandy said eagerly. "Why don't you come over and have dinner with Russ and me? We'd love to have you, wouldn't we, Russ?"

Her brother's hesitation was just long enough to convey his message.

"It's the neighborly thing to do," Mandy prompted.

"You're welcome to come, if you want," Russ said finally, and Taylor had the impression it took a great deal of resolve to echo his sister's invitation.

There wasn't any question that Taylor should refuse. But something perverse in her, something obstinate and a bit foolish, wouldn't allow her to do so. Perhaps it was because she recognized the same mulish streak in him that she knew so well in her father. Whatever the reason, Taylor decided she was going to enjoy this dinner. "Why, thank you. I'd be honored."

"Great." Mandy beamed. "We live about ten miles east of town."

"East?" Taylor repeated, turning in a full circle in an

effort to orient herself. She wasn't sure which way was east, at least not from where she was standing in the grocery store.

"Take the main road and go left at the stand of syca-more trees," Mandy continued. "That's just past Cole Creek, only don't look for any water because it's dried out at this time of year."

Further directions only served to confuse Taylor. She wasn't even all that confident she could tell a sycamore from an oak. And how was she supposed to identify a dried-out creek bed? Usually Taylor was given directions that said she should go to the third stoplight and take a left at the Wal-Mart.

"Why don't you ride along with us?" Mandy suggested next, apparently sensing Taylor's confusion. "Russ can drive you back into town later."

"It'll probably work better if I follow you," Taylor said. "My car's at the house, but it would only take a minute for me to swing by and get it."

"It wouldn't be any trouble. Russ has to come back, anyway. Besides, I wouldn't want you to get lost once it turns dark."

Taylor noted that Russ didn't echo his sister's sugges-tion. The temptation was too great to ignore, and once more Taylor found herself agreeing to Mandy's plan.

"My truck's parked outside," Russ grumbled. He didn't seem very pleased by this turn of events. But then he hadn't looked all that thrilled about anything from the moment they'd met.

Russ's truck was a twenty-year-old dented Ford that most folks would have hauled to the scrap heap a year earlier. The bed was filled with supplies. Grain sacks were stacked in one corner, fertilizer in another.

The front fender was badly bent and had begun to rust.

The license plate was missing, and Russ had to completely remove the passenger door for the two women to climb inside. Once they were seated he replaced the door and latched it shut.

Taylor squirmed around in the bench seat, searching for the seat belt.

"There aren't any," Russ explained as he slipped in next to her and started the engine.

The seat was cramped, and Taylor had to dig her elbows into her ribs. Her shoulders were touching his on the left side, his younger sister's on the right. It had been a long time since Taylor had sat this close to a man. At first she tried to keep her thigh from grazing his, but it was nearly impossible. So their thighs touched. Big deal.

Only it soon got to be.

There must've been something in all that fresh country air that was adversely affecting her brain cells. Without much difficulty, Taylor could actually imagine herself smitten with this man. *Smitten?* Oh dear, her mind was doing it again, tormenting her with this old-fashioned country jargon....

Suddenly they turned off the main road and headed down a lengthy rut-filled section that tossed her up and then down. Every time they hit a dip, Taylor would bounce off the seat as if it were greased. It was all she could do not to land on top of Russ or Mandy. They were obviously accustomed to this thrashing about, and each managed to stay neatly in place. Taylor, on the other hand, was all over the inside of the cab.

Whenever the truck hit an uneven patch, some part of Taylor's anatomy came into intimate contact with Russ's. Their thighs stroked each other. Their shoulders collided and their waists jostled together. Again and again their bodies were slammed against each other.

Taylor couldn't help noticing how firm and muscular Russ felt. She didn't want to acknowledge it. Nor did she want to experience the heat of his body and the warm muskiness of his skin. He felt solid. Strong. Virile. A host of sensations, long dormant, sprang to life inside her.

Not once had Russ Palmer purposely touched her, and yet Taylor felt as though his hands had caressed her everywhere.

"Would you mind slowing down?" she cried. She hated having to ask.

"Why?" Russ asked, his voice filled with amusement.

"Russ," Mandy snapped, "Taylor's not used to this."

Amused or not, Russ slowed the vehicle, and Taylor went weak with relief. She could feel a headache coming on, but she wasn't sure it had anything to do with the skipping, hopping and jumping she'd been subjected to for the past ten minutes.

They arrived at the ranch house a couple of minutes later, at just about dusk. The first thing Taylor noticed was the huge red barn. It was the largest she'd ever seen, but that wasn't saying much. She knew next to nothing about barns, although this one seemed enormous. The house was sizable, as well. Four gables stood out against the roof of the huge white structure, and the windows were framed by bright red shutters.

Taylor climbed out of the truck on the driver's side after Russ, not wanting to be trapped inside while he walked around to remove the passenger door. It took her a minute to steady her legs.

Mandy bolted ahead of them. She raced up the back steps that led into the kitchen, holding open the door for Taylor. "The stew's in the Crock-Pot."

Taylor saw that Russ had gone in the opposite direction, toward the barn, probably to see about unloading the contents of the truck bed. Her gaze followed him, and she wondered briefly if the close confines of the truck had affected him the same way they had her. Probably not. He looked a lot more in control of himself than Taylor felt.

A thin sheen of perspiration moistened her upper lip. What the hell was the matter with her? Groaning silently, Taylor closed her eyes. She knew precisely what was wrong, and she didn't like it one bit.

Two

Russ remained silent for most of the meal. He didn't like this schoolteacher. But he didn't exactly dislike her, either. She was as pretty as Harry had claimed, and her hair was thick and rich. A couple of times he'd been tempted to lift a strand and let it slip through his fingers, but that would've been impossible. And what she did to a pair of jeans ought to be illegal. On the ride to the ranch he'd purposely driven over every pothole he could just because he liked the way her body had moved against his.

"You're from Seattle?" Russ asked. He'd been trying to ignore her for most of the meal, not because he wasn't interested in learning what he could about her, but because—dammit—he was as taken with her as Harry had been.

Taylor nodded, smiling. "I was born and raised in the shadow of the Space Needle."

"Ever had snow there?"

"Some."

The thought of her smooth pale skin exposed to the elements knotted his stomach.

"I understand winters are harsher here than in western Washington," she said stiffly. "I came prepared."

"I doubt that you have a clue how severe winters can get in these parts." Russ had seen too many cases of frostbite to have any illusions.

It was clear that Taylor resented the way he was talking to her. He didn't mean to imply that she was stupid, only unaware, and he didn't want her learning harsh lessons because no one had warned her.

One quick look told him he'd raised Taylor's hackles. She seemed to need several minutes to compose her response, then she set her fork next to her plate, placed her elbows on the table and joined her hands. Staring directly at him, she smiled with deceptive warmth and said, "You needn't worry, Mr. Palmer. I'm perfectly capable of taking care of myself. I've been doing so for many years. I may be a city girl, but let me assure you, I'm both intelligent and resourceful."

"Do you know what happens to skin when it's exposed to temperatures below thirty degrees? How about the symptoms for hypothermia? Would you be able to recognize them in yourself or others?"

"Mr. Palmer, please."

"Russ." Mandy's outraged eyes shot from him to Taylor and then back again. "You're being rude to our guest."

Russ mumbled under his breath and resumed eating. Maybe he was overreacting. Perhaps his motives weren't so lily-white. Perhaps he was more angry with her than concerned about her welfare. She'd certainly done enough to upset him in the past few hours. Taking Mandy's side on that makeup issue had bothered him, but that hardly mattered after the way she'd pressed herself against him during the ride from town. He couldn't get the feel of her out of his mind. Her skin was soft and she smelled like wildflowers. That thought led to another. If she smelled so good, he couldn't help wondering how she'd taste.

Like honey, he decided, fresh from the comb, thick and sweet. The knot in his stomach tightened. If he didn't curb his mind soon, he'd end up kissing her before the night was through.

"You're an excellent cook," Taylor said to Mandy in a blatant effort to lighten the strained atmosphere.

Mandy beamed at the compliment. "I try. Rosa and her husband retired last year, and I talked Russ into letting me do the cooking, and it's worked out pretty well, hasn't it, Russ?"

He nodded. "There've been a few nights best forgotten, but for the most part you've done an excellent job."

"She took over all the cooking at age thirteen?" Taylor asked, obviously astonished, although Russ had trouble figuring out why. He'd long suspected that city kids didn't carry anywhere near the responsibility country kids did.

Mandy eyed Russ. He knew that look well by now, and it meant trouble. He bit his tongue as she opened her mouth to speak.

"It seems to me that any girl who can rustle up a decent meal every night is old enough to buy her own clothes without her older brother tagging along, don't you think?"

The way things were going, Mandy was angling to be sent to her room without finishing dinner. "That's none of Taylor's concern," he said tightly, daring their guest to challenge his authority with his younger sister.

"You agree with me, don't you, Taylor?" Mandy pressed.

"Uh…" Taylor hedged, looking uncomfortable. "I have a limit of answering only one leading question per day," she explained, reaching for another piece of bread. "I don't think it's a good idea to get on Russ's bad side twice in only a few hours. I might end up walking back to town."

"Russ would never do that."

Want to bet? Russ mused. Okay, so he wouldn't make her walk, but he'd sure as hell hit every pothole he could. The problem there was that he'd be the one likely to suffer most.

"What do you honestly think?" Mandy repeated.

"*I* think you should eat your dinner and leave Taylor out of this," Russ ordered harshly. The girl had turned willfulness into an art form.

"I… Your brother's right, Mandy," Taylor said, lowering her gaze to the steaming bowl of rich stew. "This is something the two of you should settle between yourselves."

"Russ and I'll settle it all right," Mandy responded defiantly, "but he won't like the outcome."

Russ didn't take the bait. "More stew, Taylor?"

"Ah…no, thanks. My bowl's nearly full."

"When did you start buying your own clothes?" Mandy asked, clearly unwilling to drop the issue.

Russ stared at Taylor, daring her to question his authority a second time. She glanced nervously away. "As I recall, I had the same problem with my father at this age. I got around him by taking a sewing class and making my clothes."

"When was this?"

"Oh, about the eighth grade or so. To this day I enjoy sewing most of my own things. It's economical, too."

"The eighth grade?" Mandy cast Russ a triumphant look. "You were basically choosing and sewing your own clothes when you were only thirteen, then."

"It's not a good idea for me to get involved in a matter

that's between you and your brother, Mandy. I did earlier and I don't think it was the right thing to do."

Russ felt a little better knowing that.

Mandy's shoulders sagged, and Russ was pleased to note that she was gracious enough to accept Taylor's word. Finally.

"I didn't mean to cause such a scene in the variety store," Mandy murmured apologetically. "All I wanted was Russ's okay to buy some lip gloss."

Russ set his napkin on the table. "I wouldn't mind letting you wear some lip gloss, but you insist on overdoing it. I walked past your bedroom the other night and I swear your lips were glowing in the dark."

Mandy glared at him, her eyes filled with indignation. What had he said *now*? Before he could ask her what was so all-fired insulting, she threw her fork and napkin onto the table and promptly rushed out of the room.

"Amanda Palmer, get back here this minute," he shouted in the same steely tone that sent his men scurrying to obey. When Mandy didn't immediately comply, he stormed to his feet, ready to follow her.

"Russ," Taylor said softly, stopping him. He turned toward her, wanting to blame her for this latest display of pique.

Taylor sighed and pushed aside her bowl. "Give her a few minutes. She'll be back once she's composed herself."

"What did I say?" he demanded, sitting back down, genuinely perplexed.

Taylor hesitated, then said, "It might've had something to do with the joke about her lips glowing in the dark."

"It's true. I told her she couldn't wear any of that war paint you women are so fond of, so she defied me and started putting it on before she went to bed."

"She's exercising her rights as a person."

"By spurning my rules? I swear that girl drives me to the edge of insanity. What's gotten into her the past couple of years? She used to be an all-right kid. Now it seems I can't say a word without setting her off."

"She's a teenager."

"What's that supposed to mean?" he barked.

"Don't you remember what you felt like at fourteen? How important it was to dress and act like everyone around you?"

"No," Russ stated flatly. His features tensed. He didn't want to discuss his sister with Taylor. She didn't know any more about raising kids than he did. The problem with Mandy was that she was getting too big for her britches.

Standing, Taylor reached for her bowl and glass. "I'll clear the table."

"Leave it for Mandy," Russ insisted.

Taylor ignored him, which was getting to be a habit with her. Russ had yet to understand what it was about women that made them constantly want to challenge him—especially in his own home.

"Why?" Taylor demanded, startling him out of his reverie. Even more astonishing was the fact that she looked angry.

"Why what?"

"Why would you want to leave the dishes for Mandy?"

"Because that's woman's work," he explained.

"You're possibly the worst male chauvinist I've ever encountered," she said, carrying what remained of the plates to the sink. "In my opinion, those who cook shouldn't have to wash dishes."

"It'll be a cold day in hell before you'll ever see me washing dishes, lady." He found the thought comical. He hadn't taken kindly to being called a chauvinist, but he refused to argue with her. They were having enough trouble being civil to each other without further provocation from him.

Taylor hurried to the sink, filling it with hot water and squirting in soap. "Since the task apparently belongs to a woman, I'll do the dishes."

"No guest of mine is washing dirty dishes."

"Fine then," she said, motioning toward the sink. "Everything's ready for you."

Although he was struggling against it, Russ was thoroughly irritated. He was standing directly in front of her. Not more than two inches separated them.

Taylor stared up at him and must have recognized his mood, because she swallowed hard. It wasn't consternation he saw in her eyes, but something that stabbed him as sharply as a pitchfork. Longing and need. The same emotions he'd been battling from the moment he'd laid eyes on her.

He saw something else. She didn't want to experience it any more than Russ wanted to feel the things he'd been feeling for her. When they'd sat next to each other in the truck, he'd never been more profoundly aware of a woman in his life. The air had been alive with tension—a tension that seemed to throb between them all evening long.

Russ felt it.

Taylor felt it.

Both seemed determined to ignore it.

Bracing her hands on the edge of the sink, she anxiously moistened her lips. Russ's eyes fell to her mouth. Her eyes reluctantly met his, and the look they exchanged was as powerful as a caress.

"I... I should be going," she whispered.

"You called me a chauvinist."

"I...apologize." Her pride was obviously crumbling at her feet. The fight had gone out of her.

He pulled his gaze back to her mouth, experiencing a small sense of triumph at the power of his will. "Where'd you ever get a name like Taylor?"

"It was my mother's...maiden name."

Once more her voice came out sounding whispery and soft. Too soft. Too whispery for comfort.

"My mother's from Atlanta, and it was an old Southern tradition to give the first daughter her mother's maiden name." By the time she finished, her voice was a mere thread of sound.

Neither of them spoke for the longest moment of Russ's life. Taking a deep, shaky breath, he was about to suggest he drive her home. Instead, Russ found himself leaning toward her.

"I'm sorry I ran out of the kitchen like that," Mandy announced, coming back into the room.

Russ frowned at his younger sister, irritated. The girl couldn't have chosen a worse time to make her entrance. For her part, Taylor appeared ready to leap across the room and hug Mandy for interrupting them.

"I was about to take Taylor back to town," Russ announced gruffly.

"Do you have to leave so soon?" Mandy asked. "It's barely even dark."

"It'll get dark anytime, and I still have a lot to do before school starts. Thank you so much for having me—both of you. You're a wonderful cook... I really appreciate this."

"You'll come again, won't you?" Mandy asked.

"If you'd like."

"Oh, we would, wouldn't we, Russ?"

He made a response that could have been taken either way.

Mandy walked to the door and down the porch steps with them. Her arms hugged her waist against the evening chill. "You're driving the Lincoln, aren't you?"

Russ gave another noncommittal reply. His truck was in the shop, having the transmission worked on, and he'd been forced to take the older one into town that morning. Mandy's implication that he'd bring Taylor home in that dilapidated thing was an insult. The look he gave her suggested as much.

"I was just asking," she said with an innocent smile.

Taylor and Mandy chatted while Russ went around to the garage and pulled out the luxury sedan. The two women hugged goodbye, and Taylor got inside the car and ran her fingertips over the leather upholstery before snapping the seat belt into place.

"You ready?" he asked more brusquely than he intended.

"Yes."

They drove a few minutes in uncomfortable silence. "How large a spread do you have here?" she eventually asked.

"A thousand acres and about that many head of cattle."

"A thousand acres," Taylor echoed.

The awe and surprise in her voice filled him with pride. He could have gone on to tell her that the Lazy P was anything but lazy. His ranch was among the largest in the southern half of the state. He could also mention that he operated one of the most progressive ranches in the entire country, but he didn't want to sound as if he was bragging.

They chatted amicably about nothing important until they got to town. Russ turned off the side street to old man Halloran's house without even having to ask where Taylor was living. If she was surprised he knew, she didn't say.

When he pulled in to her driveway, he cut the engine and rested his arm over the back of her seat. Part of him wanted her to invite him inside for coffee, but it wasn't coffee that interested him. Another part of him demanded he stay away from this schoolteacher.

"Thank you again," she said softly, staring down at her purse, which she held tightly in her lap.

"No problem."

She raised her eyes to his, and despite all his good intentions, Russ's hungry gaze fixed on her lips. He became aware that he was going to kiss her about the same time he realized he'd die if he didn't. He reached for her, half expecting her to protest. Instead she whimpered and wrapped her arms around him, offering him her mouth. The sense of triumph and jubilation that Russ experienced was stronger than any aphrodisiac. He wrapped her in his arms and dragged her against him, savoring the pure womanly feel of her.

His kiss was wild. His callused hands framed the smooth skin of her face as he slanted his mouth over hers. He kissed her again and again and again.

Her throaty plea reluctantly brought him back to reason. For an instant Russ worried that he'd frightened her, until he heard his name fall from her lips in a low, frantic whisper. It was then that he knew she'd enjoyed their kisses as much as he had.

"Do you want me to stop?" he asked, his voice a husky murmur. He spread damp kisses down her neck and up her chin until he reached her mouth. Drawing her lower lip between his teeth, he sucked gently.

"Please…stop," she pleaded, yet her hands grasped his hair, holding him against her.

But then Taylor lowered her hands to his shoulders and pulled herself away, leaving only an inch or so between them. Her shoulders heaved.

"I can't believe that happened," she whispered.

"Do you want an apology?"

"No," she answered starkly. Then, after a moment, she added, "I wanted it as much as you did. I can't imagine why. We're about as opposite as any two people can get."

"Maybe so, but I think we just discovered one way we're compatible, and it beats the heck out of everything else."

"Oh, please, don't even say that," she moaned, and pushed him away. She leaned against the back of the seat and ran a hand down her face as if to wipe away all evidence of their kissing. "This was a fluke. I think it might be best to pretend it never happened."

Russ went still, his thoughts muddled and unclear. What she'd said was true. He had no business being attracted to her. No business kissing her. She was from the city and didn't understand the complexities of his life. Not only that, she was the new schoolteacher, and not a woman the community would approve of him dallying with.

That they *were* attracted to each other was a given. Why seemed to be a question neither of them could answer. One thing Russ knew: Taylor was right. It was best to forget this ever happened.

For the next week Taylor did an admirable job of pushing Russ Palmer from her mind. It helped somewhat that she didn't have any contact with either member of the Palmer family.

Taylor didn't question what had come over her or why she'd allowed Russ to kiss her like that. Instead she'd resolutely ignored the memory of their kiss, attributing it to a bad case of repressed hormones. That was the only thing it could've been, and analyzing it would accomplish nothing.

Now that school had started, Taylor threw herself into her work with gusto, more convinced than ever that she was born to be a teacher. She was an immediate hit with her third- and fourth-grade students.

On Wednesday afternoon at about four, an hour after her class had been dismissed, Taylor was sitting at her desk, cutting out letters for her bulletin board, when there was a polite knock at her door. Suspecting it was one of her students, she glanced up to discover Mandy standing there, her books pressed against her.

"Mandy, hello," Taylor said, genuinely pleased to see the girl. "Take a seat." She waved the scissors at the chair next to her desk.

"I'm not bothering you, am I? Russ said I wasn't to visit you after school if you were busy. He thinks I'll be a pest."

"You can come and visit me anytime you want," Taylor said, as she continued to cut out blunt letters from the bright sheets of colored paper.

Plopping down on the chair, Mandy crossed her legs and smiled cheerfully. "Notice anything different about me?"

Taylor nodded. "Isn't that war paint you're wearing? And that sweater looks new. Very nice—that light green suits you."

Russ's sister giggled shyly. "I came to thank you. I don't know what you said to my brother, but it worked. The next morning he said he'd thought about it overnight and decided that if I was old enough to cook dinner and wear a little makeup, then I was mature enough to choose my own clothes without him tagging along."

Taylor wasn't convinced that Russ's change of heart had anything to do with her, but nevertheless, she was pleased. "That's great."

"I heard from Cassie Jackson that you're a really good teacher."

Cassie was a fourth-grader in Taylor's class. She smiled at the compliment.

"I hear half the boys in your class are in love with you already," Mandy told her. "I told Russ that, and I think he's a little jealous because he frowned and grabbed the paper and read it for ten minutes before he noticed it was one from last week."

The last person Taylor wanted to discuss was Russ Palmer. "I don't suppose you'd like to help me cut out letters, would you?" she asked, more to change the subject than because she needed any assistance.

"Sure, I'd love to." Within a half hour she and Mandy had assembled a bright brown, yellow and orange autumn leaf bulletin board festooned with the names of every child in the class.

Once they'd finished, Taylor stepped back, threw her arm around her young friend's shoulders and nodded happily. "We do good work."

Mandy grinned. "We do, don't we?"

Noting the time, Taylor felt guilty for having taken up so much of the girl's afternoon. "It's almost five. Do you need me to give you a ride home?"

"That's all right. Russ said he'd pick me up. He's coming into town for grain and I'm supposed to meet him at Burn's Feed Store. It's only a block from here."

Mandy left soon afterward. Taylor gathered up the assignments she needed to grade and her purse and headed toward the school parking lot. Her blue Cabriolet was there all by itself. She was halfway to the car when a loud pickup barreled into the lot behind her. From the sick sounds the truck was making, Taylor knew it had to belong to Russ.

He rolled to a stop, his elbow draped over the side window. "Have you seen Mandy?"

She nodded, her eyes avoiding his. "You just missed her. She's walking over to the feed store."

"Thanks." His gears ground as he switched them, and he looked over his shoulder, about to back out, when he paused. "Is that your car?"

"Yes." Normally Taylor walked to and from school. It was less than a mile and she liked the exercise, but it had been raining that morning, so she'd brought her car.

"Did you know your back tire's flat?"

Taylor's eyes flew to her Cabriolet, and sure enough the rear tire on the driver's side was completely flat. "Oh, great," she moaned. She was tired and hungry and in no mood to deal with this problem.

"I'll change it for you," Russ volunteered, immediately vaulting from his truck.

It was kind of him, and Taylor was about to tell him so when he ruined it.

"You independent women," he said with a chuckle. "You claim you can take care of yourselves and you're too damn proud to think you need a man. But every now and then we have our uses. Now admit it, Taylor. You couldn't possibly handle this without me." He was walking toward her trunk, as haughty as could be.

"Hold it!" Taylor raised one hand. "I don't need you to change my tire. I can take care of this myself."

Russ gave her a patronizing look and then chose to

antagonize her even more. This time he laughed. "Now that's something I'd like to see." He leaned against her fender and crossed his arms over his broad chest. "Feel free," he said, gesturing toward the flat.

"Don't look so smug, Palmer. I said I could take care of it myself and I meant it."

"You wouldn't know one end of the jack from the other."

Taylor wasn't going to argue with him about that. "Would you like to make a small wager on my ability to deal with this?"

Russ snickered, looking more pompous every minute. "It would be like taking candy from a baby. The problem with you is that you're too stubborn to admit when a man's right."

"I say I can deal with a flat tire any day of the week."

"And I say you can't. You haven't got enough strength to turn the tire iron. Fact is, lady, you couldn't get to first base without a man here to help you."

"Oh, come off it. It's about time you men understood that women aren't the weaker sex."

"Sure," Russ said, without disguising his amusement.

"All right," Taylor said slowly. She deliberately walked past him, then turned to give him a sultry smile. She narrowed her eyes. "Perhaps you don't care to place a small wager on my ability. Having to admit you're wrong would probably be more than a guy like you could take."

His dark eyes flared briefly. "I didn't want to do this, but unfortunately you've asked for it. What shall we bet?"

Now that he'd agreed, Taylor wasn't sure. "If I win…"

"I'd be willing to do something I consider women's work?" he suggested.

"Such as?"

Russ took a moment to think it over. "I'll cook dinner for you next Saturday night."

"Who'll do the dishes?"

Russ hesitated. "I will. You thought I'd have trouble going along with that, didn't you? But I don't have a thing to worry about."

"Dream on, Palmer. If I were you, I'd be sweating."

He snickered, seeming to derive a good deal of pleasure from their conversation. "Now let's figure out what you'll owe me when you realize how sadly mistaken you are."

"All right," she said, "I'd be willing to do something you consider completely masculine."

"I'd rather have you grill me a steak."

"No way. That wouldn't be a fair exchange. How about if I...do whatever you do around the ranch for a day?" Taylor felt perfectly safe making the proposal, just as safe as he'd felt offering to make her dinner.

"That wouldn't work."

"I'd be willing to try."

Russ shrugged. "If you insist."

"I do," Taylor said.

Still leaning smugly against the side of her car, Russ pointed at the trunk. "All right, Ms. Goodwrench, go to it."

Taylor opened her front door, placed her papers and purse inside and got out the key to her trunk.

"You might want to roll up your sleeves," Russ suggested. "It'd be a shame to ruin that pretty blouse with a grease stain. It's silk, isn't it?"

Taylor glared at him defiantly.

Russ chuckled and raised both arms. "Sorry. I won't say any more."

Opening the trunk, Taylor systematically searched through it until she found what she was looking for.

"A tire iron is about this size," he said, holding his hands a couple of feet apart, mocking her.

Carrying the spray can, Taylor walked around to the flat tire and squatted down in front of it. "I like my steak medium rare and barbecued over a hot charcoal grill. My baked potato should have sour cream and chives and the broccoli should be fresh with a touch of hollandaise sauce drizzled over the top." Having given him those instructions, she proceeded to fill her deflated tire with the spray can.

"What's that?" Russ asked, his hands set challengingly on his hips.

"You did say this Saturday, didn't you?" she taunted.

He scowled when she handed over the spray can for him to examine. "Fix-it Flat Tire?" he said, reading the label.

"That's exactly what it is," Taylor informed him primly. "Whatever this marvelous invention is, it fills up the tire enough so I can drive it to a service station and have the attendant deal with it."

"Now wait a minute," Russ muttered. "That's cheating."

"I never said I'd *change* the tire," Taylor reminded him. "I told you I could deal with the situation myself. And I have."

"But it's a man who'll be changing the tire."

"Could be a woman. In Seattle some women work for service stations."

"In Seattle, maybe, but not in Cougar Point."

"Come on, Russ, admit it. I outsmarted you."

He glared at her, and despite his irritation, or perhaps because of it, Taylor laughed. She got inside her car, started the engine and drove out of the parking lot. Then she circled back, returning to Russ who was standing beside his pickup.

"What do you want now?" he demanded.

"I just came to tell you I like blue cheese dressing on my salad." With that she zipped out of the lot. She was still smiling when she happened to glance in her rearview mirror in time to see Russ slam his black Stetson onto the asphalt.

Three

No doubt psychologists had a term for the attraction Taylor felt for this rancher, she decided early Saturday evening. Why else would a woman, who was determined to avoid a certain man, go out of her way to goad him into a wager she was sure to win? Taylor couldn't fathom it herself. Maybe it was some perverse method of inflicting self-punishment. Perhaps her disastrous relationship with Mark had lowered her to this level. Taylor didn't know anymore.

She'd prefer to place all the blame on Russ. If he hadn't made her so furious with his nonsense about a woman needing a man, she probably would've been able to stand aside and smile sweetly while he changed her tire. But he'd had to ruin everything.

During dinner at least, Mandy would be there to act as a buffer.

"What do you mean you're going over to Chris's?" Russ asked his sister.

"I told you about it Thursday, remember?"

Russ frowned. Hell, no, he didn't remember. He needed Mandy to help him with this stupid dinner wager he'd made with Taylor. The woman had tricked him.

In his view, she should be cooking, not the other way around. He would've been happy to take her to dinner in town and be done with it, but he knew better than to even suggest that. She'd insisted he make dinner himself.

"What's so important at Chris's that you have to do it now?"

"We're practicing. Drill team tryouts are next week, and I've got to make it. I've just got to."

She made it sound like a matter of life or death. "Couldn't the two of you practice some other time?"

"No," Mandy said. "I want to see Taylor, but I can't. Not tonight."

Grumbling under his breath, Russ opened the refrigerator and stared inside, wondering where the hell he should start. Make the salad first? Cook the broccoli? Earlier in the day he'd bought everything he was going to need, including a packet of hollandaise sauce mix.

"I'm sorry, Russ," Mandy said. "I'd offer to help..."

His spirits lifted. "You will? Great. Just don't let Taylor know. If she found out, she'd have me strung from the highest tree for allowing another woman to slice lettuce for me."

"I *can't* help you, Russ. That would be cheating."

"All I want you to do is give me a few pointers."

"It wouldn't be right." She lowered her voice to a whisper. "Don't slice the lettuce, and I shouldn't even be telling you that."

"What do you do with salad if you don't chop it?" Russ asked wearily. He followed Mandy into the living room where she collected her homemade pom-poms. "What am I supposed to do with the lettuce?"

"I can't answer that," she said, looking apologetic.

"You can't tell me how to make a salad?" he roared. His temper was wearing precariously thin. "Why not?"

"It'd be unfair. You're supposed to prepare this meal entirely on your own. If I gave you any help, you'd be breaking your agreement with Taylor." A car horn blared from the backyard, and Mandy grabbed her jacket. "That's Chris's mom now. I've got to go. See you later, and good luck with dinner."

She was out the door before Russ could protest.

Russ wandered around the kitchen for the next five minutes, debating what to do first. Grilling the steaks wouldn't be a problem. Anyone with half a brain knew how to cook a decent T-bone. The baked potato wasn't a concern, either. It was everything else. He took the head of lettuce and a bunch of other vegetables from the refrigerator and set them on the counter. Without giving it much thought, he reached for an apron and tied it around his waist. God help him if any of the ranch hands walked in now.

Taylor was impressed with the effort Russ had made when she arrived at the Lazy P. He opened the door for her and jerked the apron from his waist.

"I hope you're happy," he muttered, looking anything but.

"I am. Thanks for asking," she said, but inwardly she was struggling not to laugh. This entire scene was almost too good to be true. Next to her own father, Russ was the biggest chauvinist she'd ever met. The sight of him working in a kitchen, wearing an apron, was priceless.

"Something smells delicious," she said.

"I'll tell you it isn't the hollandaise sauce. That stuff tastes like sh—" He stopped himself just in time. "You can figure it out."

"I can," she said. Smiling, she strolled across the kitchen

and set a bottle of wine on the counter. "A small token of my appreciation."

She couldn't hear his reply as he furiously whipped the sauce simmering on the front burner. "Maybe it'll taste better once it's boiled," Russ said, concentrating on the task at hand.

The table was set. Well, sort of. The silverware was piled in the center between the two place settings. The water glasses were filled.

"The broccoli's done." Russ turned off the burner. "It looks all right from what I can tell." He drained the water and sprinkled a dash of salt and pepper over the contents of the pan.

"I'll open the wine, if you like."

"Sure," Russ said absently. He opened the oven door, and Taylor felt the blast of heat clear from the other side of the room.

"What's in there?"

"The baked potatoes," he said, slamming the door. "How long does it take to cook these things, anyway? They've been in there fifteen minutes and they're still hard as rocks."

"Normally they bake in about an hour."

"An hour?" he echoed. "Dammit, the sauce!" he cried. Grabbing a dish towel, he yanked the saucepan from the burner. He stirred frantically. "I hope it didn't burn."

"I'm sure it'll be just fine. Where's Mandy?"

"Gone," he grumbled. He stuck his finger in the sauce and licked it, then nodded, apparently surprised. "She's over at Chris's practicing for drill team. And before you ask, she didn't help me any."

"Mandy's not here?" Taylor said. A sense of uneasiness gripped her hard. After what had happened the first time she was alone with Russ, she had reason to be apprehensive.

She was overreacting, she told herself. It wasn't as if she was going to fall spontaneously into Russ's arms simply because his sister wasn't there to act as chaperone. They were both mature adults, and furthermore, they'd agreed to forget the night they'd kissed. The whole thing was as much of an embarrassment to Russ as it was to her. *She* certainly wasn't going to bring it up.

"Don't think I had anything to do with Mandy being gone, either."

"I didn't," she said with a shrug of indifference, implying that it hadn't even crossed her mind—which was true, at least before Russ mentioned it.

He was scowling as if he expected her to argue with him.

"Can I do anything to help?" she asked in an effort to subdue her nervousness.

"No, thanks. This meal is completely under control," he boasted. "I'm a man of my word, and when I said I was going to cook you the best steak you've ever eaten, I meant it."

"I'm looking forward to it." Wordlessly she opened a series of drawers until she located the corkscrew and proceeded to agilely remove the cork from the wine.

"I know it's traditional to serve red wine with beef, but I prefer white. This is an excellent chardonnay."

"Whatever you brought is fine," he mumbled as he swung open the refrigerator and took out a huge green salad.

It looked as if there was enough lettuce to feed the entire town, but Taylor refused to antagonize him by commenting on the fact.

"I want you to know I didn't slice the lettuce," he said proudly as he set the wooden bowl in the center of the table, shoving aside the silverware.

"Oh, good," Taylor responded, hoping she sounded appropriately impressed. The second cupboard she inspected contained crystal wineglasses. Standing on tiptoe, she brought down two. They were both thick with dust, so she washed and rinsed them before pouring the wine.

"I wanted to bring dessert, but there isn't a deli in Cougar Point," she said conversationally as she handed Russ his wineglass.

He stepped away from the stove to accept the wine. Scowling, he asked, "You were going to buy dessert at a deli?"

"It's the best place I know to get New York cheesecake."

Russ muttered something she didn't quite catch before returning to the stove. He turned down the burners and took a sip of his wine. "Since it's going to take the potatoes a little longer than I realized, we might as well sit down."

"Okay," Taylor agreed readily, following him into the living room. The furniture consisted of large, bulky pieces that looked as if they'd been lifted from the set of an old western series on television. *Bonanza,* maybe.

A row of silver-framed photographs lined the fireplace and, interested, Taylor walked over to examine them. A picture of Russ, probably from his high school graduation, caught her attention immediately. He'd been a handsome young man. Boyishly good-looking, but she could easily tell that his appeal was potent enough to cause many a young woman more than one sleepless night.

"That's my dad and Betty," he said, pointing out the second large portrait. "It was taken shortly after they were married." The resemblance between father and son was striking. They possessed the same brooding, dark eyes, and their full mouths were identical. She looked at Russ's high school picture again and found herself zeroing in on his youthful features. Even back then, there'd been a wildness about him that challenged a woman. No man had provoked, defied or taunted her the way Russ had, and she barely knew him. By all rights she should stay as far away from him as possible, yet here she was in his home, studying his picture and theorizing about his secrets.

She turned away from the fireplace and sat in an over-stuffed chair. "You were telling me before that you've got a thousand cattle," Taylor said, making conversation while her fingers moved nervously against the padded arm of the chair.

"I've sold half the herd. I'm wintering five hundred head, but by summer the numbers will be much higher."

"I see." She didn't really understand what he meant but didn't know enough to ask intelligent questions. Thankfully Russ seemed to grasp her dilemma and explained of his own accord.

"The men are rounding up the cattle now. We keep them in a feed ground."

"A feed ground?"

"It's a fenced pasture with no irrigation ditches."

"Why? I mean, don't they need water?"

"Of course, but the heavy snows start in December, sometimes earlier. When the ground's covered, the cattle can't see the ditches, and if a steer falls into one, he often can't get out, and I've lost a valuable animal."

"If the snow's that high, how do you get the feed to them?"

"Sometimes by sleigh."

Taylor smiled at the thought of riding through a snow-covered field. She could almost hear the bells jingling and Christmas music playing while she snuggled under a warm blanket, holding tight to Russ.

Shaking her head to dispel the romantic fantasy, Taylor swallowed, furious with the path her daydreams had taken. She drank some of her wine, hoping to set her thoughts in order before they became so confused that she lost all reason. "That sounds like fun."

"It's demanding physical labor," Russ told her gruffly.

His tone surprised her, and she raised her eyes to meet his.

He might be saying one thing, but Taylor would bet her first paycheck that he was battling the same fiery attraction she'd struggled with from the moment he'd first kissed her. He continued to stare at her in that restless, penetrating way that unnerved her.

He seemed impatient to escape from her, and unexpectedly vaulted to his feet. "I'd better check on dinner."

Once he was out of the room, Taylor closed her eyes and sagged against the back of the cushion. This evening had seemed safe enough until she'd learned Mandy was gone. The air seemed to crackle with electricity despite even the blandest conversation.

Taylor heard Russ move back into the room, and assuming dinner was ready, she leapt to her feet. "Let me help," she said.

Russ caught her by the shoulders.

"The potatoes aren't done."

As she tilted her head, her hair fell over her shoulder and down her back. Mark had liked it styled and short, and in an act of defiance, she'd allowed it to grow longer than at any other time in her life.

"You have beautiful hair," Russ murmured, apparently unable to take his eyes from it. He slid his hand from her shoulder to the dark curly mass, and ran his fingers through its length. The action, so slow and deliberate, was highly exciting. Against every dictate of her will, Taylor's heart quickened.

Soon his other hand joined the first and he continued to let his fingers glide through her hair, as if acquainting himself with its softness. Taylor seemed to be falling into a trance. His hands, buried deep in her hair, were more sensual than anything she'd ever experienced. Her eyes drifted shut, and when she felt herself being tugged toward him, she offered no resistance. His mouth met hers in a gentle brushing of lips. Their breaths merged as they each released a broken sigh.

"Tell me to stop," Russ said. "Tell me to take my hands away from you."

Taylor knew she should, but emotions that had been hiding just below the surface overwhelmed her. She meant to push him away, extract them both from this temptation—and yet the instant her hands made contact with his hard, muscular chest, they lost their purpose.

"Russ..."

His answer was to kiss her, a kiss that felt anything but gentle. His hands were tangled in the wavy bulk of dark hair as he bent her head to one side and slanted his demanding mouth over hers.

Their kisses were tempestuous, intense, exciting, and soon they were both panting and breathless.

Suddenly Russ tore his mouth from hers. His eyes remained closed. "I haven't stopped thinking of you all week," he confessed, not sounding very pleased about it. "I didn't want to, but you're there every night when I close my eyes. I can't get rid of the taste of you. Why *you?*" he asked harshly. "Why do I have to feel these things for a city girl? You don't belong here and you never will."

Taylor's head fell forward for a moment while she thought about his words. He was right. She was as out of place in this cattle town as…as a trout in a swimming pool. She raised her head while she had the courage to confront him. Anger was her friend; it took away the guilt she felt for being so willing to fall into his arms.

"You think I'm happy about this?" she cried. "Trust me, a cowpoke is the last person in the world I want to get involved with. A woman in your life is there for your convenience, to cook your meals and pleasure you in bed. I knew exactly what you were the minute we met and I could never align my thinking with yours."

"Fine then, don't," he barked.

"I don't have any intention of getting involved with you."

"Listen, lady, I'm not all that thrilled with you, either. Go back to the big city where you belong, because in these parts men are men and women are women. We don't much take to all that feminist talk."

Taylor was becoming more outraged by the minute. Russ clearly had no conception that they weren't living in the nineteenth century anymore.

"Let's eat," he snarled.

Taylor had half a mind to gather her things and leave. She would have if she'd thought she could get away with it. But Russ had made this dinner on a wager, and Taylor strongly suspected he'd see to it that she ate every bite. Knowing what she did about Russ, Taylor wouldn't put it past him to feed her himself if she backed out now.

Taylor wasn't sure how she managed to force down a single bite. Yet the salad was undeniably good. The broccoli was excellent, the sauce marginal, the baked potato raw, but the steak was succulent and exactly the way she liked it—medium rare.

Silence stretched between them like a tightrope, and

neither seemed inclined to cross it. At least ten minutes passed before Russ spoke.

"I shouldn't have said that about you not belonging here," he murmured, stabbing the lettuce with his fork.

"Why not?" she asked. "It's true and we both know it. I *am* a city girl."

"From everything I hear, you're a fine teacher," he admitted grudgingly. "The kids are crazy about you and I don't blame them."

She lifted her eyes to his, uncertain if she should believe him, feeling both surprise and pleasure.

"Word has it you're enthusiastic and energetic, and everyone who's met you says nothing but good. I don't want you thinking folks don't appreciate what you're doing. That was just me running off at the mouth."

Her voice dropped to a raspy whisper. "I didn't mean what I said either, about not wanting anything to do with you because you're a cowpoke."

Their eyes met, and they each fought a smile. Knowing she was about to lose, Taylor lowered her gaze. "I will confess to being a little shocked at how well you managed dinner."

Russ chuckled softly. "It wasn't that difficult."

"Does that mean you'd be willing to tackle it again?"

"No way. Once in a man's lifetime is more than enough. I may have lost the wager, but I still consider cooking a woman's job."

"I thought for a moment that our wager would change your mind. But at this point, why do anything to spoil your reputation as a world-class chauvinist?"

Russ chuckled again, and the sound wasn't extraordinary, but it gladdened Taylor's heart. Something about this cowboy intrigued her. He wasn't like any other man she'd ever dated. His opinions were diametrically opposed to her own on just about every subject she could mention. Yet whenever he touched her, she all but melted in his arms. There wasn't any logic to this attraction they shared. No reason for it.

Russ helped himself to more salad and replenished their wineglasses. "Now that you know what Cougar Point thinks about you, how are you adjusting to us?"

"It's been more of a change than I expected," she said, holding the wineglass with both hands. She rotated the stem between her palms. "It's the lack of conveniences I notice the most."

He arched his brows in question. "Give me an example."

"Well, I came home from work the other night, exhausted. All I wanted to do was sit down, put my feet up and hibernate until morning. The problem was, I was starving. My first impulse was to order a pepperoni pizza, and when I realized I couldn't, I felt like crying with frustration."

"The bowling alley serves a decent pizza."

"But they don't deliver."

"No," Russ agreed, "they don't."

Feeling a twinge of homesickness, Taylor finished her wine and stood. "I'll help you with the dishes," she said, feeling sad and weary as she glanced at Russ. Even in the friendliest conversation their differences were impossible to ignore.

"I'll do them," he responded, standing himself.

"Nope, you made dinner," she said firmly. "You're exempt from washing dishes—this time." She turned on the tap and squirted a dash of liquid soap into the rushing water. Monster bubbles quickly formed, and she lowered the water pressure.

She was clearing off the table when Russ suggested, "How about a cup of coffee?"

"Please," she said, smiling over at him.

He busied himself with that while Taylor loaded the dishwasher with plates and serving dishes, leaving the pots and pans to wash by hand.

"Here," he said from behind her, "you might want this."

She turned around to discover Russ holding the very apron he'd been so quick to remove when she'd arrived. Her hands were covered with soapsuds. She glanced at them and then at Russ.

"I'll put it on for you," he said.

She smiled her appreciation and lifted her arms so he could loop the ties around her waist and knot them behind her back.

Russ moved to within two steps of her and hesitated. Slowly he raised his eyes to her face. Hungry eyes. They delved into hers and then lowered just as slowly until they centered on her lips.

Unable to resist, Taylor swayed toward him. Once more she found herself a willing victim to his spell.

Their eyes held for a long moment before Russ roughly pushed the apron at her. "You do it."

With trembling hands, Taylor shook the suds into the sink and deftly tied the apron behind her. "I wish Mandy was here," she murmured, shocked by how close they'd come to walking into each other's arms again. Obviously they both enjoyed the lure of the forbidden. Whatever the attraction, it was explosive, and she felt as though they'd been stumbling around a keg of lit gunpowder all evening.

"I think I'll call her and tell her to come home," Russ said, but he didn't reach for the phone.

Once the dishwasher was loaded, Taylor vigorously scrubbed the first pan, venting her frustration on it.

"Are you going to the dance?" Russ asked her next, grabbing a dish towel and slapping it over his shoulder.

"I...don't think so."

"Why not? It'll give you a chance to meet all the young guys in town and you can flirt to your heart's content."

"I'm far beyond the flirting stage," she returned coolly.

He shrugged. "Could've fooled me. Fact is, you've been doing an admirable job of trifling with *me* from the moment we met."

Taylor's hand stilled. "I beg your pardon?"

"Take those jeans your wearing."

"What's wrong with these jeans?"

"They're too tight. Stretched across your fanny like that, they give a man ideas."

Closing her eyes, Taylor counted to ten. The effort to control her temper was in vain, however, and she whirled around to face him.

"How *dare* you suggest anything so ridiculous? You nearly kissed me a minute ago and now you're blaming *me* because *you* can't control yourself. Obviously it's all my fault."

He grunted and looked away.

"My jeans are too tight!" she echoed, her voice still outraged. "What about my sweater? Is that too revealing?" She bunched her breasts together and cast a meaningful look in their direction. "Did you notice how far the V-neck goes down? Why, a mere glimpse of cleavage is enough to drive a man to drink. Maybe I should have you censor my perfume, as well. It's a wonder the good people of Cougar Point would allow such a brazen hussy near their children. And one with a big-city attitude, no less."

"Taylor—"

"Don't you say another word to me," she cried, and jerked off the apron. Tears sprang to her eyes as she hurriedly located her purse. "Good night, Mr. Palmer. I won't say it's been a pleasure."

"Taylor, dammit, listen to me."

She raced down the stairs to her car, barely able to see through the tears in her eyes. The whole world looked blurred and watery, but Taylor was in too much of a hurry to care. This man said the most ridiculous things she'd ever heard. Only a fool would have anything more to do with him. Taylor had been a fool once.

Never, never again.

Russ sat in the living room, calling himself every foul name he could think of, and the list was a long one. When the back door opened, he knew it would be Mandy and reached for a newspaper, pretending to read.

"Hi!" She waltzed into the room. "How'd dinner go?"

"Great," he mumbled, not taking his eyes off the front page.

"Has Taylor already left?"

"Yeah."

"Oh, shucks, I wanted to talk to her. Do you want to see the routine Chris and I made up?"

Russ's interest in his sister's drill team efforts was less than nil. Nevertheless, he grinned and nodded. "Sure."

"Okay, but remember it's not the same without the music." She held the pom-poms to her waist, arms akimbo, then let loose with a high kick and shot her arms toward the ceiling. She danced left, she leaped right, her arms and legs moving with an instinctive grace that astonished Russ. This was Mandy? Fourteen-year-old Mandy? She was really quite good at this.

She finished down on one knee, her pom-poms raised above her head. Her smiling eyes met his, seeking his approval. "So?"

"There isn't a single doubt in my mind that my sister's going to make the high school drill team."

"Oh, Russ," she shouted, "thank you!" She vaulted to her feet and threw her arms around his neck. "Just for that I'll finish the dishes."

"Thanks," Russ said absently. He didn't want to think about dinner or anything else connected with this disastrous evening. That would only bring Taylor to mind, and she was the one person he was determined to forget. He'd suffered enough. All week she'd been nagging at his conscience. He'd even dreamed of her. He hadn't felt this way about a woman since he was sixteen years old.

Then he had to go and say those stupid things. The reason was even worse. He'd been jealous. The thought of her attending the Grange event and dancing with all the men in town was more than he could bear. Other men putting their arms around her. Someone else laughing with her.

If anyone was going to dance with Taylor Manning, it would be him. Not Harry Donovan. Not Les Benjamin. Not Cody Franklin.

Him.

"Russ?"

He turned and found his sister staring at him. "What?"

"You've been pacing for the past five minutes. Is something wrong?"

"Hell, no," he growled, then quickly changed his mind. "Hell, yes." He marched across the kitchen and grabbed his hat, bluntly setting it on his head.

"Where are you going?" Mandy demanded, following him.

"To town," he muttered. "I owe Taylor an apology."

Mandy giggled, seeming to find that amusing. "You going to ask her to the dance?"

"I might," he said, his strides long and purposeful.

"All right!" his sister cheered from behind him.

Four

"Taylor!" Russ pounded on the front door with his fist. This woman sure was stubborn. "I know you're in there. Answer the door, will you?"

"I can't," a soft, feminine voice purred from the other side. "I'm wearing something much too revealing." The purr quickly became an angry shout. "Army boots and fatigues!"

"I need to talk to you," Russ insisted.

"Go away."

Exhaling loudly, Russ pressed his palms against the door. "Please," he added persuasively, knowing few women could resist him when he used that imploring tone.

"If you don't leave, I'm calling the police."

"The deputy's name is Cody Franklin, and we went to school together."

"That doesn't mean he won't arrest you."

"On what charge? Wanting to apologize to my lady?"

The door flew open with such force that Russ was surprised it stayed on its hinges. Taylor's index finger poked him in the chest and he stumbled back a step.

"I am not your lady! Understand?" Deep blue eyes sliced straight through him.

Russ's grin was so big, his face ached. "I figured that comment would get a reaction out of you. I just didn't think it would be quite this zealous. Did anyone ever tell you you've got one hell of a temper?"

"No." She obviously resented being tricked. She crossed her arms protectively around her waist and glared at him. "There's only one other man in this world who can make me as angry as you do and I'm related to him."

"Which means you can't avoid him, but you *can* avoid me."

Taylor rolled her eyes skyward. "The cowboy's a genius."

Russ removed his hat and rotated the rim between his fingers. "I'm here to apologize for what I said earlier. I don't know what came over me," he hesitated, realizing that wasn't entirely true. "All right, I have a good guess. I was jealous."

"Jealous," she exploded. "Of what?"

This wasn't easy. Confronting her was one thing, but admitting how he'd been feeling... An uncomfortable sensation tightened his chest. "I was thinking about other men dancing with you and it bothered the hell out of me," he said in a low murmur, none too proud of it.

"That makes as much sense as my jeans being too tight. I already told you I wasn't going to the dance."

"Yes, you are," he countered swiftly. "You're going with me."

To his consternation, Taylor threw back her head and laughed. "In your dreams, Palmer."

There were any number of women in town who'd leap at an invitation to attend the Grange dance with him; he could name four off the top of his head. So it didn't sit right that the one woman he really wanted to take had mocked his invitation. He could feel the red burning his ears, but he swallowed his protest. Still, he supposed he and Taylor were even now.

"Some women might appreciate those caveman tactics of yours," she informed him, smiling much too broadly to suit his already wounded pride. "But I'm not one of them."

"What do you want me to do? Get down on one knee and beg? Because if that's the case, you've got a hell of a long wait!" He slammed his hat back on his head.

Some of the amusement and indignation left her eyes.

Russ tried once more, softening his voice. "There isn't anyone in Cougar Point I'd rather attend the dance with," he said. Their eyes held for a few seconds longer before Russ added, "Will you go with me, Taylor? Please?" That wasn't a word he said often; he hoped she realized that.

It was clear she was wavering. Maybe she needed some inducement, Russ decided. He settled his hands on her shoulders and brought her against him. She remained as stiff as a branding iron, refusing to relax. He could kiss her; that might help with her decision. Every time his mouth settled over hers it was like drinking rainwater, sweet and fresh from the heavens. He rested his chin on the crown of her head and felt some of the fight go out of her. A smile twitched at the edges of his mouth. He knew she'd come around once she'd had a chance to think about it.

"Taylor?" he whispered, lifting her chin so he could look into her eyes. What he saw puzzled him. Russ expected to find submission, perhaps even a hint of desire. Instead he discovered bewilderment and distress.

When she spoke, her voice was a little shaky. "I...it'd be best if you asked someone else, Russ."

"You're going to the Grange dance, aren't you?" Mary Beth Morgan asked, popping into Taylor's room after class on Wednesday afternoon.

Taylor shook her head and riffled through a stack of papers on her desk. "I don't think so."

"But, Taylor," the other teacher said, "everyone in town will be there."

"So I heard." Taylor stood and placed the papers inside her folder to take home and grade that evening.

"Why wouldn't you want to go?"

Taylor hedged, wondering how she could explain. "First, I don't have anything appropriate to wear, and second—" she hesitated and lifted one shoulder in a half shrug "—I don't know how to square dance."

Mary Beth smiled and shook her head. "You don't have a thing to worry about. You could show up at the Grange in a burlap bag and you'd have more offers to dance than you'd know what to do with. As for the square dancing part, put that out of your head. This isn't a square dance."

"I'll think about it," Taylor promised.

"You'd better do more than that," Mary Beth said. "I personally know of three young men who'll be mighty disappointed if you aren't at that dance."

"I suppose I could sew a dress," Taylor said, her spirits lifting. She knew the minute she arrived that Russ would believe she was there because of him, but the thought of staying home while everyone else was having fun was fast losing its appeal.

"Listen, Taylor, there aren't that many social functions in Cougar Point. Take my advice and enjoy yourself while you can because there probably won't be another one until Christmas."

"Christmas?"

"Right," Mary Beth said with a solid nod. "Now I'll tell you what I'll do. My husband and I will pick you up at seven."

"I know where the Grange Hall is," Taylor said, brightening. "You don't need to give me a ride."

Mary Beth laughed. "I just want to see if it's Russ Palmer, Cody Franklin or Harry Donovan who takes you home."

True to her word, Mary Beth and Charles Morgan came by to pick up Taylor promptly at seven on Saturday night.

"Oh, my, we're in for a fun evening," Mary Beth said as she walked a full circle around Taylor. Slowly she shook her head. "That dress is absolutely gorgeous."

Taylor had been up until midnight two evenings straight, sewing. There was an old-fashioned dry goods store in town, where she'd found a respectable—and surprisingly inexpensive—assortment of fabrics and notions. She'd chosen a pattern for a western-style dress with a tight-fitting lace-up bodice and snug waist. The skirt flared out gently at her hips and fell to midcalf. An eyelet-ruffled petticoat of white dropped three inches below the lavender dress. Brown boots complemented the outfit.

"Yup, we're in for a really good time tonight." Mary Beth chuckled as she slipped her arm through Taylor's and led her out the door.

The music coming from the Grange Hall could be heard even before they parked the car. Bright lights poured out from the large brick structure on the highway outside town. The parking lot was filled with trucks and four-wheel-drive vehicles. Without meaning to, Taylor started looking for Russ's truck, then quickly chastised herself.

She was hardly in the door when Mandy flew to her side. The girl's face was glowing with a warm smile.

"I knew you'd come! Russ said you wouldn't be here, but I was sure you would. Oh, Taylor," she whispered wide-eyed when Taylor removed her coat. "Where did you ever find a dress that pretty?"

Taylor whirled around once to give her the full effect. "You like it? Well, I told you before there are advantages in knowing how to use a sewing machine."

"You *made* your dress?"

"Don't look so shocked."

"Could I ever sew anything that complicated?"

"With practice."

"If I took all the money I've been saving for a new saddle and bought a sewing machine, would you teach me to sew? I'm not taking home economics until next term, and I don't want to wait that long to learn. Not when I can make clothes as pretty as yours."

"I'd be happy to teach you."

"Howdy, Taylor." A young man with soft ash-blond hair stepped in front of her, hands tucked into the small front pockets of his jeans.

"Hello," she said, not recognizing him, although he apparently knew her.

"I was wondering if I could have the next dance?"

"Ah…" Taylor hadn't even hung up her coat yet, and she would've liked to find her way around and talk to a few people before heading for the dance floor.

"For crying out loud," Mandy muttered. "Give Taylor a minute, will you, Harry? She just got here."

Harry's cheeks flushed with instant color. "If I don't ask her now," he said, "someone else will and I won't get a chance the rest of the evening." He blushed some more. "So can I have this dance?"

"Ah…sure," Taylor said, not knowing what else to do. Mandy took her coat and Harry led her to the dance floor, smiling broadly as if he'd pulled off a major coup.

Once they reached the dance floor, Harry slipped his

arm around her waist and guided her through a simple two-step. They hadn't been on the floor more than a few minutes when the music ended. Reluctantly Harry let his arm drop.

"I don't suppose you'd consider dancing the next one with me?" he asked hopefully.

Taylor hesitated. The room was growing more crowded, and she still hadn't talked to anyone.

"I believe the next dance is mine," a deep masculine voice said from behind her. Taylor didn't need a detective to know it was Russ. She stiffened instinctively before turning to face him.

Russ stood directly in front of her in a gray western-tailored suit with a suede yoke, his gaze challenging hers. His look alone was enough to silence the denial on her tongue. His eyes moved over her like a warm caress, tiny glints of mischief sparking in their depths.

The music started again, and as Harry stepped away, Russ placed his arms around her. There wasn't an ounce of protest left in Taylor as he caressed the small of her back. She closed her eyes and pretended to be engrossed in the music when it was Russ who held her senses captive.

Several minutes passed before he spoke. His mouth was close to her ear. "I knew you'd come."

Taylor's eyes shot open, and she jerked away from him, putting several inches between them. "Let me tell you right now that my being here has absolutely nothing to do with you, and—"

He pressed a finger over her lips, stopping her in midsentence.

Slowly Taylor lifted her gaze to his. Deeply etched lines from long hours in the sun crinkled around his eyes.

"Thank you for coming," he whispered, and his warm breath tinged her cheek. Then he removed his finger.

"It wasn't for you," she felt obliged to inform him, but the indignation in her voice was gone. "Mary Beth Morgan…invited me."

Russ's mouth quirked just a fraction. "Remind me to thank her."

His grip tightened, and although Taylor was determined to keep a safe, respectable distance from this man, she found herself relaxing in his embrace. He slid his hand up and down the length of her back, sending hunger shooting through her. She eased closer, reveling in the strength she sensed in the rugged, hard contours of his body. She didn't mean to, didn't even want to, but when he tucked her hand between them and rested his face against her hair, she closed her eyes once again. He smelled of rum and spice, and she breathed in deeply, inhaling his scent.

When the song ended, it was Taylor who swallowed a sigh of regret. Dancing like this was a lost art in the city. The last time she'd danced with a man who'd placed his arms around her so tenderly, she'd been with Mark, early in their relationship. She'd almost forgotten how good it was to feel so cherished.

Russ refused to release her; if anything, he pulled her closer. "Let's get out of here for a few minutes."

Taylor groaned inwardly. She couldn't believe how tempted she was to agree. "I…can't. I just got here. People will talk."

"Let them."

"Russ, no." Using her hands for leverage, she pushed herself free. He didn't offer any resistance, but the effort it had cost her to move away left her weak. And furious. How dare he assume she'd go into the parking lot with him—and for what? She'd bet cold hard cash he wasn't planning to discuss cattle breeding techniques with her.

"I want it understood that I'm not going anywhere near that parking lot with you, Russ Palmer."

"Whatever you say." But a smile tugged insolently at his mouth.

The music started again, and they stood facing each other in the middle of the dance floor with couples crowding in around them. Russ didn't take her in his arms, nor did she make a move toward him.

Amusement flickered in his eyes. There was no resisting him, and soon Taylor responded to his smile. He slipped his hands around her waist, drawing her back into the circle of his arms. They made a pretense of dancing but were doing little more than staring at each other and shuffling their feet.

No woman in her right mind would deliberately get involved with an avowed chauvinist like Russ Palmer, yet here she was, a thoroughly modern woman, so attracted to him that she ached to the soles of her feet.

The music came to an end, and his arms relaxed. A careless, handsome grin slashed his mouth. "Enjoy yourself," he whispered. "Dance with whomever you like, but remember this. I'm the one who's taking you home tonight. No one else. Me."

An immediate protest rose in Taylor's throat, but before she could utter a single word, Russ bent forward and set his mouth over hers. She clenched her fists against his gray suit jacket while his lips caressed hers. Taylor could hear the curious voices murmuring around them, and she gave a small cry.

Russ ended the kiss, smiled down on her and whispered, "Remember."

Then he walked off the floor.

Taylor felt like a first-class fool, standing there by herself with half a dozen couples staring at her. When the hushed whispers began, she smiled blandly and all but ran from the dance floor.

Taylor was so mortified that she headed directly for the ladies' room and stayed there a full five minutes, trying to compose herself. If there'd been a sofa, she would have sat down and wept. Wept because she'd been so tempted to let Russ take her outside. Wept because she felt so right in his arms. Wept because she hadn't learned a thing from her disastrous affair with Mark Brooks.

Once she reappeared at the dance, she didn't lack for attention. She waltzed with Cody Franklin, chatted over punch with Les Benjamin, another rancher, and even managed a second two-step with Harry Donovan. She smiled. She laughed. She pretended to be having the time of her life, but underneath everything was a brewing frustration she couldn't escape. Every now and then she'd catch a glimpse of Russ dancing with someone else. Usually someone young and pretty. Someone far more suited to him than she'd ever be. Yet, each time, she felt a stab of jealousy unlike anything she'd ever experienced.

By the time the evening started to wind down, Taylor decided the best way to thwart Russ was to accept someone else's offer to drive her home.

Only no one asked.

Of the dozen or so men she danced with, not a single, solitary one suggested taking her home. Charles and Mary Beth Morgan had already left by the time Taylor realized she had no option except to find Russ.

He was waiting for her outside, standing at the bottom of the Grange steps, looking as arrogant and pleased as could be.

"I want to know what you said to everyone," she demanded, marching down the steps. It was more than a little suspicious that she'd been virtually abandoned without a ride.

Russ's eyes fairly shone with devilment. "Me? What makes you think I said anything?"

"Because I know you, and I want one thing clear right now. You can take me home, but nothing else. Understand?"

"You insult me, madam!"

"Good. Now where's Mandy?" Taylor asked.

"She's spending the night with Chris," Russ explained. "However, rest assured, you're perfectly safe with me."

"I'd be safer in a pit of rattlesnakes," she said wryly. "Do you have any idea how humiliating it was when you kissed me on that dance floor and then took off?" Her voice was a low hiss.

"I promise I'll never do it again," he vowed, and led her across the parking lot where he held open the truck door.

This was a newer model than the one she'd ridden in earlier. She paused and glanced inside and was relieved to see it had seat belts. However, the truck stood probably three feet off the ground, and there wasn't any way she'd be able to climb inside without assistance.

"Here," Russ said, "I'll help you up." His hands closed around her waist and he lifted her effortlessly off the ground.

Once she was inside and Russ had joined her, she asked him, "Where do you drive this thing? Through the Rockies?"

Russ chuckled and started the engine. "You'd be surprised the places this truck has been."

"I'll bet," Taylor grumbled.

She didn't say a word during the short drive to her rented house. Russ didn't, either.

He pulled in to her driveway, cut the engine and was out of the cab before she could object. Opening her door, Russ helped her down. But when her feet were firmly planted on the ground, he didn't release her.

His eyes held hers in the dim light from a nearby streetlamp, and a current of awareness flowed between them. "You were the most beautiful woman there tonight."

"I'm surprised you even noticed." The minute the words escaped, Taylor regretted having spoken. In one short sentence she'd revealed what she'd been doing all evening.

Watching him.

She'd counted the number of women he'd danced with and, worse, envied them the time they'd spent in his arms.

Russ didn't answer her. Not with words, anyway. Instead he pulled her into his arms and kissed her. His mouth was hard, his kiss thorough. When he lifted his head, their panting breaths echoed each other.

"Invite me inside," he whispered, his voice husky.

Taylor felt powerless to do anything other than what he asked. Her hands were shaking as she drew the keys from her purse. Russ took them from her and unlocked the door, pushing it open for her to precede him.

She walked through the living room and to the kitchen, turning on the lights. "I'll…make some coffee."

"No," Russ said, stopping her. His arms anchored her against the wall. "I don't want any coffee and neither do you."

Taylor gazed into his face and recognized his hunger, aware that it was a reflection of her own. Closing her eyes, she leaned against the wall, feeling needy and weak.

"Trust me," Russ whispered. "I know what you're thinking. We're both crazy. I should stay as far away from you as possible. You don't want to feel these things for me any more than I want to feel them for you. We argue. We fight. But, lady, when we kiss, everything else pales by comparison."

"What we're experiencing is just physical attraction," she whispered as her fingers sank into his thick, dark hair.

"Physical attraction," he repeated, seconds before his mouth came crashing down on hers. Low, animal sounds came from deep within his throat as his mouth twisted and turned over hers.

Braced against the wall, she could feel every hard, rugged inch of him.

Restlessly she moved against him as her hands clenched fistfuls of his hair.

"Russ," she panted, lifting her head. "I… I think we should stop now."

"In a minute." Grasping her by the waist, he dragged her against him and groaned.

Taylor did, too.

He was so hard. She was so soft.

Man to woman.

Cowboy to lady.

They fit together so perfectly.

Drawing in deep, shuddering breaths, Russ buried his face in the curve of her neck. It took him several seconds to regain control of himself.

It took Taylor even longer.

He raised his head and smoothed the hair from her face. "I've changed my mind," he murmured. "I will take that coffee, after all."

Grateful for something to occupy herself, Taylor

moved to the counter where she kept her coffeemaker. While waiting for the aromatic coffee to drip through, she got two mugs and placed them on a tray. She was so absorbed in her task that when she turned around she nearly collided with Russ.

He took the tray from her hands and carried it into the living room. "I think it's time we cleared the air," he said, setting their mugs on the oak coffee table.

"In what way?" Taylor asked, perching on the edge of the sofa cushion.

"Above all else, we've got to be honest with each other."

"Right."

Taylor sipped from her mug, the scalding coffee too hot to savor or appreciate.

"Are you wearing a bra?" he asked unexpectedly.

"What?" She jerked forward, setting her cup back on the tray to avoid spilling hot coffee down her front. It sloshed over the edges of the mug.

Taylor's mouth gaped as she glared at him. "Is *that* the kind of honesty you're interested in?" Unable to sit still, she got up and started pacing, so furious she was tempted to throw him out of her home.

"I'm sorry. Forget I asked. I was holding you and it felt as if you weren't and the question just…slipped out. You're right—that was a stupid question."

He lowered his eyes, and Taylor noted that his ears were red. As red as Harry Donovan's had been when he'd asked her to dance. Russ Palmer embarrassed? The very thought was inconceivable.

Stepping around the low table, Taylor sat back down and reached for her coffee. "As a matter of fact, no."

Russ closed his eyes as though in pain. "You shouldn't have told me." He took a gulp of coffee, then stood abruptly. "Maybe it'd be best if I left now."

"I thought you wanted to talk. I refuse to answer personal questions like the last one, but I think you're right about us being honest with each other."

Now it was Russ's turn to do the pacing. He stood and stalked across her living room carpet and then back again as if he intended to wear a pattern in it.

"Russ?"

He rammed his fingers through his hair and turned to face her. "If you want honesty, I'll give it to you, Taylor, but I'll guarantee you aren't going to like what I have to say."

She wasn't sure she was up to this. But, on the other hand, she didn't want him to leave, either. "Just say it."

"All right," he said sharply. "Right now, I want you so damn much I can't even think straight." He raked one hand down his face. "Does that shock you?"

"No," she cried softly.

"Well, it should."

Holding the mug so tightly that it burned her palms, Taylor gathered her courage. "Earlier I objected when you called me your lady. The lady part wasn't what offended me. It might be an old-fashioned term, but I *am* a lady. And I'll always be a lady."

Russ frowned. "I know that, Taylor. No one can look at you and not realize the kind of woman you are."

"I have no intention of falling into bed with you, Russ. I wish I understood why we're so attracted to each other, but I don't. I do know we're playing with fire. Unfortunately, if we continue like this, one of us is going to get burned."

Russ closed his eyes and nodded. "You're right, of course." He inhaled deeply. "Does this mean you want me to leave?"

"No," she said, smiling at her own lack of willpower. "But I think you should, anyway."

Five

"Mandy, I'm not going near that horse."

"Taylor, please. I want to do something to thank you for all the sewing lessons you've given me."

As far as Taylor was concerned, the chestnut gelding looked as huge as the Trojan horse. He didn't seem all that friendly, either. Her palms were sweating, and her throat felt dry from arguing with the persistent teen.

"Shadow is as gentle as they come," Mandy assured her, stroking the white markings on the horse's face. "You don't have a thing to worry about."

"That's what they said to Custer, too," Taylor muttered under her breath. This whole episode had started out so innocuously. Taylor had spent an hour after school helping Mandy cut out the pattern for a vest. Then, because Russ was busy with an errand in Miles City, Taylor had dropped her off at the ranch. One of the men had been exercising a horse, and Taylor had innocently inquired about the stock. Before she knew how it had happened, Mandy was insisting on teaching her to ride, claiming she couldn't accept sewing lessons from Taylor without giving her something in return.

"Once you climb into the saddle, you'll feel a whole lot better about it," Mandy told her.

"I'm not much of a horse person," Taylor said.

"That doesn't matter. Shadow's gentle. I promise you."

"Another time perhaps," Taylor murmured.

"But today's perfect for riding."

Before Taylor could answer, she saw Russ's truck speeding down the driveway, leaving a trail of dust in its wake. Taylor hadn't seen Russ since the night of the Grange dance, and she hated the way her pulse immediately started to race.

Russ pulled to a stop and leaped out of the truck, but he paused when he saw Taylor's Cabriolet parked near the barn. Setting his hat farther back on his head, he changed his direction and walked toward them.

"Hello, Taylor," he said, bowing his head slightly.

"Russ."

"Maybe you can talk some sense into her." Mandy gestured toward Taylor, looking wistful. "I think she should learn to ride. Here she is giving me all these sewing lessons, and I want to repay her."

"You've already had me over for dinner," Taylor reminded the girl. "Really, horses just aren't my thing. The last time I sat on a horse was on a carousel when I was ten years old."

"If Taylor's afraid…"

"What makes you say that?" Taylor demanded. "I'm not *afraid* of horses. It's just that I'm unfamiliar with them. I don't think now is the time for me to do more than gain a nodding acquaintance with Shadow here, but I most certainly am not afraid."

"Then prove it," Russ challenged. He patted Shadow on the rump. The gelding returned the greeting with a nicker and a swish of his thick tail.

"I promise you'll enjoy it," Mandy said.

Grumbling under her breath, Taylor took the reins from Mandy's hands. "Why do I have the sinking suspicion I'm going to regret this?"

"You won't," Mandy vowed.

"This kid is much too free with her promises," Taylor told Russ. Lifting her left foot and placing it in the stirrup, Taylor reached for the saddle horn and heaved herself up.

"You might need some help," Mandy said. "Russ, help her."

"She seems to be doing fine without me."

Taylor had hoisted her weight halfway up when she started to lose her grip. Russ was behind her in an instant, supporting her waist. "All right, Annie Oakley, I'll give you a hand."

Swinging her leg over the back of the horse, Taylor held on to the saddle horn as if it were a life preserver and she was lost at sea.

"See?" Mandy cried triumphantly. "There isn't anything to it. Didn't I tell you?"

Russ adjusted the stirrups for her. "You look a little green around the gills. Are you okay?"

"It's…a little higher up here than I imagined. Can I get down now?"

Mandy giggled. "But you haven't gone anyplace yet."

"Isn't *this* enough to prove I'm not afraid? You didn't say anything about actually moving."

"Josh, bring me Magic," Russ instructed the hand who'd saddled Shadow earlier. A large black gelding was led from the barn, and with Josh's assistance Russ saddled and bridled the horse.

"You go ahead and take Taylor out and I'll start dinner," Mandy suggested. "By the time you two get back, everything will be ready."

"Uh… I'm not so sure this is the best time for me to ride," Taylor said, struggling to hide the panic in her voice. "I've got papers that need to be corrected and a couple of loads of wash…and other things."

"It's Friday," Mandy announced over her shoulder as she strolled toward the house. "You can do all that to-morrow."

"Of course," Taylor muttered. "I should've thought of that."

"Don't look so terrified. This is going to be a good ex-perience for you," Russ told her, his expression far more smug than she liked.

He mounted the black gelding, gave instructions to the hands to unload the pickup, then turned to Taylor. "We'll take it nice and easy. You haven't got a thing to worry about."

"If that's the case, why do I feel like I'm about a mile off the ground?"

Russ's returning chuckle warmed her heart. She'd missed him this week—although she'd had to search her soul to even admit that. With Mandy stopping in after school, three days out of five, Taylor had been kept well-informed about Russ's activities. He'd done the order-ing on Tuesday and was grumpy most of the night, and Mandy didn't have a clue why. Thursday he was out on the range, looking for strays, and Friday he'd traveled into Miles City for supplies. Taylor had never openly asked about Russ, but she was always pleased when Mandy slipped her small pieces of information.

Russ, riding Magic, set the pace, and once they were past the barn, he pointed out a trail that led toward roll-ing hills of fresh, green grass. "We'll head this way."

"Do you mind if we go a bit slower?" She swayed

back and forth, beginning to feel a little seasick with the motion.

"If we went any slower, we'd be standing still."

"What's wrong with that?" she muttered. "By the way, if it isn't too much to ask, where are you taking me?"

Russ waggled his eyebrows suggestively. "*Now* she asks."

"And what's that supposed to mean?"

"Nothing." But his dark eyes were twinkling—a look Taylor had seen before, once too often.

She pulled back on the reins several minutes later, mildly surprised when Shadow slowed to a stop. "I don't trust you, Russ. Tell me this minute exactly where we're going."

Russ leaned back in the saddle, nonchalantly throwing one leg around the saddle horn and clasping his hands behind his head. He was as at ease in a saddle as he was in his own living room. "No place in particular. You want to stop and rest a minute? There's a valley about a quarter mile from here."

Taylor hated to admit how sore her posterior already felt. And they hadn't even gone very far. If she squinted, she could just make out the back of the red barn in the distance.

"Yes, let's stop and rest," she agreed. "But no funny business."

Theatrically Russ removed his hat and pressed it over his heart with a roguish grin. "Once again you insult me, madam."

Taylor said nothing, unwilling to take part in his performance.

"Mandy says you're helping her sew a vest," Russ said conversationally a few minutes later. He slowed Magic and swung down with a grace Taylor could only envy. It had taken all her strength just to raise herself into the saddle. If Russ hadn't given her a boost, she would've been caught with one foot in the stirrup and the other madly waving in midair—until she crashed to the ground.

"Need any help?"

"I can do it myself," she announced, not the least bit confident. Surely climbing out of the saddle would be less of a strain than getting into it had been. Besides, if Russ lent her a hand, he'd use it as an excuse to kiss her. Not that she'd mind, but for once she'd enjoy having a relaxed conversation without falling into his arms like a love-starved teenager.

Taylor was pleased at how easy dismounting turned out to be. Her legs felt a little shaky, but once her feet were on the ground and she'd walked around a bit, she decided this horseback riding business wasn't as difficult as she'd assumed.

"I don't expect many more warm days like this one," Russ said. He tilted his hat back on his head and stared into the distance. Several cattle were grazing on a hill across from them.

Taylor joined him, and he slipped an arm around her waist as familiarly as if he'd been doing so for years.

"Thank you for everything you're doing for Mandy."

"It's nothing."

"It's a lot. Teaching her to sew. Encouraging her. She comes home high as a kite after she's been with you, chattering a mile a minute." A boyish grin lifted his mouth. "For that matter, I come home happy, too."

Taylor lowered her eyes. "I think her making the drill team is what boosted her spirits more than anything. She could've walked on water the day she learned she'd been chosen."

"Only three freshmen made the squad," Russ said, smiling proudly.

Linking her hands behind her back, Taylor strolled over to a large tree. Leaning against the trunk, she raised one knee and rested her booted foot behind her. "I've enjoyed working with Mandy this week. She reminds me of my sister, Christy, when she was fourteen. Unfortunately I was sixteen at the time and considered Christy a major pest."

"Mandy told me you came from a large family."

"By today's standards, I guess you could say that. I have three older brothers, Paul, Jason and Rich. Paul's the only one who's married, and believe me, the rest of us are eternally grateful to him because he quickly presented my parents with twin sons. Now that Mom and Dad have grandchildren, the rest of us are off the hook, at least for a while."

"You're close to your family, aren't you?"

Taylor nodded. "I can't believe how much I miss them. They must be feeling the same way because I've heard from them practically every day."

Russ lowered himself to the grass, stretching his legs in front of him and crossing his ankles. "Mandy said something about how your father reminds you of me."

"Is nothing sacred?" she teased. If his sister had been dropping tidbits about him, she'd also done a bang-up job of keeping Russ informed of their conversations. "My dad's a born chauvinist. I don't think he's sure it was a good thing that women were granted the vote."

Russ didn't laugh the way most people would. "I don't mind if women vote. It's holding public office that concerns me."

Taylor shoved away from the tree so fast, she nearly fell. Her mouth worked for several seconds before any words came out. "I can't *believe* you just said that. Why *shouldn't* a woman hold public office?"

"My, my, you're always so touchy."

"Who can blame me when you say something so ludicrous?"

"Think about it, Taylor. A woman is the very heart of a home and family. What kind of wife and mother would she be if she was so deeply involved in politics that she couldn't tend to her family?"

"I'm not hearing this," she muttered.

"Don't you think a woman's place is with her children?"

"What about a father's place?"

"The husband's got to work in order to support the family."

Taylor covered her face with both hands. Even if his opinion was half-meant to be provocative, arguing with him would do no good. She'd tried often enough with her father, but to no avail. The two men were equally out of date in their views, equally stubborn and difficult.

Not knowing what possessed her, she leaped forward, jerked Russ's hat from his head and took off running.

"Taylor?" Russ vaulted to his feet in one smooth movement and chased after her. "What are you doing with my hat? What's gotten into you?"

Walking backward, keeping a safe distance from him, Taylor hid the Stetson behind her. "You're narrow-minded and the second-worst chauvinist I've ever known."

"You stole my hat because of that?"

"Yes. It was the only way I could make you suffer."

Russ advanced toward her, taking small steps. "Give me back the hat, Taylor."

"Forget it." For a good part of her life, Taylor had been

playing keep-away with her brothers. She might not be as big as Russ and not nearly as agile, but she was quick.

"Taylor, give me the hat," he said again. His gaze narrowed as he advanced toward her, holding out his hand.

"No way. Women don't have any business holding public office? I can't let something that outrageous pass without making you pay."

Laughter flashed from his eyes as he lunged for her. Taylor let out a playful shriek and darted sharply to the left. Russ missed her by a yard.

Russ turned and was prepared to make another dive toward her when Taylor tossed the black cowboy hat with all her might into the sky. "Catch it if you can!" she shouted, bobbing past him. She was in such a rush that she stumbled and would have crashed face-first onto the grass if Russ hadn't captured her around the waist and brought her against him. The full force of her weight caught him off balance. He twisted so that he took the brunt of the impact, and they toppled onto the ground.

Within a heartbeat, Russ had reversed their positions, pinning her hands above her head. Taylor looked up into the dark warmth of his eyes and smiled. Her breasts were heaving with excitement.

"Who's making whom pay?" Russ demanded. He pressed his mouth to her neck, running the tip of his tongue over the smooth skin of her throat. Sensation wove its way down her spine, and she moaned softly and bucked. "No..."

"You're going to be doing a lot more begging before I'm through with you," Russ whispered. He kissed her then, his lips teasing and taunting hers with soft nibbles, promising but never quite delivering.

Arching her back, she struggled and was immediately released. With her hands free, she buried her fingers in his hair, raised her head and fused her mouth to his. She could feel herself dissolving, melting against him.

Russ kissed her mouth, her eyes, her throat. Taylor felt as if she were on fire, her whole body aflame with need. His hand found her breast, and Taylor sighed as a fresh wave of fiery sensation engulfed her.

"Oh, Russ," she pleaded, not sure what she was asking of him. The physical urge was strong and compelling, but there had to be so much more before she could freely give herself to him. A merging of their hearts. Commitment. Love.

She had no time to voice her concerns. Russ kissed her, and a swift, acute sensation of hot, urgent desire rose up in her, blocking out everything but her awareness of Russ and her growing need.

She wanted him to continue—and yet…

"Either we stop now or we finish." His breathing was raspy as he slid his hands from her hips to her shoulders. "The choice is yours."

Taylor squeezed her eyes shut. Her throat was tight as she slowly shook her head. She didn't need to think twice; the decision had been made for her the moment she met Russ. He was as much a part of this landscape as the sycamore trees around them. She was as misplaced as a hothouse flower. But beyond that, Russ was a chauvinist. There was no other word for it. After the years of battling with her father, Taylor had no intention of falling in love with a man who shared the same outdated attitudes toward women.

She gave a shake of her head.

Russ exhaled sharply. "That's what I thought." His breath left him in a defeated rush and he stroked her hair. "Were you hurt when we hit the ground like that?"

She shook her head a second time, wishing she could

hide her face in her hands and never look at him again. She certainly hadn't intended to let things go this far. One moment she was teasing him, playfully tossing his hat into the air, and the next...

"Are you sure you're all right?"

"Of course." But that was far from the truth. Taking his cue, she moved away from him and sat on the grass.

"Mandy's probably wondering about us," she said, doing her best to keep her voice from trembling as badly as her hands did.

"Don't worry. She won't send out a search party."

To Taylor's way of thinking, it might have been better if Mandy had.

It seemed everyone was looking at Taylor when she rode back into the yard. The ranch hands' curiosity about her was probably due to her precarious seat atop Shadow more than anything. As soon as she was able to stop the horse, she tossed the reins over his head and slid ingloriously from the saddle. Her feet landed with a jarring thud when she connected with the ground.

Mandy came out of the house, waving. "Gee, what took you guys so long?" she called, walking toward them. "I've had dinner ready for ages."

"We stopped and rested for a bit," Russ said, sharing a secret smile with Taylor, who was confident the color in her cheeks spelled out exactly what they'd been doing.

"I thought you were going to be back right away, so I fixed soup and sandwiches for dinner. That's all right, isn't it?"

"Actually, I should be getting back to town," Taylor said, eager to make her escape. Only when she was alone would she be able to analyze what had happened. Of one thing she was sure: there wouldn't be a repeat of this.

All her good intentions to take the time to heal her

broken heart properly were like dust particles caught in the wind, blowing every which way. She had no business getting involved with Russ.

"Oh, please, don't go yet." Mandy's face fell at Taylor's announcement.

"I really have to," Taylor insisted. Spending any more of this day with Russ would have been agonizing, reminding her of what she couldn't allow herself to have.

Taylor hadn't been in her rental house five minutes when she felt the urge to talk to her mother. But it was her father who answered on the third ring.

"Hi, Dad."

"Taylor, sweetheart, how are you?" No matter what his mood, he always sounded gruff.

"Fine."

The pause that followed was brief. "What's wrong?"

Taylor smiled to herself. She'd never been very good at keeping anything from her parents. "What makes you ask?"

"You don't call home very often."

"Dad," she whispered, closing her eyes, "is Mom around? I'm in the mood for a mother-daughter chat."

"Your mother's shopping. Just pretend I'm her and talk."

"I can't do that." She loved him dearly, but they were constantly arguing. Of all the Manning children, Taylor was the one who didn't hesitate to stand up to him. Her bravery had won her the esteem of her siblings.

"Why can't you talk to me? I'm your father, aren't I? You're the one who's always throwing equality of the sexes in my face. So talk."

"But, Dad, this is different."

"Hogwash. I haven't been married to your mother

for the past thirty-five years without knowing how she thinks. Tell me what you want and I'll respond just as if I were your mother."

"It's nothing really, but, well…" She decided to jump in with both feet. "What would you say if I told you I met a cowboy I think I might be falling in love with? The problem is, I'm not sure I could even get along with this man. From the moment we met he set my teeth on edge."

"I take it the situation has changed?"

"Not really," she mumbled, knowing she wasn't making much sense. "He still says things that make me so mad I could scream, but then at other times he'll do something so sweet and sincere I want to cry." Her voice shook. "I realize it probably goes back to Mark, and you're going to say I'm on the rebound. Russ and I are as incompatible as any two people could be. I can't even believe I'm so attracted to him." She pulled in a deep breath once she'd finished. There was silence on the other end. "Dad?"

"I'm here."

"Well, say something."

"You want me to say something?" he repeated, but he didn't sound like himself. He paused and cleared his throat. "In this case I think you might be right—talk this over with your mother. She knows about these things."

Taylor laughed softly into the phone and shook her head. For the first time in recent history she'd won an argument with her father.

On Tuesday afternoon, as Taylor walked home, she stopped at the grocery store, then mailed her electric bill payment at the pharmacy. She loved going into Cougar Point's drugstore. Not only could she have a prescription filled, but she could buy just about anything she needed. A tiny branch of the post office operated there, as well as a liquor store. In Seattle one-stop shopping generally referred to a large mall, but in Cougar Point it meant going to the pharmacy.

As she carried her groceries home, she noticed that the leaves were starting to change and wondered how long this pleasant fall weather would continue. Turning off Main Street and onto Oak, she saw Mandy sitting on her front porch.

"Mandy?" The girl's eyes were red and puffy from crying. "Sweetheart, what's wrong?"

Russ's sister leaped to her feet and wiped her eyes. Her chin was tilted at a proud, indignant angle and her mouth trembled. "I'm leaving."

"Leaving?"

"Running away," she explained in a tight voice. "But before I go, I thought I should tell someone so Russ won't send Cody Franklin out looking for me."

Six

"Come inside," Taylor urged the girl. "I think we should talk about this."

Mandy hedged, keeping her eyes downcast. "I don't really have time."

"It'll just take a few minutes. I promise." Withdrawing the key from her purse, Taylor opened the door, walked inside and deposited her groceries on the kitchen counter.

Mandy followed, clearly anxious to be on her way.

Pulling out a chair, Taylor indicated she should sit down. Then she grabbed them each a can of cold soda as inducement and took the chair opposite Mandy.

"It's Russ," the girl said in a choked whisper. "He's making me quit the drill team."

Taylor struggled to hide her dismay. "Is it your grades?"

"No. I've always been high honor roll. We got our uniforms this afternoon and I tried mine on and Russ happened to come into the house. He saw me and got all bent out of shape, saying the skirt was too short. I tried to tell him the skirts have been the same length for the past hundred years, and that just made him madder."

"I don't think your brother appreciates sarcasm."

"No kidding. He insisted I drop the hem on the skirt

five inches. I know I should've been more subtle, but I couldn't help it. I laughed and told him he was being ridiculous."

"I can't imagine that pleased him."

"No," Mandy said, shaking her head. She clutched the can with stiff fingers, but as far as Taylor could see she hadn't taken a sip. "Then he said this wasn't an issue we were going to discuss. He was ordering me, as my legal guardian, to lower the hem of the skirt, and he didn't want any arguments."

"Naturally you refused."

"Naturally. What else could I do?" Mandy yelped. "I'd look totally asinine with a drill team skirt that went to midcalf. I'd be the laughingstock of the entire school district, and all because my bullheaded brother won't listen to reason."

"Is that when he issued the ultimatum?"

"H-how'd you know?"

"I know Russ, or at least someone a whole lot like him. The way I figure it, he suggested that either you lower the hem or you quit the drill team, and then he stalked out of the house."

Mandy blinked, then took a deep swallow of the soda. "That's exactly what happened."

"You've gotten into plenty of arguments with your brother before without deciding to run away. Why now?"

Mandy's green eyes clouded with tears as she lifted one shoulder in a halfhearted shrug. "Because."

"That doesn't tell me much." Taylor stood and reached for a box of tissues, setting it on the table.

"He doesn't want me around."

"That isn't true," Taylor said. "We were talking about you making the drill team just the other day, and Russ was so proud. He loves you, Mandy. I'm sure of it."

"I'm not. At least not anymore. He's so stubborn."

"Opinionated?"

"That, too, and…" She hesitated, searching for another word.

"Unreasonable?"

Mandy slowly raised her eyes to Taylor. "I didn't realize you knew Russ so well."

"I told you before that my father and I had trouble getting along when I was your age, didn't I?"

Mandy nodded and jerked a tissue from the box, as though admitting that she needed one was a sign of weakness.

"Sometimes I swear my father and your brother were cut from the same cloth. It would be easier to change the course of the Columbia River than to get them to alter their opinions." Raising her feet onto the edge of the chair, Taylor looped her arms around her bent knees. "The family money was limited and my parents couldn't afford to pay for all five of us to go to college. So he decided that educating the boys was more important. He assumed they'd be supporting families, while Christy and I would end up with husbands."

"But you went to college."

"Indeed I did, but I paid for every cent of it myself. It took me eight years to complete my education. I worked summers in Alaska when I could, in addition to nights and weekends during the school year. Once I was a senior, I was able to get on as a dorm mother, and that took care of my room and board."

"But, Taylor, that's not fair!"

"In my father's eyes it was. Granted, if Christy and I had been the only two, I'm sure he would have gladly paid for our education, but Dad was financially strapped paying for the boys."

"Yeah, but your brothers will probably end up getting married, too."

Mandy's logic was closely aligned with Taylor's own. "Yes, but as my father said, they won't be having babies, and it's unlikely they'll have to delay whatever career they choose in order to raise a family."

"Women are entitled to a career if they want one!"

"Of course. But it wasn't only college that my father and I argued over. It started with the usual things, like clothes and makeup and friends, but later we found ourselves at odds over just about everything else."

"W-what about boyfriends? Did your dad find reasons to dislike them all?"

"No. Just one." Now Taylor lowered her eyes. From the moment her father had met Mark, he hadn't liked the up-and-coming financial planner. When Taylor had questioned him about his instant dislike, Eric Manning had given her the most nonsensical reply. Her father had claimed Mark was too smooth. Too smooth! He'd made Mark sound like a used car salesman. Her father had refused to look past the friendly smile and the easy laugh to the talented man beneath. Mark had tried hard to win him over; Taylor gave him credit for that. The more effort he'd put forth, the more she'd loved him. Taylor and her father had argued constantly over Mark.

Then one day she'd learned that everything her father had guessed about Mark was true. She'd gone to him and broken into bitter tears. For the first time he hadn't said I told you so. Instead, he'd held her in his arms and gently patted her head while she wept. She'd heard later from her brothers that their father had wanted to confront Mark and tell him what a bastard he was. It had taken some fast talking on their parts to convince him it was best to leave the situation alone.

"You've had arguments with Russ before," Taylor said again, tearing herself away from the memories of a painful past.

Mandy plucked out another tissue, noisily blew her nose and nodded. "Lots of times, especially lately. He's always finding things to gripe at me about."

"But why run away now?"

"I have my reasons."

Her words were so low that Taylor had to strain to hear. "Where will you go?"

"I have an aunt in New Jersey.... I'm not exactly sure where. She was my mother's half sister, and she sent me a birthday present once before my mom died. I think she might let me live with her."

Taylor didn't bother to point out the numerous holes in Mandy's plan. "Wouldn't it be a good idea to contact her first?" she asked.

"I...was hoping to surprise her."

"You mean show up on her doorstep so she can't say no?"

"Something like that," Mandy admitted.

The phone rang, and standing, Taylor walked over to answer it. Apparently Mandy thought this was a good time to use the bathroom and left the kitchen.

"Hello."

"Taylor, this is Russ. I don't suppose you've heard from Mandy, have you?" He sounded impatient and more than a little worried. "I'm at my wit's end with that girl. I've called practically everyone in town. I've got enough to do without playing hide-and-seek with her."

"She's here."

"We had another one of our fights and—" He stopped abruptly. "She's there? In town? With you?"

"That's what I just said."

"How'd she get there?"

"I assume she either walked or hitchhiked."

"Into town?" He groaned. "Listen, keep her there. I'll be at your place in ten minutes. You can warn her right now, she may be on restriction for the rest of her natural life."

"Russ, there seems to be a lack of communication here."

"You're damn right there is. She can't go running to you every time she needs someone to champion her cause. And while I'm on the subject, I refuse to listen to your arguments regarding this skirt issue. I'm not going to have any sister of mine running around half-naked."

"Mandy didn't ask me to champion her cause," Taylor said, having trouble holding back her own quick temper. "She came to tell me she was running away."

Russ's response was a short, harsh laugh. "We'll see about that," he said, and slammed down the receiver.

Stifling a groan herself, Taylor hung up.

"I should be leaving," Mandy said when she returned to the kitchen.

"What about clothes?"

"I packed a bag and hid it in the bushes outside. I wasn't going to tell you I was running away at first. I only came to thank you for being my friend. I… I think Russ likes you and I hope that you two…well, you know." She smiled bravely, but tears rolled down her face and she smeared them across her cheeks with the back of her hand.

"Money?" Taylor tried next, thinking fast. She had to stall Russ's sister until he arrived, although in his present frame of mind, she wasn't sure he'd help matters any.

"I have enough."

"How much is enough?"

"A couple of hundred dollars. I was saving it for a new saddle, but after I saw the dress you made for the dance

I was going to buy a sewing machine. Now I'll need it to get to New Jersey."

"But, Mandy, that won't even pay for a bus ticket."

"I'll...think of something."

"I've got some cash," Taylor said, reaching for her purse. "It's a shame you're leaving. I was asked to be a chaperone when the drill team goes to Reno next month. I was looking forward to seeing you perform."

"You were?" Mandy brightened somewhat. "It's going to be fun. We've been practicing early every morning for this competition, and by next month we should be really good. The larger high schools almost always win, but all the girls who go have such a good time." Some of the excitement left her, and her shoulders sagged. She forced a smile. "At least in Reno you'll be able to use your American Express."

"And order pizza. I would kill for a good pepperoni pizza on a Friday night."

"The bowling alley makes a decent one. You should try it sometime."

"I suppose I will," Taylor said, rummaging through her wallet. "Are you sure you won't change your mind? Mandy, sweetheart, it's a cold, cruel world out there. If you like, you can call your aunt from here and feel her out before you leave Cougar Point."

"I guess maybe I should," Mandy murmured, not looking certain about anything. She hesitated, then turned huge appealing eyes on Taylor. "I was wondering...do you think maybe I could live with you? No, don't answer that," she said quickly. Regretfully. "Russ would never allow it, and, well, it wouldn't work. Forget I asked."

"I'd love it if you did, but, honey, that isn't any solution."

Mandy tucked her chin against her collarbone. "I'll leave in a few minutes, okay?"

"Mandy." Taylor stopped her. She couldn't continue this pretense. "That was Russ on the phone a few minutes ago. He's on his way to talk to you."

The pale green eyes widened with offense. "You told him I was here? How could you, Taylor? I thought you were my friend. I trusted you...."

"I am your friend. I care about you and can't let you ruin your life because you've had a spat with your brother."

"It's more than that."

"I know. Trust me, I know," Taylor said gently, resisting the urge to pull Mandy into her arms. "What I'd like to suggest is that when your brother arrives you stay in the kitchen, and I'll keep him in the living room and try to talk some sense into him."

"He won't listen," Mandy cried. Tears ran unrestrained down her cheeks, and she clenched her fists at her sides. "It would be best if I just left now."

The sound of Russ's truck screeching to a stop outside the house was a welcome relief, at least to Taylor. "Give me ten minutes alone with him," she said.

"All right," Mandy reluctantly agreed. "But that's all the time I've got." She made it sound as if she had a plane to catch.

Taylor was at the front door before Russ could even knock. What she saw didn't give her any hope that this matter could easily be put to rest. His fury was all too evident; his face was red and his steps were quick and abrupt as he let himself in the house. Taylor practically had to throw herself in front of the kitchen door to keep him in the living room.

"Where is she?"

"Before you talk to Mandy, you and I need to discuss something."

"Not now," he said, looking past her. "I've never raised a hand to that girl, but I'll tell you she's tempting fate. Running away? That's a laugh. And just where does she intend to go?"

"Russ, would you stop shouting and listen to me." Taylor used her best schoolteacher voice and placed her hands threateningly on her hips as if to suggest one more cross word and she'd report him to the principal.

"I have somewhere to go, so you needn't worry," Mandy yelled from the kitchen.

"Sit down," Taylor said, pointing at her sofa. "We've got a problem here that isn't going to be settled by you hollering threats at your sister."

"They're a lot more than threats." Russ continued pacing the floor, occasionally removing his hat long enough to angrily plow his fingers through his hair.

"Mandy didn't come to me about the length of the drill team uniform—"

"It's a damn good thing because I'm not changing my mind. No sister of mine is going to parade around a field in that skimpy little outfit." His frown informed Taylor that he didn't appreciate her interference in what he considered a family affair.

"I'm leaving!" Mandy shouted from the other room.

"Over my dead body," Russ retaliated. "I'll drag you back to the ranch if I have to."

"Then I'll run away tomorrow. You can't force me to live with you."

"She's right, you know," Taylor whispered.

Russ shot her a look hot enough to boil water.

"Listen to what she's really saying," Taylor pleaded.

Russ advanced a step toward the other room. Taylor's

hand on his arm stopped him. He glanced down at her and blinked as though he'd almost forgotten that she was there. "This is between me and my sister," he growled.

"Listen to her," Taylor repeated, more forcefully this time. "Hear the doubt and pain in her voice. She doesn't want to leave any more than you want her to go."

"Then why…?"

"Because she's convinced you don't love her and you don't want her living with you anymore."

Russ removed his hat and slapped it against the coffee table. "Of all the foolish…" Suddenly he seemed at a loss for words. "That's the most ridiculous thing I've ever heard."

"Mandy," Taylor called, "come out here and sit down." She gestured toward Russ, motioning for him to do the same. "The only way I can see that'll do any good is for the two of you to clear the air. You need to talk face-to-face instead of hurling insults at each other."

Mandy hesitantly moved into the living room. She sank slowly into a chair and picked up a women's magazine sitting on the arm, absently flipping through the pages.

Russ sat on the other side of the room, looking nonchalant and relaxed. He propped his ankle on one knee and spread his arms across the back of the davenport as if they were discussing the abrupt change in weather rather than the future of his only sister and their relationship.

"Mandy, why do you want to move in with your aunt?" Taylor asked.

"Because my pigheaded brother is so unreasonable."

"You've gotten along with him up until now."

"No, I haven't." Her voice grew smaller and smaller. "Besides, I'm just in the way."

"Russ," Taylor said, twisting around to confront him, "is Mandy in the way?"

"Hell, no, I need her."

"Sure, to cook your meals and wash your clothes. You can hire someone to do that. I bet Mary Lu Randall would do it for free. She's had a crush on you forever."

"You're all the family I've got," Russ countered gruffly.

"I'm nothing but a problem," Mandy said, rubbing the tears from her eyes. "You think I don't notice, but I do. There isn't a single thing you like about me anymore. You're always complaining. If it isn't my hair, it's my clothes or I'm wearing too much makeup or spending too much time with my friends."

Russ dropped his leg and leaned forward, hands clasped. He studied Mandy, then started to frown. "I'm just trying to do the best job I can to make sure you turn into a responsible adult."

Mandy looked away. Unable to stand still, Taylor crossed the room, sat on the arm of the chair and placed her own on Mandy's thin shoulders.

"I love you, Amanda," Russ said starkly. "Maybe sometimes I don't show it the way I should, but I do. You're as much a part of my life as the Lazy P. I need you, and not to do the cooking and laundry, either."

Mandy sniffled in an effort not to cry, and Taylor reached inside her pocket for a fresh tissue, handing it to the girl.

"I...didn't realize this drill team thing was so important to you," Russ went on. "I suppose Taylor's going to tell me I should've been more sensitive." Russ paused, shaking his head. "When I saw you all dressed up like that, it made me realize how grown-up you're getting, and I guess I didn't want to face the fact you're going to be a beautiful young woman soon. It kind of scares me. Before long, the boys are going to be swarming around the ranch like ants."

"I-if you really want me to quit the drill team, I will," Mandy offered in a thin, raspy voice.

"No, you can stay on the team. If the other parents are willing to let their daughters prance around a playing field in those little outfits, then I'll just have to get used to the idea." Russ stood up and walked across the room, standing in front of his sister. "Friends?"

Mandy nodded, fresh tears streaking her face. She jumped up and moved into Russ's arms, hugging him tight. "I didn't really want to live with Aunt Joyce in New Jersey."

"That's good because the last I heard she retired someplace in Mexico."

"She did? How come you never told me?"

"Maybe because I was afraid you'd think it was an exotic, fun place to be and decide you'd rather live with her. I meant what I said about loving you, Mandy. You're going to have to be more patient with me, I guess, but I promise I'll try harder."

"I…will, too."

Russ slowly shut his eyes as he hugged his sister close.

Taylor felt her own eyes fill with tears. She hadn't expected Russ to be so open about his feelings for Mandy. When he'd first arrived, she'd been convinced everything was going to go from bad to worse. Russ was so proud and so furious, but once he'd stopped to listen to his sister and heard her fears, he'd set the anger aside and revealed a deep, vulnerable part of himself that Taylor had never even suspected was there.

"Say, how about if I treat my two best girls to dinner?" Russ suggested.

"Yeah," Mandy responded. "Pizza?"

"Anything you want," he said, smiling down on his sister. He raised his eyes to Taylor, and they softened perceptibly.

"I...can't," she said, declining the invitation. "Anyway, this should be a time for the two of you to talk. I'd just be in the way."

"No, you wouldn't. We'd never have been able to do this without you," Mandy insisted. "I really want you to come."

"Another time," Taylor promised. "You two go and have fun."

Russ squeezed Mandy's shoulders. "I don't know about you, but I'm famished. If Taylor wants to turn down an offer for the best pizza in town, there's only one thing we can do—let her suffer."

"It's your loss," Mandy told Taylor on their way out the door.

"Yes, I know," she said, standing behind the screen door. Mandy bounded down the front steps and ran around the side of the house, where she'd apparently hidden her bag of clothes.

While Russ was waiting for his sister to reappear, he turned to Taylor and mouthed the words, "Thank you." Then he touched his fingers to his lips and held his hand out to her. She pressed her open palm against the screen door.

The following evening Taylor sat at the kitchen table with her feet propped on a chair, stirring a bowl of soup. "You're in deep trouble here," she muttered to herself. "If you don't watch it, you're going to fall in love with a cowboy. You're already halfway there. Admit it."

She vigorously stirred her chicken noodle soup until it sloshed over the rim of the bowl. Setting the spoon aside, Taylor leaned her elbows on the table and buried her face in her hands.

The whole purpose of coming to Montana was to avoid relationships. She hadn't been in town a week when she'd met Russ. And from there everything had quickly gone downhill. From the first time he'd kissed her she'd known she was headed for disaster. But had that stopped her? Oh, no. Not even the cool voice of reason—or the memory of Mark's betrayal—had given her pause. Instead she was walking straight into his arms, knowing full well that nothing could ever come of their relationship. She wouldn't have an affair with him. Marriage was out of the question; Russ would agree with her there. So exactly where was their relationship going?

Nowhere.

"Nowhere," she repeated out loud. "Save yourself some heartache," she told herself, then sat back and wondered if she was wise enough to follow her own advice, immediately doubting that she was. The voice in her heart was so much louder than anything her brain was telling her. She'd been a fool once. Hadn't she learned anything? Apparently not!

The phone rang, startling her. She dropped her legs and stood to answer it, afraid it might be Russ and not knowing what she'd say.

It was.

"Hi," she said, forcing some enthusiasm into her voice. The man had no idea of the turmoil he was causing her.

"I'm calling to thank you for what you did for Mandy and me yesterday."

"It wasn't anything," she said lightly. Her hand tightened around the telephone receiver as she supported herself against the kitchen wall. She hated the way her pulse reacted to the sound of his voice. If he had a voice like other men, it wouldn't affect her so strongly. His was deep and so sexy....

"You were right about me not being aware of her doubt and fear," he went on to say. "I don't know what I did to make her think I don't want her around anymore, but she's totally wrong."

"You were wonderful with her." Taylor meant that. She hadn't expected him to be half as understanding or sensitive to his sister's needs. Perhaps it would be easier to walk away from him if she could continue to view him as a difficult male, but he'd shown her another side of his personality, one so appealing that she found her heart softening toward him.

"I felt bad because I'd overreacted to the whole issue of her drill team uniform," Russ explained. "I'd come into the house, and seeing Mandy dressed in that outfit caught me by surprise. My nerves were on edge, anyway. We'd just found a dead calf, and when I saw Mandy, I took my frustration and anger out on her. She didn't deserve that."

"But you apologized. And taking her out to dinner was nice."

"I wish you'd come along. We both owe you."

"Nonsense. That was your time with Mandy."

Taylor could sense Russ's smile. "I will admit that we did have fun. I'd forgotten what a kick my sister can be. She's a sweet kid, but she's growing up too fast." There was a pause. "Listen, I didn't call you just to talk about Mandy. How about dinner Friday night?"

Taylor closed her eyes. The lure of the invitation was as strong as the pull of the tide. Squaring her shoulders, she shook her head.

"Taylor?"

"I don't think it's a good idea for us to see each other again," she said flatly.

Seven

"What the hell do you mean?" Russ demanded. He didn't know what kind of game Taylor was playing, but he wasn't about to become a participant. If there was a problem, he wanted it out in the open.

"Exactly what I said," she returned, sounding shaky and unsure. "I don't think it's wise for us to continue seeing each other."

"Why not?" He tried to keep his voice even, but dammit, Taylor was irritating him, not that this was anything new.

Russ had never met a woman like Taylor Manning before. She could make him madder than anyone he'd ever known, but when he kissed her, the earth moved, angels sang, and whatever else people said about moments of passion. Russ didn't understand it. No one had ever affected him the way Taylor did.

He'd tried staying away from her. Tried exercising a little more self-control, but five minutes with her and his good intentions went the way of all flesh. He wanted her in his bed, her hair spread out over his pillow. He thought about that a lot, far more than he should. Not for the first time, the image brought with it the stirrings of arousal. How could this teacher—and worse, one from a big city—inspire such hunger in him? It made no sense.

He'd run into a cocktail waitress friend when he'd been in Miles City the week before. It had been an uncomfortable encounter. April had expected him to come home with her for what she called "a little afternoon pleasure." Instead, Russ couldn't get away from her fast enough. Not that he didn't crave being with a woman. But deep down he'd known that the only woman he wanted was Taylor.

That afternoon Russ had seen April for what she was, jaded and cold, and he wanted nothing to do with her. He'd escaped and hurried back to the Lazy P, only to discover Taylor there with his sister. He'd wanted her so badly that day. There was no use lying to himself about it. Even now, almost a week later, when he closed his eyes, he could still smell the fragrance of her perfume. Her mouth had parted beneath his, eager for his kisses. Every touch had hurled his senses into chaos.

"I...don't want there to be any misunderstandings between us," Taylor said, cutting into his thoughts.

Reluctantly Russ pulled himself from his musings. "I don't, either. If you won't have dinner with me, I'd like to know why. That's not such an unreasonable request, is it?"

"I...think the reason should be obvious."

"Tell me, anyway."

Russ felt her hesitation, and when she spoke again, her voice was a little raspy, as if she found it difficult to share her thoughts. "Our personality differences should be more than adequate reason for us to use caution."

She sounded exactly like the schoolteacher she was. "That hasn't stopped us before. Why should it now?" he asked.

"Darn it, Russ Palmer," she cried. "You aren't going to make this easy, are you?"

"All I want is the truth."

Her sigh sang over the wire. "I can't give you anything less than the truth, can I?"

"No," he said softly. "I'll admit we're different. Anyone looking at us could be able to see that. Our opinions on most subjects are completely opposite, but frankly, I'm willing to work around that. I like you, Taylor."

"I know," she whispered dismally. That knowledge seemed to cause her distress rather than celebration.

Russ wasn't pleased, but he refused to make an issue of it. "There are plenty of girls in Cougar Point who'd be mighty pleased if I invited them out to dinner," he added, thinking that might set her back some, help her realize she had competition.

"Ask them out then," she said tartly.

"I don't want to. The only woman who interests me is you."

"That's the problem," she mumbled, and it sounded like she was close to tears.

The thought of Taylor crying did something funny to Russ's stomach. His protective urges ran deep when it came to this woman. "Taylor, maybe I should drive into town and we can talk face-to-face."

"No," she returned abruptly. "That would only make this more difficult." She paused, and Russ had to restrain the yearning to put the phone aside and go to her immediately.

"Is this about what happened the other day?" he asked. "I know our kissing went further than it should have, but that wasn't intentional. If you want an apology…"

"No, that's not it. Oh, Russ, don't you see?"

He didn't. "Tell me."

"I like you too much. We both know where this is going to lead—one of these days we're going to end up in love and in bed together."

That didn't sound too tragic to Russ. He'd been dreaming about it for weeks. "So?"

"So?" she shouted, and her voice vibrated with anger. "I'm not interested in a permanent relationship with you. You're a wonderful man—and you'll make some woman a terrific husband. But not me."

He let a moment of tense silence pass before he commented. "If you'll recall, the invitation was for dinner. All I was asking for was a simple meal together. I'm not looking for a lifetime commitment."

"You're doing your best to make this difficult, which is all too typical. I will not have an affair with you, and that's exactly where our relationship is headed. People are already talking, especially after the Grange dance. And then we went horseback riding and… Before I know it, you're going to be telling me how to vote and insisting a woman's place is in the home." She paused only long enough to inhale a quick breath. "I'm sorry… I really am, but I don't think we should have anything to do with each other. Please understand."

Before Russ could say another word, the line was disconnected. He held the receiver in his hand for several minutes in disbelief. His first response was anger. He didn't know what Taylor was muttering about. Her words about voting and a woman's place were utterly nonsensical.

He had every right to be upset with her; no one had ever hung up on him before. Instead he felt a tingling satisfaction. Slowly, hardly aware that it was happening, Russ felt a smile creep over his face.

Mandy strolled past him just then. "Hey, what's so funny?"

"Taylor," he said, grinning hard. "She likes me."

Russ was riding the range, looking for strays, when he saw his lifelong friend come barreling toward him in a battered pickup. Removing his hat, Russ wiped his forearm across his brow. He'd been in the saddle since morning, and he was wearier than he could remember being in a long while. He hadn't been sleeping well; Taylor was constantly on his mind, and he still hadn't figured out what to do about her. If anything, he'd delayed confronting her, thinking it was best to give her time. But he was growing anxious. In the past couple of days Russ had faced a few truths about the two of them.

"Cody, good to see you," Russ greeted him, dismounting from Magic. "Problems?"

"None to speak of," Cody said, opening the cab door and getting out.

"You didn't come looking for me to discuss the weather."

Cody wasn't wearing his sheriff deputy's uniform, which was unusual. Instead, he had on jeans and a thick sweater. He was about the same height as Russ, but he kept his dark hair trimmed short.

"It's been nice the past week or so, hasn't it?" Cody said, gesturing toward the cloudless blue sky. He tucked his fingertips into the hip pocket of his Levi's and walked to the front of the truck. Leaning his back against the grille, he raised one foot and rested it on the bumper.

For early October the weather had been unseasonably warm. They'd experienced several Indian summer days, and while Russ appreciated the respite before winter hit, he knew better than to take anything about Montana weather for granted.

"What's up?" he asked. "It isn't like you to beat around the bush."

Cody nodded, looking slightly chagrined. "I came to talk to you about the new schoolteacher."

"What about her?" Russ asked, tensing. He moved over to the truck and put his foot on the bumper, meeting Cody's eyes.

The deputy glanced away, but not before Russ saw the troubled look on his face.

"We've been friends a lot of years, and the last thing I want is for a woman to come between us."

"I take it you want to ask Taylor out?"

Cody nodded. "But only if you have no objection. Word is the two of you aren't seeing each other anymore."

"Who told you that?" Russ demanded, fighting to repress the surge of instant jealousy that tightened around his chest. He'd resisted the temptation to rush into town and talk some sense into Taylor, assuming she'd have second thoughts by now. Apparently that wasn't the case. Truth be known, Russ had been doing some thinking about their situation. They were both mature adults and they weren't going to leap into something that would be wrong for them. Okay, so they were strongly attracted—that much was a given—and not seeing each other wasn't going to change the situation, not one bit.

It came as a shock for Russ to admit he was falling in love with Taylor. There wasn't any use in fighting it—hell, he didn't even want to. Nor was he going to pretend he didn't care about her.

"Mary Beth Morgan said something to me this morning," Cody continued. "Mary Beth said she and Taylor were having coffee in the faculty lounge and she inquired about the two of you. Evidently Taylor told her you'd decided not to see each other again."

"Taylor came right out and said that?"

"I don't know her exact words. Hey, I'm repeating what someone else repeated to me. How close it is to the truth, I wouldn't know. That's why I'm here."

The mental image of Cody holding Taylor in his arms brought a sudden flash of rage so strong that for a moment Russ couldn't breathe. Shoving away from the truck, he returned to Magic, reached for the reins and leaped onto the gelding's back.

"Russ?" Cody asked, frowning.

"Go ahead and ask her out."

Taylor couldn't remember Friday nights being so lonely before moving to Cougar Point. It seemed she'd always had something to do, someplace to go. But that wasn't the case anymore. Her entertainment options were limited. The town sported one old-time theater. One screen. One movie. The feature film for the week was a comedy Taylor had seen six months earlier in Seattle. By now it was probably available on video in most parts of the country.

There had been an offer for dinner from Cody Franklin, which had been a surprise, but she'd turned him down. In retrospect she wished she hadn't been so quick to refuse him. He was certainly pleasant. They'd met at the dance, and she'd found him reserved, and perhaps a little remote.

If she was looking for some way to kill time, she could sew, but Taylor simply wasn't in the mood. After a long week in the classroom, she was more interested in doing something relaxing.

Well, she could always read, she supposed. Locating a promising romance, she cuddled up in the armchair and wrapped an afghan around her legs. She hadn't finished the first chapter when her eyes started to drift closed. Struggling to keep them open, she concentrated on the text. After the third yawn, she gave up, set the open book over the arm of the chair and decided to rest for a few minutes.

The next thing she knew someone was pounding at her front door.

Taylor tossed aside the afghan and stumbled across the room, disoriented and confused. "W-who is it?" she asked. The door didn't have a peephole; most folks in town didn't even bother to lock their front doors.

"Russ Palmer," came the gruff reply.

Taylor quickly twisted the lock and opened the door. "What are you doing here?" she insisted. It took all her willpower not to throw her arms around him.

Now that Russ was standing in the middle of her living room, he didn't look all that pleased about being there.

The wall clock chimed, and Taylor absently counted ten strikes. It was ten! She'd been "resting" for nearly two hours. Good grief, she'd been reduced to falling asleep at eight o'clock on a Friday night.

"Russ?" she prodded. He was frowning, and she had no idea why. "Is something wrong?"

"No." He gave her a silly, lopsided grin. "Everything's wonderful. You're wonderful. I'm wonderful. The whole world's wonderful."

"Russ?" She squinted up at him. "You've been drinking."

He pointed his index finger toward the ceiling. "Only a little."

She steered him toward the sofa and sat him down. "How much is a little?"

"A couple of beers with a bunch of guys." His brows drew together as he considered his words. "Or was that a couple of guys and a bunch of beers? I don't remember anymore."

"That's what I thought," she murmured. He'd obviously downed more than two beers! "I'll make you some coffee."

"Don't go," he said, reaching out and clasping her around the waist. "I'm not drunk, just a little tipsy. I had this sudden urge to visit my lady, and now that I'm here, I want to hold you."

He effortlessly brought her into his lap. Her hands were on his shoulders. "I thought we agreed this sort of thing had to stop," she whispered.

His mouth found the open V of her shirt, and he kissed her there, gliding his tongue over her warm skin, creating sensations that were even warmer.

"We weren't going to see each other anymore, remember?" she tried again. Her nails dug into the hard muscles of his shoulders as she exhaled slowly.

"I've been thinking about that," Russ said between nibbling kisses that slid along the line of her jaw. "I haven't thought of anything else all week."

"Russ, please stop," she whimpered.

To her surprise, he did as she asked. Her hands were in his hair, and she reluctantly withdrew them. "You shouldn't be driving."

"I know. I left the truck at Billy's and walked over here. Only I didn't realize where I was headed until I arrived on your doorstep."

Billy's was one of the town's three taverns—the most popular, according to what Taylor had heard. During the summer months, they brought in a band every third Friday, and apparently every adult in town showed up.

"You shouldn't have come," she whispered. Then why

was she so glad he had? Taylor didn't want to analyze the answer to that, afraid of what she'd discover.

"You're positively right," Russ concurred. "I have no business being here. Go ahead and kick me out. I wouldn't blame you if you did. Fact is, you probably should."

"If you promise to behave yourself, I'll put on a pot of coffee." She squirmed off his lap and moved into the kitchen. She'd just poured cold water into the automatic drip machine when Russ stole up behind her. He slipped his arms around her waist and buried his face in the curve of her neck.

"Russ...you promised."

"No, I didn't."

"Then...you should leave."

He dropped his arms, walked over to the chair, turned it around and straddled it. He was grinning, obviously pleased. "Cody told me," he announced.

Taylor busied herself bringing down two mugs from the cupboard and setting them on the counter. Apparently there were no secrets in this town. Taylor regretted not accepting Cody Franklin's dinner invitation. She certainly wished she had now.

"You turned him down. Why?" His dark eyes held hers with unwavering curiosity, demanding a reply.

"I...don't think that's any of your business."

He shrugged, his look indifferent. "I'd like to think it *is* my business."

"You don't own me." She pressed her hands into the counter behind her.

He grinned. "Not for lack of trying." He held out his arms to her, beseeching her to walk over. "We've got a good thing going, and I can't understand why you want to throw it away." His eyes continued to hold hers, but he was no longer smiling. "The first time I met you, I recognized trouble. That didn't stop me, and it didn't stop you, either, did it?"

She lowered her gaze rather than answer. When she raised her head, she discovered Russ standing directly in front of her.

"Did it?" he repeated. He grabbed her around the waist, and with one swift movement set her on top of the counter.

She stared at him, wondering about his mood. "Russ?"

He slanted his mouth over hers, kissing her long and hard, and when he'd finished, she was panting. "Did it?" he asked a third time.

He reached for her shoulders again, intent on another kiss—and more.

"Russ, you're drunk." From somewhere she found the strength to stop him, although it felt like the most difficult task of her life.

Ever so slowly he tilted back his head. His grin was sultry and teasing. "I'm not that drunk."

"You shouldn't have come here."

"Yes, I know." His hands were in her hair. He couldn't seem to leave it alone. Every time they were together, he ran his fingers through it. Carefully he removed the combs, then arranged it over her shoulder, smoothing it with his callused fingertips. Then his hands framed her face and he kissed her once more.

Unable to resist him, she parted her lips in welcome, and they clung to each other.

When he finally dragged his mouth from hers, he smiled at her. "Go ahead and give me that coffee, and then you can drive me home."

Without question, Taylor did as he asked. They drank their coffee in silence, and its sobering effect hit her immediately. After all her intentions to stay away from him, she'd been giddy with happiness when he'd arrived. It hadn't mattered that he'd been drinking. It hadn't mattered that he took liberties with her. All that mattered was seeing him again. Taylor had never thought of herself as a weak person, but that was how Russ made her feel. Spineless and indecisive.

Russ fell asleep on the drive out to the ranch. Taylor was glad to see that the back porch light was on when she pulled in to the yard. She parked the car and hurried around to the passenger side.

"Russ," she said, shaking him by the shoulders. "Wake up."

His eyes opened slowly, and when he recognized her, he grinned, his gaze warm and loving. "Taylor."

"You're home."

His arms circled her waist. "Yes, I know."

Taylor managed to break free. "Come on, let's go inside, and for heaven's sake, could you be a little less noisy? I don't want anyone to know I brought you here."

"Why not?" He inclined his head as if the answer demanded serious concentration.

"There's enough talk about us as it is. The last thing I need is for someone to report seeing my car parked at your house late on a Friday night."

"Don't worry. No one can see the house from the road."

"Just get inside, would you?" She was losing her patience with him. Despite the coffee, his actions were slower than before. He moved with the deliberateness of inebriation, taking unhurried wobbly steps toward the house.

The back door was unlocked, and Russ slammed it shut with his foot. The sound ricocheted through the kitchen like a blast from a shotgun, startling Taylor.

"Shh," Russ said loudly, pressing his finger over his lips. "You'll wake Mandy."

Taylor wished the teenager *would* wake up and come to help her. Russ was increasingly difficult to handle.

"You need to go to bed," she said and prepared to leave.

"I'll never make it there without you." His smile was roguish and naughty, and he staggered a few steps as though that was proof enough. "I need you, Taylor. No telling what might happen to me if I'm left to my own devices."

"I'm willing to chance that."

"I'm not." With his arm around her waist, he led her toward the stairs. He stumbled forward, bringing Taylor with him. She had no choice but to follow. She didn't know if it was an act or not, but he really did seem to need her assistance.

They were two steps up the stairs when Russ sagged against the wall and sighed heavily. "Have I ever told you I think you're beautiful?"

"I believe the word was wonderful," she muttered, using her shoulder to urge him forward.

"You're both. A man could drown in eyes that blue and not even care."

"Russ," she said in a whisper, "let's get you upstairs."

"In bed?" He arched his brows suggestively.

"Just get upstairs. Please."

"You're so eager for my body, you can hardly wait, can you?" he asked, then chuckled softly, seeming to find himself exceptionally amusing. He leaned forward enough to kiss the side of her neck. "I'll try to make it worth your while."

Taylor was breathless by the time they reached the top of the stairs. "Which room is yours?" she asked.

Russ turned all the way around before raising his arm and directing her to the bedroom at the end of the hall. "There," he said enthusiastically, pointing straight ahead as if he'd discovered uncharted land.

With her arm firmly around his middle, Taylor led him to the room. The hall was dark, lit only by the light of the moon visible through an uncurtained window. She opened the door, and together the two of them staggered forward, landing on the bed with a force that drove the oxygen from her lungs.

Russ released a deep sigh and rolled onto his back, positioning Taylor above him. His unrelenting dark eyes stared up at her.

"I...should be going."

"Not yet," he whispered. "Kiss me good-night first."

"Russ, no." She tried to move, but his hands were on her hips, holding her fast.

"All I'm asking for is one little kiss. So when I wake up in the morning I'll remember you were here and that'll make me feel good."

She rolled her eyes. "The only thing you're going to feel in the morning is a world-class headache."

"If you won't kiss me, then you leave me with no option but to kiss you."

He began to kiss her lips, tiny nibbling kisses that promised so much more than they delivered. Then he changed tactics, drugging her with prolonged kisses that chased away all grounds for complaint.

For some reason he stopped. Suddenly. He threw back his head and dragged in several deep breaths.

"Does this prove anything?" he asked urgently.

"That...that I should have left you to your own devices. You didn't need my help."

"I did. I do. I always will."

She shook her head, but Russ ignored that.

"In case you haven't figured it out yet," he informed her, "you belong in my bed, and that's exactly where you're going to end up."

With what remained of her shredded dignity, Taylor pushed herself free. She bolted off the bed and paced the room. As she did, Russ sat up on the bed, leaning against the bunched pillows, looking smug and arrogant. "You're so beautiful."

It was all Taylor could do not to throw her hands in the air and scream. "This doesn't change a thing," she insisted. "Not a thing."

His answering grin was filled with cocky reassurance. "Wanna bet?"

Eight

"Hi, Taylor," Mandy said as she stepped into Taylor's classroom early the following week.

"Howdy."

Mandy grinned. "You're beginning to sound like a country girl."

That gave Taylor cause to sit back and take notice. "I am?"

Mandy nodded. "Russ told me just the other day that he's going to make a country girl out of you yet." Mandy walked over to the front row of desks and sat on the edge of one as she spoke.

At the mention of Russ, Taylor began to fiddle with the pencils on her desk.

"Do...you remember the day I was thinking about running away?" Mandy asked, and her voice lowered.

"Of course," Taylor said.

"I asked you what your father thought about the boys you dated, and you told me he'd generally approved of your boyfriends." She pressed her books close to her chest, and Taylor noted how tense her hands were. "There was...a reason I asked about that. You see, there's this boy in school—he's a junior and his name is Eddie and...

well, he's really nice and my family knows his family and we've known each other almost all our lives and—"

"You like Eddie?"

Mandy's responding nod was fervent. "A whole lot, and I think he likes me, too. We've only talked in the hall a couple of times, but this morning when I was putting my books in my locker, he walked up and we started talking…not about anything in particular, at least not at first, then all of a sudden he asked if I wanted to go to the movies with him Saturday night."

"I see." Taylor did understand her dilemma. All too well. Mandy was only fourteen, and Russ would surely consider a high school freshman too young to date. In fact, Taylor agreed with him, but she'd been fourteen once herself and attracted to a boy who'd liked her. He'd been older, too, and had asked her to a party, which her father had adamantly opposed her attending. The memory of the argument that had followed remained painfully vivid in her mind.

"I really, really want to go to the movies with Eddie, but I'm afraid Russ will get upset with me for even asking. I mean, he's been trying hard to listen to my point of view, but dating is something that's never come up before and…well, I have a feeling we aren't going to be able to talk about me having a boyfriend without…an argument." She sighed heavily. "What should I do, Taylor?"

Taylor wished she had an easy answer. "I really don't know."

"Will you talk to him for me?"

"Absolutely not."

"Oh, please! You don't know how much this would mean to me. Don't you remember what it's like to be fourteen and have a boy like you?"

That was the problem; Taylor *did* remember. "When

I was your age, a sixteen-year-old boy invited me to a party. My father made it sound as if he wanted to drag me into an opium den. More than anything in the world, I wanted to go to that party."

"Did you?"

Taylor shook her head sadly. "I was too young to date."

Mandy's shoulders sagged with defeat. "It's only a movie, and I don't understand why it would be so bad if Eddie and I went to a show together."

Crossing her arms, Taylor started to pace her classroom, her thoughts spinning. "What about a compromise?"

"H-how do you mean?"

"What if Russ were to drop you off at the theater, you paid your own way and then you sat next to Eddie? With Russ's approval, of course."

Mandy looked more perplexed than relieved. "Eddie could buy me popcorn, though, couldn't he?"

"Sure. It wouldn't be like a real date, but you'd still be at the movies with Eddie."

Mandy's hold on her schoolbooks relaxed. "Do you think Russ would go for it?"

"He's a reasonable man." Taylor couldn't believe she was actually saying this, but in some instances it was true, and he was trying hard with his sister. "I'm sure he'd at least take it into consideration."

Mandy nodded, but her lips were still pinched. "Will you talk to him about it?"

"Me?" Taylor returned spiritedly. "You've got to be joking!"

"I'm not. Russ listens to you. You may not think so but I know he does. It's because of you that I'm allowed to wear makeup and buy my own clothes. Russ and I are trying hard to get along, but I'm afraid this thing with Eddie will ruin everything. Oh, Taylor, please. I'll do

anything you want. Cook your meals, do your laundry…
all year, anything. *Please*."

"Russ will listen to you."

"Maybe," Mandy agreed reluctantly, "but this is too
important to mess up. I told Eddie I'd have to talk it over
with my brother, and he said I should let him know tomorrow. I'm afraid if I put him off he'll ask some other
girl, and I'd die if he did."

Against her better judgment, Taylor felt herself weakening. She hadn't seen Russ since Friday night when
she'd dropped him off at the house, taken him up the
stairs and put him to bed. That whole episode was best
forgotten as far as Taylor was concerned.

"Please," Mandy coaxed once more.

"All right," Taylor muttered. When she was growing
up, she'd been able to go to her mother, who'd smooth
things over with her father. Mandy didn't have anyone
to run interference for her. Taylor didn't really mind—
although she worried that Russ would use this opportunity to press her with a few arguments of his own, ones
that had nothing to do with his sister.

Russ had been having a bad day from the time he'd
woken up that morning. The minute he'd stepped out of
the house he'd encountered one problem after another, the
latest being a calf standing two feet deep in mud. After
an hour of fruitless effort, Russ had lost his patience and
accepted the fact that he was going to need help. He'd
contacted a couple of his hands by walkie-talkie and was
waiting for them to arrive.

Every calf was valuable, but this one, trapped and
growing weaker, had been marked for his breeding herd.
Like most of the ranchers in Cougar Point, Russ kept two
herds. One for breeding purposes, which he used to pro-

duce bulls that he often sold for a handsome profit. Bull calves that didn't meet his expectations were turned into steers and raised for beef. His second herd was strictly grade cattle, sold off at the end of the season.

This particular calf had been the product of his highest quality bull and his best cow. Russ had great expectations for him and sure didn't want to lose him to a mud hole.

Russ checked the sun and wondered how much longer he'd have to wait. He'd sent his two best hands out to mend fences, a tedious but not thankless task.

There was still a lot of work left to complete before winter set in, and he didn't have time to waste. Miles of fence to inspect and mend, which was no small chore. If the fences weren't secure, Russ would soon be dealing with the elk that come down from the mountains in winter. If elk could get through his fence, they'd eat his oats and hay. No rancher could afford to feed elk, and a good fence was the best protection he had.

If Russ had to choose his favorite time of year, it would be autumn. The sun was still warm, but the air was crisp, and morning frost warned of encroaching winter. When he drove his cattle into the feed ground, it was like a homecoming, a culmination of the year's efforts.

The calf mewled, reminding Russ of his predicament.

"I know, fellow," Russ muttered. "I've tried everything I can think of. I'm afraid you're stuck here until one of the other men swings by and lends me a hand."

No sooner had the words escaped his mouth than he saw a truck heading slowly in his direction. He frowned, wondering who'd be coming out this way, knowing all his men were on horseback. Maybe there'd been trouble at the house.

After the day he'd been having, Russ didn't look forward to dealing with any more problems. As the blue ranch truck approached, Russ realized it was Taylor at the wheel.

He walked out of the mud and stood with his hands on his hips, waiting for her. He hadn't seen her since the night she'd driven him home. The truth was, he didn't feel proud of the way he'd finagled her into his bedroom. Yes, he'd had too much to drink, but he hadn't been nearly as drunk as he'd led her to believe.

"Hello," Taylor said as she climbed awkwardly out of the cab. She was dressed in jeans, but they were several inches too short and a tad too small. The sweater looked suspiciously like one of Mandy's.

Russ pulled off his gloves. "What brings you out here?" He didn't mean to sound unfriendly, but he was frustrated, tired and hungry. Despite that, he was damn glad to see her.

She didn't answer him right away, but instead focused her attention on the calf, which mewled pitifully. "Mandy suggested I drive out so I could talk to you," she muttered, then pointed at the mud hole. "That calf's stuck."

"No kidding."

"There's no need to be sarcastic with me," she announced primly. As she stood there, he couldn't help noticing just how tight those jeans were.

"Aren't you going to do something?" she demanded.

Undressing her occurred to him.... Russ brought his musings to an abrupt halt. "Do something about what?" he asked.

"That cow. She needs help."

"She's a he, and I'm well aware of the fact."

"Then *help him*," Taylor ordered, gesturing toward the calf as though she suspected Russ was simply ignoring the problem.

"I've spent the past hour helping him."

"Well, you certainly didn't do a very good job of it."

He raised his eyebrows. "Do you think you can do any better?"

She looked startled for a moment, then said, "I bet I could."

"Here we go again." He took off his hat long enough to slap it against his thigh and remove the dust. "Because you're a woman, an independent, competent woman, you're convinced you can handle this problem, while I, a chauvinist and a drunk, am incapable of even assessing the situation."

"I... I didn't exactly say that."

"But it's what you implied."

"Fine," she agreed. "I'll admit I can't see why you aren't helping that poor animal."

"I guess I just needed you. Go to it, lady."

"All right, I will." Cautiously she approached the edge of the mud hole. She planted her boots just outside the dark slime and leaned forward slightly. In a low voice she started carrying on a soothing, one-sided conversation with the calf as if she could reason him out of his plight.

"You're going to have to do a lot more than talk to him," Russ couldn't resist telling her. He walked over to the truck, crossed his arms and leaned against the side. Already he could feel his sour mood lifting. Just watching Taylor deal with this would be more entertainment than he'd enjoyed in a long while.

"I'm taking a few minutes to reassure him," Taylor returned from between clenched teeth. "The poor thing's frightened half out of his wits."

"Sweet-talkin' him is bound to help."

"I'm sure it will," she said, giving him a surly look.

"Works wonders with me, too," Russ had to tell her, although he couldn't keep the humor out of his voice.

"However, it's my belief that actions speak louder than words. When you're finished with the calf, would you care to demonstrate your concern for me?"

"No."

Russ chuckled softly. "That's what I thought."

Taylor cast him a furious glance before walking around the edges of the mud-caked hole. The calf continued to mewl, not that Russ could blame him. The fellow had gotten himself into one heck of a quandary.

"It appears he's completely trapped," Taylor announced in formal tones.

It had taken Russ all of three seconds to come to that conclusion.

"Can't you put a rope around his neck and pull him out?" She motioned toward Russ's gelding. "You could loop one end around the calf and the other around the saddle horn and have Magic walk backward. I saw it done that way in a TV rerun. Trigger, I think it was Trigger, saved Roy Rogers from certain death in quicksand doing exactly that."

"It won't work."

Taylor gave an indignant shrug of her shoulders. "Why won't it? If it worked for Roy Rogers, it should work for this poor little guy."

"With a rope around his neck, he'd probably strangle before we budged him more than a few inches."

"Oh." She gnawed on her lower lip. "I hadn't thought of that."

Russ hated to admit how much he was enjoying this. She'd outsmarted him once before with that flat tire business, but Taylor was on his turf now, and Russ was in control. "I don't suppose you'd care to make a wager on this?"

"No more bets."

"What's the matter? Are you afraid you'll lose?"

Taylor firmly shook her head. "I'm just not interested, thanks."

"How about this? If you get the calf out, I'll come willingly to your bed. If you don't, then you'll come willingly to mine."

"Does everything boil down to *that* with you?"

"*That,* my sweet lady, is exactly what we both want."

"You're impossible."

"If you were honest with yourself, you'd admit I'm right."

Her mouth was pinched so tightly that her lips were pale. "You're disgusting."

"That isn't what you said the other night," Russ murmured.

"If you don't mind, I'd prefer it if we didn't talk about Friday night."

"As you wish," he said with a grin.

Taylor frowned, studying the calf. "Couldn't we prod him out?"

"*We?* It was my understanding that you could do this all on your own."

"All right," she flared, "if you won't help me, then I'll do it myself." She took two tentative steps into the thick, sticky mud and wrinkled her nose as she moved warily toward the distressed calf. "For being such a great rancher, you certainly seem to be taking this rather casually," she accused him, glancing over her shoulder. Her arms were stretched out at her sides as though she was balancing on a tightrope.

Russ shrugged. "Why should I be concerned when you're doing such a bang-up job?"

Taylor took two more small steps, her face wrinkled with displeasure.

"You're doing just great," Russ called out to her. "In another week or so you'll have reached the calf."

"I never realized how sarcastic you were before now," she muttered.

"Just trying to be of service. Are you sure you're not willing to stake something on the outcome of this?"

"I'm more than sure," she said. "I'm absolutely, totally positive."

"That's a shame."

She glared at him. "It seems you've forgotten that this calf belongs to you. The only reason I'm doing anything is because I find your attitude extremely callous."

"Extremely," Russ echoed, and laughed outright. He tried to disguise it behind a cough, but the irate look she shot him told him he hadn't succeeded.

The sound of pounding hooves caught his attention, and Russ turned to see two of his men galloping toward him.

"Who's coming?" Taylor demanded. She twisted around to glance over her shoulder and somehow lost her balance. Her arms flailed as a look of terror came over her. "Russ…"

Russ leaped forward, but it was too late. He heard her shriek just as she tumbled, hands first into the thick slime. For a shocked second he did nothing. Then, God forgive him, he couldn't help it, he started laughing. He laughed so hard, his stomach hurt and he clutched it with both arms.

A long string of unladylike words blistered the afternoon air when he waded into the mud. Taylor was sitting upright, her knees raised, holding out her hands while the gunk oozed slowly between her fingers. At least the upper portion of her body had been spared.

"Get away from me you…you—" She apparently

couldn't think of anything nasty enough to call him. "This is all your fault." Taking a fistful of black mud, she hurled it at him with all her strength, using such force that she nearly toppled backward with the effort.

The mud flew past Russ, missing him by several feet. "Here, let me help you," he said, wiping tears of mirth from the corners of his eyes.

"Stop laughing," she shouted. "Stop right this second! Do you understand me?"

Russ couldn't do it. He'd never seen anything funnier in his life. He honestly tried to stop, but he simply couldn't.

Taylor was so furious that despite several attempts she couldn't pull herself upright. Finally, Russ moved behind her and, gripping her under the arms, heaved her upward.

The second they were out of the mud, Taylor whirled around, talking so fast and so furiously that he couldn't make out more than a few words. From those he recognized, he figured he was better off not knowing what she had to say.

Russ's two hands, Slim and Roy, stood by, and when Russ met their eyes, he saw that they were doing an admirable job of containing their own amusement. Unfortunately Russ wasn't nearly as diplomatic.

"You two can handle this?" he said, nodding toward the calf.

"No problem," Slim said.

"Taylor didn't think she'd have a problem, either," Russ said, and started laughing all over again.

Both Slim and Roy were chuckling despite their best efforts not to. They climbed down from their horses and leaned against the side of the truck, turning away so Taylor couldn't see them. It wasn't until then that Russ noticed she was missing. He discovered her walking in the direction of the house, which by his best estimate was a good three miles north. Her backside was caked with mud, and her arms were swinging at her sides.

"Looks like you got woman problems," Roy said, glancing at Taylor.

"Looks that way to me, too," Slim said, reaching for his kerchief and wiping his eyes. "I'd be thinking about what Abe Lincoln said if I were you."

"And what's that?" Russ wanted to know.

"Hell hath no fury like a woman scorned."

"That wasn't Abe Lincoln," Roy muttered. "That was Johnny Carson."

Whoever said it obviously knew women a whole lot better than Russ did. The way he figured it, if he ever wanted Taylor to ever speak to him again, he was going to have to do some fast talking of his own.

Taylor had never been angrier in her life. That mud was the most disgusting thing she'd ever seen, and having it on her clothes and skin was more horrible than she even wanted to contemplate. She was cold and wet, and all Russ had done was laugh.

He'd laughed as if she was some slapstick comedian sent to amuse him with her antics. To add to her humiliation she couldn't find the key to the stupid truck. She'd thought she'd left it in the ignition. One thing she did know: she wasn't going to stand around and listen to those men make fun of her.

The least Russ could've done was tell her he was sorry! But he hadn't. Oh, no! He'd roared so loud she swore she'd hear the echo for all eternity.

The sound of the pickup coming toward her did nothing to quell her fury. She didn't so much as turn and look at him when Russ slowed the truck to a crawl beside her.

"Want a ride?"

"No." She continued, increasing her pace. She was already winded, but she'd keel over and die before she'd let Russ know that.

"In case you're wondering, we're about three miles from the ranch house."

She whirled around. "What makes you think I'm going there?"

He shrugged. "Would it help if I said I was sorry?"

"No." Her voice cracked, and her shoulders started to shake while she tried to suppress the tears. Her effort was for naught, and they ran down her face, hot against her skin. Forgetting about the thick mud caked on her hands, she tried to wipe off the tears and in the process nearly blinded herself. The sobs came in earnest then, and her whole body shook with them.

She heard Russ leap out of the pickup, and before she could protest, he was wiping the mud from her face, using a handkerchief. She only hoped it was clean, and once she realized how preposterous that was, she cried harder.

"I hate you," she sobbed, and her shoulders heaved with her vehemence. "I hate Montana. I hate everything about this horrible place. I want to go home."

Russ's arms came around her, but before she could push him away, he'd picked her up and carried her to the truck.

"I...can't sit in there," she wailed. "I'll ruin the upholstery."

Russ proceeded to inform her how little he cared about the interior of his truck. He set her inside the cab, with her feet hanging out the door, then reached into the back and grabbed a blanket and placed that around her shoulders.

"You're cold," was all he said.

"I'm not cold. I'm perfectly—" She would've finished

what she was going to say, but her teeth had started to chatter.

Russ brushed the hair from her face, his fingers lingering at her temple. "I am sorry."

"Just be quiet. I'm in no mood for an apology."

Russ moved her legs inside, then closed the door. The blast of heat coming from the heater felt like a warm breeze straight from paradise, and tucking the blanket more securely around her, Taylor hunched forward. She didn't want to know where this tattered old blanket had been.

Russ hurried around the front of the truck and climbed in beside her. "Hold on," he said. "I'll have you at the house in two minutes flat."

"Where did you find the truck key?" she asked grudgingly.

"I always carry one on my key chain."

"What about the poor little calf?"

"Don't worry. The guys'll get him out. And they'll bring Magic back for me."

If Taylor had thought the ride from town the day they'd met had been rough, it was a Sunday School picnic compared to the crazy way Russ drove across the pasture.

Mandy must have heard them coming, because she was standing on the back porch steps when Russ pulled in to the yard and screeched to a halt. He turned off the engine and vaulted out of the cab.

Taylor couldn't seem to get her body to move. Russ opened the door and effortlessly lifted her into his arms.

"What happened?" Mandy cried, racing toward them.

"Taylor fell in the mud. She's about to freeze to death."

"I… I most certainly am not going to freeze," she countered. "All I need is a warm bath and my own clothes."

"Right on both counts," Russ said, bounding up the back steps with her in his arms. He paused at the top and drew in a deep breath. "How much do you weigh, anyhow?"

"Oh," Taylor cried, squirming in his arms, struggling to make him release her.

Her efforts were in vain as Mandy held open the door and Russ carried her through the kitchen and down a narrow hallway to the bathroom.

"How'd it happen?" Mandy asked, running after them.

Russ's eyes met Taylor's. "You don't want to know the answer to that," Taylor informed the teenager.

"I'll tell you later," Russ mouthed. When they reached the bathroom, Mandy opened the door wider so Russ could haul Taylor inside.

"Boil some water and get the whiskey bottle from the top cupboard," he instructed.

Mandy nodded and dashed back to the kitchen.

"Put me down," Taylor insisted. If it wasn't for this egotistical, stubborn, *perverse* man, she wouldn't be in this humiliating position in the first place.

Russ surprised her by doing as she asked. Gently he set her feet on the tile floor, then leaned over the tub to adjust the knobs, starting the flow of warm water.

For the first time Taylor had an opportunity to survey the damage. She looked down at her legs and gasped at the thick, black coating. A glance in the mirror was her second mistake.

Her lower lip trembled and she sniffled, attempting to hold back the tears.

"You're going to be just fine in a few minutes," Russ said in an apparent effort to comfort her.

"I'm not fine," Taylor moaned, catching her reflection in the mirror again. "I look like the Creature from the Black Lagoon!"

Nine

"Taylor!" Russ shouted from the other side of the bathroom door, "close the shower curtain. I'm coming in."

Resting her head against the back of the tub until the warm soothing water covered her shoulders, Taylor turned a disinterested glance toward the door. She felt sleepy and lethargic. "Go away," she called lazily, then proceeded to yawn, covering her mouth with the back of her hand.

"If you don't want to close the curtain, it's fine with me. Actually, I'd be grateful if you didn't."

The doorknob started to turn and, muttering at the intrusion, Taylor reached for the plastic curtain and jerked it closed.

"Damn," Russ said from the other side, not bothering to hide his disappointment. "I was hoping you'd be more stubborn than this."

"Why are you here?" she demanded.

"I live here, remember?"

"I mean in the bathroom! You have no business walking in on me like this." Actually Taylor should have been out of the bathtub long ago, but the water was so warm and relaxing, and it felt good just to sit there and and soak.

"I'm taking these clothes out so Mandy can put them in the washing machine," he said, and his voice faded as he went down the hall.

All too soon he was back. "Stick out your arm."

"Why?"

"You'll find out."

Taylor exhaled sharply, her hold on her temper precarious. "May I remind you that I'm stark naked behind this curtain."

"Trust me, lady, I know that. It's playing hell with my imagination. Now stick out your arm before I'm forced to pull back this shower curtain."

Grinding her teeth, Taylor did as he asked, knowing full well he'd follow through with his threat given the least provocation. Almost immediately a hot mug was pressed into her palm. She brought it behind the curtain and was immediately struck by the scent of whiskey and honey mixed with hot water. "What's this for?"

"It'll help warm you."

"I wasn't really that chilled." Actually she'd been far too angry to experience anything more than minimal discomfort.

"If you want the truth," Russ said in low, seductive tones, "I was hoping the drink would help take the edge off your anger."

"It's going to take a whole lot more than a hot toddy to do that."

"That's what I thought," he muttered. "I've left a couple of Mandy's things here for you to change into when you've finished. There's no hurry, so take all the time you want."

"Are you leaving now?" she asked impatiently.

"Yes, but I'll be waiting for you."

"I figured you would be," she grumbled.

Taylor soaked another ten minutes until the water started to turn cool, then she reluctantly pulled the plug and climbed out of the tub.

A thick pale blue flannel robe that zipped up the front was draped over the edge of the sink, along with a pair of fuzzy pink slippers. After Taylor had finished drying, she slipped into those, conscious that she wore nothing underneath.

Russ was sitting at the kitchen table. "Where's Mandy?" she asked, doing her best to sound casual and composed, as if she often walked around a man's home in nothing more than a borrowed robe.

"She's on the phone, talking to Travis Wells's boy."

This must be the famous Eddie who'd caused Taylor so much grief. Not knowing what she should say or do, she walked over to the counter and filled her empty mug with coffee. She'd just replaced the pot when Russ's hands settled on her shoulders. He turned her around and gazed into her eyes.

"I shouldn't have laughed." His voice was husky, his expression regretful.

She lifted one shoulder in a delicate shrug. "I don't think you could've helped it—laughing was a natural reaction. I must have looked ridiculous."

"Do you forgive me?"

She nodded. Her sojourn in the bath had washed away more than the mud; it had obliterated her anger. She acknowledged that she hadn't been completely guiltless in this fiasco, either. "You weren't really to blame. I did it to myself with my stubborn pride. You're the rancher here, not me. I was a fool to think I could free that poor calf when you couldn't. I brought the whole thing on myself, but you were handy and I lashed out at you."

Russ lifted her chin with his index finger. "Did you mean what you said about hating Montana?"

Taylor didn't remember saying that, although she'd muttered plenty about Russ and his stupid cows and everything else she could think of.

"Not any more than I meant what I said about everything else."

"Good." Russ obviously took that as a positive answer. He raised his finger and traced it slowly over her cheek to her lips. His touch was unhurried and tender as if he longed to ease every moment of distress he'd caused her, intentionally or otherwise. His eyes didn't waver from hers, and when he leaned forward to kiss her, there wasn't a single doubt in Taylor's mind that this was exactly what she wanted.

His mouth settled over hers, and she sighed softly in hopeless welcome. His kisses, as always, were devastatingly sensual. Taylor felt so mellow, so warm.

"I could get drunk on you," Russ murmured in awe.

"It must be the whiskey," she whispered back.

He shook his head. "I didn't have any." His hands were in her hair, his lips at her throat, and the delicious, delirious feelings flooded her.

Sliding her hands over the open V of his shirt, she wound her arms around his strong neck. He leaned her against the counter and pressed himself against her, creating a whole new kaleidoscope of delectable sensations. Taylor let her head fall back as he continued to kiss her. He was so close she could feel the snap of his jeans. He was power. Masculine strength. Heat. She sensed in him a hunger she'd never known in any man. A hunger and need. One only she could fill.

Then, when she least expected it, Russ stilled his body

and his hands and roughly dragged his mouth from hers. Not more than a second had passed when...

"Oops...oh, sorry," Mandy said as she walked into the kitchen. "I bet you guys want me to come back later. Right? Hey, no problem." She backed out of the kitchen, hands raised.

Russ's arms closed protectively around Taylor, but she broke free and managed a smile, then deftly turned toward the teenager. "There's no reason for you to leave."

"Yes, there is," Russ said. "Taylor and I have to talk."

"No, we don't," she countered sharply. "We've finished...talking."

Russ threw her a challenging glance that suggested otherwise, and Taylor, who rarely blushed, did so profusely.

"We haven't even started *talking*," Russ whispered for her ears alone. Taylor wasn't going to argue with him, at least not in front of his sister.

Mandy stared down at the linoleum floor and traced the octagonal pattern with the toe of her tennis shoe. "You've already talked to Russ?" she asked, darting a quick glance at Taylor. Her soft green eyes were imploring.

"Not yet," Taylor said pointedly.

"Disappear for a while, Mandy," Russ urged, turning back to Taylor.

"No," Taylor said forcefully. The minute the girl was out of the room, the same thing would happen that always did whenever they were alone together. One kiss and they'd burst spontaneously into a passion hot enough to sear Taylor's senses for days afterward.

"No?" Mandy echoed, clearly confused.

"I haven't talked to Russ yet, but I will now."

The fourteen-year-old brightened and nodded eagerly.

She pointed toward the living room. "I'll just wait in there."

"What's going on here?" Russ demanded once Mandy was out of the room.

"Nothing."

"And pigs fly."

"Sit down," she coaxed, offering him a shy smile. She got a second mug and filled it with coffee, then carried it to the round oak table where Russ was waiting for her. His arm slipped around her waist, and she braced her hands against his shoulders.

"You're supposed to talk to me?" he asked.

She nodded.

"This has to do with Mandy?"

Once more Taylor nodded.

Russ frowned. "That was why you drove out to see me earlier, wasn't it?"

"Yes," she answered honestly. He kept his arms securely around her waist, but he didn't look pleased. Taylor felt the least she could do was explain. "Mandy came to talk to me after school, and she asked me to approach you about...something."

"She isn't comfortable coming to me herself?" Russ muttered, looking offended. "I've been trying as hard as I can to listen to her. I can't be any fairer than I've already been. What does she want now? To get an apartment in town on her own?"

"Don't be silly," Taylor answered, riffling his hair, seeking some way to reassure him. "Mandy knows you're trying to be patient with her, and she's trying, too. Only this was something special, something she felt awkward talking to you about, so she came to me. Don't be offended, Russ. That wasn't her intention and it isn't mine."

He nodded, but his frown remained. From the first,

Taylor hadn't been sure she was doing the right thing by approaching Russ on Mandy's behalf. She'd only wanted to help, but regretted her part in this now. Look where it had led her! Two feet deep in mud.

Positioning herself on his lap, she rested her arms over his shoulders, her wrists dangling. "You're right," she said, and kissed him long and leisurely by way of apology.

His eyes were still closed when she'd finished, his breathing labored.

"Mandy," Taylor called, embarrassed by how noticeably her voice trembled.

The teenager raced into the kitchen so fast she nearly skidded across the polished floor. "Well?" she asked expectantly. "What did he say?" She seemed a little startled to see Taylor sitting on her brother's lap, but didn't mention it at all.

"I haven't said anything yet," Russ growled. "I want to know what's going on here. First of all, Taylor drives out to talk to me, and from what I can tell she's wearing your clothes."

"I couldn't very well send her out there in the dress she was wearing at school. I'm certainly glad I insisted she put on something of mine, otherwise look what would've happened!" Mandy declared.

"What's that got to do with this?"

"You were supposed to be back early today, remember?" Mandy reminded him pointedly. "You said something about driving over to Bill Shepherd's this afternoon—"

"Oh, damn," Russ muttered, "I forgot."

"Don't worry. He phoned while you were out with Taylor, and I said you'd probably run into some trouble. He's going to call you back tonight."

Russ nodded. "Go on."

"Well, anyway, I thought it might even be better if Taylor talked to you when I wasn't around, so I suggested she take the truck and—"

"How'd you know where I was?" Russ asked his sister, clearly confused.

"I heard you speaking to Slim this morning about checking the south fence lines. I just headed Taylor in that direction. I knew she'd find you sooner or later."

Russ's gaze shot to Taylor. "She found me all right. Now tell me what you were going to talk to me about." The tone of Russ's voice suggested he was fast losing patience.

"Mandy, I'm holding him down, so you do the talking," Taylor said, smiling at Russ.

"You ask him, Taylor. Oh, please…" the girl begged.

"Nope, you're on your own, kiddo."

"Will the two of you stop playing games and tell me what's going on here?"

"Okay," Mandy said, elevating her shoulders as she released a deep breath. She pushed up the sleeves of her sweater, not looking at her brother, and launched into her request. "You know Travis Wells, don't you?" She didn't give Russ time to respond. "His son Eddie goes to school with me."

"Eddie's older than you."

"He's sixteen," Mandy returned quickly. "Actually he's only twenty-two months and five days older than I am. If he'd been born in October and I'd been born in August we might even have been in the same class together, so there's really not that big a difference in our ages." She paused as though waiting for Russ to comment or agree.

"All right," he said after an uncomfortable moment.

Mandy looked at Taylor pleadingly, silently asking her to explain the rest. Taylor shook her head.

"Eddie's been talking to me lately…in the halls and sometimes at lunch. Yesterday he sat with me on the bus." This was clearly of monumental significance. "Eddie was the one who encouraged me to try out for the drill team, and when I made it, he said he knew I would."

"That was him on the phone earlier, wasn't it?"

A happy grin touched the girl's mouth. "Yes—he wanted to know if I'd talked to you yet."

"About what?" Russ asked, then stiffened. His eyes narrowed. "You're not going out with that young man, Amanda, and that's the end of it. Fourteen is too young to date, and I don't care what Taylor says!"

If she hadn't been sitting on his lap, Taylor was sure Russ would have jumped to his feet. Framing his face with her hands, she stroked the rigid muscles of his jaw. "There's no need to yell. As it happens, I agree with you."

"You do?"

"Don't look so shocked."

"Then why were you coming to talk to me about it? Because I'll tell you right now, I'm not changing my mind."

"I'm not, either," she said softly, "so relax."

"Mandy?" Russ turned to his sister, his frown threatening.

"Well…as you've already guessed, Eddie asked me out on a date. Actually he just wanted me to go to the movies with him."

"No way," Russ said without so much as a pause.

Mandy's teeth bit her trembling bottom lip. "I thought you'd feel that way. That's the reason I went to Taylor, but she said she agreed with you that fourteen's too young to date. But while we were talking she came up with a... compromise. That is, if you'll agree."

"I said no," Russ returned resolutely.

Taylor felt she should explain. "When I was fourteen, my father—"

"You're from the city," he said in a way that denigrated anyone who lived in a town with a population over five hundred. "Folks from the country think differently. I don't expect you to understand."

His harsh words were like a slap in the face to Taylor. She blinked back the sharp pain, astonished that he would offend her so easily.

"Russ," Mandy whispered, "that was a terrible thing to say."

"What? That Taylor's from the city? It's true."

"You're right, of course." She slipped off his lap and looked at Mandy. "Are my clothes in your room?"

The girl nodded. "I hung them in my closet."

Drawing in a deep breath, Taylor looked at Russ. "I apologize. I should never have involved myself in something that wasn't my affair. I went against my better judgment and I was wrong. Now if you'll excuse me, I'll change clothes and get out of here." The way she felt at the moment, she never intended to come back. What Russ had said was true; he was only repeating what she'd been saying to him from the first. They were fooling themselves if they believed there was any future in their relationship.

Mandy's bedroom was on the main floor, next to the bathroom. Taylor shut the door and walked over to sit on the bed. Her hands were trembling, and she felt close to tears. Raised voices came from the kitchen, but Taylor couldn't make out the words and had no intention of even trying. If anything, she was regretful that she'd become yet another source of discord between brother and sister.

Taylor was dressing when someone tapped politely on the door. "I'll just be a minute," she said, forcing a cheerful note into her voice.

Slipping the dress over her head, Taylor walked barefoot across the room and opened the door. Mandy came inside, her face red and stained with tears. Sobbing, she threw both arms around Taylor's waist.

"I'm sorry," she whispered. "I'm really sorry…it was so selfish of me to involve you in this. Look what happened. First you fell in that terrible mud—"

"But, remember, I was wearing your clothes."

"I don't care about that." She lifted her head to wipe the tears from her face. "You could take all my clothes and put them in a mud hole if you wanted."

"If you don't mind, I'd prefer to avoid any and all mud holes from now on."

Mandy's responding chuckle sounded more like another sob. "Russ should never have said what he did."

"But it's true," Taylor said lightly, pretending to dismiss the entire incident.

"Maybe so, but it was the way he said it—as if you're not to be trusted or something. You're the best thing that's ever happened to my brother—and to me. All the kids in school are crazy about you and…and for Russ to say what he did was an insult."

"Don't be so hard on him. You can take the girl out of the city, but you can't take the city out of the girl," she joked.

"He'll be sorry in a little bit," Mandy assured her. "He always is. He's the only man I know who slits his own throat with his tongue."

"There's no need for him to apologize," Taylor said,

hugging the teenager close. She broke away, slipped on her shoes and reached for her jacket. She draped her purse over her shoulder. "Chin up, kiddo. Everything's going to work out for the best."

Mandy bobbed her head several times.

Russ wasn't around when Taylor walked through the kitchen and out the back door. For that she was grateful. She opened her car door, but didn't get inside. Instead she found herself studying the house and the outbuildings that comprised the Lazy P, giving it a final look. Sadness settled over her and she exhaled slowly.

This was her farewell to Russ and to his ranch.

If the day Taylor fell in the mud hole had been full of problems, Russ decided, the ensuing ones were just as impossible. Only now the difficulties he faced were of his own making.

Taylor had been on his mind for the past three days. Not that thinking about her constantly was anything new, but now, every time he did, all he could see were her big blue eyes meeting his, trying so hard to disguise the pain his words had inflicted. He'd been angry with Mandy for going to Taylor, and angry with Taylor for listening.

Unfortunately Russ didn't have time to make the necessary amends. Not yet, anyway. Slim and Roy had set up cow camp in the foothills, and Russ and two of his other hands were joining them. They were running cattle, branding the calves born on the range, vaccinating and dehorning them. It would be necessary to trim hoofs, too; otherwise the snow, which was sure to arrive sometime soon, would clump in their feet.

There'd been snow in the mountains overnight, and there was nothing to say the first snowfall of the season couldn't happen any day. With so much to do, he didn't have time for anything but work. The cattle buyers would show up right after that, and Russ would be occupied with them, wheeling and dealing to get the best price he could for his beef.

He'd contact Taylor later and apologize.

When Russ returned to the house, it was after seven and he was exhausted. Mandy was sitting at the kitchen table, doing her homework.

"Any calls?" he asked hopefully. Maybe Taylor had finally decided to forgive him, although he doubted it.

"None."

Russ frowned. That woman was too stubborn for her own good—or his.

"Dinner's in the oven," Mandy said, not looking at him. She closed her book and inserted pages into her binder.

Russ took the plate from the oven with a pot holder, then set it on the table. "I've been thinking over what you suggested about this thing with Eddie," he said while he took a glass from the cupboard and poured himself some milk.

Mandy's eyes rose to search his. "It wouldn't be like a real date. I'd be paying for my own ticket and all Eddie and I would be doing is sitting together. It'd be just as if we'd accidentally met there. If Eddie wants, I'd let him buy me some popcorn—but only if you think it would be all right."

"I'd drop you off and pick you up at the theater?"

"Right."

Russ pulled out a chair and sat down. "This is a sensible compromise," he said as he spread the paper napkin across his lap. "This idea shows maturity and insight on your part, and I'm proud of you for coming up with it."

"I didn't."

Russ finished his first bite and studied his sister, who was standing across the table, her hand resting on the back of the chair. "Taylor's the one who suggested it first. She tried to explain it to you…. Actually, we both did, but you wouldn't listen."

The bite of chicken-fried steak stuck halfway down Russ's throat, and he had to swallow hard before he could speak normally. "Taylor came up with the idea?"

"I think her parents were the ones who thought of it because she was telling me that's what they did with her and her sister when they were fourteen and boys began asking them out."

"I see."

"Just think, Russ," Mandy murmured sarcastically. "Taylor's parents are from the big city, and they managed to come up with this all on their own. Naw, on second thought, I bet someone from the country suggested it."

Normally Russ wouldn't have tolerated his sister talking to him in that tone of voice. The kid sure knew all the right buttons to push. But this time Russ didn't react as he usually did. The pressure that settled on his chest made it difficult to concentrate on anything else.

His appetite gone, Russ pushed his plate away, propped his elbows on the table and stared straight ahead.

He'd done it now. Taylor would never speak to him again. Unless…

Another lonely Friday night, Taylor mused as she sat at the kitchen table with paper and pen. She owed everyone letters, and it wasn't as though she had anything pressing to do.

She leaned back in the chair and reread the long letter from Christy, chuckling over her youngest sibling's warmth and wit.

Someone knocked at the door and, laying aside the letter, Taylor went to answer it. A smiling Mandy stood on the other side.

"Mandy? Is everything all right?"

"It's perfect. Well, almost..." she said, beaming. She seemed in a hurry and glanced over her shoulder.

Taylor's gaze followed hers, and she noticed Russ's truck parked alongside the curb. He was sitting in the cab.

"Russ said I could meet Eddie at the movies and sit with him under one condition, and I'm afraid that involves you."

Taylor couldn't have heard Mandy correctly. "I beg your pardon?"

"Russ seems to feel that Eddie and I are going to need a couple of chaperones."

"That's ridiculous."

"No, it isn't," Mandy insisted much too cheerfully to suit Taylor. "At least I don't mind if you guys sit on the other side of the theater from Eddie and me."

"You guys?"

"You and Russ. He said I can only do this if you agree to sit with him during the movie so he doesn't look like a jerk being there all by himself."

"You can tell your brother for me—"

"Taylor," Mandy cut in, leaning forward to whisper as if there was a chance Russ might overhear. "This is the *only* way Russ could think of to get you to talk to him again. He's really sorry for how he acted and the things he said."

"Sending you to do his apologizing for him isn't going to work," Taylor said matter-of-factly. "Neither is this little game of blackmail."

Mandy thought about it for a moment, then nodded. "You know what? You're absolutely right!" Placing her hands on her hips, she whirled around to face the street. *"Russ!"* she yelled at the top of her lungs.

Russ leaned across the cab of the pickup and rolled down the window.

"If you want to apologize to Taylor, you're going to have to do it yourself!" Mandy shouted. Taylor was certain half the neighbors could hear. Her worst fears were confirmed when she saw the lady across the street pulling aside her drape and peeking out.

"*And* Taylor says she refuses to be blackmailed."

Taylor was mortified when the doors to several more homes opened and a couple of men stepped onto their porches to investigate the source of all the shouting.

"What are you going to do about it?" Mandy yelled.

By this time Russ had climbed out of the truck. He was wearing the same gray suit jacket with the suede yoke he'd had on the night of the Grange dance.

"Hey, Palmer, what's going on with the school-teacher?" one of Taylor's neighbors heckled.

Two or three others came off their porches and onto the sidewalk. A low murmur followed Russ's progress toward Taylor.

"Hey, Russ, apologize, would you?"

"Yeah," another chimed in. "Then we can have some peace and quiet around here."

Russ paid no attention. When he reached the end of the walk, he looked straight at Taylor, then leaped up the steps. "You want a formal apology?" he asked. "Fine, I'll give you one, but after that we're going to the movies."

Ten

"**I**'m not going to the movies with you, Russ Palmer. That's all there is to it," Taylor said, and gently closed the door. She turned the lock just to be on the safe side and went back to the kitchen where she'd started a letter to her sister.

A few minutes later, she heard the faint strains of a guitar and someone singing, badly off key. Good grief, it sounded like… Russ. Russ singing?

Deciding the only thing she could do was ignore him, Taylor returned to her letter-writing project.

Apparently Russ wasn't going to be easily foiled, and when she didn't immediately appear, he countered by singing and playing louder. His determination was evident in each word of his ridiculously maudlin song. He was completely untalented as a singer, and his guitar-playing abilities weren't anything to brag about, either.

Covering her ears, Taylor slid as low as she could in her chair. The man's nerve was colossal. If she'd learned anything during her time in Cougar Point, it was that cowboys didn't lack arrogance. To assume that she'd be willing to forget everything simply because he serenaded her was downright comical.

It was then that the phone rang. Taylor answered it on the second ring, grinning at Russ's impertinence, despite her irritation.

"For heaven's sake," her neighbor shouted over the line, "do something, will you? His singing is making my dog howl."

No sooner had Taylor replaced the phone than it rang again. "My china's starting to rattle. Would you please kiss and make up before my crystal cracks?" Taylor recognized the voice of Mrs. Fergason, the lady from across the street.

Grinding her teeth with frustration, Taylor tore across the living room and yanked open the door. "Stop!"

Russ took one look at her and grinned broadly. He lowered the guitar, obviously delighted with himself. "I see you've come to your senses."

"Either stop singing or I'm calling the police. You're disturbing my peace and that of my neighbors. Now leave."

Russ blinked, apparently convinced he'd misunderstood her. "I wish I could, but I owe you an apology and I won't feel right until I clear the air."

"Okay, you've apologized. Now will you kindly go?"

He rubbed his hand down his jaw. "I can't do that."

"Why not?" Taylor jerked back her head hard enough to give herself whiplash. "I don't believe it. Why are you doing this?"

"Because I'm falling in love with you."

A lump immediately formed in Taylor's throat. This was the last thing she'd wanted. Living in Cougar Point was supposed to give her a chance to heal from one disastrous relationship, not involve her in another.

"Russ," Mandy called, leaning out the window of the truck, "hurry or we'll be late for the movie."

"Are you going or not?" Mrs. Fergason shouted. "Decide, will you? *Jeopardy*'s about to start, and I don't want to miss Alex Trebek."

Taylor was still too stunned to react. "Don't love me, Russ. Please don't love me."

"I'm sorry, but it's too late. I knew the minute you went headfirst into that mud hole that we were meant for each other. Now are you going to ruin Mandy's big night with your stubbornness, or are you going to the movie with me?"

If she'd had her wits about her Taylor would never have agreed to this blatant form of blackmail, but Russ had taken all the wind from the sails of her righteousness. Before she realized exactly how she'd gotten there, she was inside the Cougar Point Theater, sitting in the back row with Russ, munching on hot buttered popcorn.

"We've got to talk," she whispered as the opening credits started. She'd seen the movie months earlier, and although she'd enjoyed it, she wasn't eager to see it a second time—especially now, after Russ's shocking declaration.

His large callused hand reached for hers, closing around her fingers. "We can talk later."

How she managed to sit through the entire film, Taylor didn't know. Her mind was in a chaotic whirl. All too soon the closing credits were rolling and the house lights came up. The theater began to empty.

Mandy dashed down the aisle, the famous Eddie at her side. "Would it be all right if we went over to the bowling alley? Chris's mom and dad offered to buy everyone nachos. Lots of other kids are going."

"How long will you be?" Russ asked.

Mandy looked at Eddie. "An hour," the boy said firmly,

perhaps expecting Russ to argue with him. He was over six feet tall and as lean as a telephone pole, yet Mandy gazed at him as if he were a Hollywood heartthrob.

"All right," Russ said, apparently surprising them both. "I'll pick you up in exactly one hour."

"Thanks," Mandy said, and impulsively kissed his cheek.

"That gives us forty-five minutes to settle our differences," Russ said, smiling over at Taylor, his eyes filled with silent messages.

By now Taylor felt more than a little disoriented. It was as if her entire world resembled the flickering frames in a silent movie. Everything had a strange, staccato feeling, and nothing seemed real.

"Where are we going?" she asked when Russ opened the truck door for her.

"Back to your place. Unless you object."

Russ had ignored every one of her objections from the moment they'd met, and there was no reason to assume he was going to change at this stage.

When Russ parked his truck, Taylor half expected her neighbors to file out of their homes and line the sidewalk, offering advice. But all the excitement earlier in the evening had apparently tired everyone out. It was only nine, and already most of the houses were completely dark.

"I'll make us some coffee," Taylor said, finding her voice. She unlocked the door, but before she could flip on the living-room lights, Russ gently turned her around and pulled her into his arms.

He closed the front door with his foot and pressed her against the wall. Their eyes adjusted to the dark, and met. "You're so beautiful," he whispered reverently. He lifted his hands to her hair, weaving the thick strands through his fingers. Taylor felt powerless to stop him. She closed her eyes and savored the moment. Savored the exquisite sensations Russ evoked within her.

"Please don't fall in love with me," she pleaded, remembering the reason for this discussion. "Don't love me."

"I can't help myself," he whispered, kissing the taut line of her jaw. "Trust me, Taylor, I wasn't all that happy about it myself. You belong in the city."

"Exactly," she said, breathing deeply. It never seemed to fail: Russ would hold her and she'd dissolve in his arms. Her breathing became labored, and her heart went on a rampage. She tried to convince herself that they were simply dealing with an abundance of hormones, but no matter how many times she told herself that, it didn't matter.

Russ *couldn't* love her. He just couldn't. Because then Taylor would be forced to examine her own feelings for him. She'd be compelled to face what she intuitively knew would be better left unnamed.

"You're a West Coast liberal feminist."

"You're a small-town Montana redneck."

"I know," he agreed, continuing to kiss her jaw, his mouth wandering down the side of her neck.

Listing their differences didn't seem to affect their reactions to each other. Russ raised his head and traced his thumb across her lower lip. It was all Taylor could do not to moan. No man had ever incited such burning need.

Taylor took Russ's finger between her teeth and slowly drew it into her mouth, sucking lightly. He closed his eyes and smiled, then sighed from deep within his chest.

With his hands cupping her face, he kissed her, and it was incredibly sweet, incredibly sexy. Every time Russ took her into his arms, he eliminated all the disparities between them, took everything in their lives and reduced it to the simple fact that they were man and woman.

She gripped his wrists and held on tightly. "Russ, no more...please." With a strength she didn't realize she had, Taylor broke off the kiss.

"I've just begun," he warned.

His lips remained so close to hers that she inhaled his moist, warm breath.

"Why does everything come down to this?" she murmured. Her knees were slightly bent as she struggled to hold on to what little strength she still possessed.

"I don't know," he answered honestly. "I can't seem to keep my hands off you." As though to prove his point, he trailed a row of kisses across the curve of her shoulder.

"Russ..."

"Not here... I know." His voice was so husky Taylor barely recognized it. Without any difficulty, he lifted her into his arms.

"What are you doing?" she demanded.

"Carrying you into the bedroom."

"No," she whispered, close to tears.

"Rhett Butler carried Scarlett—I can't do any less for you. I thought all women, even you feminist types, went for this romantic stuff."

"We can't do this.... Russ, listen to me. If we make love, we're both going to regret it later." She was nearly frantic, desperate to talk some sense into him. Talk some sense into herself. All the while, Russ was walking along the hallway to her bedroom.

Her weight must have gotten to be too much for him, because he paused and leaned heavily against the wall. Before she could argue, insist that he put her down, his mouth sought hers, his lips sliding back and forth over hers with mute urgency. Whatever objection Taylor was about to raise died the instant his mouth took hers. She entwined her arms around his neck and boldly kissed him back.

"I thought that would shut you up," he murmured triumphantly as he shifted her weight in his arms and carried her directly into the bedroom.

There was ample time to protest, ample time to demand that he stop, but the words, so perfectly formed in her mind, were never spoken. Instead she leaned her head against his shoulder and sighed heavily. She couldn't fight them both.

Russ placed her on the bed. Taylor closed her eyes, hating this weakness in her. At the same moment, savoring it. "I can't believe we're doing this."

"I can," he said. "I haven't stopped thinking about it since the day we met. I haven't been able to stop thinking about *you,*" Russ murmured, "day and night, night and day."

She smiled softly up at him and slipped her arms around his neck. "You've been on my mind, too."

"I'm glad to hear it. But it's more than that," he continued between kisses. "I can't seem to rid myself of this need for you. I want to make love to you more than I've wanted anything in my life."

Taylor felt his moist breath against her cheek and sighed audibly as he began kissing her again, creating magical sensations. Scorching need.

Her arms and legs felt as if they were liquid, without strength. Russ continued to hold her, to rain kisses over her face. Then he nuzzled her neck. Taylor tried to immerse herself in his tenderness, but as hard as she tried, she couldn't seem to block out the fact that their lovemaking would only lead to pain. It had been months since she'd seen Mark, and she was still suffering. How could she do this to herself a second time when she was all too aware of the emotional aftermath?

She'd tried so hard to fight her attraction to Russ. Yet here she was, inviting even more pain, more doubts, more questions. She wasn't the type of woman who leaped into bed with a man just because it felt good.

"Russ…no more," she pleaded, pushing with all her strength against the very shoulders she'd been caressing only moments earlier. "Stop…oh, please, we have to stop."

He went still, and slowly raised his eyes. They were darker than she'd ever seen them. Hotter than she'd ever seen them, but not with anger.

"You don't mean that." Lovingly, tenderly, he ran his hands over her face and paused when he discovered the moisture on her cheeks.

"You're crying."

Taylor hadn't realized it herself until he'd caressed her face. His eyes questioned hers, filled with apprehension, misgivings. "What's wrong?"

She placed the tips of her fingers on his cheek. "I can't make love with you…. I can't."

"Why not?" His voice was little more than a whisper, and gruff with anxiety. "I love you, Taylor." As if to prove it, he kissed her again, but even more gently this time.

Twisting her head away, Taylor buried her face in the curve of his neck, dragging in deep gulps of air as Russ held her close.

"I don't want you to love me," she sobbed. "If we continue like this, it'll only cause problems—not just for me, but for you, too."

"Not necessarily."

How confident he sounded, how secure, when she was neither.

"I've been in love before...and it hurts too much."
She raised her head and swallowed a sob, then wiped
the tears from her face. "His name was Mark—and he's
the reason I moved to Montana. I had to get away...and
heal.... Instead, I met you."

The sobs came in earnest then. Huge heaving sobs that
humiliated and humbled her. She wasn't crying for Mark;
she was over him. Yet the tears fell and the pain gushed
forth in an absolution she hadn't expected. Pain she'd
incarcerated behind a wall of smiles, and then lugged
across three states.

Russ obviously didn't know what to think. He stroked
her hair, but he didn't say anything, and she knew her
timing couldn't have been worse. Bringing up the subject of Mark now, tonight, was insane, but she'd had to
stop Russ. Stop them both. She'd had to do *something*.

Still sobbing, she rolled off the bed. Finding her foot-
ing, she gestured in his direction, miming an apology and
at the same time pleading with him to go. She needed
to be alone.

"I'm not leaving you."

Unable to find the strength to go on standing, Taylor
lowered herself to the edge of the bed. "Do you always
have to argue with me? Just for once couldn't you do
what I want?"

"No." He eased himself behind her and wrapped his
arms around her shoulders, holding her carefully. "I love
you," he told her again.

"Please don't."

"The choice was taken from me long ago."

"No...don't even say it. I can't bear it if you love
me—I can't deal with it now. Please, try to understand."

His arms tightened slightly, pulling her back against

him. "I wish it wasn't so, for your sake, but my heart decided otherwise. I can't change the way I feel."

"I refuse to love you! Do you understand?" Taylor cried. "Look at us! We're a pair of fools. It won't work, so why should we put each other through this? It doesn't make sense! Oh, Russ, please, won't you just leave me alone?"

"Loving you makes sense. We make sense. I love you, Taylor. Nothing will change that."

"Don't tell me that. I refuse to love you," she repeated. "Do you understand? Nothing has changed. Nothing!"

"It doesn't matter."

If Russ had been angry or unreasonable, it would've helped her. Instead he was gentle. Loving. Concerned.

While she was angry. Angrier than she'd ever been.

"Leave me alone. Go!" She pointed to the door in case he wasn't convinced that she meant what she said. "Stay away from me. I don't want to get involved with you."

Russ studied her for several nerve-racking minutes, then sighed and stalked out of the room.

The whole house went quiet, and it reminded her of the hush before a storm. Russ had left; he'd done exactly what she'd asked. She should be glad. Instead, the ache inside her increased a hundredfold and the emptiness widened.

Clutching her stomach, Taylor sobbed while she sat on the bed and rocked. Back and forth. Side to side. She wept because of one man she no longer loved. She wept for another she was afraid of loving too much.

She lost track of time. Five minutes could have been fifty-five; she had no way of telling.

A noise in her kitchen alerted her to the fact that she wasn't alone. Curious, she righted her clothes, wiped her face with a corner of the sheet and walked out of the bedroom.

Russ was sitting in the kitchen, his feet balanced on a chair, ankles crossed. He was drinking a cup of coffee. Apparently he'd made it himself.

"You didn't leave?"

"Not yet."

"What about Mandy?"

"I called the bowling alley and told her to kill another hour." Dropping his legs, he stood and poured Taylor a mug, then set it down for her. "Feeling any better?"

Embarrassed, she looked away and nodded. She would rather he'd left when she'd asked, but that would have created other problems. Eventually she'd need to explain, and the sooner the better. "I'm…sorry. I shouldn't have yelled at you."

"Do you want to talk about it?"

"Not really, but…" She shrugged, then pulled out a chair, sat down and reached for the coffee. Cradling the mug, she warmed her hands with it.

"I suppose I should've suspected something," Russ said after a moment. "Someone like you wouldn't accept a teaching position in this part of the country without a reason. You didn't come to Montana out of a burning desire to learn about life in the backwoods of America."

Her gaze continued to avoid his, but she did manage a weak smile.

"So you were in love with Mark. Tell me what happened."

She sighed. "How much do you want to know?"

"Everything. Start at the beginning, the day you met him, and work through to the day you moved to Cougar Point. Tell me everything—don't hold back a single detail."

Taylor closed her eyes. He wouldn't be satisfied with anything less than the truth, the whole truth. He wanted names, places, dates, details. Gory, painful details. The man was wasted on a cattle ranch, she thought wryly; he should've been working for the Internal Revenue Service. Or the FBI.

"I can't," she whispered as the ache in her heart increased with the memories. "I'm sorry, Russ. If I talked to anyone about Mark, it would be you, but he's behind me now and I'm not about to dredge up all that pain."

"You wouldn't be dredging it up," he told her. "You've been carrying it with you like a heavy suitcase all the way to Cougar Point. Get rid of it, Taylor."

"You think it's that easy?" she responded tartly. "You're suggesting I casually take what little remains of my pride and my dignity and lay it out on the table for you to examine. I can't do it."

The heat in the kitchen felt stifling all of a sudden. Taylor stood abruptly and started pacing. "I wanted to get away—that's understandable, isn't it? I read everything I could find about Montana, and the idea of living here for a year or so appealed to me. I thought... I hoped I could use these months to recharge my emotions, to mend."

"It hasn't worked, has it?"

She hung her head. "No."

"Do you know why?"

"Of course I know why!" she cried. "Meeting you has messed up everything. I wasn't in town a week and you were harassing me. Goading me. I'd be a thousand times better off if we'd never met. Now here you are, talking about loving me, and I'm so afraid I can't think straight anymore."

"Are you looking for an apology?"

"Yes," she cried, then reconsidered and slowly shook her head. "No."

"That's what I thought."

She reached for her coffee, downed a sip and set the mug back on the table. The hot liquid burned her lips and seared its way down the back of her throat. "I met Mark while I was student-teaching." She folded her arms around her waist and resumed pacing. "Between working and school I didn't have a lot of time for relationships. For the first four years of my college education, I might as well have been living in a convent."

"Why was Mark different?"

"I...don't know. I've asked myself the same question a hundred times. He was incredibly good-looking."

"Better-looking than me?" Russ challenged.

"Oh, Russ, honestly, I don't know. It isn't as if I have a barometer to gauge the level of cute."

"Okay, go on."

"There isn't much more to tell you," she said, gesturing with her hands. "We became...involved, and after a couple of months Mark brought up the idea of us living together."

Russ frowned. "I see."

Taylor was sure he didn't; nevertheless she continued. "I loved him. I truly loved him, but I couldn't seem to bring myself to move in with him. My parents are very traditional, and I'd never come face-to-face with something that contradicted my upbringing to such an extent."

"Mark wanted you to be his 'significant other'?"

"Yes. He wasn't ruling out the idea of marriage, but he wasn't willing to make a commitment to me, either, at least not then."

"Did you agree to this?"

It took Taylor a long moment to answer, and when she did, her voice was low and husky. "No. I needed time to think over the decision, and Mark agreed it was a good idea. He suggested we not see each other for a week."

"So what did you decide?"

Russ's question seemed to echo through the room. "Yes... I reached an intelligent, well-thought-out decision, but it didn't take me a week. In fact, five days was all the time I required. Having made my choice, I planned to contact Mark. I'd missed him so much that I went over to his apartment the following evening after work...." The floor seemed to buckle, and she reached out and grabbed the back of a chair. "Except that Mark wasn't alone—he was making love with a girl from the office." The pain, the humiliation of that moment, was as sharp now as it had been several months earlier. "Correction," she said in a breathy whisper. "In his words, he was 'screwing' the girl from the office. But when he was with me, he was making love."

Russ stood and walked over to her side, then drew her into his arms.

Clenching her hands in tight fists, Taylor resisted his comfort. The burning tears returned. Her breath seemed to catch in her throat and released itself with a moan. "You don't understand," she sobbed. "You don't know... no one does. No one ever asked."

"I do," Russ whispered, brushing the tendrils from her face. "You'd decided to move in with him, hadn't you?"

Sobbing and nearly hysterical, Taylor nodded.

Eleven

Every part of Russ longed to comfort Taylor. He wasn't immune to pain himself. His mother had run off and abandoned him when he was still a child. He'd been unable to understand what had driven her away, unable to understand why she hadn't taken him with her. Then, several years later, his father met and married Betty. Mandy was born and Russ was just beginning to feel secure and happy when Betty had died. His father had buried himself in his grief and followed not long afterward. Russ had been left to deal with his own anguish, plus that of his young sister, who was equally lost and miserable.

Emotional pain, Russ had learned during the next few years, was a school of higher learning, a place beyond the instruction of ordinary teachers. It was where heaven sagged and earth reached up, leaving a man to find meaning, reconciliation and peace all on his own.

Taylor sobbed softly, holding him close. Russ shut his eyes. The ache he felt for this woman cut clear through his heart. Taylor had loved another man, loved him still. Someone who didn't deserve her, someone who didn't appreciate the kind of woman she was. The overwhelming need to protect her consumed him.

Lifting her head, Taylor brushed the confusion of hair from her face. "I think you should go now," she said in a voice thick with tears.

"No," he answered, his hands busy stroking her back. He couldn't leave her. Not now. Not like this.

"Please, Russ, I want to be alone. I need to be alone."

"You'll never be alone again," he promised her.

Her head drooped, and her long hair fell forward. "You don't understand, do you? I can't... I *won't* become involved with you. I'm here to teach, and at the end of my contract I'm leaving. And when I do, I don't want there to be any regrets."

"There won't be. I promise you." Russ tried to reassure her, but when he bent to kiss her, she broke away from him and skittered over to the other side of the kitchen, as if that distance would keep her safe.

"It would be so easy to let myself fall in love with you," she whispered. "So easy..."

Witnessing her pain was nearly Russ's undoing. He moved toward her, but for every step he advanced, she retreated two. He hesitated. "All I want to do is love you."

"No," she said firmly, holding out her arm as if that should stop him. Russ found little humor in her pathetic attempt. *He* wasn't the one who'd cheated on her. He wasn't the one who'd abused her love and her trust. And he damn well refused to be punished for the sins of another.

"Taylor, listen to me."

"No," she said with surprising strength. "There isn't anyone to blame but me. From the moment you and I met I realized we were in trouble, and we've both behaved like fools ever since. Me more than you. I've said it once, and apparently you didn't believe me, so I'm saying it again. I don't *want* to become involved with you."

"You're already involved."

"I'm not—not yet, anyway. Please, don't make this any more difficult than it already is. I'm not asking you this time. I'm telling you. If you care about me, if you have any feelings toward me whatsoever, you'll forget you ever knew me, forget we ever met."

Her words seemed to encircle his heart and then tighten like barbed wire. If he cared for her? He was crazy in love with her! His breath felt frozen in his chest.

"Am I supposed to forget I held you and kissed you, too?"

She nodded wildly. "Yes!"

Russ rubbed the back of his neck while he contemplated her words. "I don't think I can forget."

"You've got to," she said, and her shoulders heaved with each pleading syllable. "You have to."

Walking out on her then would have been like taking a branding iron and burning his own flesh. Despite everything she'd claimed, and asked for, Russ walked to her side, took her by the shoulders and pulled her against him. She fought him as though he was the one responsible for hurting her so terribly. As if he was the one who'd betrayed her.

Her fists beat against him, but he felt no pain. None. Nothing could hurt him as much as her words.

Gripping her by the wrists, he pinned her hands behind her back. She glared up at him, her eyes spitting fire. "Why do you have to make this so difficult? Why?"

"Because I don't give up easily. I never have." He raised his hand and glided his fingertips over the soft contours of her face. He traced her stern, unyielding mouth, and with his hand at the small of her back, pressed her forward until her body was perfectly molded to his. Then he buried his face in her sweet-smelling hair and inhaled deeply.

"Russ," she pleaded, bending her head to one side, "don't do this."

He answered by sliding his mouth over hers. His hand freed her wrists as he held her against him. The fight had gone out of her, and her arms crept up his chest, pausing at his shoulders, her nails digging hard into his muscles. But Russ still felt no pain.

A moment later, she pulled away from him, looking into his eyes. "Do I have to walk out on my contract, pack my bags and leave town to convince you I mean it?" she asked. "Is that what it's going to take?"

"If you want me out of your life, just say so," Russ said, shoving his hands in his pockets.

"What do you think I've been trying to do for the past weeks? Stay away from me, Russ! I've got to get my head straightened out. I'm not ready to fall in love again, not with you, not with anyone. I can't deal with this—with you—right now. I may not be able to for a long time."

"All right," he said gruffly. "I get the message. Loud and clear." He stalked out of the kitchen, paused long enough in the living room to reach for his hat, and then he was gone.

But as he closed the door, he heard Taylor's sobs. He forced himself to walk away from her, but he hesitated on the porch and sagged against the pillar. Regret and pain worked through him before he was able to move.

Once more he had to find meaning, reconciliation and peace in the aftermath of pain.

"Cody Franklin just pulled in to the yard," Mandy told Russ as though that was earth-shattering news.

Russ grumbled something in reply, and his muscles

tensed involuntarily. If Cody was stopping by to talk, Russ knew what—who—the subject was bound to be.

Taylor.

"I don't understand you," Mandy said, clearly at the end of her wits. "Why don't you just call Taylor and put an end to this nonsense? You've been walking around like a wounded bear all week."

"When I need your advice, I'll ask for it," Russ bit out, and stood up so fast, he nearly toppled the kitchen chair. "Stay out of it, Amanda. This is between me and Taylor."

"She obviously isn't doing any better. She called in sick twice this week."

"How many times are you going to tell me that?" Russ muttered. "It doesn't change the situation. She doesn't want anything to do with me. If and when she does, she'll contact me. Until then it's as if we never met."

"Oh, that's real smart," Mandy said, her fists digging into her hips. "You're so miserable, it's like having a thundercloud hanging over our lives. You love Taylor and she loves you, so what's the problem?"

"If Taylor feels anything for me, which I sincerely doubt, she'll let *me* know. Until then I have nothing to say to her." It gnawed at him to admit it, but the truth was the truth, no matter how many different ways he chose to examine it. Taylor had claimed she wanted nothing to do with him often enough for him to believe her. He had no other choice.

"Save me from stubborn men," Mandy groaned, as she headed for the door, pulling it open for Russ's friend.

"Howdy, Amanda," Cody Franklin said as he walked into the kitchen. He removed his cap and tucked it under his arm. He was dressed in his uniform—green shirt and coat and tan slacks. His gunbelt rode low on his hips.

"Hello, Cody." Mandy craned her neck toward Russ.

"I hope you've come to talk some sense into my bull-headed brother."

Cody seemed uneasy. "I'll try."

Mandy left the two of them alone, a fact for which Russ was grateful. He didn't need a letter of introduction to deduce the reason for his friend's latest visit. One look at Cody confirmed what Russ had already guessed. The deputy had stopped by as a courtesy before going out with Taylor himself.

"So you intend to ask her for a date?" Russ forestalled the exchange of chitchat that would eventually lead to the subject of Taylor.

Cody's eyes just managed to avoid Russ's.

"Frankly, Cody, you don't need my permission. Taylor is her own woman, and if she wants to date you that's her business, not mine."

Having said as much, Russ should have felt relieved, but he didn't. He'd been in a rotten mood from the moment he'd left Taylor's nearly a week before, and Cody's coming by unannounced hadn't improved his disposition any.

Cody must have sensed his mood, because he gave Russ a wide berth. He walked over to the cupboard, brought down a mug and poured himself coffee before he turned to face Russ.

"Sit down," Russ snarled. "I'm not going to bite your head off."

Cody grinned at that, and it occurred to Russ that Cougar Point's deputy sheriff wasn't bad-looking. Handsome enough to stir any woman's fickle heart. Plenty of women were interested in him, but he took his duties so seriously that no romantic relationship lasted more than a couple of months. Cody Franklin didn't smile very often, and Russ thought he knew why.

The two men went back a long way, and Russ didn't want their friendship to end because of one stubborn woman. "You're planning on asking Taylor out, aren't you?" he demanded when Cody didn't immediately respond.

Cody joined Russ at the table. "Actually, I wasn't going to do anything of the kind. I asked her once already, and she turned me down. I figured she wasn't interested, so I was willing to leave it at that."

"Then why are you here?"

"Because she phoned the other day and asked *me* to dinner Friday night." He paused to rub the side of his jaw. "I don't mind telling you, I was taken aback by that. I've never had a woman ask me for a date."

"What did you tell her?"

Cody looked uncomfortable. "I said I needed some time to think it over."

"So Taylor's the one who called you?" Russ was surprised his voice sounded so normal.

"I've never had a woman approach me like this," Cody went on to say a second time. "I'm not sure I like it, either. It puts me in one hell of a position." He twisted the mug around in his hands, as though he couldn't locate the handle. "From what she said, I assume she intends to pay, too. I've never had a woman pay for my meal yet, and I'm not about to start now."

"Don't blame you for that," Russ felt obliged to say, although he couldn't help being slightly amused. He didn't need a script to realize what Taylor was doing. She'd asked Cody Franklin to dinner to prove something to herself and possibly to him.

"You've got feelings for her, haven't you?" Cody asked, eyeing him suspiciously.

"You could say that," Russ confirmed, understating

his emotions by a country mile. He had feelings, all right, but he wasn't willing to discuss them with his friend.

Cody grinned, revealing even white teeth. Crow's-feet crinkled at the corners of his eyes. "So, what do you want me to say to her?"

"That you'll be happy to let her buy you dinner."

Cody hesitated before taking a sip of his coffee. "You don't mean that," he finally said.

"Yes, I do. In fact, I've never been more serious in my life."

"But—"

"Taylor Manning doesn't want anything to do with me."

"And you believe her?"

Russ shrugged. "The way I see it, I don't have any choice. If she wants to go out with you, fine. That's her decision."

Cody shook his head. "I can't believe I heard you right."

"You did. Trust me, dealing with this woman isn't easy."

Cody set his half-finished coffee on the table and stood. "Okay, but I have the feeling you're going to regret this."

Cody Franklin was as nice a man as Taylor had ever met. And a gentleman to boot. He arrived promptly at seven, dressed in a suit and tie. He really was handsome. Considerate. And Taylor was badly in need of some tender loving care. She'd just spent the most miserable week of her life, and an evening with a man who didn't pose the slightest emotional threat was exactly what she needed to pull herself out of this slump. At least that was what she kept telling herself.

"I hope I'm not too early," Cody said, stepping inside and glancing around. Apparently he approved of what he saw, because he gave her a smile.

"No, this is perfect." She reached for her coat, but Cody took it from her hands and held it for her so she could slip it on. With a murmured thanks, she picked up her purse.

"Before we leave," he began, then cleared his throat, "there's something I'd like understood. If we go to dinner, I pay the tab."

"But I invited you," Taylor reminded him, somewhat surprised at the vehemence with which he spoke.

"I pay or we don't go."

Taylor couldn't see any point in arguing. She'd encountered enough stubborn male pride with Russ to know it wasn't going to do her any good. "If you insist."

"I do."

Once that was resolved, they managed to carry on a pleasant conversation while Cody drove to the restaurant. He'd chosen Larry's Place, the one halfway decent eating establishment in town. Taylor hadn't eaten there before, but she'd heard the food was good—and the company was exemplary. For the first time in a week she found herself smiling and talkative.

The hostess escorted them to a table, and they were handed menus. It took Taylor only a moment to decide. Her appetite had been nonexistent for days, and she was determined to enjoy this evening no matter what.

"Hello, Cody. Taylor."

Russ's voice came at her like a blast of cold air. She drew in a deep breath before turning toward the man who'd dominated her thoughts all week. "Hello, Russ," she said coolly.

"Russ," Cody said, standing. The two exchanged handshakes. "Good to see you again, Mary Lu."

"Have you met Taylor Manning?" Russ asked his date. His hand was casually draped over the other woman's shoulder as he smiled down on her. "Taylor's the new schoolteacher."

"Pleased to meet you," Mary Lu said, and she actually sounded as if she was.

Taylor smiled and nodded. The woman didn't reveal a single shred of jealousy, she mused darkly. Surely by now everyone in town knew there was something going on between her and Russ. The least the other woman could do was look a little anxious. But then, why should she? Mary Lu was the one with Russ. Taylor was with Cody Franklin.

Cody reclaimed his seat. "Would you two care to join us?"

Taylor's heart shot upward and seemed to lodge in her throat. Seeing Russ accompanied by another woman was painful enough without having to make polite conversation with them for the rest of the evening.

"Another time," Russ said. His thoughts apparently reflected her own.

Taylor was so grateful, she nearly leaped from her chair to thank him with a kiss. It wasn't until he'd left the table that she realized how tense she was. Smiling in Cody's direction, she forced herself to relax. Elbows on the table, she leaned toward her date. "So how long have you been in law enforcement?"

"Since I graduated from college," he answered, but his concentration wasn't on her. Instead, his gaze followed Russ and Mary Lu to the other side of the restaurant.

His frown disturbed her. "Is something wrong?" she asked.

"I don't know yet."

Taylor sighed. This whole evening was a mistake. She'd phoned and asked Cody to dinner for two reasons. The first and foremost was simply because she was lonely, and the thought of spending another weekend alone was more than she could bear. The second was to prove that... She was no longer sure what she'd hoped to accomplish.

Cody sipped his water. "You're in love with him, aren't you?"

This man certainly didn't pull any punches. The least he could've done was lead into the subject of Russ Palmer with a little more tact. Taylor considered pretending she didn't know what he was talking about, but that would've been ridiculous.

She lowered her gaze to the tablecloth. "I don't know if I love him or not."

"What's there to know? I saw the look in your eyes just now. Russ walked in with Mary Lu, and I swear you nearly keeled over."

"You're wrong. I was mildly surprised, that's all."

"It doesn't bother you that he's with Mary Lu?"

She managed a casual shrug. "Not really. I wasn't expecting to see him. If I reacted, which I don't think I did, it was due to that and that alone."

"So what are you going to do about it?"

"Do about what?"

"The way you feel for Russ."

"I'm not going to do anything." She didn't need time to make that decision; it had been made weeks earlier. All the arguments she'd put forth, time and again, crowded her mind. All the reasons a relationship with him couldn't work... Yet she couldn't turn her eyes away from Russ, couldn't stop gazing at him with an emotional hunger that left her trembling.

"He loves you, too," Cody whispered. He reached across the table and took hold of her hand. "I don't know what drove you two apart, but I'm here to tell you right now, it's eating him alive." His smile was gentle, concerned. "It seems to be having the same effect on you."

"It's not that simple," she whispered.

A long moment passed before Cody spoke again. "Nothing worthwhile ever is."

"Taylor, do you realize what time it is?" her sister, Christy, groaned after she answered the phone on the fifth ring.

"I'm sorry... I should've checked," Taylor said, feeling utterly foolish and completely miserable.

Christy yawned loudly. "It's three in the morning! Why are you phoning at this hour? Are you all right? You're not in trouble, are you?"

If only Christy knew! "I...was calling to see if you were going to be free next weekend."

"Are you flying home? Oh, Taylor, it would be so good to see you. I can't believe how much I miss you. Paul, Jason and Rich, too. Mom and Dad don't say much, but know they feel the same way."

"No, but I'll be in Reno, and I thought that, well... I was hoping I could talk you into joining me. There are a bunch of cheap flights out of Sea-Tac and I thought maybe you could meet me in Nevada."

Christy slowly released her breath. "I can't. I'm really sorry, but I can't possibly swing it at this late date. What will you be doing in Reno?"

"Nothing much. The drill team is competing there, and I volunteered to be a chaperone—but apparently the team will be busy for two days and I'm going to have a lot of time to kill. I thought it would be fun if we got together."

"All right, Taylor," Christy said after a moment. "What's wrong? And don't try to tell me *nothing.* The last time you called me at three in the morning was when... I'm sure you remember."

"This doesn't have anything to do with Mark."

"Thank God for that." Her voice lowered slightly with concern. "What's wrong, then?"

Taylor reached for a tissue and blew her nose loudly. "I...think I'm in love."

Christy groaned again. "You've got to be kidding. Who?"

"His name is Russ Palmer and he owns a cattle ranch."

"I was afraid of that. I read your last letter to Mom and Dad and it was full of that cowboy! It was Russ this and Mandy that. Taylor, get control of yourself. You don't want to spend the rest of your life on a ranch out in the wilds of Montana, do you?"

"Of course not!" Taylor sobbed. "The last thing I intended to do was fall in love—especially with someone who thinks just like Dad."

"Your cowboy believes women shouldn't have the right to vote?" Christy asked, aghast.

Taylor started to laugh even while she was crying. "He said he doesn't care if we vote. It's females holding public office that bothers him." She paused. "He knows how much I hate it when he says stuff like that. He does it to get a rise out of me and it works every time."

She could hear Christy taking a deep breath and imagined her mentally counting to ten. "Listen, Taylor, you're my sister and my dearest friend. What you feel isn't love. It's a natural and common emotion following the breakup of any romance."

"That's what I thought…at first."

"You were right. For most of your life your judgment was totally sound. Nothing's changed all that much. So you made a mistake with Mark. So what? But when you come out of a long-term relationship, there's an emptiness and the normal reaction is to immediately find someone to fill it."

"I don't think that applies in this case," Taylor argued. In the beginning she'd assumed the same thing, but not anymore. This ache she felt went deeper than anything she'd ever experienced.

"You've spent the past six weeks in a town where no one even accepts American Express," Christy reminded her. "Taylor, this thing with the cowboy is all due to what happened with Mark. You're away from your family. You're lonely and vulnerable, and it's only natural to find yourself attracted to another man. I know I would be if the situations were reversed."

"You would?"

"Of course," Christy said smoothly and with conviction. "Just hold on for another week, and once you're in Reno, where there are real stores and real people, you can reevaluate your feelings. I'm sure being there will help clear your mind."

"Do you honestly think so?"

"I know so," Christy said without the least qualm. "Now take two aspirin, go to bed and call me next week when you get back from Reno. Ten to one, you're going to feel a lot different than you do tonight."

"Okay," Taylor said. After a few more minutes she replaced the receiver, convinced her sister was right.

The next week flew past, the days blending as Taylor threw herself into her job. Friday afternoon, her suitcase packed, she headed for the school bus and the twenty girls who comprised the Cougar Point High School Drill Team.

The first girl she saw was Mandy, who flew across the yard and hugged Taylor close. "I'm so glad you're going with us."

"Me, too," Taylor said, meaning it.

Mandy reached for Taylor's suitcase, setting it beside the others. "Everyone's here except the driver." She paused and rolled her eyes. "But then he's always late."

The girls gathered around Taylor, and soon they were chatting away like old friends. Taylor knew many of the team members as well as their coach.

"Everyone ready?" a male voice called out.

Taylor recognized it immediately as Russ's. She swallowed and turned toward him, frowning. "What are you doing here?" she demanded.

He tossed one suitcase into the compartment on the side of the bus and then another. "The same thing as you," he said without the least animosity. "You're a chaperone, and I happen to be driving the bus."

Twelve

It wasn't the twenty boisterous, exuberant high school girls who were driving Russ crazy. They sang, they cheered and they shouted as he drove the school bus across three states.

No, it wasn't the girls—it was Taylor. Taylor, who laughed and sang. Taylor, who joked and teased as if she hadn't a care in the world.

Each and every one of those girls adored her. The problem was, so did Russ.

Other than their brief exchange before they'd boarded the bus, she hadn't said more than a handful of words to him. True, there hadn't been a lot of opportunity. They'd stopped in Billings for something to eat and she'd sat in a booth surrounded by teenagers. Russ had eaten with Carol Fischer, the drill team coach, and another of the chaperones. Carol and he had exchanged a few pleasantries, but the entire time they were eating, Russ had found his gaze drawn again and again to the table next to his where Taylor was seated.

He would've liked nothing better than to get Taylor alone for a few hours. Then, and only then, would he have the chance to talk some sense into that stubborn head of hers.

Okay, she'd gone and fallen in love with the wrong man. Everyone made an error in judgment at some point, but that was in the past and Russ was very much part of the present. Although he told himself this a hundred different times and in as many different ways, the thought of Taylor aching, wanting, crying over another man felt like a knife slicing deep into his heart. It hurt so much that for a moment he couldn't breathe normally. Hell, he hadn't been breathing normally from the second he'd stumbled upon Taylor in the five-and-dime last September.

The long, lonely miles sped past. The girls gave up singing even before they left Montana. Around midnight the only one on the bus who wasn't sleeping was Russ.

"Do you want some coffee?"

Taylor's soft voice behind him sounded like an angel's, Russ thought gratefully.

"Russ?"

"Please." He waited to speak until she'd poured him some from the thermos she carried and he'd sipped it, appreciating the way it revived him. "I figured everyone was asleep."

"They are."

"What's keeping you awake?" He'd love it if she admitted he'd been in her thoughts for two desolate weeks and that she couldn't let another hour pass, or even another second, without telling him how she felt.

"I never could sleep in a moving vehicle."

"Oh," he said, trying to disguise his disappointment. He should know by now that Taylor wasn't going to fulfill his fantasies by saying all the things he longed to hear.

"How have you been?"

They'd barely said a word to each other in two weeks, he mused darkly, frowning, and she was asking about his health!

Briefly he wondered what she'd say if he told her he wasn't sleeping well, his mood was sour and he couldn't sit down to a single meal without suffering indigestion afterward. All these ailments he attributed entirely to her stubbornness.

"I'm fine," he said instead. "How about you?"

"Fine, just fine."

"Now we've got that settled, what else would you like to talk about? The weather seems a safe enough subject, doesn't it?"

"I… I think I'll go back and check on the girls."

"You do that," he muttered, then immediately wanted to kick himself for being such an idiot. At least Taylor had been willing to talk to him, which was a lot better than the strained silence that had existed between them up to this point.

It wasn't until midafternoon the following day that they pulled in to the congested streets of Reno. The girls were leaning out the windows, shouting at tourists, while Carol and the other adults attempted to calm their rampant enthusiasm.

Carol and Russ had traded off driving, but like Taylor, Russ didn't sleep well in a moving vehicle. He leaned back, shoved his hat low over his face and did a fair job of pretending, but he hadn't slept a wink in over twenty-four hours.

When Russ pulled in to the parking garage at Circus Circus, the hotel where they were booked, he heaved a giant sigh of relief. He was exhausted, mentally and physically. With the help of two bellboys, he unloaded the ton of luggage the girls had found indispensable for this short trip. While he was busy with that, Carol and the other chaperones, accompanied by the entire drill team, checked in. As soon as he was finished, Carol handed him his room key and suggested he get some sleep.

Russ didn't need to be told twice. He practically fell asleep in the elevator on the way up to his floor. Taylor and several of the girls rode with him, and just before he entered his room, Russ saw that she'd been assigned one on the same floor.

Some of his tiredness vanished when he discovered that Taylor would be sleeping down the hall from him. Not bothering to unpack his bag he tossed his hat onto the small table and collapsed on top of the bed. Bunching up the pillow, he closed his eyes and savored the quiet, the peace. It wasn't until sleep began to overtake his mind that he realized he had two whole days in which to convince Taylor she loved him.

Taylor couldn't remember a time when she'd been more exhausted. Other than brief stops, the bus had spent nearly twenty hours on the road, and she hadn't gotten more than a catnap the entire distance. Carol, bless her heart, had insisted Taylor go upstairs to bed while she and the assistant coach managed the girls. Taylor didn't offer a single argument.

From the moment they pulled in to the hotel, the girls' schedule was packed. In less than two hours they were meeting several other out-of-state teams, who would also be competing the following day, for a social. Then, first thing the next morning, Carol would be driving the drill team to a local high school and they'd be there the entire day until their performance, which was scheduled late that evening. After a good night's sleep, they'd be back on the road again, heading home to Montana.

Yawning, Taylor ran a tub of hot bathwater and soaked

in it, struggling to stay awake. When she got out, she crawled between clean, crisp sheets, already half-asleep.

There was noise and confusion around her for part of the time, since her room adjoined one with teenagers, but she hardly noticed. She woke at eight the next morning, just in time to see the team off and wish them well.

"You're coming to watch us, aren't you?" Mandy pleaded.

"Wild horses couldn't keep me away," Taylor promised.

"Do you think Russ will want to come?"

Taylor nodded. "I'm sure of it."

Beaming, Mandy hugged Taylor and then rushed to join her teammates.

Once the Cougar Point High School Drill Team had departed the hotel, Taylor wandered downstairs to the casino, where most of the gambling took place. Bells jingled incessantly and smoke rose like a sacrificial offering to the unpredictable gods of chance and good fortune. Row upon row of slot machines lined the brightest, reddest carpeting Taylor had ever seen.

She'd never gambled much, but the excitement that crackled through the room lured her toward the slot machines.

Trading her hard-earned cash for several rolls of nickels, she grabbed a plastic container and picked out a one-armed bandit at the end of a long row of identical machines.

"A fool and her money are soon parted," she muttered, seating herself on a stool.

She inserted three nickels and gingerly pulled down on the handle. Oranges, plums and cherries whirled past in a blur, then came to an abrupt halt.

Nothing.

She tried again and again and was rewarded by several minor wins. Two nickels here, ten there.

Someone slid onto the stool next to hers, and when she glanced over, a ready smile on her lips, her eyes clashed with Russ's. He looked well-rested and so devastatingly handsome that her breath jammed in her throat. The lazy grin he gave her was more potent than any of the free drinks she could have ordered.

"How are you doing?" he asked.

"Fine...good, really good." She plopped three more coins into the appropriate slot and pulled the lever with enough energy to dismantle the machine.

"How much have you won?"

She looked down at the small pile of nickels.

"Actually, I think I'm out a couple of bucks."

He grinned. "I'm down about the same. I don't suppose I could talk you into having some breakfast with me? You wouldn't consider that a breach of protocol, would you?"

"I...that would be fine." Taylor didn't know how a grown woman, a college graduate and teaching professional, could be so flustered around one man. The way her heart was jitterbugging inside her chest, anyone might assume Russ had asked her to join him in bed instead of in a restaurant.

Neither of them appeared to have much to say until they'd been seated by the hostess and handed menus.

Russ chose quickly and set his aside. "So how did your dinner with Cody Franklin go last weekend?"

"Cody's a wonderful man," she answered, glancing over her menu. Their eyes met briefly and she quickly switched her gaze back to the list of breakfast entrées.

"So you plan on seeing him again?" Russ demanded. Then he shook his head. "I'm sorry. I didn't have any right to ask you that. Whom you choose to date is your business."

Actually, she'd decided against dating Cody again, but not because she hadn't enjoyed his company. He'd been polite and gentlemanly all evening. After they'd left the restaurant, she'd invited him in for coffee and he'd accepted, but to her dismay their entire conversation then, as it had through most of dinner, centered on Russ. Cody hadn't kissed her good-night, nor had he asked her out again. Why should he? Taylor mused. She'd spent the evening with one man, while longing to be with another.

The waitress came by for their order and filled their coffee cups. Taylor took a sip of hers, and decided if Russ could question her, she should feel free to inquire about his own evening out. She carefully returned her cup to the saucer. "How was your dinner with Mary Lu Randall?"

"Great," Russ answered. "She's a lovely woman. Interesting, fun to be with, thoughtful…"

Taylor's throat constricted painfully as she nodded. Everything Russ said was true. Mary Lu Randall was known as a generous, unassuming woman.

"I won't be seeing her again, though," Russ muttered, drinking his coffee.

Despite everything she'd hoped to prove to this man, Taylor sighed with relief. "You won't? Why not?"

Russ set his coffee cup down hard enough to attract attention, and several heads turned in their direction. Russ glanced apologetically at those around him.

"Why?" he asked in a heated whisper. "Do you honestly need me to explain the reason I won't be dating Mary Lu again?" He threw his head back and glared at the ceiling. "Because I'm in love with you is *why*. In addition, you've ruined me for just about any other woman I might happen to meet."

"I've ruined you?" she echoed vehemently. She leaned toward him, managing to keep her voice low enough not to attract further attention.

The waitress delivered their meals, and Russ dug into his fried eggs as though he hadn't eaten in a week. He'd eaten both eggs before Taylor had finished spreading jelly across her toast, which she did with jagged, awkward movements.

"I would've thought Mary Lu was perfect for you," she said, unwilling to let the subject drop. "She's sweet and gentle and *deferential,* and we both know how important that is to a man of your persuasion."

"I used to think that was what I wanted until I met you." He stabbed his fork into his fried potatoes. "I'll be damned if you didn't ruin me for decent women."

"Ruined you for decent women?" Taylor cried, not caring whose attention she drew.

"That's right. *You.* This is all your fault. No woman ever challenged me and dared me the way you do, and I'm having one heck of a hard time adjusting. Compared to you, every other woman has the appeal of watered-down soup." He jammed his index finger against the top of the table before continuing. "Mary Lu's one of the nicest women in Cougar Point, and any man she married would consider himself lucky."

"But it won't be you," Taylor stated, hating the way her heart gladdened at that.

"How can it be when I'm crazy about you?"

The irritation drained out of Taylor as quickly as it had risen. She set her slice of toast aside and dropped her eyes, suddenly close to tears. "I wish you wouldn't say that."

"Why? Because you don't like hearing it? Fine, I won't say it again, but that isn't going to change a thing. If you want to put us both through this hell, then go ahead. There's nothing I can do to stop you. But I love you, Taylor, and like I said, that's not going to change."

"But I don't *want* you to love me."

"Don't you think I know that? Trust me, lady, if I had any choice in the matter, you'd be the last woman I'd fall in love with. Do you honestly believe I need this aggravation in my life? If so, guess again."

"There's no need to be angry."

Russ pushed his near-empty plate aside and downed the last of his coffee in a single gulp, apparently doing his best to ignore her.

"Thank you for breakfast," Taylor said, pushing her own plate aside after a moment. She'd only managed a few bites of egg. The toast she'd so carefully spread with jelly remained untouched.

"You're welcome." Leaning back in his chair, Russ rubbed a hand over his eyes. When he dropped his hand, it was clear that he was forcing himself to put their disagreement behind him. He smiled. "What are your plans for today?"

"The first thing I'm going to do is shop. There's a fingernail hardener with epoxy that I need to find," she said, glancing down at her carefully groomed nails. "Not a single store in Cougar Point carries it."

"Don't they use epoxy in glue?" Russ frowned as he stared down at her hands. "If you want to go putting that stuff on your pretty nails, far be it from me to stop you."

"Thank you," she said graciously, resisting the urge to roll her eyes. "After that, I thought, since I was in town, I'd pick up a few other things for the sheer joy of using my American Express card."

Russ chuckled. "Would you mind if I tagged along?"

"Of course not," she said promptly. She didn't mind. In fact—perversely—the prospect delighted her.

Over the past few weeks and all the disagreements, Taylor had forgotten what pleasant company Russ could be. He was good-natured and patient to a fault as she dragged him from one store to the next. He was more than tolerant while she tried on a series of dresses, and after she chose one, he went with her to the shoe department and helped her pick out a comfortable pair of heels.

Taylor tried to return the favor and help him choose new work shirts. Russ seemed to be of the opinion that if he found one shirt that suited him, he might as well buy five exactly like it. Taylor made a concerted effort to convince him otherwise.

"Where would you like to go for lunch?" Russ asked four hours later. His arms were loaded with a large number of bags and packages as he led the way down the street.

"Since you asked," Taylor said, smiling up at him, "I'm dying for a good pepperoni pizza, only—"

"Only what?"

"Only my favorite pizza chain doesn't have inside seating."

Russ looked at her as if she were deranged. "How do they do business then?"

"It's take-out and delivery only."

"All right," he said, mulling over this information. "Then I suggest we go back to the hotel. You can drop off the packages in your room while I phone and order a large pepperoni pizza."

Taylor agreed without realizing what she'd done until it was too late. After returning to her room, she piled her shopping on the double bed, then sat on the edge while she considered this latest development. She'd agreed to join Russ in his room. In the middle of the day. With no one else around.

Walking into the bathroom, she ran a brush through her hair. She toyed with the idea of finding an excuse, phoning Russ's room and canceling the whole thing. The hotel was filled with restaurants. The food was good and so reasonably priced it was a shame to order out.

Taylor slumped against the bathroom sink and closed her eyes dejectedly. Who was she kidding? Certainly not herself. She was in love with Russ and had been for weeks. They had no business falling in love, but it had happened, and instead of fighting it she should be grateful. Her attitude should be one of thanksgiving that she'd come across a man as fundamentally honest as Russ. There was no comparison to Mark, none whatsoever.

Five minutes later, she knocked on Russ's door. He let her in but had obviously been having second thoughts of his own. He marched to the other side of the room as though he feared she was carrying some dangerous virus.

"I phoned that pizza place and ordered," he said, apparently trying to sound casual. He tucked his hands into his pockets as if he suddenly didn't know what to do with them. "They said they'd be here in thirty minutes or less." He checked his watch. "That gives them nearly twenty-five minutes."

"Good," Taylor said, walking farther into the room. His was almost identical to her own. One queen-size bed, a dresser, one small table and two chairs.

"Make yourself at home," he said, pulling over a chair. Then he walked around the bed, averting his eyes.

"That was quite a morning we had, wasn't it?" he asked, rubbing his palms together. Heaving a sigh, he whirled around and faced her. "Listen, Taylor, this isn't going to work. If you want to have your pizza, fine, but I've got to get out of here."

"You don't have to leave," she said as she sauntered across the room, making sure her hips swayed just a fraction more than normal. When she turned to look at Russ, she was well rewarded for the little extra she'd put into her walk. His jaw was tight, and the edges of his mouth had whitened. His hands were knotted into fists at his sides.

"I...don't think you understand," Russ said faintly.

She moved close so that she was almost directly in front of him. Standing on her toes, she raised her arms and slid them around his neck, then molded her body against his.

Russ held himself completely rigid. Then he brought up his hands and closed them around her wrists, ready to pull her away from him. For some reason he hesitated. His gaze was hot and questioning when it locked with hers. "Just what kind of game are you playing?"

"The seductress. How am I doing?"

His gaze narrowed, and she noted that his breathing had become ragged. "Good. Too good."

He gazed down on her, his look a mixture of doubt and wonder. "Do you love me?" he asked.

She found herself lost, the words confusing her before they even reached her lips. Before she could tell him everything, before she could explain what was in her heart, Russ sighed and hauled her back in his arms.

His hands were in her hair, and his mouth was seeking hers. "It doesn't matter," he whispered brokenly. "I love you enough for both of us. It doesn't matter," he said again, just before his hungry lips claimed hers.

The passion between them was explosive. Tears clouded her eyes and fell down her face without restraint.

But these were tears of joy, tears of thanksgiving and discovery, surging from deep within.

"I love you, I love you," she chanted silently as she felt the tremors that went through Russ. He pulled her against him and held on as if he'd jerked her from the jaws of death and feared losing her a second time.

For the longest moment he didn't move.

"Russ?" she whispered. "What's wrong?"

The merest hint of a smile turned up the corners of his mouth. He leaned forward and with infinite care he brushed the hair from her brow. His callused, work-roughened hands had begun to shake.

"Russ?" she repeated, growing alarmed. Her hands framed his face, and he dragged one palm across his cheek to his lips and kissed the inside of her hand.

"I need to explain something first," he whispered, and the words seemed to be pulled from the farthest reaches of his soul. "If we make love now, there'll be no turning back."

Taylor blinked. She heard the desperation in his voice and read the havoc in his handsome face.

Her own mind was reeling, her thoughts jumbled. Had she been able to speak, her words would have made no sense.

Russ lowered his mouth to hers, but his kiss was featherlight. "Look at me," he whispered. "I want you so much I'm shaking like a newborn calf. All these weeks I've dreamed of this moment, of making you mine, and when the time arrives, I discover... I can't."

Not according to the evidence pressing against her thigh. Taylor didn't know a delicate, or even indelicate, way of mentioning the fact.

"I know your career is important to you, and it should

be. You worked too hard for your education to give it up now," he said.

"That's r-right," Taylor returned, puzzled.

Holding her hand in his own, Russ whispered, "And another thing…"

"There's more?"

"Lots more," he said, grinning down at her. His mouth brushed hers in a lazy, affectionate kiss. "I know you haven't come to appreciate Cougar Point yet, but that's all right. I promise you will in time. There's something about standing outside on a crisp autumn night and seeing the moonlight through the branches. Or hearing the crunch of snow under your boots in winter. In spring it's newborn animals, the smell of the earth and the rush of wind as it blows over the treetops. Those are the things I love most."

Taylor frowned in confusion. Her hands went back to his face and she studied him, seeking some meaning to his words. "Why are you telling me all this?"

"Because I want you to love my home as much as I do. I want you to love the country. Cougar Point will never rival Seattle. It won't even rival Reno, but it's a good place to live, a good place to raise a family."

Taylor had no argument with that. None. From the first, she'd seen how strong the sense of family was in this small community. "In the beginning I was so lost. Moving to Montana was like visiting a foreign country. Time seemed to have been turned back thirty years."

"What about ranch life?"

Again she wasn't sure what he was asking. "In many ways it's beautiful. I never thought I could say that and mean it. At first all I saw was the harshness of the land, and how unforgiving it could be. I saw how hard you and the others work. How busy you are. I learned a little about the problems and wondered why anyone would bother when ranching's such a demanding way of life."

"And now?"

"Now...there's still a great deal I don't understand about your kind of life, and I probably never will, but I see the contentment of knowing you've worked hard." She hesitated, surprised at how well-formed her thoughts actually were since she'd never voiced them before. "I moved to Cougar Point looking for one thing and found something else entirely. In the past few weeks I've learned what's important in life and what isn't."

Russ smiled and rewarded her with a lengthy kiss. "Now that we've got that subject all cleared up, I want you to know that I consider babies a woman's business...."

Bracing her hands against his chest, Taylor lifted her head. "What are you talking about? Honestly, Russ, I have no idea where this conversation is going."

His mouth dropped open. "You don't?"

She shook her head.

"Good grief, I thought you knew all along. I'm asking you to marry me."

Thirteen

"**M**arriage!" Taylor said, stunned. "You're joking."

"Trust me, a man doesn't joke about something like this."

All at once Taylor's knees didn't feel as if they would support her anymore, and she slumped onto the bed. Breathless and light-headed. She held her hand over her heart in an effort to calm its erratic beating, but that didn't seem to help.

"Taylor, what's wrong?" Russ knelt in front of her and took both her hands in his own. "You look like you're about to faint."

"Don't be ridiculous."

"What's wrong?"

She pointed at his door. "When I walked into this room, I wasn't thinking about getting married. Not for a second."

"Do you mean to say you came here after my body? Well, and the pizza, of course," he added with a laugh.

"Your body? Don't go all righteous on me," she muttered. "You've been after mine for weeks."

"I've reconsidered," Russ said with infuriating calm.

"I want more than an occasional tumble with you. A whole lot more."

"Isn't marriage carrying this a little too far?"

"No. Is it so wrong to want to wake up with you at my side?"

"You shouldn't hit a woman with this kind of talk. I'm not prepared for it." She pulled her hands from his and waved them dramatically. "Out of the blue he starts talking about marriage."

Russ ignored her outburst and sat beside her on the bed. "When I come into the house after a hard day's work, it's you I want to find."

Taylor's gaze narrowed. "I suppose it's me you want cooking your dinner and laundering your clothes!"

"Yes," he said matter-of-factly. "Because I'll have spent the past twelve or more hours building a good life for us. But if washing a load of clothes bothers you so much, I'll bring someone in. I'm not marrying you for your domestic talents."

He was serious. "Russ," she whispered, running her hands down his face, "marriage isn't something we should discuss now. Let's talk about it later…much, much later." Leaning forward, she slanted her mouth over his. Russ resisted her at first but quickly surrendered. His response was gratifying.

He wrapped his arms around her, and his returning kiss was urgent, charged with unleashed passion. As their kissing intensified, Russ eased her onto the bed and positioned himself above her.

"Taylor…" He lifted his head and groaned. He looked like a man who didn't know what to do, a man trapped in one world, seeking entrance to another. His eyes were shut.

Taylor had no answers to give him. All she knew was that she was tired of fighting this feeling, tired of living

a life filled with denial. She hadn't meant to fall in love
with Russ Palmer, but she had. Her fingers tangled in his
hair as she directed his lips back to hers.

She yearned for more of him. He kissed her again,
and she felt it in every part of her body, from the crown
of her head to the soles of her feet.

When she least expected it, he started kissing her in
a fierce and raging storm of his own, and then without
warning, he moved away from her.

With shaking hands, Taylor said, "Russ?" She kissed
him lightly. "Why did you stop?"

"I already told you. If we're going to make love, even
once, there's no turning back. I've got to have more from
you than your body.... I want you for my wife."

"Does it have to be all or nothing?"

"Yes," he said forcefully.

"But why talk about marriage now?" she asked gently.
"Isn't that something we could consider later?"

"No...it'll be too late to think about it afterward," he
said fervently. "If we're going to make love, there's got
to be a commitment between us."

"But, Russ..." She wasn't sure why she was fighting
him so hard; the reasons had escaped her. She'd already
admitted she loved him, and if she'd gone that far, then
accepting responsibility for their feelings was the next
logical step. Only she felt as if she'd just learned to walk
and Russ was signing her up for a marathon.

Russ took her by the shoulders. "I realize things are
done differently in the city. Men and women change
partners as often as they do their sheets. I've read about
'swinging singles' and 'hooking up.'"

"That's not true," Taylor argued. "At least not for me.
There's only been one other man in my life, and it was
the biggest mistake I've ever made."

"Then don't repeat it. I'm offering you what Mark never would have, because I don't want anything less. When we make love, there won't be any doubt in your mind about my commitment to you. It's complete and total. When I told you I loved you, that wasn't a momentary thing based on physical attraction or a case of overactive hormones. It's something that's been growing from the first moment we met. It's not going to change or go away. I love you, and it's the first time I've ever said that to a woman and truly meant it."

A lump formed in Taylor's throat, and tears brimmed in her eyes. "But we're so different...."

"Of course we are," Russ said, tucking both her hands between his. "That's the crazy part in all this. At first I thought those differences would doom any chance of a lasting relationship between us. I figured we didn't have any business joining our lives together when our views are so far apart. Then I realized that being with you, fighting with you, has brought balance into my life. You've shown me and taught me things I needed to know. There's a lot I still disagree with, but we can face those issues when they arise. Basically I'm coming around to your way of thinking."

That was news to Taylor. He still seemed as obstinate as ever in several areas. But then again, he'd allowed Mandy to wear makeup and he'd changed his opinion about the drill team uniform and even agreed to her compromise on the dating issue. There'd been other changes, too. Subtle ones. When she argued with him now, Russ listened and weighed her argument, which was something she'd never gotten her father to do. Her mother had always lent a willing ear, but never her father.

"I can see the changes in you, too," Russ continued. "Remember how you felt when you first moved to Cougar Point? As I recall, you said it was the farthest corner of the known world. Yet just a moment ago you were telling me you've come to appreciate some of the qualities of small-town living. True, no merchant in town accepts American Express, but who knows? And if you really get a craving to use that card, Billings isn't all that far."

"It's three and a half hours," she muttered, resisting the urge to laugh. She was actually considering this crazy proposal of his! What he said about Mark had hit home. The months apart had given her perspective. Russ was right; Mark would never have married her.

"Billings is only three hours, and that isn't far," he explained eagerly. "If you like, we'll make a regular weekend trip of it and spend our days shopping and our nights making love. I'm willing to compromise. If doing housework offends you—"

"That's not it!"

"Then what is?"

For the life of her, Taylor couldn't think of a single argument that made sense. She stuck with one that was tried and true. "It's the idea of a woman working for a wage and then being expected to do everything else at home, too. If a wife works outside the home, her husband should do his share of the housework and rearing the children."

"I agree," Russ murmured, although it looked as if he'd had to swallow a watermelon to say so. "But that's also why I feel a mother's place is in the home."

"Oh, please, let's not get into that again."

"Right," Russ said emphatically. "We could inadvertently start another war, and the last thing I want to do is fight with you. I love you, Taylor. Heaven help me, but it's true."

She raised her hand and caressed the side of his face. "I love you, too."

Russ pressed his own hand over hers and sighed deeply. "I knew you did. I couldn't believe anything else because it hurt too damn much. I swear to you, Taylor, I've never been a jealous man, but when you were having dinner with Cody Franklin last weekend, it took every ounce of restraint I possess not to march across that restaurant, pick you up and carry you out of there."

Taylor smiled and leaned forward until their foreheads touched. Her lips brushed his. "I'm not much for the green-eyed monster myself, but Mary Lu Randall should consider herself a lucky woman. I felt like tearing her hair out."

"Does this mean you'll marry me?"

Taylor closed her eyes and waited for a list of sound, rational arguments to convince her otherwise. To her surprise there were none. "Yes...."

With a triumphant shout loud enough to crack the windows, Russ bolted to his feet, taking her with him. With his arm at her waist, he whirled her around until Taylor, laughing, begged him to stop.

Instead, he lifted her higher and higher until she supported her hands on his shoulders and threw back her head.

The knock on the door caught them both by surprise. Taylor's eyes found Russ's. She didn't even want to imagine who was on the other side.

"Who is it?" Russ demanded, carefully lowering her to the floor.

"Pizza delivery."

Taylor hurriedly arranged her clothes and paused to smile when she heard that. She'd completely forgotten about the pizza.

Russ paid for their meal and brought the cardboard

box and a stack of napkins inside. The scent of pepperoni and melting cheese filled the room.

Taking the box from Russ, Taylor placed it on the table and immediately opened it, inhaling deeply. She was grateful for the napkins the delivery boy had included, and pulled a slice free for Russ. Next she helped herself, savoring the first delicious bite.

"Taylor," Russ groaned, sitting in the chair across from her, "we're having the most important discussion of our lives. How can you eat at a time like this?"

"The pizza is hot *now*," she said, and gobbled down two extra bites, in case he convinced her to put it aside.

"I suppose we're going to have to figure out how to get your pizza fix, too, aren't we?"

She nodded. "At least once a month, please." She closed her eyes. "Oh, my goodness, I'd forgotten how wonderful a pizza can taste. Russ, I'm sorry, but I can't marry you unless we arrange to have a decent pepperoni pizza every few weeks."

"The bowling alley—"

"Makes a great breakfast, but someone has to let those people know that good pizza is made fresh and doesn't come out of the freezer."

Russ jammed his fingers through his hair. "I'll do what I can. Anything else?"

"When are we going to announce the engagement? Christmas time?"

Russ stood abruptly and started pacing. He didn't look at her and seemed to be composing his thoughts.

"Russ?"

He turned to face her. "Taylor, I want us to get married this afternoon. I know you're entitled to a big wedding with the fancy dress and the dinner and dancing and everything else, but dammit all, we could be married within the hour if you'd agree."

The pizza that had seemed so important a few minutes before was forgotten. "You want us to get married *now*? *Today?*"

"We're in Reno, aren't we? What else do folks do in this town?"

She shrugged, and when she started to speak, her voice sounded as though she'd suddenly been struck with laryngitis. "I understand gambling is a big interest."

"Okay," Russ said, rubbing the side of his jaw, clearly calling upon all his powers of self-control. "Rushing you wouldn't be fair. I've been thinking for weeks about us getting married, but for you it's coming out of the blue. If you want to wait until Christmas, then fine. I can accept that. I don't like it, and I don't know how I'm going to keep my hands off you till then, but I'll try."

"You know what they say: marry in haste, repent at leisure," she felt obliged to remind him.

"Right," he returned with a complete and total lack of conviction. "When we look back on our wedding day, I don't want there to be any regrets. None."

"I certainly wouldn't want you to have any, either."

"The best thing to do is take this nice and slow," he said, raising both hands. "You're a teacher, so you tend to be methodical, and although you've seen evidence to the contrary, I'm not normally one to act on impulse, either."

"I don't think you heard me correctly," Taylor murmured, because he really had misunderstood her. "I thought we'd *announce* our engagement this Christmas."

Russ whirled around and stared at her, looking even more disgruntled. "Are you saying you'd like to be a traditional June bride?"

"School will be out, and it makes sense, doesn't it? But then, I'm not really much of a traditionalist."

He grinned at that and bent to kiss her. "You're more of one than you realize, otherwise you wouldn't have had any qualms about moving in with Mark." Once more he knelt in front of her. "I plan to do everything right for you, Taylor. Set whatever date you want for the wedding."

His eyes were filled with such intensity that Taylor saw herself mesmerized by the love she saw there. "I don't know…" she whispered, feeling overwhelmed by his willingness to commit his life to her. "We're both in Reno now. We're in love, but there are problems…."

"Nothing we can't settle," he suggested with an eagerness that brought a smile to her lips.

Closing her eyes, Taylor leaned forward and slipped her arms around Russ's neck. "Are you *sure* you want to marry me? You haven't met a single member of my family, and my father's opinionated enough to test the patience of a saint."

"It's not your family I'm marrying—it's you." He drew her hand to his mouth and kissed her knuckles. "As for whether I'm sure about marrying you, I've never felt more confident of anything in my life."

Despite everything, Taylor felt equally certain. "Now that you mention it, today does have appeal, doesn't it?"

"Yesterday had appeal, too, as does tomorrow and all the rest of my tomorrows."

"Oh, Russ, sometimes you say the most beautiful things."

"I do?" He seemed completely surprised by that. "I wasn't trying." With his hands at the small of her back, he drew her forward until she was perched on the very edge of the chair. "I love you, Taylor, and I'm going to love you all the days of my life." His mouth captured hers, and he worshiped her in a single kiss.

When he pulled away, Taylor felt like clay in his arms, her will shaped and molded by his. "I'll wear my new dress."

"One more question," he whispered close to her ear. "Are you on birth control?"

Her eyes flew open. "No. Are you?"

He jerked his head back and stared at her, open-mouthed. Then his face relaxed into a lazy smile. "I'm beginning to know you, Taylor Manning, soon to be Taylor Palmer. You're telling me birth control isn't just a woman's responsibility."

She rewarded him with a long, slow, leisurely kiss.

"I'll stop at the drugstore," he murmured when she'd finished.

"No," she whispered between nibbling kisses. "I don't want you to."

"But you might get pregnant."

"Yes, I know." She found his earlobe and sucked it gently. "I'd like it if I did. What about you?"

"I'd like it, too.... Taylor," he moaned, "stop now while I've still got my sanity."

She pressed her breasts against him, loving the feel, savoring the sensations the action aroused.

"Taylor," Russ groaned once more. "Stop...please."

"In a moment."

"Now." He clasped her around the waist and stepped back.

He stood, clutching the back of the chair. "I'll go find us a preacher," he said, and his voice was shaking. "Can you be ready in an hour?"

Taylor stood in the foyer of the wedding chapel, holding a bouquet of small pink rosebuds. The minister who'd married her pointed out the line on the wedding certificate where she was supposed to sign. Taylor did so with a flair, then smiled at her husband and handed him the pen. Russ in turn gave the pen to the receptionist and clerk who'd served as their witnesses.

Russ hurriedly signed the document, and when he'd finished, he shook the minister's hand and guided Taylor out of the chapel.

"I don't think I've ever seen you more beautiful," he said, sliding his hand around her waist and drawing her close. His eyes shone with a light that had been transmitted straight from his heart, a message of joy.

"I don't think I've ever seen you more handsome," Taylor told him.

His eyes didn't stray from her. "What would you like to do next? Have dinner? See a show?"

Taylor chuckled. "You've got to be kidding. You know what I want because it's the same thing you want. Besides, we've only got a few hours."

"A few hours. Why?"

"Because," she said, leaning forward to press her mouth over his, "the drill team is scheduled to perform at eight, and Mandy would never forgive us if we weren't there for her big moment."

Russ grumbled something under his breath and quickened his pace, leading her back to the hotel.

"You seem to be mighty eager, Mr. Palmer," she said as they entered into the hotel elevator.

"Move your hips like that one more time and I'll show you how eager I can be."

"And I'd let you."

Russ reached for her then, dragging her against him. His mouth took hers, and he gave her a glimpse of the pleasure that awaited her. The elevator had stopped at their floor, and the doors had glided open before either of them was aware of it.

As soon as they stepped into the long, carpeted hallway, Russ lifted her in his arms. "You didn't get the big fancy wedding, with the bridesmaids and orange blossoms and the organ music, but there are some traditions I can and will provide."

However, opening the door with Taylor in his arms proved to be awkward, and after a frustrating moment, Russ tossed her over his shoulder like a bag of grain.

"Russ," Taylor cried, "put me down this minute."

"Be patient," he said, crouching down in an effort to insert the key into the lock. Apparently he was having trouble, because it was taking him forever.

A middle-aged couple strolled past, and mortified, Taylor covered her face with both hands.

"Dear," the woman whispered to Taylor, "do you need help?"

"Not really," she answered. "Just don't ever let your daughters grow up to marry cowboys."

"You're recently married?" the woman asked as if that was the most romantic thing she'd ever heard. "Did you hear that, John? They just got married."

The door finally opened, and Russ walked inside with Taylor still dangling over his shoulder. "We've been married for all of about fifteen minutes," Russ told the couple. "Now, if you'll excuse us, we're going to have our honeymoon." With that he shut the door.

"Russ Palmer, put me down," she ordered him again.

"With pleasure."

He walked to the bed and released her. Taylor went flying backward, a cry hovering on her lips. Chuckling, Russ lowered himself over her.

"Was that really necessary?" she asked, feigning indignation.

"If I wanted to get you inside this room, it was. And trust me, I wanted you in this room."

A smile twitched at the edges of Taylor's mouth.

"Oh, Taylor," Russ groaned, "I'm so crazy about you." He set his long fingers in her hair and pulled up her head to receive his kiss. His mouth was hard over her own, hard with passion and with need.

"Oh, sweet Taylor," he murmured as he tore his mouth free and nestled his face in the delicate curve of her neck. He kissed her there, his lips hot and moist. His hands were gentle as he helped her stand and slip out of her dress. It fell to the floor in a pool of silk and lace. He picked it up and set it aside.

Their mouths met once more in another kiss, a kiss that promised passion about to be assuaged—and a love that would last through all the seasons of their lives.

An hour later, just before they left for the drill team performance, Taylor used the phone in Russ's room to call her family.

Russ stood behind her, his hands caressing her shoulders. Without her ever having said a word, Russ seemed to know how difficult this discussion would be for her.

"Mom?" she said excitedly when her mother answered. "If Dad's home, get him on the other phone. I've got some important news."

Taylor heard her mother's hurried call. Within a minute, Eric Manning was on an extension.

"Taylor," her father's voice boomed over the long-distance line, "what is it? Is anything wrong? Listen, I've been reading between the lines in your letters, and I'm worried about you and this cowpoke. Christy said you called and talked to her, but she never told us exactly why. Just said you were having trouble with that cowboy."

"Dad...stop a minute, will you?"

"Now you listen to me. If he gives you any more problems, I want you to let me know because your brothers and I will deal with him."

"Eric," her mother interrupted, "Taylor called because she has some news."

It took Taylor a tense moment to compose herself.

"Mom and Dad," she said after swallowing hard, "congratulations are in order.... I was married today." A second of stunned silence followed her announcement. "I'm afraid I married that cowboy." She handed the receiver to Russ.

Fourteen

Russ took the telephone receiver, worried about the way she was frowning, wondering what her parents had said. It looked as if she wanted to advise him, but there wasn't time.

"Hello," Russ said. "I'm Russ Palmer."

"What the hell have you done?" a loud male voice shouted at him.

Russ moved the phone away from his ear. "I married your daughter," Russ explained, doing his best to keep his tone even and controlled. He didn't much take to being yelled at, but he could understand Eric Manning's feelings.

"Taylor's just broken off one relationship, and the last thing she should do is get involved in another, especially with—"

"A cowboy," Russ finished for him. Taylor was sitting on the edge of the bed, her hands clasped tightly in her lap, her blue eyes staring up at him.

"That girl of mine should have her head examined. She doesn't understand what she's done and—"

A soft, feminine voice interrupted the tirade. "Eric, dear, all this shouting isn't going to settle anything.

They're already married. Didn't you hear Taylor tell you that?"

"And we intend to stay married," Russ added, in case there was any doubt in the older man's mind.

"It's too soon," Taylor's father continued, his voice less menacing. "Surely you realize she married you on the rebound. You may be a perfectly fine young man, but my daughter—"

"Is twenty-six and old enough to know her own mind."

"She's always been a hothead. No doubt her sister told her I was dead set against her having anything to do with you."

"I can understand your concern," Russ said, now that his anger had worn off. "You don't know me from Adam."

"What about your family?" Eric thundered anew. "What do they have to say about this?"

"The only family I have is a younger half sister. We haven't told her yet, but Mandy will be delighted."

"You don't have any family?" Eric shouted. "How are you supposed to know what's right? By the way, how old are you?"

"Thirty-five."

"Thirty-five! You're nine years older than Taylor— that's too much."

"Now, Eric," Elizabeth Manning broke in. "You're being ridiculous. If you recall, you're seven years older than I am. Russ, you'll have to excuse my husband's temper. It's just that he loves Taylor and is terribly proud of her, except he has trouble letting her know that."

"You don't need to go telling *him* that."

"Russ is family, dear."

"Not if I have anything to say about it."

"Frankly, Mr. Manning," Russ said firmly, "you don't. The deed is done. Signed, sealed and delivered."

"We'll see about that."

"Stop it now, the pair of you. Eric, either you be civil to Taylor's husband or you can get off the phone. I won't have you speaking to him that way." Her words were followed by the click of a telephone receiver.

Russ waited a moment to compose himself. Taylor had mentioned the type of man her father was more than once, but butting heads with him had been even more of a challenge than Russ had anticipated.

"Mrs. Manning, believe me, I can understand your concern, and I can't say I blame you. But I want you to know I love Taylor, and I have every intention of being a good husband."

"I'm sure you do. Please forgive my husband. Personally I think he was disappointed that he didn't get to walk Taylor down the aisle. Only one of our sons is married, and I think Eric was looking forward to taking part in a wedding for one of his daughters."

"I'm sorry to have cheated him out of that."

"Don't worry about it. There's always Christy, and we expect she'll be engaged to an attorney friend of hers soon. Now, before you think the worst of us, I want to offer you a hearty welcome to the family, such as it is."

"Thank you," Russ said, and smiled reassuringly at Taylor, who was looking more anxious by the minute.

"Would you mind putting Taylor back on the line?"

"Of course not." Russ's eyes found Taylor's as he held the receiver out to her. "Your mother wants to talk to you."

"Was it bad?" she whispered, sounding guilty when there was no reason for it.

"No, I think your father and I will get along just fine."

"The two of you are quite a bit alike."

Russ figured it was probably a good thing that he'd first been introduced to Taylor's father over the phone.

Had they met in person it was entirely possible that they would have swung at each other.

Taylor took the phone and relaxed visibly as she started talking to her mother. Russ was relieved to see her good spirits return. This was their day, the one he'd been thinking about for weeks, and he didn't want anything or anyone to ruin it.

The problem, Russ decided an hour later, was that he'd reckoned without Mandy, his cantankerous younger sister.

"You did *what?*" the teenager shrieked in outrage.

"We got married," Taylor explained softly, holding out her ring finger, adorned with a simple gold band, as proof. He could tell that she was equally surprised by his sister's response. "I thought you'd be pleased."

"You did it without even talking to me?" Mandy cried. She stood with her hands on her hips as though she were the adult and they were recalcitrant children. "I can't believe the two of you." She whirled around and confronted Carol Fischer. "Did you hear what they just did?" Mandy demanded.

Carol had trouble containing a grin. "Yes, I did," she said, and stepped forward to hug Taylor. "Congratulations."

"You didn't so much as consult me," Mandy reminded him, her eyes narrowing. "Can you imagine how I feel? I'm your sister, and I should've been in on this! Good grief, you wouldn't have even *met* Taylor if it hadn't been for me!"

"Do you mind our getting married so terribly much?" Taylor asked softly.

"Of course I don't mind. Marrying you is the smartest thing Russ has done in his whole sorry life. It's just that…" She paused, and tears clouded her pretty green eyes. "I would like to have been there. You couldn't have waited until after the drill team performance?"

"Yes, we could have. We should have," Russ agreed, stepping closer to his sister. "I'm sorry if we offended you. That wasn't our intention."

"We were so lost in each other that we forgot everyone else," Taylor said.

"I can't believe it. When we left this morning, you were barely talking to each other, and the next thing I know, you're married. I just don't understand it."

Taylor placed her arm around Mandy's shoulders. "I've been in love with your brother from the first, but I was fighting it because…well, because I didn't think I'd fit into his life. Then we started talking and I realized I couldn't even remember why I was fighting him so hard when I love him so much. This probably doesn't make a lot of sense to you, and I'm sorry."

Mandy lifted one shoulder in a halfhearted shrug. "In a way it does make sense. I just wish you'd waited a little longer. I would've liked to throw rice or birdseed or something."

"We were just thinking about going out for a wedding dinner. We'd like it if you came."

With her arms folded, Mandy cocked her head to one side. "Are you sure I wouldn't be intruding?"

"More than sure," Russ told her. "I'm going to order a bottle of champagne and you can have a virgin daiquiri if you want. It isn't every day a brother can share his wedding dinner with his sister, and we have a lot to celebrate, don't we? In fact, Taylor's and my wedding day wouldn't be complete if you weren't here to share part of it with us."

"You're just saying that," Mandy said with a regal tilt to her chin. "However, I'm going to let you get away with it because I really am pleased." She dropped her arms and threw herself against Russ with such force that he nearly toppled backward. "Hey," she cried, wiping tears from her cheeks with the back of her hand, "did you see how great the team did? Aren't we fabulous?" She didn't wait for a response, but reached for Taylor, slipping an arm around her waist and the other around Russ. "Now listen," she said, serious once more. "A wedding is one thing, but if you're going to start having babies, I want to be consulted. Understand?"

Three weeks later, early on a Saturday morning, Taylor nestled close to her husband under a layer of quilts, seeking his warmth. When she'd first arrived in Montana, Russ had warned her about the winters, but nothing could have prepared her for the bitter cold that had descended upon them in the past ten days.

Russ stirred, rolled over and pulled her into his arms. Taylor smiled contentedly as she repositioned herself so that her head rested on his shoulder. She settled her hands over his chest. Married life certainly seemed to agree with him—and she knew it agreed with her. From the moment they'd said their vows in Reno, Russ had been a devoted and loving husband, with the accent on the word *loving*. He couldn't seem to get enough of her, which was fine with Taylor, since she couldn't get enough of him, either.

With Mandy living with them, it sometimes became embarrassing. More than once after their wedding, Russ had insisted he was exhausted and dragged Taylor upstairs practically before they'd finished clearing the dinner dishes. Mandy loved to tease Russ about his sudden need for extra sleep since he'd returned from Reno.

At one point Taylor had felt it was necessary to talk to Russ's sister. Her fear was that Mandy would feel excluded, and that was the last thing Taylor wanted.

"Are you kidding?" Mandy had said, exchanging a smile with Taylor. "I think getting married is the best thing that's happened to Russ. He should've done it years ago. He's too mellow to fight with me anymore. Keep him happy, okay? Because when he's happy, I'm happy."

Keeping Russ happy made Taylor feel delirious with satisfaction herself. Every now and then they clashed over some issue, but that was to be expected. Both seemed willing, however, to listen to the other's point of view.

"Good morning," Russ whispered. His hand found her breast, and she sighed at the instant surge of pleasure.

"They seem fuller," he whispered.

"I know what you're thinking," she said, snuggling closer. "But it's much too soon to make that kind of assumption."

"Taylor," Russ groaned, kissing her hungrily. "We haven't used any kind of protection. Not once. Have you...you know, started yet?"

"Not yet, but I'm often a few days late."

Russ smoothed the hair about her face. "You know the problem, don't you?"

"The problem is you and your sexy ways," she muttered.

"You've never complained before."

"I'm not complaining now. I'm just telling you."

"Actually, the problem I'm talking about is your parents. They'll be here next week for Thanksgiving, and you don't want to have to tell them you're pregnant."

"My father will assume the worst."

"Let him. We know the truth."

"My father's always been ridiculously protective of us girls, and if he even suspects I was pregnant before we were married, he's going to raise the roof."

"Do you think I care?" Tenderly he rested his hand

on her abdomen, and the smile that came to his face was filled with an abundance of pride. "I bet this baby's a boy."

"What a terrible, chauvinistic thing to say."

"I can't help it. Every time I think about you having my son I get all warm. I still have trouble believing we're really married. It seems like a dream."

"We could very well have a girl. In fact, I'd be pleased if we did."

"So you're willing to admit you might be expecting."

Taylor was expecting, all right, but not the way Russ meant. She was waiting for trouble, and the minute her parents arrived there was bound to be plenty of it. Not once since she'd phoned to tell her mom and dad that she and Russ were married had Taylor spoken to her father. Her mother had phoned about the possibility of visiting for Thanksgiving, and Taylor had readily agreed. But she knew the real reason for this visit, and that was so her father could confront Russ about their rushed marriage. Several times in the past three weeks Taylor had tried to prepare Russ for the meeting, but he seemed to let everything she said roll off him. Either he really wasn't concerned or he was living in a world of his own. After doing battle with her father for most of her life, Taylor was nervous. Seldom did she back down from Eric Manning, but this was different. She wanted her family to love and appreciate Russ the way she did.

It wasn't that her father was such a monster, but he tended to be opinionated and hotheaded, especially when it came to his daughters. After Taylor had broken up with Mark, her father had taken pains to introduce her to a handful of eligible young men. All of them were professionals. Taylor didn't doubt for a moment that her father would consider Russ an inappropriate husband for her.

"And for another thing," she said stiffly, reminding him of the ridiculous statement he'd made when they were discussing marriage, "babies are *not* just a woman's business."

"Oh? And what am I supposed to do?"

"Plenty!"

"Come on, Taylor, be sensible. There's not a lot I can do with a baby. They're too…tiny."

"You can change a diaper."

"You've got to be joking."

She rolled away from him and buried her face in the pillow, embarrassed by the tears that sprang to her eyes. Even if she was pregnant, it would be months before the baby was born, and there was plenty of time to deal with the issue of Russ's role as a parent.

"Taylor?" Russ asked softly, his hand on her shoulder. "Are you crying?"

She refused to admit it. "Of course not."

"I've been doing a little reading on pregnancy and birth, and I understand that tears are perfectly normal. Women become highly emotional during this time."

"I suppose you're going to be quoting facts and statistics to me for the next eight months," she said, then immediately regretted her waspish tone. Turning back to Russ, she sobbed and threw her arms around his neck. "I'm sorry… I didn't mean that. It's just that I'm worried about you meeting Dad."

Russ gently kissed the tip of her nose. "There isn't going to be a problem, sweetheart. I promise you."

"You can't say that—you don't know my dad."

"I won't let there be a problem. We have one very important thing in common. We both love you. Two men of similar persuasion are going to get along famously. So stop borrowing trouble, all right?"

She nodded. "Okay, but I don't think we should say anything about the possibility of me being pregnant until after Christmas. Agreed?"

"If that's the way you want to handle it." He eased her more fully into his arms. "But I'm afraid I might inadvertently give it away. I'm so happy about it I have trouble not shouting every time I think about us having a son."

"Or daughter."

"I still think it's a boy."

"Whichever it is, I'd better tell Mandy. Otherwise we'll be subjected to her wrath—just like after the wedding. Weren't we given specific instructions to clear the idea of having kids with her first?"

"I already told her."

"Russ?" Taylor levered herself up on one elbow.

"I hadn't intended to, but we were sitting at the table one afternoon and apparently I was wearing a silly grin and—"

"It was probably more of a satisfied smirk," Taylor interrupted. Then she said, "Go on."

"Anyway, I was sitting there minding my own business and she wanted to know what I found so funny. Of course, I said I didn't find anything funny, and before I knew it, I was telling her about the book I'd picked up at the library about pregnancy and birth and how I thought you were going to have a baby. She was delighted. By the way, I told her the baby's probably a boy."

"Russ, you don't know that!"

"Somehow I do. Deep in my heart I feel he's a boy. Do you think your father will settle down if we promise to give the baby some family name of yours?"

"We've got to get him accustomed to the fact that we're married first. That might take some time." She made a wry face. "You know, like approaching a wild animal slowly..."

"Right," Russ grumbled. "I forgot." He reached for her and pulled her close. "If you're looking for ways to tame *this* wild beast, I might be able to offer a few suggestions." He wiggled his eyebrows provocatively.

Giggling, Taylor encircled his neck with her arms. "I tamed you a long time ago."

"That you did," he whispered as his mouth sought hers. "That you did."

The Wednesday before Thanksgiving Eric and Elizabeth Manning pulled their thirty-foot RV into the yard of the Lazy P.

Since school had been dismissed at noon, Taylor was home. The instant she recognized the vehicle, she called out to Russ, threw open the back door and flew down the steps, hardly taking time to button her coat. Russ followed directly behind her.

Standing by the door, Russ felt Eric Manning's eyes on him. The two men quickly sized each other up, and Russ descended the steps. He waited until Taylor had welcomed each of her parents before he placed his arm protectively around her shoulders.

If her parents didn't immediately guess she was pregnant, he'd be surprised. Taylor positively glowed—just like they said in the books. And he felt no less happy himself. Only rarely had he been this content. This *complete*. Taylor had filled all the dark, lonely corners of his life.

He hadn't been joking when he told her he felt all warm whenever he thought about the child growing inside her. At odd moments of the day he'd think about his wife and how much he loved her, and he'd actually feel weak with emotion. Some nights he'd lie awake and cherish these peaceful moments with Taylor sleeping at his side. She'd been sleeping a lot more lately. The books had told him she'd be extra-tired. He would prefer it if she'd quit work, but the one time he'd suggested it, she'd almost bitten his head off. Moodiness. That was something else the books had addressed. Russ decided he'd let Taylor decide when and if she should stop teaching. She knew her own limits.

"Mom and Dad," Taylor said, slipping her arm around Russ's waist, "this is my husband, Russ Palmer. You'll meet his sister, Mandy, this evening."

Russ stepped forward and extended his hand to Taylor's father. The older man muttered something unintelligible, and the two exchanged hearty handshakes.

"Come inside," Russ invited, ushering everyone into the warmth of the kitchen. He took their coats and hung them in the hall closet while Taylor settled her parents in the living room.

There had been lots of small changes in the house since she'd moved in. She had a natural flair for decorating and had rearranged the furniture and done other things that gave the living room a fresh, comfortable feel.

"Would you like some coffee?" she asked.

"No, thanks. We just had some, honey," her mother said.

Elizabeth Manning was an older version of her daughter. They both had the same intense blue eyes and long, thick dark hair. Eric Manning was as big as a lumberjack, tall and muscular, intimidating in appearance. It was important to Russ to win over this man. Important for Taylor. She'd fought with her father for most of her life. She'd often gone against his will, but she loved him, and his approval meant a great deal to her.

"Eric," Elizabeth Manning said softly, looking at her husband.

The older man cleared his throat. "Before I say anything more to get myself in hot water, I want to apologize for the way I behaved when we last spoke. It's just that finding out my daughter had married without a word to either of her parents came as a surprise."

"I understand," Russ said, "and I don't blame you. If my daughter had done that, I don't think I would've behaved any differently."

The two men shared a meaningful look.

"There's something you should both know," Taylor said, sitting on the arm of Russ's chair. She gave him a small smile, her eyes wide. "I'm pregnant. Now, Daddy, before you assume the worst," she added in a rush, "this baby was conceived in love with a wedding band on my finger. I swear to you it's the truth."

Russ stared up at his wife in shock. For days she'd been schooling him on the importance of keeping their secret until the Christmas holidays. Again and again she'd insisted the worst thing they could do was announce her pregnancy the moment her parents rolled into the Lazy P. Then, with barely a second's notice, Taylor had spilled it all.

"Oh, Taylor, that's absolutely wonderful." Her mother was clearly delighted. One look told Russ that wasn't the case with her father.

"Daddy?" Taylor turned expectantly to her father. She took Russ's hand and held it tightly. "I love him, Dad, more than I ever dreamed it was possible to love a man."

"He's good to you?"

"Damn right I'm good to her," Russ muttered. He wasn't sure what was going on between father and daughter, but he resented being left out of the conversation.

"That true?" Eric asked, tilting his head toward Russ.

"Yes, Dad."

Eric opened his arms to her, and Taylor flew across the room, to be wrapped in a bear hug by her robust father. The older man's gaze found Russ's. "She's more trouble than a barrel of monkeys. Opinionated and strong-willed, and has been from the day she was born. I suggest you keep her barefoot and pregnant."

"Daddy!" Taylor tore herself away from her father, hands on her hips. "What century are you living in?"

"The same one I am," Russ said, and chuckled boisterously when Taylor whirled around to glare at him.

The two men smiled at each other. Taylor understood what Russ was doing but couldn't help reacting anyway.

"If the two of you think you can run my life, I want you to know right now that—"

She wasn't allowed to finish. Russ gently turned her around, draped her over his arm and kissed her soundly.

"I can see our daughter married the right man," Russ heard Eric Manning inform his wife. "The right man indeed."

* * * * *

THE SHERIFF TAKES A WIFE

One

"What do you *mean* you're in labor?" Christy Manning asked her sister.

"I didn't say that...exactly," Taylor Palmer said, her palms flattened against her protruding abdomen. She lowered her eyelashes, taking a long, slow breath.

"You can't be in labor! I just got here. My suitcases are still in the trunk of my car." Christy bolted to her feet and shoved the dark curls away from her face with both hands. She'd been driving for nearly three days to be with her sister for the birth of this baby, but she hadn't counted on the blessed event happening quite so soon.

"What do you want me to do?" she asked, regaining her poise. In her opinion, there was plenty of reason for alarm. The Lazy P, Russ and Taylor's cattle ranch, was miles outside Cougar Point, the closest town. And there wasn't a neighbor in sight.

Taylor's husband, Russ, was driving his sister, Mandy, over to a friend's house and doing a couple of errands before heading back to the ranch. At most he'd be gone only an hour, or so he'd claimed.

But a lot could happen in an hour.

"I'm not convinced this is the real thing," Taylor said

in an apparent effort to reassure Christy, but her hands caressed her stomach as she spoke. "I've never been in labor before, so I'm not exactly sure what to expect."

Trying to gather her scattering wits, Christy circled the kitchen table. First and foremost, she needed to keep calm. Mentally she reviewed the recent classes she'd taken through the local library. She knew CPR and enough karate to defend herself. Great. She could knock someone out and then revive him. A lot of good either of those skills was going to do her in this situation.

She swallowed a feeling of impending panic. She wasn't even supposed to be in Montana. Her mother was the one who'd planned to make the trip, only Elizabeth Manning had taken a fall and broken her leg. She was having trouble getting around and would be little or no help to Taylor. Since Christy had a couple of weeks of vacation due, she'd volunteered to come and stay with her sister. It wasn't any sacrifice on her part; Christy and Taylor had always been close.

Unfortunately no one had bothered to tell her she was going to be stuck alone on a cattle ranch with her nine months' pregnant sister, who was "feeling funny."

It all seemed unreal. Christy had arrived late the night before. Too late to do more than greet everyone, haul her overnight bag into the guest bedroom and fall exhausted into bed.

"Stop looking like you expect to deliver this baby on your own," Taylor said, smiling up at her sister.

"But, Miss Scarlett, I don't know nothin' about birthin' no babies," Christy wailed in a Southern drawl. She might be teasing, but what she said was the honest-to-goodness truth.

None of this was supposed to be happening—at least not like this. Taylor should be living in Seattle with the rest of her family. Instead, Christy's older sister had gone to Montana a year earlier and to everyone's surprise married a cattle rancher three months later.

At the time, Christy couldn't imagine what had possessed her cultured, cosmopolitan sister to marry someone like Russ Palmer. Especially in Reno, without a single family member present.

Their father hadn't been pleased at being cheated out of the chance to walk his daughter down the aisle, but once he'd met Russ, the rancher had won him over. Russ had reassured everyone in the family without even trying. Taylor and her husband had flown to Seattle at the end of May to celebrate her parents' wedding anniversary. It was then that he'd met Christy and her three brothers.

Taylor winced and her eyes drifted shut again. Her display of pain effectively cut off Christy's thoughts. She held her breath until she saw the tension slowly ease from her sister's body. "What happened?"

"I felt a funny pain, that's all. Don't worry. It wasn't anything."

"A funny pain? And you don't want me to worry?" Christy echoed. She couldn't keep the panic out of her voice. "Then why do I have this urge to boil water?"

Taylor, forever calm and serene in a crisis, grinned. "Don't worry. I've been having these pains off and on for the past week, but…"

"But what?" Christy asked.

"But these feel…different. I don't know how to explain it." She rose haltingly to her feet. "I think it might be a good idea if I got dressed."

"Right," Christy said, as if the idea was a stroke of genius. "Me, too." With her arm around what remained of Taylor's waist, Christy led her sister down the hallway that went to the master bedroom. "Do you need any help?"

"Don't be ridiculous!" Almost before the words had left her lips, Taylor let out a cry and pressed one shoulder to the wall while clutching her stomach.

Christy was instantly alarmed. "What is it?"

"Oh…my." Wide-eyed, Taylor turned toward Christy. "Hurry and get some towels. My water just broke."

"Your water broke," Christy repeated in a stupor. She threw her hands toward the ceiling. "Her water just broke." Rushing into the bathroom, she returned with enough towels to soak up a flood.

Taylor was still leaning against the wall, breathing deeply, her eyes closed. Christy dropped the towels onto the floor, far more concerned about Taylor than she was about a little water. "Are you all right?"

Her sister answered with a nod that said otherwise.

"I'm calling the doctor," Christy told her. "Don't you dare move. Understand?" The panic was stronger than ever, but Christy managed to swallow it. Taylor needed her; there wasn't time to be concerned with her own fears.

Taylor's doctor was in Miles City, sixty miles away, and the hospital was there, too. As far as she could tell, they were an hour or more from help. Christy spoke to Dr. Donovan briefly, and when she explained what had happened, the doctor suggested Taylor come to the hospital immediately.

"I'm not going without Russ," Taylor insisted when Christy relayed her conversation. "Russ will be back any minute."

Christy started to balk. It wasn't her fault that Taylor's husband had such a bad sense of timing.

"You don't know Russ the way I do," Taylor said, even before Christy had a chance to reason with her. "If he came home and found us gone—"

"I'll leave him a note. He'll understand. Then as soon as he's back, he can join us."

"No."

Christy had heard that tone of voice often enough to realize these was no way she could budge that stubborn streak of Taylor's. "We can't just sit here and wait," Christy moaned.

"Of course we can. Now relax!"

"Me, relax? You're the one having the baby."

"I'm fine. Baby Palmer and mother are both calm and prepared."

Baby Palmer. Her only sister was about to become a mother. This wasn't new information, but until this moment Taylor's pregnancy had seemed abstract. Yet here they were alone together, and suddenly this baby was very real. This tiny life depended on Christy, and the thought was terrifying. Yet nothing she said would convince Taylor to leave for the hospital without Russ.

The next thirty minutes felt like thirty years. Christy changed into jeans and a sweatshirt, forced down another cup of coffee and looked out the kitchen window every three seconds.

Outwardly Taylor still seemed calm, but Christy could tell from the pain that flashed on her sister's face that the intensity of the contractions was increasing.

"Maybe you should call the feed store. If Russ isn't there, then contact Cody."

"Great idea!" Christy leaped at the possibility of bringing someone else into the picture. The sooner the better. "Just a minute," she said. "Who's Cody?"

"Cody Franklin…he's the newly elected sheriff and a good friend. I don't know what his schedule is, so try the office first. If he's not at work, his home number's written in the front of the phone book."

Calling anyone, including the National Guard, sounded like an excellent plan to Christy. She found the impossibly thin phone book in the drawer. Good grief, she'd ordered from menus thicker than this.

Christy phoned the feed store first. The lady who answered said Russ had left a half hour earlier, and she hadn't a clue where he'd gone. Christy accepted this with a shrug. At the rate things were developing, she was about to take an advanced course in childbirth.

Christy found the sheriff's home number right where Taylor said it would be. She punched it out and waited impatiently for someone, anyone, to answer.

"Hello," a groggy voice muttered on the fourth ring.

"Hi, oh, thank God you answered." Christy was so relieved, she wanted to weep. She gulped in one giant breath and rushed to explain. "You don't know me. I'm Christy Manning, Taylor Palmer's sister, and Russ left an hour ago and promised he'd be back but he isn't and Taylor's water broke and she's in labor. She keeps insisting she won't leave for the hospital until Russ comes home, but he isn't here, and I don't know anything about delivering babies."

A short silence followed. "Taylor's in labor?"

"That's what I just finished saying. The second and equally important factor is that Russ, the father of this about-to-be-born-baby, isn't here. He said he'd only be gone an hour, but he's late, and Taylor really should be leaving for the hospital."

"Where did he say he was going?"

"The feed store. But he left there thirty minutes ago and…and *disappeared*." That might be an exaggeration, but the situation called for a minor stretching of the truth, although she realized she'd made it sound as if he'd been abducted by aliens.

"I'll find him and be there as soon as I can."

The relief that washed over Christy felt like a cool evening rain after the hottest day of summer. Taylor needed her, and the last thing Christy wanted to do was reveal how much this situation frightened her. She'd made this trip to help Taylor with the baby. As in diaper, hold, burp. Not *deliver*.

She coaxed Taylor into the living room and had her lie down on the sofa. The ease with which Christy was able to convince her revealed a great deal about Taylor's condition. Although she struggled to disguise it, her dauntless older sister was scared. The pains were obviously far stronger than Taylor was willing to admit.

A whole lifetime seemed to pass before Christy heard a car barreling down the driveway. Taylor sighed audibly and relaxed against the pillows Christy had placed behind her back. "That's Russ now."

Christy hurried to the back door. She didn't recognize the car as Russ's, but that was the least of her worries. The four-wheel-drive Cherokee hadn't even come to a stop before her brother-in-law leaped out of the front seat.

He raced up the steps. "Where's Taylor?" he demanded.

Numb with relief, Christy sagged against the doorjamb and pointed toward the living room. She was about to follow her brother-in-law when a second man climbed out of the driver's seat.

Christy couldn't pull her eyes away from this tall, long-limbed stranger. It was all she could do not to throw her arms around him in thanks. "You must be Cody."

He touched the rim of his Stetson. "At your service. You must be Taylor's sister," he said, sauntering toward her.

"Christy Manning," she said in an authoritative voice, as if she had the situation completely under control and frequently delivered babies while vacationing. She stepped forward to offer the sheriff of Custer County her hand. In truth she was so grateful he'd found Russ that she was close to tears.

A few seconds later, Russ came out, carrying Taylor. "You ready?" he asked his friend.

"Russ, put me down," Taylor insisted. "I'm too heavy."

"We'll argue later, but at the moment you're about to give birth to my son," Russ reminded her with a worried frown.

"Our baby could very well be a girl," Taylor began. "You're still so pigheaded you refuse to—"

"I swear you're the only woman on God's green earth who'd argue with me at a time like this."

"I'd think you'd be used to it by now," Taylor mumbled, but her voice faded as a fresh contraction overtook her. She closed her eyes, pressed her hands to her belly and breathed deeply.

Russ's distraught gaze connected with Christy's.

"I'll get her suitcase," Christy said as she rushed into the master bedroom. When she reappeared, Cody took the single bag from her hands and put it inside the car. Taylor and Russ were already situated in the backseat, and the passenger door was open for Christy. Without another word, she climbed inside and snapped the seat belt in place.

The ride to the hospital took a full hour. Christy didn't need to look at the speedometer to know Cody was traveling well above the speed limit. If anything, she had to stop herself from pleading with him to go even faster.

Taylor did an admirable job of disguising the extent of her discomfort, but it was apparent to all that the sooner she was under medical supervision the better. Russ was calm and collected.

It turned out that the carburetor in Russ's truck had started acting up, and he'd pulled over to the side of the road. Cody had found him bent over the engine, trying to fix it so he could make it back to the ranch.

Christy held herself tense until they reached the outskirts of Miles City. Only then did she feel herself start to relax.

Within ten minutes of their arrival at the hospital, Taylor was in the labor room with Russ at her side. Cody and Christy were relegated to the waiting room, where they leafed through six-month-old issues of *Time* magazine.

Soon bored with those, Christy found her gaze wandering to Cody. Fine lines fanned out from the corners of his dark eyes, and sharply cut grooves bracketed his mouth. He was tanned, his skin weathered by the sun and wind. He had the kind of rich bronze coloring that others strived to achieve under a sunlamp. His hair was thick and as dark as his eyes and cut military short. He wasn't handsome or stunning or anything else she could easily put a name to, but he was beyond a doubt the most uncompromisingly masculine man she'd ever seen. Immediately she experienced a faint stirring of guilt.

James. Dear, sweet James. Always so patient and understanding. She shouldn't even be *looking* at another man, not when she had James.

Cody glanced up from his magazine, and their eyes met. Christy managed to fake a smile. He returned it with a smile of his own and went back to reading. Christy made a pretense of doing the same thing. Despite her best efforts, her gaze wandered back to the sheriff again and again. It was somewhat embarrassing to realize that she wasn't studying him as a representative of law and order but as a man. Cody Franklin was incredibly male. Incredibly...incredible. Everything about him spoke of strength and purpose: his walk, the square set of his jaw, even the way he sat with his ankle resting over his knee. Disturbed by her unintended focus on the sheriff, she flipped through the pages of a two-year-old issue of *People*. Something was definitely wrong with her. No doubt it had to do with Taylor and the baby. Babies were said to stir up lots of feelings and buried emotions. What astonished her was that she should find this man so attractive.

Enough!

More determined than ever, Christy reached for another magazine and gazed unseeing at its pages.

"I take it you just arrived in Cougar Point?" Cody surprised her by asking.

"Last night," Christy said, setting aside the dog-eared issue of *People*. "Actually, it was early this morning when I went to bed. Russ left the house about the time I came down for coffee, and the next thing I knew, Taylor was telling me she was having these 'funny' pains, only I wasn't laughing, and neither was she."

"How long after that did you call me?"

"Too long," Christy said vehemently. "Taylor claimed the pains were nothing to worry about. I knew I shouldn't have listened to her. Good grief, what does she know?"

Cody smiled, and her eyes were immediately drawn to his full sensual mouth. Frustrated with herself, she quickly looked away.

"Don't be so hard on yourself. You handled the situation exactly the way you should have." He turned back to the periodical. Christy picked up another one herself, but when she glanced up, she saw Cody studying her. "I don't mean to stare," he apologized, "but I can't get over how much you and Taylor resemble each other."

That was almost worth a laugh. She'd hardly been able to keep her eyes off Cody Franklin from the moment they got to the hospital, and *he* was apologizing for staring at *her!* As for the part about the two sisters looking alike, Christy took that as a compliment. Taylor was stunning.

In fact, Christy couldn't remember a time when her sister had been more beautiful than she was right now. Taylor was the beauty, not Christy. She didn't mean to sell herself short; she knew she was reasonably attractive. Perhaps the biggest difference was that Taylor had spunk. Her older sister had always displayed such tenacity, such mettle. When it came to dealing with their headstrong father, Taylor had more courage than the rest of them put together.

Anyone looking at the two sisters would know they were related; Christy was willing to grant the sheriff that much. Their deep blue eyes were a distinct family trait, also shared by their three older brothers, as was the slightly upturned nose.

The two sisters styled their hair differently. Taylor kept her thick chestnut hair long, whereas Christy preferred hers short in a breezy wash-and-wear style.

Christy was about to make some comment along the lines of what a peaceful community Cougar Point seemed to be when they saw Russ.

Cody and Christy stood as Russ approached, his eyes slightly dazed.

"Taylor's ready to go into the delivery room."

"So soon?" Christy's heart was in her throat. "We just got here." She paused long enough to check her watch—and restrain her panic. "We've only been here twenty minutes. How could she possibly be ready for the delivery room?"

"I don't know.... The nurse told me the baby's coming *now*."

"It wasn't supposed to be this soon."

Russ wiped a hand down his face. "You're telling me? If Cody hadn't found me when he did..." He left the rest unsaid, but the implication was obvious.

Christy slumped back into the chair, her knees about to buckle. From everything she'd read and heard, babies were supposed to take their time, especially the first one. What about those twenty-hour labors her friends had described in minute detail? What about all the talk of first labors dragging on and on? Apparently Taylor hadn't been listening.

Russ returned to the double doors, then looked back into the waiting room. He swallowed hard, and Christy realized that if she'd been shaken by the news, it had affected Russ far more profoundly.

"Are you all right?" Cody asked her.

"Of course," she lied. "I'm not the one who's having a baby minutes after I arrive at the hospital." A fact for which Christy was eternally grateful. She wasn't nearly as courageous as Taylor; in fact, when it came right down to it, she considered herself a watered-down version of her older sister. All her life Christy had admired Taylor, wanting to be more like her. Instead, she was complacent and congenial, never causing her parents a moment's concern. Their father once claimed he owed every gray hair on his head to Taylor and every laugh line to Christy. His two daughters were the joy of his life, he often said.

"You look like you're going to faint," Cody said, watching her closely.

"Don't be ridiculous," she snapped, then instantly regretted her sharp tongue. She darted Cody an apologetic smile.

"Come on," Cody suggested, "let's walk. It'll help pass the time."

"Pass what time?" she muttered. "We've been here for about twenty minutes, and already Taylor's being wheeled into the delivery room."

"Come on, you could do with some activity—get your circulation going."

Christy merely nodded. Emotions were coming at her

from every direction. Her first concern was for Taylor and the baby. The thought of this precious life, created in love, stirred a realm of deep feelings inside Christy. Her stomach started churning, her palms were sweating, and her heart seemed to be doing a jig. She couldn't have uttered a word had her life depended on it.

They walked the entire length of the hallway and stopped in front of the nursery. Christy carefully studied the row of newborns swaddled in pink and blue blankets and unexpectedly found tears clouding her eyes. Normally she wasn't sentimental or weepy. She didn't dare look over at Cody. He'd assume… She hadn't a clue what he'd assume, but it wouldn't be good.

"Christy?"

"The babies are really beautiful, aren't they?" she whispered, her gaze on the five infants.

"Yes, they are," he answered softly. He stood behind her and rested his hands on the curve of her shoulders. His touch was light, but it offered her a steadiness and comfort that had been lacking all morning. He didn't say anything when she brushed the telltale moisture from her cheeks, and Christy was grateful.

She didn't know what had come over her in the past few hours. She turned to face Cody, placed her hands on his forearms and stared up at him, her eyes bright with unshed tears.

Nothing seemed real anymore. It was as if she'd been walking around in a dream. A living fantasy was beginning to unfold right before her. Perhaps she'd spent too many hours on the road. Otherwise she wouldn't be looking into the darkest brown eyes she'd ever seen and thinking the things she was thinking.

Cody was staring back at her with the same wonder and surprise. He seemed about to say something important when the doors at the other end of the hall opened and Russ stepped out, wearing a green surgical gown and a large smile. Seeing him, both Christy and Cody rushed forward.

"It's a boy," Russ announced, his eyes shimmering with tears. He let out a wild shout of joy, grabbed a shocked Christy around the waist and boisterously whirled her around.

"Congratulations," Cody said, coming forward. The two men exchanged hearty handshakes, then hugged, slapping each other on the back.

Russ didn't speak for a moment and seemed to be composing himself. "He weighed in at eight pounds, three ounces, and he's the ugliest little critter you ever saw. Taylor kept saying how beautiful he is, and all I could see was this furious pink face bawling as loud as anything. His legs were pumping like an oil rig. That boy is madder than a wet wasp."

Christy felt tears in her eyes as she pressed her fingers to her lips. "How's Taylor?"

"She's fine…more than fine. That woman's incredible. I don't know what I ever did to deserve her, but I intend to thank God every day for the rest of my life." He half turned toward the doors he'd come through. "I've got to get back. They're taking Eric into the nursery now, and the delivery room nurse said I could watch him being washed and dressed. If I have anything to say about it, I'll do the washing and dressing myself."

"You're naming him Eric?" Christy asked as she moved one step forward.

Russ nodded. "Eric Russell, after your father and me. Taylor insists."

"That sounds like a perfectly wonderful name to me," Christy whispered, surprised at the emotion that clogged her throat. Her father would be so proud, the buttons would pop right off his shirt.

"If you two walk over to the nursery, you might be able to see him, too," Russ added excitedly. "Taylor will be out of the delivery room anytime. I know she'll want to talk to you both, so stick around for a little bit, okay?"

Christy and Cody had already started in that direction when Russ stopped them. "Hey, one last thing. Taylor and I talked it over, and we want the two of you to be Eric's godparents."

Christy exchanged a meaningful glance with Cody before they simultaneously nodded.

"We'd be honored," Cody answered for them.

"Truly honored," Christy repeated, her throat tightening even more.

In her excitement Christy whirled around to face Cody—except that she hadn't realized he was quite so close. She flattened her hands against his chest as she smiled up at him, her joy overflowing now that her nephew was safely born.

Cody returned the smile. His dark eyes were alive with emotion.

Slowly, moving as if he were hypnotized, Cody slipped his arms around her waist and raised her from the ground. Her hands clutched his shirt collar as his eyes delved into hers.

"I believe congratulations are in order, don't you?"

"Yes," she said, hugging him, afraid he was going to kiss her, equally afraid he wouldn't.

How would she ever explain kissing another man to James? How would she rationalize allowing Cody to hold her like this when she'd promised to spend her life loving someone else?

Two

"**O**h, Taylor, he's so beautiful," Christy whispered. "Russ held him up for me to see and…" She paused, unable to continue. The minute she'd seen Eric, her heart had swollen with such a profound sense of love that it had been impossible to suppress her tears.

"You're crying," Taylor said softly.

Christy rubbed her cheeks. She reached for her sister, and they hugged with an intensity she'd never felt before. This wealth of emotion, of happiness, took Christy by storm.

"I love you, Taylor. I really do. And I love Eric, too. He's beautiful, perfect. I feel absolutely ecstatic." She straightened and gave a breathy laugh. "I want to throw open the windows and tell the world my sister just had a beautiful baby boy."

"Did you get a chance to talk to Mom and Dad?"

Christy nodded. The moment her mother heard the news she'd started weeping and then her father had taken the phone. His own voice hadn't sounded all that steady, either. Russ had done most of the talking with Christy crowded close beside him. When it was her turn, she seemed to jabber on like a magpie, but couldn't stop herself.

Following the conversation, Russ and Cody had gone to the hospital gift shop to buy a box of cigars. Christy had spent these few moments alone with her sister.

"I'm sorry I frightened you," Taylor said apologetically, "but I didn't want to leave for the hospital without Russ."

"I understood. I wasn't worried." On the contrary, Christy had been nearly frantic, but it didn't matter now that everything had turned out so well.

Her sister sighed. "I'm glad you were able to meet Cody."

At the mention of the other man's name, Christy abruptly looked away, feeling uneasy. She hadn't had the chance to tell Taylor and Russ about her engagement to James Wilkens. Unfortunately the diamond ring James had given her was still at the jeweler's being sized. If she'd been wearing the ring, it would've been a logical introduction to her announcement. She'd meant to surprise her sister and brother-in-law with the big news as soon as she'd arrived, but it had been so late and everyone was exhausted. Then, before Christy knew it, it was morning and Taylor had gone into labor.

Now the timing was all wrong. Tomorrow, she promised herself, she'd tell Taylor. Everything would be less hectic then. But even as she formed that decision, Christy hesitated, not fully understanding why.

Her head spun and her thoughts skidded to a halt. Who did she think she was fooling?

She *did* know why.

Cody Franklin had hugged her when Russ had come to tell them about Eric. Now, an hour later, the way she'd felt in his arms still caused her pulse to accelerate. He'd pulled her close, and the feeling of being held by this man was completely and utterly natural, as instinctive as breathing or sleeping. It was as if they'd known each other all their lives. As if their relationship was one of long standing.

Without his saying a thing, Christy knew he'd experienced the same lavish range of sensations. They'd stared openly at each other, neither speaking. If Russ hadn't been there, Christy couldn't help wondering what would've happened. What they would've said to each other. If anything.

But Russ had been there, and after an awkward moment, Cody had released her. He'd dropped his arms with a reluctance that sent blood pounding through her veins until she grew dizzy simply remembering.

James was her fiancé! Yet she had to struggle to bring his image to mind. Her parents had been thrilled with the news of their engagement, but Christy had known they would be. Her father had told her often enough that James, an attorney, would make her an excellent husband. They'd been dating on and off for nearly two years, almost from the first week Christy had been hired as a paralegal at James's law firm. Their relationship, however, hadn't turned serious until three months ago. Until then, their dates had been casual get-togethers with mutual friends. Then they'd started working together on an important case. It had been a real coup for James to be assigned to defend Gary Mulligan against the Internal Revenue Service, and if everything went well, it could mean a partnership for him.

"Christy?"

She turned to her sister. "Sorry. Were you saying something?"

"Just that I'm glad you met Cody today."

"He...seems very nice," Christy answered, and sighed with relief when the nurse walked into the room, distracting her sister's attention from the subject of the sheriff. The woman brought in a huge bouquet of red roses in a tall crystal vase.

"Oh, my," Taylor breathed, reaching for the card. She tore open the small envelope and read the message. Immediate tears filled her eyes. "They're from Russ."

"How sweet."

Taylor smiled softly as a faraway look came into her eyes. Christy speculated that her sister was recalling the first time she'd met Russ and all that had happened since. Russ might not have been the man her family would've chosen for Taylor, but one fact had been clear from the instant they flew to Seattle to attend their parents' anniversary party. Russ Palmer loved Taylor. Beyond question. Beyond doubt. Whatever reservations Christy and her brothers held regarding this marriage had been quickly dissolved.

Footsteps from behind Christy told her Russ and Cody had returned.

"Russ…" Taylor held out her arms to her husband. "The roses are so beautiful. Thank you."

Christy's brother-in-law walked across the room, and his eyes closed as he took his wife into his arms. He whispered something in her ear; Taylor smiled and nodded. The scene was an intimate one, and Christy felt like an intruder. She backed away, not looking at Cody until it was impossible to avoid him.

"Hello, again," he said. His voice was low and his smile contained a warmth and depth that multiplied a hundredfold all the sensations she'd experienced earlier, the very feelings she was trying to put out of her mind. Once again Christy was struck by the possessiveness she felt looking at him, studying him. For the past hour she'd been trying to understand why she should feel anything toward him. Nothing had come to her. No insights. Nothing.

They were barely more than strangers, and yet she felt completely comfortable with him. At the same time, he rattled her composure unlike anyone she'd ever met. It seemed absurdly ironic to be so flustered by a man and still feel so sheltered.

Cody glanced toward Russ and Taylor. "Would you like to go down to the nursery to view our godson?"

She nodded, gladly accepting an excuse to leave husband and wife alone.

Together she and Cody walked down the familiar corridor until they stood in front of the large nursery window. But it wasn't the newborns that captured their attention. They made comments about little Eric and the other babies, but what interested them most was each other. After a while they gave up the pretense of looking at the newborns.

"Russ phoned the ranch and is having a couple of his hands drive a car over for him," Cody said after a while. "He's planning to spend the day with Taylor."

Once more Christy nodded. It seemed all she was capable of doing. Being this close to Cody felt like being trapped in a magnetic force field. It didn't matter how much she resisted, she was drawn to him.

With a determined effort, she diverted her attention to Eric again. The infant was sleeping, swaddled in a pale blue receiving blanket. A long-sleeved T-shirt covered his tiny arms and fists. He was so small, so adorable.

Cody's eyes followed hers, and when he spoke, his voice was filled with astonishment. "He's really something, isn't he?"

"Yes." Her voice was a whisper. "And to think we could've ended up delivering him."

"We?" Cody joked. "In all my years of law enforcement I've been spared that. Thank God."

Standing behind her, Cody's large hands held her shoulders, as if he'd been holding and touching her for a lifetime. It felt right and good to have this man so close. A small shudder skimmed down her spine at the innocent contact.

Cody must have noticed it, because he turned her around to face him, his eyes narrowing slightly. "You're trembling."

She couldn't deny it. This man she hardly knew confused her, bewildered her. The worst part was that she couldn't understand why. She'd met and dated any number of attractive, compelling men before. Yet none of them had ever overwhelmed her the way Cody did.

"Are you cold?"

"No," she answered quickly, flustered by his questions.

"What's wrong?"

How could she possibly explain something she couldn't grasp herself? "Nothing."

His eyes found hers, and she could've sworn they went several shades darker. "Does this happen often?"

"No." She shook her head. "Does it to you?" Christy swallowed, astonished she'd had the courage to ask him such a personal question.

"No," he answered after a moment. "Never."

She pulled her gaze away, baffled by his openness. His honesty. It was exactly what she'd longed to hear. And what she'd feared.

"I... I need to get back to the ranch," she said, seeking an excuse to do something, anything to end this heightened awareness between them. "Taylor asked me to make some phone calls for her."

Cody lowered his eyes to her lips, his look, unhurried

and sensual, as intimate as a kiss. Christy's stomach became a churning mass of doubts, mingled with an abundance of misgivings. She wanted to blame this feeling on the chaotic events of the day.

Slowly, almost unaware of what she was doing, Christy raised her own eyes to meet Cody's. He didn't look too comfortable. In fact, he seemed as perplexed and hesitant as she.

"I need to get back myself," he murmured.

Not until that moment did Christy realize the only way she had of returning to Cougar Point was with Cody. A sinking feeling assailed her. She couldn't possibly avoid an hour or more with him in the intimate confines of his vehicle.

Cody Franklin had no idea what was happening between him and his best friend's sister-in-law. To be honest, he hadn't paid Christy Manning much attention until they were in the hospital waiting room. She'd been terribly agitated, flipping through one magazine after another. Cody doubted she'd read a single word.

Then Russ had appeared and said that Taylor was ready for the delivery room, and Cody had watched as Christy started to completely unravel.

He'd suggested they take a short walk in an effort to help her relax. He didn't know how much comfort he'd be to her, since he was a stranger, but the least he could do was try. He knew from his years as a lawman that some physical activity might help take her mind off her sister.

It was when they'd stopped to look at the babies in the nursery that Cody had felt the faint stirring of something more. Faint stirring, hell, it was like a fist to his gut!

From that moment on, some emotion had started to awaken deep within him. He experienced a lost sensation, as if he were charting unknown land, and each turn led him farther away from all that was familiar. He was suddenly at a loss for words; he'd planned to involve her in conversation, occupy her with inane chitchat about Seattle and her job to keep her from thinking about Taylor, but he hadn't asked a single question.

Every time Cody started to speak, he got lost in her eyes. He'd never seen a woman with eyes quite this blue. They reminded him of the coldest days of winter, when everything around him seemed to anticipate the promise of spring. When she smiled, those same blue eyes brightened even more, and it was like watching sunshine emerge after rain.

She'd look at him, and Cody swore he could see all the way to her soul. She was guileless and genuine and so lovely, it was all he could do not to stare at her, something he'd already apologized for once that day.

Twice he'd placed his hands on her shoulders. It wasn't his habit to comfort women with physical gestures, and he didn't understand his own actions. When he'd first held her, she'd obviously been shaken by Russ's news about Taylor, and he'd reached out in an effort to steady her.

The moment his hands had closed over her shoulders, his heart had begun racing like a runaway train. That hadn't happened since he was thirteen and had kissed a girl for the very first time.

Twenty-two years had passed, and the impact now was nearly as strong. Every minute with her he learned something new about himself, and every emotion he discovered only bewildered him more.

"I'm sorry if it's an inconvenience for you to take me out to the ranch," Christy said, sliding into the front seat of his four-wheel drive.

"It isn't a problem." The only difficulty it created was

of his own making. He was caught in some mysterious web of yearning. Perhaps, in some strange way, this all had to do with Russ and Taylor. He couldn't help envying the happiness his friends had found. Taylor was the best thing that had ever happened to Russ Palmer, and now Russ was a father.

Cody paused, half expecting to feel a twinge of jealousy or resentment. When he was introduced to Taylor a year ago, he'd wanted to date her himself, but she'd already met Russ and it was clear that she was falling in love with him. Cody had stood on the sidelines and watched their romance unfold, amused at the way they'd both fought it so hard.

No, jealousy hadn't prompted these feelings; he was convinced of that. His only reaction was happiness for his friends—a pure sense of shared joy.

The drive, which had seemed like four hundred miles earlier in the day with Taylor and Russ in the backseat, went quickly on the return trip. Christy said little, but neither seemed uneasy with the silence. Occasionally Cody would look over at her, and their eyes would meet. Each time, some magic would pass involuntarily between them, some entrancement. After a while it became a challenge to discover what fascinated him about Taylor's sister, and he found his gaze repeatedly drawn to her as he attempted to analyze his attraction.

She was pretty, but no prettier than any number of women he'd dated. Not as beautiful as Becca. He paused, surprised that he didn't immediately feel a jolt of pain as he thought about her. It had been three years since Becca had turned his life upside down. He tried not to think of her at all, tried to ignore her memory as though he'd never known her at all. For the most part he succeeded... For the most part.

"Would you like to stop and get something to eat?" Cody asked as they neared Cougar Point. He wasn't hungry so much as reluctant to leave her.

He should've been exhausted. He'd had only a couple of hours sleep in the past forty-eight. Instead he felt alive. Reborn.

All he knew was that he'd met a woman, a warm, caring, generous woman, and he felt as if his life was starting over again.

"I'm starved," Christy said enthusiastically. "I was so concerned about Taylor this morning that I forgot to eat breakfast."

"I haven't had anything, either."

"I got you out of bed when I phoned, didn't I?"

Cody nodded. Hell, he'd give his right hand to have her wake him every morning. "I worked the graveyard shift last night."

"You must be exhausted."

On the contrary, Cody had never felt more energetic. "Not at all," he said, mustering a smile to reassure her. "There are a couple of decent restaurants in town, but if you're interested in breakfast, the best place to eat is the bowling alley."

"Great."

Cody had expected her to laugh or to question his choice. She was, after all, a city girl, and he doubted that anyone in Seattle had ever taken her out to eat at a bowling alley. But she accepted his choice enthusiastically.

Since it was midafternoon by this time, the parking lot was nearly deserted. Christy didn't wait for him to come around and open the door for her, a fact that didn't surprise him. Taylor hadn't waited for him to open her door the one time he'd gone out with her, either.

Cody chose a booth toward the back of the restaurant

and slid into the red vinyl seat. Christy sat across from him and reached for the menu, which was tucked between the sugar bowl and the salt and pepper shakers.

"Howdy, Cody," Mary Andrews said as she came over to the table, carrying two water glasses. She glanced curiously at Christy.

"This is Taylor's sister, Christy Manning. Christy, Mary Andrews."

"I don't suppose Taylor had her baby, did she?" Mary asked.

Christy's eyes softened as she nodded. "This morning. Eric Russell Palmer weighed in at eight pounds, three ounces."

Mary grinned from ear to ear. "That's terrific. You don't mind if I let folks know, do you?"

Christy shook her head. "Please do."

Still grinning, Mary pulled a small pad from her apron pocket. "What can I get for you two?"

"I'll have the breakfast special," Christy said, closing her menu. "With coffee."

"So will I," Cody said, sliding his own menu back into place.

Mary wrote down their order, then walked back to the kitchen.

For a long time Cody said nothing. Partly because he didn't know what to say and partly because he didn't feel the need to fill the silence with small talk. He was comfortable with Christy. He hadn't felt that way with any woman, ever. He looked over at her and wondered if she was experiencing this same sense of serenity, and instinctively knew she was. "What are you thinking?" he asked as Mary filled two cups with coffee.

Christy added cream to hers, took a sip and smiled.

"If we're Eric's godparents, does that mean the two of us are related?"

A grin lit his face. "I suppose it does. I'm just not sure how."

"Me, neither."

One thing he did know: the idea of being linked to Christy pleased him immeasurably. "Tell me about yourself." He wanted to know everything there was to know about her from the time she was in preschool to the present.

"I'm the youngest of five."

"Spoiled?"

"Terribly."

He deliberately drew his gaze away from her mouth, which had fascinated him for several minutes. Beyond question, he knew he was going to kiss her. He didn't know when. Soon, if possible. Nor did he know where. Only that it was quickly becoming an obsession.

"What about you?" Christy asked, pulling a napkin from the holder and spreading it across her lap, taking time to smooth it out. She seemed to be avoiding eye contact with him. That didn't surprise Cody. He'd been blatantly staring at her every chance he got. Her mouth enthralled him as nothing ever had. Soft. Pink. Moist. Just right for kissing.

"What about you?" she repeated, and the question seemed to echo.

"I was born in Miles City," he said, focusing on his coffee. "In the same hospital as Eric, as a matter of fact."

"Was your father a rancher?"

"No. He was a lawman, just as his father was before him. The Franklins have a long tradition of upholding law and order in Custer County."

"Did you always want to work for the sheriff's department?"

"Always. For as long as I can remember I dreamed of wearing a badge."

"They must be proud of you," she said in a way that made his heart quicken. What she was said was true. But his father and grandfather would never know he'd been elected sheriff; his two younger sisters were the only family he had left.

Cody didn't want to talk about himself, not when there was so much to learn about her. "What did *you* want to be when you were a kid?"

"Not a paralegal," she said, then looked away, as if the words had slipped out before she could stop them. "I didn't even know what they were until high school. Sad to say, my dreams were far more traditional. I wanted to be a mommy."

"And now?"

"And now," she repeated in a whisper, frowning.

She was saved from having to answer by Mary, who brought two platters to their table. Each was heaped high with steaming hash browns, scrambled eggs, sausage and toast.

Their conversation ceased as they both picked up their forks. Neither spoke for several minutes.

"I didn't realize how hungry I was," Christy said, reaching for the small container of jam. She peeled back the cover and scooped out the preserves with her knife.

"Where's Mandy?" Cody asked, remembering Russ's teenage sister, who lived with Russ and Taylor, for the first time that day.

"She's with a friend. Russ phoned from the hospital and told her about Eric. She had lots of questions and was sorry she missed all the excitement."

Cody pushed his empty plate aside. Mary stopped by

the table to refill their coffee mugs and take away Cody's plate.

"You might as well take mine, too," Christy said, leaning back in the booth. She placed her hands over her flat stomach and sighed. "I can't believe I ate all that."

"Can I get you anything else?" Mary asked.

"Nothing, thanks," Cody answered for them.

Mary set the bill on the table and walked away with a quick backward wave.

They left the restaurant a few minutes later. Cody opened the door for Christy, insisting on the courtesy because he enjoyed doing something, however small, for her.

She seemed preoccupied and anxious on the ride to the Lazy P. He started to ask her how long she planned to stay, but even before he'd finished the question, he knew she wasn't listening.

"I'm sorry. What did you say?" she asked, glancing at him.

"It wasn't important." He pulled off the main road and headed down the long, dusty driveway. This time of year the road was filled with ruts deep enough to send them both bouncing around the interior of his Cherokee if he wasn't careful to watch where he was driving. In several spots he slowed down to ten or so miles an hour. Then he was forced to ask himself if it was his car he was concerned about—or the fact that the sooner he arrived at the ranch, the sooner he'd have to leave Christy.

Once he reached the ranch yard, he turned off the engine and climbed out of the cab. Christy had opened the car door, offering him just the excuse he needed to touch her. His hands slid around her slim waist and he lifted her down.

She hadn't been expecting his help and, caught off

guard, she fell forward. She made a small sound as her hands came into contact with his chest.

Neither moved. Cody couldn't believe how good it felt to have her in his arms again.

"I'm sorry," she whispered.

"I'm not." Cody had never been one to beat around the bush, as the saying went. "Not in the least," he added.

Her hands were against his chest, and he wondered if she could feel how fast his heart was beating, wondered if she had even an inkling of what he was feeling.

"Thanks for breakfast and the ride home," she murmured, but made no effort to move away from him.

Heat radiated from where her hands were touching him, warming him in ways he couldn't understand but didn't question. She tensed her fingers as if to pull away, but if that was her intention, she didn't follow through.

Cody raised his hand to the side of her neck. His fingers stroked the kitten-soft skin there, and he watched, fascinated, as she slowly closed her eyes.

Once more his gaze sought her mouth. Her lush, vulnerable mouth. Never had it looked more inviting than it did at that moment.

It seemed only natural to kiss her. Hell, he'd been thinking about doing exactly that for hours, but now that the opportunity presented itself, he hesitated. It was as if an inborn defense mechanism flashed a warning through his system. Kiss Christy Manning and you'll never be the same again, it seemed to be saying.

But the words of caution counted for nothing. Cody couldn't have stopped himself if he'd wanted to. Whatever came after, whatever life held for him, whatever the cost, he was going to kiss this woman.

Unhurriedly, deliberately, he pressed his lips over hers.

She murmured something, Cody didn't know what, and he felt the movement against his mouth.

Her lips were everything Cody had dreamed they would be. Warm. Moist. Devastating. With a whimper she responded immediately. It was as if he'd never kissed a woman before this moment.

Her arms made their way around his neck as she leaned into him. Her softness melded into his hardness, and white-hot sensation seemed to explode inside him. Cody kissed her again and again, his hands in her hair, cradling the back of her head. He kissed her until his breathing became labored. Until he heard her moan, and then realized it was his own sigh of longing that echoed in his ears. Still he didn't release her. He held her against him, never wanting to let her go.

Only when Christy stiffened did Cody slacken his hold. Slowly he opened his eyes to discover her looking up at him, her beautiful eyes bright with tears. He frowned because he didn't understand. Then, in a heartbeat, he did. The kissing had affected her as profoundly as it had him.

"I know what you're thinking," he whispered, lifting her chin with his finger, dropping his mouth to hers, unable to resist.

"You don't," she said. "You couldn't possibly know."

"But I do," he countered. "You're thinking this is the craziest thing that's ever happened to you. I know because that's exactly what I'm thinking. We just met this morning, and yet I feel I've known you all my life."

Her eyes widened as if his words had hit their mark.

"All of this is because of Taylor and Russ," she told him. "Their happiness, their excitement must be rubbing off on us. Don't you see how foolish this is?"

"No." He didn't mean to be blunt or obtuse. He was

nearly thirty-five years old and long past the age of playing games. Christy was younger, but she knew, the same way he did. She might choose to deny it, but he wouldn't.

"Are you saying you didn't want me to kiss you?" he asked, trusting her to be honest, because he didn't believe she could be anything else.

It took her a minute to answer him, and when she did her voice was raspy. "That's the problem.... I've never wanted anything more."

Three

Christy woke early the next morning after a restless night's sleep. She'd tossed and turned so frequently that the sheets had been pulled loose from the bed and the bedspread had slipped onto the floor. Staring up at the ceiling, Christy slowly expelled her breath while mulling over the events of the day before.

So much had happened.

Taylor's son had been born, and Christy had been introduced to the newly elected sheriff of Custer County.

However, Christy had more than *met* Cody Franklin. He'd taken her to breakfast late in the afternoon, and when he dropped her off at the ranch, he'd kissed her—and she'd let him. More than *let* him; she'd encouraged him. What she'd told him was true. She'd never wanted anyone's kiss more.

Admitting as much certainly wasn't one of her more intelligent moves, but then it hadn't been her mind doing the talking. It had been her heart.

Once again she tried to focus her thoughts on James. He'd been so sweet the evening he'd given her the engagement ring. They'd gone out for dinner, sitting at the table with candlelight flickering and soft music playing in the background. Christy had noticed that he'd barely touched his meal. He seemed nervous, then started talking nonstop. Normally James was a calm, quiet man, not easily agitated. He'd been rambling for about fifteen minutes, and Christy couldn't figure out where the discussion was leading. She'd told him so. Then James had gotten flustered.

Before Christy could react, James pulled a ring box from the inside of his suit pocket. He'd been so endearing, so wonderfully sweet as he held out the diamond, letting the ring speak for him.

By then Christy had become so flustered herself that all she could do was stare at the lovely solitary diamond glittering up at her. James had withdrawn it from its velvet bed, and without a word she'd given him her hand.

The entire thing hadn't taken more than a few seconds. She'd promised to become his wife, promised to pledge her life to him without a word of love spoken between them. James cared for her, Christy felt assured of it. He wouldn't have offered her the ring if he didn't. By the same token, she loved him. Otherwise she wouldn't have accepted his proposal.

Afterward, James had been ecstatic as he'd hugged and kissed her. The ring was too large and had nearly slipped off her finger as she'd shown it to her parents that same night. Both Eric and Elizabeth Manning had been thrilled with the news of Christy's engagement to the up-and-coming attorney.

It wasn't until two days later, just before she left for Montana, that the first of the doubts had come. She loved James, she reminded herself, repeating it again and again on the endless drive across three states.

James was a good man. He'd been a friend long before they'd become romantically involved, and judging by everything she'd read, friends made the best husbands.

Perhaps the most convincing argument for this marriage was how comfortable Christy felt with him. Her parents thought the world of James; in fact, they seemed more excited than she was about the prospect of his joining the family. Her father talked of little else, promising Christy the wedding of the year.

But if she'd been experiencing a few niggling doubts before she left Seattle, they'd multiplied a hundredfold since she'd arrived in Montana and met Cody Franklin.

Cody.

For more reasons than she dared explore, she struggled to push every thought of the sheriff from her mind.

With a determination born of pride and a sense of fairness and truth that had been ingrained in her from birth, Christy decided to tell Russ, tell someone, anyone, about her engagement. She climbed out of bed and got dressed, then went in seach of her brother-in-law.

Russ, however, had already left the house. A note was propped against the sugar bowl, explaining he'd be with his men that morning, and she shouldn't look for him before noon. He also wrote that he wouldn't be able to visit Taylor and the baby until that evening. He signed his name, adding that Christy should make herself at home.

Defeat settled over Christy. She couldn't keep quiet about herself and James much longer and still hold her head high.

It took only an hour to straighten up the house. She cooked herself some eggs, then realized she wasn't hungry. Russ, on the other hand, had apparently fixed himself a breakfast large enough to feed five men. He'd made a minimal effort to clean the kitchen; clearly, he'd been in a rush.

With time to spare, Christy wandered outside, wanting to investigate what she could of the grounds. Since Russ was visiting Taylor that evening, she'd drive to the hospital in the afternoon.

One hand leading a chestnut horse paused and stared at her when she appeared.

"Good morning," Christy said cheerfully.

"Howdy." The lanky cowboy straightened and touched the rim of his hat. He looped the reins around a fence-post, then walked toward her. A fistful of cigars with pale blue bands was sticking out of his shirt pocket, evidence of Russ's eagerness to spread the news of his son's birth.

"You must be part of Mrs. Palmer's family."

"Christy Manning," she said, holding out her hand. "I'm Taylor's sister."

The middle-aged man took pains to remove his thick leather glove and clasped her soft palm in his callused one. "Pleased to make your acquaintance. Russ is out this morning, but I s'pect he'll be back soon. Most folks call me Billy Joe."

"Good to meet you, Billy Joe," Christy said, looking toward the barn. Several horses stuck their sleek heads over the stall doors, glancing at her with open curiosity.

"If you'll excuse me," Billy Joe said, backing away from her. His horse was saddled and waiting, prancing in place. "This gelding's anxious to be on his way."

"Of course. I'm sorry. I didn't mean to hold you up."

"No problem." He mounted the gelding in a single smooth motion. Pulling back on the reins, Billy Joe nodded at her once more, then galloped out of the yard.

Left to her own devices, Christy wandered toward the barn, stopping in front of the first stall. The name Shadow was burned into a wood plaque above the door.

"Howdy, Shadow," Christy said. "You look like a

friendly horse." Friendly enough, at any rate, for her to venture petting his nose. She stroked it a few times while the gelding took pride in revealing his teeth and nickered his approval.

Seeing a large barrel of grain near the middle of the barn, Christy stepped over to it, intending to reach for a handful of oats. She didn't know much about horses, but figured a handful of oats would win approval.

"I thought I might find you in here," a deep male voice said from the barn door.

Christy's heart shot to her throat. Cody. She turned to see him silhouetted against the morning sunlight. Tall, lean and dark. He wore jeans and a western shirt with a string tie and was so strikingly handsome that for a moment all she could do was stare.

"Hello," she said, returning to her task, her hands trembling. It wasn't fair that he should have this effect on her. But then, she was learning that little in life was fair.

Her hand loaded with grain, she walked back to Shadow's stall.

"Be sure to feed that to him with your palm flat, otherwise he might inadvertently bite you," Cody warned, moving toward her.

Christy was grateful for the advice and did as he suggested. Shadow ate the oats quickly, and when he'd finished, Christy wiped her hand on her jeans. Her heart was hammering so hard, she was certain Cody could hear it.

"Did you sleep well?"

"No," she answered honestly. Her back was to him, but that didn't help. She felt warm and dizzy just knowing he was there.

"I couldn't, either." His voice was soft and raspy. Sensual. "I only had a couple of hours of sleep the night before, so I should've nodded off the minute my head touched the pillow. But I didn't. I couldn't."

Christy found a strange comfort in knowing his sleep had been as unsettled as her own. "I...tossed and turned most of the night, then finally drifted off toward morning."

"Me, too."

When he'd left her the night before, she'd stood inside the house and watched him drive away, feeling restless and uneasy. That disquiet hadn't dissipated until the moment he'd stepped into the barn. Cody spoke, and instantly the emptiness had started to leave her, as if a sense of order had been restored to her life.

Except that it wasn't right. Everything was very, very wrong.

"We need to talk."

"Yes," she whispered. She'd meant to tell Russ about James, knowing her brother-in-law would mention the fact to Cody. But this was better. She could tell Cody herself. Explain before either of them got hurt. Before things went too far.

Honesty really was the best policy. She'd grown up believing that. Practicing it.

Christy was searching for just the right words, irritated with herself for not having thought this out beforehand. There should be an easy way to say it. The truth shouldn't be this difficult.

Then Cody was behind her, so close she could feel the heat radiating from his body. His hands settled over her shoulders, his touch light and warm and reassuring. Slowly he turned her around so she faced him.

Their eyes locked, and Christy's throat went tight. His were beautiful, as dark and rich as the finest coffee. They were the eyes of a man who'd only recently learned to dream. Wistful eyes. Pensive eyes.

"Every time I'd try to sleep, all I could think about was you." His tone said that he'd struggled long and hard against allowing her to dominate his thoughts.

"It was the same with me." She shouldn't have told him that. Shouldn't admit his effect on her in one breath and then tell him about James in the next. "But I—"

"I couldn't stop thinking about how good you felt in my arms."

She knew exactly what he was saying because she'd experienced the same thing herself. He felt good to her, too, the kind of good that made everything feel right even when it was wrong. The kind of good that never diminished, never ceased.

"You felt it, didn't you?" He seemed to need confirmation from her.

She gave it reluctantly, breathlessly, lowering her eyes. "Yes."

They lapsed into silence then, as though neither of them knew what else to say. There didn't seem to be any need for words. Christy understood what Cody was thinking and feeling as clearly as if he'd spoken.

I need to kiss you again and discover if last night was real. He asked her with his eyes.

No, her heart cried. She couldn't allow it. If Cody kissed her again, she'd be forced to confront issues she dared not face. Cody Franklin was a stranger. James was her fiancé. Her friend.

I've frightened you.

No, came the cry from the farthest corner of her heart. *Yes,* she countered immediately. Cody stirred emotions she didn't know she was capable of feeling. Emotions she'd never experienced with any man. Each time they were together, her awareness of him became more intense. This shouldn't be happening to her. Not now. Not *ever.* She was engaged to another man.

Frowning, Cody took one step toward her. Christy's heart surged.

Don't, please, don't, she pleaded silently. *I can't refuse you. I can't refuse myself.*

But Cody had apparently given up listening to the cries of her heart. When she looked at him, he was both watchful and silent.

Before another second could pass, he reached for her, and whatever resistance she'd been able to muster burst like the white filaments of a dandelion in the wind. His mouth found hers, smooth and firm against her softness. She moaned in protest, but her small cry soon became a sigh of welcome, of need, of pleasure.

A tenderness blossomed within her, the sensations so exquisite they shocked her even more than they had a day earlier. It shouldn't be this good, this wonderful, she told herself over and over, wanting to weep with frustration. Yet it was better than anything she'd ever experienced.

Cody continued to kiss her with a passion and an excitement that left Christy clinging to him.

"I can't believe this," he murmured, and her mind echoed his words. She was struggling with reality, and felt lost and weak.

Cody bent his head and dropped a succession of kisses down her neck and along her jaw until she moaned. He responded with a small, throaty sound and quickly joined their mouths again, kissing hers softly.

Christy went weak with need. She was melting from the heat. Burning up with fever. Consumed with a sweet warmth that threatened to devour her. "No," she whimpered. "We can't do…this."

Cody raised his hands and held them against the sides of her face.

He was going too fast for her. Her own body was going too fast for her. She felt as though she were sitting on a runaway horse, galloping out of control, being propelled farther and farther away from reason.

"I feel as if I've been waiting for you all my life," Cody whispered, wrapping his arms completely around her. His hand reached up to smooth the hair from her temple. "I can only imagine what you must think of me coming here like this."

Her eyes remained closed, and her dark world continued to spin without restraint. Even when she opened her eyes, everything was blurred and out of focus, her thoughts hopelessly addled.

"I didn't mean to shock you," he said.

"You didn't. I shocked myself."

Cody worked his thumbs sensuously across the high curve of her cheekbones. He frowned as he felt her tears. "I hurt you?"

"No..." she murmured, looking away. Now she understood the restless feeling she'd experienced all night. She'd been haunted by his kiss, haunted by the emotions and the need he'd created within her.

All of this had to stop. Now. This instant. She pressed her forehead against his solid chest, needing his strength in order to find the courage to say what she had to say.

His hand lifted her hair, his touch gentle as though fingering strands of silk.

"I fall apart when you kiss me," she confessed.

His throaty laugh was filled with amusement and tenderness. "*You* fall apart?" He captured her hand and pressed it over his heart. "See what you do to me?"

She didn't need to touch him to realize how his pulse

was churning beneath her palm. Unable to watch the disillusionment in his eyes when she told him about James, she closed her own.

"I've never felt anything for anyone as strongly as I have for you," she said softly. Then she didn't say anything more for a long moment, carefully formulating her words.

Cody obviously sensed that she felt troubled because he tucked his finger under her chin and raised her head. His gaze caressed her. "Christy?"

"Please listen," she whispered, her voice trembling. "There's something you should know, something I meant to tell you from the first, only—"

"Cody, what are you doing here?" Russ's voice echoed through the barn like thunder. "Everything's all right with Taylor, isn't it?" Christy's brother-in-law stopped abruptly when he saw Cody's arms around her waist. He removed his Stetson and wiped his forehead with the back of his hand. "I wasn't interrupting anything, was I?"

"Your timing couldn't be worse," Cody barked, glaring at his friend.

Russ didn't appear the least bit concerned. He tossed a load of baling wire into his pickup and promptly reached for another. If anything, he looked amused.

"This isn't funny."

Russ paused. "Now that's where I disagree. You just met Christy. Until yesterday you hadn't so much as set eyes on her. I don't mind telling you, Franklin, I've never known you to work so fast."

"Shut your fool mouth before you say something I'll make you regret," Cody grumbled. His threat wasn't worth a dime and Russ knew it, but he felt he had to respond.

"She is a pretty little thing, isn't she?" Another wheel of wire landed on top of the first with a loud, discordant clang. He turned to stare at Cody when he didn't answer right away. "Isn't she?" he repeated.

"Yes," Cody admitted grudgingly.

"For a moment there, it looked like the two of you had been kissing." Once more Russ paused, a grin turning up the edges of his mouth.

"I *was* kissing her," Cody said, challenging Russ to make something of the fact if he wanted to. He was as uncomfortable as he could ever remember being with his friend. Russ was curious to learn what was going on between him and Christy, but unfortunately Cody could think of no way of explaining his feelings for Christy, especially with the mood Russ was in. His friend seemed to find the situation downright comical.

"I guessed as much." Russ wiped the sweat from his brow, but Cody had a sneaking suspicion that he did so to cover a smile. Not that Russ had any trouble poking fun at him and letting him know it.

After Russ arrived, and the three of them had exchanged pleasantries, Christy excused herself and left, saying that she was driving to Miles City to visit Taylor and Eric. Cody would have offered to go with her, but he was working swing shift and it wasn't likely that he'd be back before he was scheduled to go on duty.

"You're not going to get closemouthed with me now, are you?" Russ was asking. "I can't say I've ever seen you take to a woman the way you have to Taylor's sister. What's different about Christy?"

"What was different about Taylor?"

Russ chuckled. "Touché. But if you remember correctly, all Taylor and I could do at first was argue. Never met a woman who could irritate me as much as she did."

"You didn't stay angry at her for long."

Russ shook his head. "No, can't say I did. She'd make

me so furious I couldn't think straight. Before I could stop myself, I'd say or do some fool thing I'd end up regretting. That certainly doesn't seem to be the case with you and Christy, though. You two can't seem to keep your hands off each other."

Cody decided it was best to ignore that comment. "You and Taylor worked things out, and that's what matters."

Some of the humor disappeared from Russ's dark eyes. "We did, didn't we?" A faraway expression came over him. "Did you get a good look at him, Cody?"

Before Cody could respond Russ continued. "The nurse handed me Eric, and I swear something happened to my heart. It was the craziest thing, holding that baby in my arms and loving him so much my throat got all clogged up. I couldn't have said a word if my life depended on it. Before I knew what was happening, tears were rolling down my face. *Me.* I can't remember the last time I cried. I've never felt anything as incredible as holding my son.

"You know, I loved Taylor before the baby was born, but it pales in comparison to what I felt for her as she struggled to give birth to Eric. I've always thought of women as the weaker sex, but I was wrong." He shook himself as if waking from a deep sleep, his eyes as somber as Cody had ever seen.

"You have reason to be proud."

"I bought every box of cigars the gift shop owned."

"I know. I was with you."

"Hell, I don't even smoke."

Cody laughed. "I know that, too." He hesitated, uncertain how to proceed. "About Christy… You don't have any objection to my seeing her, do you?"

"So you plan to take her to Sitting Bull Lookout?"

The ridge above the town had been their favorite necking place as teenagers.

"Probably," Cody answered, trying to hold back a grin.

Russ tucked his hands in his hip pockets. "Then you really are serious?"

"I've never been more serious in my life," Cody admitted without a pause.

Taylor was sound asleep when Christy got to the hospital. Her sister's long hair spread out over the white pillows like spilled coffee. Her eyes were closed, her breathing deep and even.

Tiptoeing into the room so as not to disturb her, Christy pulled out the lone chair and sat. Although she'd been on the road for more than an hour, she remained as upset and nervous as when she'd left the house.

She felt like weeping. She felt like rejoicing. No woman should experience such conflicting emotions.

The obedient, do-what's-right-at-all-costs part of her kept reminding her of James. Loyal, hardworking James, who loved her.

All her life Christy had done what was right. She'd never been rebellious. She'd been a model child. A model sister. Respectful. Considerate. Thoughtful.

She felt none of those things now.

The look Cody had given her just before Russ stepped into the barn would be forever burned in her mind. It was the kind of look a woman dreams of receiving from a man sometime in her life. A lover's look. One so intimate and personal that it could never be explained to another.

If this intense feeling between her and Cody was wrong, then why did Christy feel so good inside? Why did she long to throw up her arms and shout for joy? If this was being rebellious or disrespectful, then all Christy could say was that she was entering puberty later than the normal teenager. About ten years later.

Taylor stirred and opened her eyes. "Christy," she said, yawning. "When did you arrive?"

"About five minutes ago."

"You should have woken me."

"And interrupted your nap?" she teased. "How are you feeling?"

"Wonderful." A soft smile touched her eyes. "Eric spent most of the morning with me. Oh, Christy, he's so adorable. We became acquainted with each other. I counted his fingers and toes, and he taught me about breast-feeding."

"You look happy."

"I am... I really am."

Christy settled farther down in the chair. Trying not to be obvious, she stared at the floor, studying the pattern in the white tile. "Cody took me out to eat when we left here yesterday."

"In Miles City?"

"No. We went to the bowling alley in Cougar Point."

"I'm glad." There was a pause. "He's a good man."

Christy knew that instinctively. "I thought so, too. I like him, Taylor. I really do."

"Why do you look so guilty?"

How could she look or feel anything else? But Taylor wouldn't understand. Her sister had no way of knowing about the lovely engagement ring being sized at the Seattle jewelers.

They chatted for a few minutes before Taylor settled back against the pillows and sighed.

"What was that all about?"

"What?"

"That sigh," Christy said.

"Oh… I was just thinking about you and Cody. I'm really pleased you like him so much. Frankly, I've been concerned about you seeing so much of James."

Christy was surprised she didn't give everything away right then and there. "Oh?" she managed.

"He's nice, don't get me wrong, but he's so boring. To be honest, I've never understood what you saw in him."

"But he's kind."

"So is Big Bird!" Taylor argued. "I think James is a nice guy, but he isn't the right one for you, and I can't understand why you continue to date him."

"How can you say that?" Christy demanded, forcing the argument. James had been a child prodigy, a recognized genius by age ten. He graduated from high school in his early teens, and from law school at twenty. At twenty-five he was close to becoming the youngest partner in Atwater and Beckham's long, distinguished history. "James is a a really nice man."

"True," Taylor agreed readily enough. "But he isn't the right one for you," she said again.

"You're wrong." A simple way to end this argument would be for Christy to announce her engagement, yet she hesitated, interested in hearing her sister's opinion.

"James is everything you say, but you're not in love with him and never have been," Taylor announced with a challenging smile.

"You sound so confident of that."

"I am. You couldn't possibly be in love with James if you're this interested in Cody Franklin."

Any objection Christy might have posed died a quick and quiet death.

"I think," Taylor said, holding out her hands to her sister, "you came to Montana at exactly the right time."

Four

"Can I hold Eric?" Mandy Palmer asked minutes after Taylor was home from the hospital. "I barely got a chance to look at him before," she added, casting an accusing glance in the direction of her older brother.

"Of course," Taylor said, leading the teenager into the living room. Russ followed, leaving Christy standing alone in the kitchen with Cody.

She busied herself at the stove, praying the sheriff would go with the others.

He didn't.

"You've been avoiding me," he said softly, leaning against the kitchen counter and crossing his arms over his chest. It was all Christy could do not to stare at him. If she did, he'd be able to read the longing in her eyes, and he'd realize she'd been miserable and unhappy and at odds with herself.

She'd needed these two days to think. To come to grips with herself. To decide.

The answers hadn't come easily. She'd wrestled with the most momentous decision of her life. The resolution had come, but not without a price. She felt exhausted, frightened and on the verge of tears.

She couldn't deny Cody's words. She *had* been avoiding him. She'd astonished herself at how clever she'd been about it. Clever enough so no one would have guessed.

Except Cody.

"Why didn't you answer my calls?" he asked.

"I came to spend time with Taylor, to help her. I've been busy...."

No one had bothered to tell her that Cody had been invited to Taylor and Eric's welcome-home dinner. She wasn't prepared for this.

From the way everyone had disappeared the minute Taylor arrived, Christy shouldn't be surprised to find herself alone with Cody. It seemed as if it had all been prearranged.

"Christy, talk to me," he pleaded, his frustration evident. "Tell me what's wrong."

"Nothing. It's just that I've been so terribly busy." So terribly confused. So terribly guilty. Cowardly, too, since she'd been juggling with her conscience, her scruples and her sense of fairness.

If anything, this time away from Cody had enlightened her. The first day she'd been trapped in the restless, lost sensation she'd experienced the night before, after he'd left.

The second day, however, she'd found peace. It was a strained peace and would be so until she went home to Seattle and talked to James. Nevertheless, she'd reached a decision.

For a good part of the afternoon, Mandy and Christy had worked together to get the house ready for Taylor's return with Eric. No one had said Cody would be returning with them.

No one had given her a word of warning. She didn't

know what to say to him just now, and the truth seemed unwieldy. Awkward.

"I don't blame you if you're frightened," Cody continued, his voice low. "I'm frightened myself. The first time we kissed I felt like I'd been hit by a freight train. The second time it was even more powerful.... Deep down I'd hoped it was somehow tied up in the emotion surrounding Russ, Taylor and the baby, but it isn't."

"I don't think it is, either."

"If you're looking for an explanation of what's going on between us, I can't give you one. All I know is what I feel."

Sometimes, Christy believed, a lifetime of doing the right thing could be subverted by pure sensation. This had certainly proved true with her and Cody.

"Talk to me."

Slowly she turned, witnessing for herself the tenderness, and the confusion, in his eyes. Without uttering a word, she walked over to him and slipped her arms around his waist. He placed his own around her, anchoring her to his chest as he expelled a harsh breath.

"Can you tell me what's troubling you?"

She nodded, almost giddy with relief and release. Raising her head, she smiled up at him, longing to reassure him. Part of her yearned to put this behind them and blurt it all out. She wanted to tell him about James and the engagement and how meeting him had turned her world inside out. But there wasn't enough time to untangle this mess before dinner. They needed privacy to discuss it in detail, time to reach an understanding.

She glanced regretfully toward the living room.

"Do you want to steal away?" Cody asked. "Go somewhere else?"

That was exactly what she did want, but they couldn't

leave. Tonight was an evening to celebrate. Taylor and Eric were home for the first time, and leaving would be selfish and thoughtless.

"Forget I asked that," Cody murmured. "I'll be patient."

"So will I. We'll make some excuse after dinner," she suggested, then on impulse lightly brushed her lips over his.

Cody, however, wanted more. Much more.

Placing his hands on each side of her neck, he pulled her tighter to him and wove his fingers through her short hair as he brought his mouth to hers.

"I swear," Russ exclaimed loudly, walking into the kitchen, "I can't leave these two alone for a moment." The words were followed by the sound of his laughter.

Languidly Cody eased his mouth from Christy's and slowly opened his eyes. "How about getting lost for the next few minutes?" Cody said.

"Fine with me," Russ agreed, "but I don't think that fried chicken's going to want to wait much longer."

"Oh, my," Christy said, abruptly breaking away. She'd completely forgotten about the dinner she and Mandy had so carefully planned. She grabbed a pot holder and moved the grease-spitting skillet from the burner. Heaving a sigh of relief, she brushed her bangs off her forehead.

"Need any help?" Mandy asked, sauntering into the kitchen. Russ's teenage sister lived with him and Taylor, and from everything Christy had heard, Mandy was the one responsible for bringing Russ and Taylor together. Because of a summer job and other commitments, Mandy had been away from the house during most of Christy's visit and Christy was only beginning to get to know her. And like her.

"No. I've got everything under control here."

Russ contradicted her under his breath, but Christy chose to ignore her brother-in-law's comment. She was relieved when the two men vacated the kitchen.

With Mandy's assistance, dinner was ready fifteen minutes later. Mandy called everyone, and they gathered around the dining room table. Russ escorted his wife, his eyes tender as he seated her.

Taylor, wearing a loose pale blue dress that complemented her eye color, looked wonderful. Every woman should look so good three days after giving birth, Christy mused.

"Oh, Christy... Mandy," Taylor said, studying the table. "This is fantastic. You must've spent the whole day cooking—and in this heat!"

"It wasn't a problem," Christy said automatically.

"Yes, it was," Mandy countered smoothly. "It took all afternoon, but we had so much fun it was worth it. Your sister's great!"

"I think so, too, but you shouldn't have gone to so much trouble." Taylor gestured at the three different kinds of salads, the platter of fried chicken and two separate desserts.

"But we did," Mandy said, reaching for the potato salad, "so you might as well enjoy it."

Christy shared a secret smile with her older sister. She admired Mandy for her openness and her honesty. Had she answered, she would've quickly allowed Taylor and the others to believe she'd managed to whip up a three-course meal in a matter of minutes without the slightest trouble.

Eric stirred just as they were finishing dinner, and Taylor immediately started to rise. Russ put his hand on her arm, stopping her.

"Let me?" He made it a question.

"He probably needs his diaper changed," Taylor warned.

"So? I can do it. Just how difficult can changing a diaper be?"

Christy and Taylor exchanged a meaningful glance. When she pulled her gaze away from her sister, Christy's eyes sought out Cody. The sheriff gave her a look of exaggerated shock.

"Did I hear correctly?" he teased. "Did Russ Palmer volunteer to change a diaper?"

"Apparently so," Taylor said, pretending to be as awed as Cody.

"All right, you guys, cut it out," Russ warned, shouting from the master bedroom.

"I don't know if I can let a moment like this pass without witnessing it myself. Does anyone have a camera?"

"You're not taking any damn picture," Russ roared, his voice booming through the house. His words were quickly followed by the squalling cry of an infant. A fraction of a second later Russ shouted for Taylor.

Christy tossed her napkin aside and left the table with her sister, wondering if she could help. Mandy was the only one content to let the others deal with the baby while she finished her meal.

The three of them crowded around the bassinet where Russ struggled with the diaper and pins. He was grumbling, and his face was creased with a deep frown as if he were performing major surgery.

"I marry the most modern woman in the world. She won't let me open a car door for her, insists on paying for her own dinner when we go out on a date, but will she use disposable diapers? Oh, no, she's got to torment me with cloth ones."

"They're better for the environment," Taylor said,

gently pushing her husband aside. She dealt efficiently with the diaper-changing, completely unfazed by the task.

"That's all there is to it?" Cody asked, making fun of his friend's inability to handle such an uncomplicated situation.

"If you think it's so easy, you try it."

"I will, but probably not for several years." Cody looked at Christy, and the mental image of Cody holding a baby in his arms, their baby, filled her mind. She looked away, not wanting anyone to witness the emotion she was feeling.

Russ watched as Taylor lifted the dirty diaper from the bassinet. "What are you going to do with that...thing?" He wrinkled his nose as he asked the question.

"I'm putting it in the diaper pail in the bathroom."

"You're not keeping those smelly diapers in there, are you?" he said as he followed Taylor down the hallway. Christy could hear him listing his objections.

Once more Christy and Cody were left alone, this time with Eric. The infant lay on his back, squinting his blue eyes as he gazed up at them. His mouth made small sucking motions.

Unable to resist, Christy reached into the bassinet and lifted Eric out. He gurgled contentedly in her arms as she sat on the end of the bed. Cody stood next to her, studying the newborn. He lovingly smoothed his large hand along the side of the baby's head. Eric's tiny hand closed around Cody's index finger.

"Look," Cody said excitedly, as if Eric had broken an Olympic record. "I think he recognizes us."

"And well he should! We're his godparents," Christy reminded him. She turned to smile at Cody and once more found herself lost in his eyes.

In that brief moment Christy saw a reflection of everything she was feeling. Until now, whenever they looked at each other, their eyes brimmed with questions and doubts.

But this time was different. Christy saw in Cody an understanding. They'd each lost the need for answers or explanations.

"How long will you be in Cougar Point?" Cody asked.

"My vacation is two weeks."

Both seemed to calculate the number of days remaining before she'd need to go home.

Cody's expression told her he wanted to spend every available moment he could with her. It was what Christy wanted, too, more than she'd wanted anything in her life.

"I'm working day shift tomorrow," he told her softly, his look tender. "What about dinner?"

"I'd like that." Which was definitely an understatement.

The air between them seemed to spark with sensuality. Cody leaned toward her, and Christy knew beyond a doubt that he intended to kiss her. He hesitated a fraction of an inch from her mouth before regretfully backing away.

"I'd bet my last dollar if I kissed you, Russ would interrupt us."

"He probably would. He seems to have an incredible sense of timing, doesn't he?"

As soon as she spoke, her brother-in-law stuck his head in the doorway. "What's taking you two so long? Mandy's got the coffee poured."

"See what I mean?" Cody whispered.

Christy nodded and stood, placing Eric over her shoulder and rubbing his back. He was so tiny, so perfect, and her heart swelled anew with love for him.

Taylor and Russ were sitting in the living room when

Cody and Christy appeared. Their looks were openly curious—as if they were waiting for the couple to make an announcement.

Christy didn't think it would do much good to try to disguise what was going on between her and Cody. Her sister knew her far too well, and clearly Russ was equally familiar with Cody.

Christy handed the baby over to Taylor, dropping a kiss on his forehead as she did. By tacit agreement, she and Cody sat at opposite sides of the room. Being close to each other only intensified the attraction, and no doubt the curiosity.

"So," Russ said, glancing from Cody to Christy, sporting a wide grin.

"Russ," Taylor warned in a low whisper.

"What?"

"Do you have to be so obvious?"

Russ blinked, apparently at a loss to understand his wife's censure. "I didn't say anything, but if I did venture to mention the obvious, I'd say something along the lines of how happy I am that my best friend and your sister have apparently hit it off so well."

"To tell you the truth, I couldn't be more pleased myself," Taylor added, smiling.

Cody crossed his legs and picked up his coffee. "I'm glad to hear Christy and I have made you two so happy."

Russ chuckled at that, amusement glistening in his eyes. "Do you remember that time in the sixth grade?" Russ asked.

"I'm not likely to forget it."

"What are you two mumbling about now?" Taylor demanded.

"We were eleven."

"You were eleven," Cody corrected. "I was ten."

"Right," Russ agreed. "We'd been good friends for several years and had started to notice some of our other buddies turning traitor."

"Turning traitor?" Christy repeated.

"Liking girls."

Since Christy was the youngest of the five Manning children, she couldn't recall her brothers sharing similar feelings. "What did you two do?" she asked.

"The only thing we could," Russ explained, grinning again. "We were losing our best friends left and right, so Cody and I made a pact and became blood brothers. We made a solemn vow never to associate with any of the guys who'd turned traitor and liked girls."

"Especially pretty ones with dark hair and bright blue eyes," Cody remarked, looking at Christy, who possessed both. His mouth quivered, and she realized he was only a breath away from laughing outright.

"And which of you broke this sacred vow first?"

"Cody did," Russ said.

"Russ," Cody responded, the two speaking almost simultaneously.

"Boys, please," Taylor said in what Christy was sure was her best schoolteacher voice.

"Cody gave Mary Lu Hawkins a valentine that year," Russ reminded him.

"My mother forced me to do it," Cody insisted. "I never liked Mary Lu Hawkins, and you know it."

"That's not what I heard."

Listening to Cody and Russ was like being present at an exchange between her own brothers. A strong sense of family was an integral part of who she was. She loved their frequent get-togethers and had missed Taylor dreadfully over the past year.

"Is it always like this between these two?" Christy asked her sister.

"Sometimes worse," Taylor answered.

"Russ was the ultimate traitor," Cody said, setting his coffee mug aside. "He married a dark-haired, blue-eyed woman, and worse, I wasn't even invited to the wedding."

"No one was," Mandy inserted as she came in from the kitchen, drying her hands on her apron skirt. "Not even me. Russ's very own sister."

"I swear you're never going to forgive me for that, are you?" Russ grumbled. "Just wait till you fall in love, little sister, then you might be more understanding."

Mandy straightened her spine and threw back her shoulders. Her eyes narrowed as she glared across the room at her brother. She reminded Christy so much of her older sister confronting their father that she nearly laughed out loud.

"It may come as a shock to you, big brother, but I've been in love several times." Mandy evidently considered herself a woman of the world.

Russ didn't hide his opinions on *that* issue. He rolled his eyes.

"Russ," Taylor said softly.

"Now what did I do?" he asked. At the rate he was going, his foot would remain permanently in his mouth. "All right, all right, I—*we* made a mistake by not including you in the wedding ceremony. There. Are you satisfied?"

"No. I want you to admit that I'm old enough to be in love."

"Mandy!"

"Admit it." It was clear that brother and sister were often at odds, yet Christy sensed the deep and abiding love they shared.

"Don't look at me, Russ Palmer," Taylor said bluntly. "You got yourself into this."

"I suppose that at fifteen a mature teenage girl may have experienced her first taste of love."

"May have?" Mandy repeated. "That's not good enough."

"Hey, the girl wants blood," Cody murmured.

"She's likely to get it, too," Taylor said, apparently for Christy's benefit.

"All right, I'll admit it. There! *Now* are you satisfied?"

Mandy smiled graciously and nodded. "Thank you, brother dearest."

"You're welcome, sister sweetest." He turned his attention away from Mandy. "Listen," Russ said, looking at Cody and Christy and then back at his friend. "If you two ever get married, whether it's to each other or anyone else, take my advice and don't elope."

"If Mandy was upset about not being at the wedding, that was nothing compared to how strongly Mom and Dad felt about it," Taylor said. "Dad seemed to feel I'd cheated him out of an important part of fatherhood by not letting him escort me down the aisle."

From somewhere deep inside, Christy forced a smile. This talk about weddings was making her decidedly uncomfortable. What her sister said was true enough; her parents had been bitterly disappointed not to hold a large wedding for their oldest daughter. It was one of the reasons they were so pleased when Christy announced that she and James would be getting married. Almost immediately they'd started talking about the church ceremony, with a reception and dance to follow.

"I think it's time for us to go, don't you?" Cody said to Christy, unfolding his long legs and standing. He walked across the room in three strides. "See you later, Taylor,

Eric. Oh, and you, too." He nodded at Russ with a grin. "Thanks for dinner, everyone."

"Where are you two headed?" Russ wanted to know, making no effort to disguise his interest.

"Out." Cody turned to Christy, and his smile was like the warm fingers of sunlight in winter. They'd known each other such a short while, and it seemed inconceivable that she could feel like this. But she did. The feelings she and Cody shared were too complex to put into words.

"When will you be back?" Russ asked his sister-in-law, as if he wasn't completely convinced his best friend was safe in her company.

"Who appointed you my guardian angel?" Cody asked sarcastically, his eyebrows raised.

"I'm only looking out for your best interests," Russ explained, continuing the game. "Good grief, man, she's pretty with dark hair and blue eyes. We learned way back in the sixth grade that those are the ones to watch out for. You've got to be careful. Look what happened to me!"

"What did happen to you?" Taylor asked, her brow wrinkling with the question.

"You should know. Before I realized it, I was saddled with a wife. I don't mind telling you, Franklin, I'm worried about you."

"If I'm responsible for the security of an entire county, you can trust me to take care of myself."

"Saddled?" Taylor asked, her voice ominously low. "You found yourself *saddled* with a wife?"

Russ instantly looked guilty. "Maybe saddled wasn't the best word."

"Then I suggest you search for another."

"Ah…" Russ rubbed his hand across his neck.

"He's talking off the top of his head," Cody said, defending his friend. He turned toward Russ. "If I were you, I'd plead for leniency and remind her how crazy in love you are."

"How about I was *favored* with a wife?" Russ muttered. He seemed quite pleased with his choice of word.

Taylor glanced at Christy, a smile playing at the corners of her mouth, then shook her head. "You'll have to do better than that."

"Taylor, come on, I'm having a serious discussion with my friend here. All I'm trying to do is impart a few words of wisdom before Cody makes the same...before he ends up..."

"Ends up what?" Taylor prompted.

It took Russ a moment to answer. "Blessed?" he offered, confident he'd smoothed things over.

"Blessed is an acceptable word."

"I think we should get out of here while the getting's good, don't you?" Cody asked, reaching for Christy's hand, entwining their fingers.

"I couldn't agree with you more." The solid ground beneath her feet seemed to shift as she realized that once they were alone she'd need to explain about James. Dragging in a steadying breath, she looked at Taylor. "I won't be gone long."

"If I get worried, I'll call the sheriff," Taylor teased.

The phone rang, and Mandy shot out of the living room.

Russ escorted Christy and Cody to the back door.

Mandy appeared, stretching the long telephone cord into the kitchen. She seemed confused as she held out the receiver to Russ. "I think it must be a wrong number. Maybe you should talk to him."

"All right."

Cody chuckled. "I never thought I'd be grateful for a

phone call. I had the impression Russ was going to make us listen to more of his pearls of wisdom."

They were all the way down the steps when the back door swung open with enough force to send it crashing shut.

"Christy." Russ stood on the top of the steps, hands on his hips, his eyes squinting against the setting sun.

"Yes?" She turned to face her brother-in-law. The humor in his eyes had been replaced with a fierce anger that transformed his handsome features.

Cody took a step forward. "What is it?"

"The phone," Russ said. "It's for Christy. Someone named James Wilkens."

She gasped softly before she could stop herself.

"He claims he's her fiancé."

Five

"Cody, please," Christy began, her heart in her eyes. "I can explain."

"You mean it's true?" Russ shouted.

"It's not as bad as it sounds—if you'd take the time to listen." Both of her hands gripped Cody's forearm as she boldly held on to him, not wanting to let him go for fear she'd never see him again.

"Are you engaged or not?" Cody asked. His dark eyes burned into hers, searing her conscience far more deeply than any words he could've spoken.

"I was going to tell you about James...."

Cody's face tensed as though she'd delivered a crippling blow to his abdomen. He lowered his gaze to her hands, which clenched his arm tightly.

"I see." The two words were cold, his voice remote.

She moistened her lips, unsure she could trust her voice. "Please let me explain."

"What's there to say? It's simple, isn't it? Either you're engaged or you're not." He pulled himself free and turned his back to her.

"Cody." She tried once more, hating the way her voice wobbled as she pleaded for patience and understanding.

One stern look told her he wasn't willing to grant her either. Her heart seized painfully as she slowly dropped her hands and stepped away from him.

Without another word, Cody climbed inside his Cherokee, slammed the door and drove away as if the very demons of hell were in hot pursuit.

Christy went completely still. She couldn't move. Couldn't breathe.

How long she stood there, Christy had no idea. Nor could she put order to her thoughts. Just a few minutes ago she'd been sitting across the room from Cody, laughing with him, sharing secret smiles, her whole being permeated with gladness and joy. How natural it had seemed to be together. As natural as the sun setting. As natural as rain.

"Are you going to talk to your fiancé or not?" Russ demanded, his voice sharp with censure.

Christy stared at him for a moment before she realized James was still on the phone. Nevertheless, she stood where she was and watched the plume of dust that trailed behind Cody's vehicle. After a while it faded away, taking with it the promise of something wonderful.

Russ waited for her at the top of the porch steps. Christy lowered her eyes as she moved past him. He didn't need to say anything for her to feel his reprimand.

The telephone receiver was resting on a small table in the hallway. Christy dragged in a deep, calming breath and reached for it. "Hello, James." She prayed her voice revealed none of her turmoil.

"Christy. How are you?" He sounded anxious, concerned.

"Fine, just fine. Taylor had the baby, but I suppose you've heard about that already. I doubt Mom and Dad could keep quiet about Eric. He really is precious." She knew she was chattering but couldn't seem to make herself stop. "Montana is a beautiful state. I haven't seen much of Cougar Point yet, except the bowling alley. I had breakfast there the other morning, only it was really the middle of the afternoon—the day Eric was born, actually."

"You ate breakfast at a bowling alley?"

"There's a restaurant there and the food's good—excellent, in fact."

"That's nice."

"How are you?" Christy felt obliged to ask.

"Fine. I miss you." He dropped his voice slightly as if he'd admitted something he shouldn't. "The office seems empty with you away."

James wasn't a man who was comfortable with expressing his emotions. Showing affection was difficult for him. The fact that he'd called and said he missed her was practically equivalent to another man standing on a rooftop and shouting at the top of his voice that he was madly in love.

"I... I've been busy."

"I was hoping you'd call me."

His disappointment echoed in each word.

"I'm sorry, James, really I am. It's just that everything happened so fast. I didn't even have a chance to unpack my bags before Taylor went into labor. She came home from the hospital today, and we...we were just having dinner." That was a slight exaggeration, but she needed an excuse to get off the phone before she did something stupid like weep uncontrollably or tell him about Cody.

"You're having dinner? Why didn't you say something sooner? No wonder it took you so long to get to the phone."

Christy leaned against the wall, closed her eyes and swallowed. She felt guilty about by her minor deception, contaminated by the way she was deceiving him in an effort to cut short this painful conversation.

James deserved so much more than this. The guilt was killing her, and it demanded all the self-control she possessed to keep from blurting everything out.

"I'll let you go, but before I do I want you to know I got the diamond back from the jeweler. It'll be ready when you return from your sister's."

"Oh, g-great," she stammered, trying to inject some enthusiasm into her voice.

"Goodbye, Christy. Give my regards to Taylor and her husband and congratulate them both for me."

"I will. Bye, James. Don't work too hard."

"No, I won't."

She replaced the receiver, her fingers curled tensely around it as she waited for the recriminations to rain down on her. She felt an overwhelming sense of wrongdoing, a surge of remorse.

Raised voices came at her from inside the living room.

"The least you can do is listen to her," Christy heard Taylor shout.

"What possible explanation could she have? Either she's engaged or she isn't."

"Listen to me, Russ Palmer. I won't have you yelling at my sister. Whatever's happening between her and Cody is her business. It doesn't have anything to do with us."

"Like hell I'm going to stay out of it. We're talking about Cody here—my best friend. I thought he was your friend, too."

"He is."

"Then you can't expect to sit idly by and watch him get hurt."

"Please," Christy said, stepping into the room. She

couldn't bear to have them arguing over her. "Please… don't fight."

The room went silent, a silence so intense it seemed to throb like a giant heart. Taylor's gaze, clouded with doubt and uncertainty, locked with Christy's. Russ's eyes were filled with reproach.

Russ and Taylor continued to stare at her. Russ was angry and made no effort to disguise his feelings. Taylor, usually so strong and confident, couldn't hide her confusion.

Christy suspected her sister was as troubled as her husband. Only Taylor wouldn't allow herself to voice her misgivings because of family loyalty.

"Sit down," Taylor suggested. She motioned toward the recliner where Christy had sat earlier. "You're so pale. Are you sure you're all right?"

"Why didn't you tell us you were engaged?" Russ asked, barely giving her time to compose herself. "And if you and James are getting married, why aren't you wearing a ring?"

"Russ, please," Taylor said, "let her answer one question before hitting her with another." Directing her attention to Christy, Taylor widened her eyes. "We're waiting."

Folding her hands in her lap, Christy squeezed her fingers so tightly they hurt. "James asked me to marry him two days before I left Seattle."

"He didn't give you an engagement ring?"

"Of course…it's being sized now."

"I see," Taylor said, frowning. "And you didn't mention it to anyone? Do Mom and Dad know? I'm your sister, for heaven's sake! The least you could've done was mention it to me."

"Taylor," Russ said gruffly, then reminded her of her own words. "She can only answer one question at a time."

"I didn't have a chance to tell you when I first arrived. Remember? Then first thing the next morning you went into labor and… I met Cody."

"You had no business leading him on," Russ snapped.

"I didn't mean to," she cried, and raked her fingers though her short hair, praying Taylor and Russ wouldn't condemn her. "It just…happened. We were both so excited about the baby and afterward we went out to eat. Then Cody drove me home and…and I knew he was going to kiss me. I realize it was a mistake not to say anything to him, but I was afraid…" Afraid that if she *had* said something he wouldn't have touched her, and she'd wanted his kiss so much.

Unable to meet her sister's eyes, she glanced at the coffee table as the tears spilled down her cheeks.

"Who's this James character, anyway?" Russ asked Taylor. "Did we meet him?"

She nodded. "He's the attorney Christy introduced to us last summer."

"Not the…" He hesitated.

"Why didn't you tell me?" Taylor apparently considered it a personal affront that Christy had kept the news to herself. "We had plenty of time to talk while I was in the hospital and you were there every day."

"I tried," Christy said in her own defense. "But every time I mentioned James, you changed the subject. And when I finally managed to drag him back into the conversation, you started telling me how dry and boring you think he is and what a mismatched couple we are. What was I supposed to do? Tell you I'd agreed to marry the man you'd just finished criticizing?"

"Oh, dear," Taylor whispered. "Now that you mention it, I do remember you trying to bring James into the conversation."

"Fine. You two got that settled, but what about Cody?" Russ stalked to the other side of the room and stared out the front window. "I can't, I *won't* let this happen to him a second time. Not when it's in my power to prevent it." Gradually he turned around, his shoulders squared and his jaw tightly clenched.

"A second time?" Christy echoed.

When Russ didn't respond right away, she looked at her sister, who was busy with Eric. Either that or she was avoiding eye contact. "Taylor?"

"It happened several years ago," Russ began grudgingly. "A woman by the name of Rebecca Morgan moved into town. She was from somewhere in the south and had the sweetest manners you can imagine. She was the type of woman a man could fall in love with. Becca was perfect. Beautiful. Demure. Charming and..." Russ shook his head. "Who would've guessed?"

"Guessed what?" Christy asked.

"Becca made it obvious from the moment she moved into town that she was attracted to Cody. Every time he turned around there she was, batting her eyes at him, doing those things you women do to let a man know you're interested."

"I could make a comment here, but I won't," Taylor muttered.

"Soon Becca and Cody were seeing a lot of each other. You have to understand, Cody isn't easily taken in, especially by a pretty woman. Until recently." He frowned at Christy as he said it. "But Becca did more than interest him. For the first time in his life, Cody was in love. It showed in everything he said and did.

"Cody's always been popular with the folks around here, and his happiness seemed to rub off on everyone. Most folks liked Becca, too. They couldn't help it. There was plenty of talk about the two of them getting married." Russ walked over to the ottoman and sat down. "A month or so after she moved into town, a series of baffling robberies started happening."

"You don't mean to say Becca…"

"Not her personally. She was part of a team. They worked a scam in small cities all across the western states. Apparently the heat was on in several of the larger cities, and she and her partner decided to try their hand in smaller towns. They were successful, too. Becca would move someplace and get involved with a deputy from the local sheriff's office. One way or another she'd get information about shipments of money to the town banks. Then she'd pass that information to her partner. It was all cleverly done. Whenever a shipment of cash was due to arrive, Becca would make sure she was nowhere nearby. Two banks were robbed, and a couple of stores lost valuable equipment all within the second month she was in town. But no one suspected her. How could they? She was just as sweet as honey."

"How long did it take Cody to realize it was Becca?"

"Not long, a few weeks, but he felt like the biggest fool who ever lived and you'll never convince him differently. He took responsibility for everything, blamed himself for not picking up on the scam sooner."

"But he loved her. Trusted her."

Russ's dark gaze collided with Christy's. "I know. He arrested her and her partner and testified against them."

"Surely no one blamed Cody!"

"No, everyone in town was as taken in by her as he was. But Cody felt as responsible as if he'd personally handed over the money. It's his job to protect and to serve and he felt he'd let the entire county down, although he worked his fool head off until every penny was returned.

Even that wasn't enough. Cody felt he had to resign from the department."

"No." Christy's response was immediate. True, she'd only known Cody a short while, but in that time she'd learned how important law enforcement was to him.

"Thankfully some of us were able to talk some sense into him. He made the mistake of falling in love with the wrong woman—but then again, it was all due to his efforts that Becca and her friend were caught. If it hadn't been for Cody, no one knows how long their little scam would've worked or how many other communities would've been bilked. Unfortunately Cody didn't see it that way."

"He's only human." Christy felt a burning need to defend him.

"Becca used him. But worse than that, she made him feel like an idiot. It's taken three years for him to live it down, at least in his own mind. The way most folks figure it, Cody did Montana a good deed by putting Becca Morgan and her partner behind bars."

"That's why he wouldn't run for sheriff until last year?" Taylor asked, shifting the baby in her arms.

"It's been his life's dream to be elected sheriff of Custer County, but it took all this time for him to agree to run. I suppose he felt he had to prove his worth all over again. The crazy part is that he could've won hands down *any* year, including the year he was involved with Becca."

"I didn't know," Taylor said softly.

"It's not something that's talked about a lot," Russ explained. "The subject is such a painful one, it's best forgotten."

"Then Becca's still in prison?" Christy managed to ask. Learning how Cody had been deceived was painful for her, too. The knowledge that justice had been done somehow made it easier to accept.

"From what I understand, she's tried to contact Cody a few times, claiming she really was in love with him, and still is. To hear her tell it, she was a helpless pawn in all this. She says she was a victim of blackmail. But Cody won't have anything to do with her."

"I can certainly understand that," Taylor said.

"You aren't comparing me to Becca, are you?" Christy asked bluntly, feeling even more wretched.

"You're no thief," Russ said abruptly. "I'm not worried about you bilking the good citizens of Cougar Point, if that's what you think. No..." He rubbed the back of his neck. "After Becca something changed in Cody. He rarely dated. He closed himself off, became more pensive, introspective. It was as if he'd lost trust in women."

Taylor nodded. "I can't say I really blame him."

"I don't, either," Christy added, realizing as she did so that she was condemning herself.

Russ frowned. "That's why I was so pleased about what happened after he met you. When he looked at you, it was like seeing the old Cody all over again, the man who smiled and joked and didn't take everything so seriously. I don't know what went on between you." He hesitated and glanced at his wife. "Taylor's right when she says it isn't any of my business, but I won't stand by and let you take advantage of him."

"I wouldn't... I couldn't."

"Then why didn't you tell him you were engaged?"

Christy felt as if she'd been backed into a corner. "I planned to. I never intended to keep it a secret, but I needed time to think. You may not believe this, but I'd hoped to talk to Cody about James tonight. I was going to tell him everything."

"Are you planning on marrying James?" Taylor asked, her eyes seeking Christy's.

The question came as a shock. "No. I couldn't—not after meeting Cody."

"Then why didn't you break the engagement when you had the chance?" Russ asked. "You were just talking to him. It would've been a simple matter to tell him then."

"I can't do it over the phone," Christy said, jerking her head upward. "James is a good man. He deserves better than that. He hasn't done anything wrong. I hate to hurt him...." She paused when hot tears threatened to spill down her face. Biting her lower lip, she drew in a shuddering breath.

"Christy's right." Taylor's words cut through the emotion of the moment. "This is a delicate situation. You can't expect her to call James and break off the engagement. That would be heartless. This is best done in person. James may be a bit dull, but he's a decent human being."

"Is...is there any chance Cody will talk to me?" Christy wanted to drive into town and explain that she had no intention of going through with the marriage.

"I doubt he'll have anything to do with you," Russ answered, confirming her worst fears.

"Wait until tomorrow," Taylor advised. "Give him an opportunity to think everything through."

"He asked me out to dinner.... But I'm not sure if he'll show up."

"He won't," Russ said. "I know him better than anyone, and I can tell you, as far as he's concerned, whatever was between you is over."

Christy's shoulders sagged with defeat. "I was afraid of that."

"Don't make it sound so hopeless," Taylor muttered.

"She's engaged, for crying out loud. What do you expect Cody to do?" Russ said. "Ignore it? He isn't going to do that."

"But I have every intention of breaking off the engagement."

"I doubt that'll make any difference to him. I'll be surprised if he even listens to you."

"That's not true," Taylor said confidently. "Cody's a reasonable man, and it's obvious that he's attracted to you."

"He isn't anymore." Russ shook his head for emphasis.

Taylor shot daggers at her husband. "Russ Palmer, kindly allow me to finish."

"Feel free, but you've got to understand. After Becca, Cody doesn't have a lot of trust in the opposite sex."

"My sister isn't another Becca," Taylor insisted.

"You and I know that."

A short silence followed before Christy said, "Cody's smart enough to know it, too." She wanted to believe that. Needed to believe it. But whether that was the case or not was something she'd soon discover.

Cody slammed his fist against the steering column. He was parked on the ridge that overlooked Cougar Point and had been sitting there for the past hour, collecting his thoughts.

Frustration and anger mounted with each passing minute. Drawing in a deep breath, he rubbed his face with both hands, certain he'd almost made a world-class fool of himself for the second time.

When was he going to learn? Women weren't to be trusted. Especially pretty blue-eyed ones who looked as pure as freshly fallen snow. On the outside they were all sweetness, but inside... His thoughts skidded to an abrupt halt despite his best efforts to think badly of Christy.

He couldn't compare Becca with Taylor's sister. The two women had little, if anything, in common. Becca was a con artist. Christy wouldn't know how to deceive anyone.

But she had.

She'd deceived him.

Once more he rubbed his hand down his face. Had she really? Hadn't she said there was something she needed to tell him? He'd stood in Russ's kitchen, looked into her beautiful eyes and had seen for himself the turmoil inside her. He'd been unable to grasp what was troubling her.

But right now all Cody could think about was himself. For the first time in years he'd been able to feel again. For the first time in years he'd been whole.

The only thing he felt now was an ache that cut far deeper than anything he'd known before. His feelings for Christy had been a cruel joke.

"You don't honestly expect Cody's going to come, do you?" Taylor asked as Christy sprayed her carefully styled hair. She'd spent the past half hour fussing with her makeup and hair, hoping that if she looked her best, it would lend her confidence.

"No. But I want to be ready in case he does."

"You've been restless all day," her sister said.

"I know. I can't help it. Oh, Taylor, I can't bear to let things end this way between Cody and me. Everything felt so…so right with us."

"It's hard, isn't it?"

She nodded, fighting the need to rush to him and make him understand. "His eyes were so cold. I didn't know anyone could look so…" She couldn't think of a word strong enough to describe her fears.

For much of the night she'd wrestled with the sheets and blankets, trying to find a comfortable position. Once she did and closed her eyes, the disdainful look on Cody's face would pop into her mind. Her eyes would fly open, and the need to explain to him would dominate her thoughts again.

She'd spent most of the night composing what she was going to say. All day she'd been mentally rehearsing it so when the time came she'd be ready.

But she didn't feel ready now. She felt uneasy and scared, as if nothing she could say or do would make a difference.

"If he doesn't come, what do you plan to do?"

"Go to him," Christy said firmly. "He made a date, and he's going to keep it whether he wants to or not."

A quick smile flashed from Taylor's eyes, and her lips quivered with the effort to suppress it. "I see."

"I mean it. If Cody isn't man enough to give me a chance to explain, then he deserves what he's going to get."

"And what's that?"

"I haven't decided yet, but I'll think of something."

"Yes, I'm sure you will," Taylor said on her way out of the bathroom.

Once she was finished, Christy joined her sister, who was busy with dinner preparations. "Let me help," she insisted, feeling guilty that Taylor was stuck with the cooking. The very reason Christy was in Montana was to help with the household chores while Taylor recuperated.

"Don't be silly. I'm perfectly fine. Besides, you might mess up your makeup." Leaning against the counter, Taylor surveyed Christy's attire. "Personally I'm betting Cody's not going to be able to take his eyes off you."

"Oh, Taylor, do you really think so?" Looking her best was important to Christy. If Cody was going to slam the door in her face, which was a distinct possibility, then she wanted him to know what he was missing.

"There's something different about you," Taylor went

on to say, her expression somber. She crossed her arms and cocked her head to one side.

"You mean the eyeliner. I'm using a different shade."

"No, this doesn't have anything to do with eyeliner. You're not the same Christy I left when I moved away from Seattle."

"I'm older," Christy said, "and hopefully more mature."

Taylor paused to consider that. "I suppose that's part of it, but there's more."

"Oh?"

"You were always the 'good daughter.'"

"You make it sound like you were the bad one, and that isn't the least bit true."

"But we both know I love an argument," Taylor said, "and Dad was always willing to comply. We were so often at odds."

"But you and Dad loved and respected each other. It wasn't like some families."

"I know. It's just that we're so different. About the worst thing I can remember you doing was running around the house with a pair of scissors in your hand."

"I did go swimming in the community pool without a bathing cap that one time, remember?"

"Ah, yes, I'd forgotten about that. You renegade!"

They laughed. Taylor was right; Christy had never caused a problem, never been in trouble. The good daughter. Too good, in some ways.

"You realize Mom and Dad are going to be disappointed when they find out you aren't going to marry James."

"Probably more disappointed than James," Christy joked.

Taylor frowned slightly. "Are you sure you're doing the right thing?"

The question was unexpected. "Of course. Very soon after I met Cody, I knew I should never have agreed to marry James. I..."

"Then why did you?"

"Well...because we're friends and we'd been working together a lot, and it just seemed...like a good idea."

"Your decision had nothing to do with Mom and Dad?"

"I...ah..."

"I don't mean to pressure you or sound like a know-it-all, but if you check your motives, I think you might discover that you accepted James's proposal for all the wrong reasons. It suited Mom and Dad for you to marry him, and you went along with it because you were trying to please them. Am I right?"

"I..." Christy lowered her eyes as a tingling extended from her stomach to her arms and down her fingers. She loved her parents so much and wanted to make them proud of her. Her marrying James would certainly have done that. Christy had been so concerned about doing what her parents thought was right that she'd never considered if it was best for her.

"Christy?"

"You make me sound so weak, so insecure."

"You're not. You're loving and gentle and good. James is a fine young man, but he's not the one for you."

Without question her parents would be upset with her, but in time they'd realize she was doing what was best for both her and James.

Christy left the Lazy P soon afterward, not waiting to see if Cody was going to come for her or not. From the way he'd left the evening before, she suspected he had no intention of keeping their dinner date.

She found his place without a problem and parked her

car. She took several minutes to compose herself before making her way to the front door.

An eternity passed before he answered her knock. "Christy?"

"I believe we have a dinner date," she said boldly, damning her voice for shaking. She didn't want him to guess how terribly nervous this confrontation made her.

"A dinner date? You and me? Forget it, sweetheart. If you want to go out, call your fiancé."

Six

"I'm not going to marry James," Christy explained in a voice that demanded Cody listen to her and at the same time begged for his understanding. Cody wasn't in the mood to do either. From the moment he'd left Christy the night before, he'd fought to push every thought of her from his mind.

With very little success.

"Who you marry or don't marry is none of my business," he said, his words sharp and abrupt.

Christy flinched at his disdain, and it was all Cody could do to keep from reaching for her and asking her forgiveness.

"Please, if you'd give me a chance to explain...."

She was so beautiful, with her cobalt-blue eyes and sweet, innocent face. Until he'd met Christy and Taylor, Cody had never seen eyes that precise shade of blue.

He groaned inwardly, struggling against the need to take her in his arms and bask in her softness. Equally strong was the instinctive urge to protect his heart and his orderly life from the havoc she was sure to bring.

Cody was the sheriff-elect, but there was little that could terrify him the way this woman did. It was essential to keep his eyes off her. Everything about her was sensual and provocative. It was difficult enough to fight her, but the battle grew even fiercer as he struggled with his own desires. This was much harder than he'd ever imagined it would be.

"At least talk to me."

Her voice was soft and compelling. The mere sound could drive him straight through the bounds of what was fast becoming his limited self-control.

"I think you should leave."

There, he'd said it. He didn't mean it, but he'd said it, and that little bit of resistance lent him a sense of control, which had been sadly lacking to this point. Christy wasn't aware of that, but he was.

"I'm not leaving until you've listened to me."

"Then you're going to have to do your talking from the street." It astonished him how forcefully he came across. He blocked the doorway as he leaned indolently against the jamb, trying his best to suggest that he hadn't a care in the world.

She hesitated, then surprised him by nodding. "Fine. If that's what it takes, I'll shout at you from the middle of the street, loud enough for the entire block to hear."

"You're wasting your time." He'd played these games with another woman once, and he wasn't about to fall into that trap a second time.

Feeling suddenly confident, he straightened, leaned forward and braced his hands against her shoulders, keeping her at arm's length. It was a risk to touch her, but one he was prepared to take. Perhaps he felt the need to convince himself that he could be close to her and not want to kiss her....

His plan backfired the instant she looked directly up at him. To complicate matters, she flattened her hands on his chest. His heart reacted immediately, and he was sure she could feel the effect she had on him. Maybe touching her wasn't such a smart move, after all.

"I meant what I said." He narrowed his eyes, hoping she'd take the hint and leave. In the same breath he prayed she wouldn't.

"You have every right to be angry," Christy continued, her eyes pleading with him. "I don't blame you. I intended to tell you about James and me. Remember when we were in the kitchen before dinner? I told you there was something I had to talk to you about."

She didn't give him a chance to answer. Not that it mattered; he did remember, all too well.

"It was never my intention to mislead you. I would've explained everything except James phoned before I had the chance."

Cody felt himself weakening. This wasn't supposed to be happening. He should be a tower of strength. A bastion of fortitude. With little more than a shrug of his shoulders he ought to send her packing. One woman had mercilessly used him before. Only an idiot would allow it to happen again.

"I realized the first time you kissed me that I could never marry James," she persisted. "Maybe even before then. I know it should've been a simple decision, but it wasn't. I had to think everything through. The answer was so obvious, so clear—but it frightened me."

She was frightened! Cody was shaking in his boots!

He dropped his hands; touching her had been a tactical error.

"So you've broken it off?" he asked, hating the way his hopes rose at the possibility that she was free.

Christy dropped her eyes. "Not exactly. But I promise you I will the minute I get back to Seattle."

Cody's blood turned to ice. So she intended to string him along. At least she was honest about it, but frankly that didn't count for much.

"I know it sounds bad," she said softly. "You might think it'd be better if I told James now. I thought so myself, but then I realized it wouldn't be right. James doesn't deserve to be treated so heartlessly. He's a good man— it would be wrong to call him and just tell him I'd met someone else. It's cruel to do it over the phone."

Cody snorted a soft laugh. She was a candidate for the loony bin if she expected him to buy into that. Either she was engaged to James or she wasn't. Either the wedding was on or it was off. As simple as that.

"All right," she said, and he could see her fighting to hold on to her composure. "If you can't accept that, I'll phone James and talk to him right now."

"Fine." He led her into the house and didn't stop until he reached the kitchen phone. Feeling slightly cocky, he lifted the receiver and handed it to her, fully expecting her not to go through with the call. She was putting on a brave front, but he was sure she had no intention of following through.

She stared at the receiver for a moment before taking it out of his hand. When she did, Cody saw how deathly pale she'd gone.

She offered him a quick, reassuring smile. "You're right," she said weakly. "I shouldn't be thinking about James's feelings at a time like this. You have feelings, too. It's probably best to get this over with now. James will understand. I know he will." As if her fingers weighed a thousand pounds, she lifted her hand and slowly punched out a series of numbers, then closed her eyes as she waited. "He's probably still at the office."

After what seemed like an inordinate amount of time,

and a short conversation with the receptionist, Christy replaced the receiver. "James already left. He must be home by now. I'll try there—only…" She looked up at him, her eyes wide and full of tension. She was willing to do this because Cody demanded it of her, but it was so hard. To know she was humiliating *James,* causing him pain…

"Only what?" he prompted.

"Could you kiss me? I seem to need it right now."

His mouth found hers even before she'd finished speaking. He'd planned to brush his lips gently across hers. This wasn't the time for anything more.

To be on the safe side, he kissed her again—just so he'd know for a fact that he could walk away from her in the blink of an eye.

That was Cody's second tactical error of the evening.

She tasted like heaven, sweet and warm. His mouth continued to move over hers until her lips parted. She sighed deeply and sagged against him. Then she buried her face in the curve of his neck. Her breathing was as hard and uneven as his own. His hands were splayed across her back, and he held on to her with what little strength he'd managed to reserve.

"Give me a moment and I'll phone James at his house," she whispered, her voice raspy.

Cody framed her face in his hands. "No," he whispered.

"No?"

"I'm not happy with the situation, but you're right. Breaking the engagement by phone would be insensitive. I can wait until you get back to Seattle and talk to him face-to-face."

She lowered her eyes in gratitude, her thick lashes sweeping her cheek. "Thank you."

He nodded.

"Oh, Cody, please believe me, I'm going to end it. I'm being as completely honest as I can."

"I know."

"You do?"

He nodded. He wrapped his arms around her and rested his chin on her head. "I don't know where that leaves us," he said. "Or even where we go from here."

"I don't, either," Christy whispered, but he felt her sigh of contentment as she relaxed against him.

"You're as jumpy as a grasshopper," Russ teased three days later. "I swear you keep looking out that window as though you expect the Mounted Police to come riding over the hill."

"Not the Mounted Police, just one handsome sheriff."

"Ah, so you're seeing Cody again."

"I've seen him every night this week." Christy could feel herself blush as she said it, which was exactly the reaction her brother-in-law was looking for.

"Quit teasing my sister," Taylor said. She was sitting at the kitchen table, Eric nestled in her arms, nursing greedily.

Every time Christy watched her sister with the baby, she felt astonished at how easily Taylor had taken to motherhood. She acted as though she'd been around infants all her life. She seemed so comfortable, so *confident* with her son, whether she was breast-feeding him or diapering or rocking him to sleep.

"Where's Cody taking you this afternoon?" Taylor asked, glancing up at her.

"He wouldn't say. It's supposed to be a surprise, but I have a sneaking suspicion we're headed into the wild blue yonder." At her sister's raised eyebrows, she explained. "I think he's planning to take me for a plane ride. He told me earlier that he has his private license and twice now he's mentioned flying."

"I thought you were afraid of planes," Taylor commented. When it was first decided that Christy would come to Montana, she'd immediately rejected the idea of flying into Miles City. Driving to Montana appealed to her far more. Neither Taylor nor their mother had pressed the issue.

"I'm not excited about flying," Christy admitted.

"But you don't mind going up in a plane with Cody?"

"No." She trusted him beyond question. Enough to place her life in his hands.

"If I were you, I'd make sure his little surprise doesn't involve horses," Russ warned, and his eyes connected with his wife's as though they were sharing some well-kept secret.

"Cody doesn't ride that often."

Russ poured himself a cup of coffee and joined Taylor at the kitchen table. He smiled at his son while speaking to Christy. "You certainly seem to know a great deal about the sheriff's habits."

"I…" Christy could feel warmth invade her cheeks. She hated the way she blushed whenever the subject of Cody was introduced.

She and Cody had spent every available moment together. With her vacation vanishing like melting snow, each day was more precious than the one before. It was as if they were cramming several months of a relationship into two short weeks.

Cody wasn't pleased that she remained technically engaged to James, but he'd graciously accepted the situation. It wasn't easy for him, but he never questioned her about the other man, or brought James into their conversation.

For his part, Cody had never said anything to Christy about Becca and the way he'd been duped by the other woman. Knowing what she did made her more sensitive to his needs, made her love him all the more.

Christy did love Cody. This wasn't infatuation or hormones or anything else. For some reason, unknown to them both, they were meant to be together. She knew it. He knew it. Yet Christy never spoke of her feelings, and neither did Cody.

She understood his hesitancy. He couldn't talk freely about their relationship while James was still part of her life.

Once she was back in Seattle and had broken the engagement to James, then and only then would she tell Cody she loved him. And he in turn would be free to tell her what she already knew.

Christy would've liked to hear it sooner, but if Cody could display this much patience, she could do no less.

"I don't know when we'll be back," Christy said. "Is there anything I can do for you before I leave?" she asked, looking at Taylor.

Her sister grinned. "Just have a good time."

"I will." She was already having the time of her life.

"I was in town earlier today," Russ said. He paused to be sure he had their full attention.

"So? You go into town at least twice a week," Taylor reminded him.

"Noah Williams, who works at the insurance agency, stopped me." Once more he hesitated as if this news was significant.

"Old Man Williams stops anybody who'll listen to him," Taylor interjected. "That man is the biggest gossip in three counties, and you know it."

Russ rubbed the side of his jaw. "Yeah, I suppose I do."

"Would you say what's on your mind and be done with it?" Taylor grumbled.

Russ chuckled. "All right. Noah claimed he'd heard that the sheriff's about to take a wife. A pretty one, too. He said word has it she's a relative of mine."

"Oh?" Christy asked, willingly playing into his hands. "And did this relative of yours have a name?"

Christy remembered Cody introducing her to the town's sole insurance agent. He'd also told her that Noah Williams was well acquainted with most folks' business, whether they were his clients or not.

"Said he didn't recall the name, but he thought it was something like Cathy or Christine. Or Christabel."

"Funny. Very funny," Christy muttered, looking out the window, hoping to see Cody's truck.

"I'm telling you right now," Russ said, chuckling again, "the secret's out. The sheriff's gonna take himself a wife."

The next afternoon, Christy was lying on her back in a meadow not far from the ranch house, chewing on a long blade of grass. Cody had taken her flying the previous day, just as she'd guessed, and the experience had been exhilarating, not frightening at all. He lay beside her now, staring at the darkening sky. A series of clouds was rolling in, obliterating the sun, but they'd both decided to ignore the threat of rain.

"Looks like there's a storm coming," Cody said.

"Let it. I don't mind, do you?"

"That depends." He rolled onto his stomach and leaned on his elbows as he gazed lovingly down at her. He didn't seem any more eager to leave the site of their picnic than Christy.

The afternoon had been ideal. Cody had arrived at the

house early in the day, and Christy had met him with a basket full of goodies. Russ complained that she was taking enough food to feed a small army...of ants.

"Depends on what?" she asked, smiling up at him.

"On who I'm with." As if he couldn't stop himself, he leaned over her and pressed his mouth to hers. Then his lips moved along the side of her face and into her hair. He paused and went still as he breathed in the scent of the cologne she'd dabbed behind her ears.

Other than the few kisses they'd exchanged over the past days, Cody hadn't touched her. It wasn't that he didn't desire her, didn't need her. But he held himself back—held himself in check.

Christy understood and in many ways approved.

The physical attraction between them was more powerful than either had ever experienced. It wasn't something to be trifled with.

He kissed her again lightly, softly, gently.

Christy slid her hands up his chest and put her arms around his neck. He kissed her again, his breath hot and quick. "We should stop now," he warned but made no effort to move away from her.

"Yes, I know," she concurred.

He brushed his thumb back and forth over her moist lips as if gathering the needed resolve to pull away from her. She gazed up into his dark, troubled eyes and saw his hesitation. His hands were trembling as he started to roll away from her.

"No." Her cry was instinctive. Urgent.

"Christy..."

"Shh." She sank her fingers into his hair at the sides of his lean, rugged face, raised her head from the soft patch of grass and touched her mouth to his.

His hands tangled with her short curls as he moved

the upper half of his body over hers, anchoring her to the ground. Their frenzied kissing seemed to go on and on.

"Enough," he said breathlessly. "We have to stop."

Christy wanted him so desperately; the hunger to love him all but consumed her, and she moved fitfully beneath him.

"Christy," he said, "we're headed for trouble if we don't stop...*now*."

"I thought sheriffs were trained to deal with any kind of trouble." Her tongue outlined his mouth even as she spoke.

Cody moaned.

Christy sighed.

There didn't seem to be anything strong enough in this world or the next to pull them apart. Christy felt as if she'd been created for this man, for this moment. The love between them was as inevitable as the setting sun. As natural as the ocean waves caressing the shore or the wind stirring the trees. Her blood seemed to vibrate in sympathy, a vibration that grew more insistent—until she realized something was amiss. It wasn't her blood that was pounding in her veins, but rain that was pounding the earth. The clouds burst over them, drenching Christy within seconds.

Cody brought his hands to her face, framing it as he slowly raised his head. His eyes sought hers.

"Cody, it's pouring!"

He responded by kissing her again. "You taste too sweet to move."

"You're getting soaked."

"So are you." He grinned. "And I don't mind if you don't."

"I don't."

"Good." Once more his mouth connected with hers.

A moment later, Christy leaned against him. "We... almost made love."

"I promised myself we wouldn't," he whispered. "And this is a promise I mean to keep." His hands closed around her upper arms. "Understand?"

Christy nodded.

"I mean it, Christy."

"Yes, sir." She teased him with a salute.

Deftly he reversed their positions, smoothly rolling over and taking her with him so she was poised above him. She straddled his hips and arched her head back as the rain pummeled her face. Brushing away her hair, she smiled at the dark, angry sky.

"I suppose I should be grateful," Cody murmured.

"For the rain? Why?"

"You know why."

"Yes," she whispered, "but in some ways I wish..." She let the rest fade, because they were aware of what would have happened if Mother Nature hadn't intervened when she did.

Seven

"You're *sure* you want to babysit?" Taylor asked, as though she expected Christy to change her mind.

"You're going," Christy said, ushering her older sister to the kitchen where Russ was waiting impatiently. It was the first time Taylor had left Eric, and she was having second thoughts.

"This night is for you and Russ."

"I know but—"

"I have the phone number to the restaurant, the home nurse, the doctor and the hospital. If anything the least bit out of the ordinary occurs, I'll phone someone, so quit worrying."

"Eric's never had a bottle," Taylor protested.

"It's still Mama's milk. He's a smart baby. He'll adjust." After Taylor had spent a long—and hilarious—afternoon learning how to operate the breast pump, each ounce was more precious than gold.

"Christy, I'm not convinced this is such a good idea, after all."

"Don't be ridiculous. Eric will probably sleep the entire time you're away."

"Are you going to let me take you to dinner or not?"

Russ's voice boomed from the kitchen. "I'd like to remind you the reservation is for six." After a hard day on the ranch, Russ got too hungry to wait much beyond that for the evening meal.

Cody was the one who'd come up with the idea of the two of them babysitting Eric while Russ and Taylor took an evening for themselves. It was Christy's last night in Cougar Point. First thing in the morning she'd start the long drive across three states. Although she'd been gone less than two weeks, it felt as if an entire lifetime had passed.

"Cody's here," Russ called out. "Just how long does it take you women to put on a little war paint, anyway?" His voice lowered, and Christy could hear him conversing with the sheriff. Her brother-in-law was saying that Taylor and Christy were the two most beautiful women in the county as it was. He contended that they didn't need makeup, and he was having a heck of a time understanding why they bothered with it.

"Hold your horses," Taylor cried, poking her head out the bathroom door and calling down the hallway into the kitchen. "I'll only be a minute."

"Famous last words if I ever heard 'em," Russ grumbled.

As it turned out, her brother-in-law was right. Taylor spent an extra five minutes fussing with her hair and adding a dash of perfume to her wrists. When she'd finished, she checked Eric, gave Christy and Cody a long list of instructions, then reluctantly left the house with her husband.

Cody brought his arm around Christy as they stood on the back porch, watching Russ hold open the car door for Taylor. Christy smiled when Russ stole a lengthy kiss.

"Well," Cody said after Russ had pulled out of the yard, "they're off."

"I don't think they'll win any races."

"No," he chuckled, "I doubt they will." He turned her into his arms and kissed her softly.

"Oh, honestly," Mandy said, scooting past them and down the porch steps. "You two are as bad as Russ and Taylor. If it was me doing these PDAs, you can bet I'd be in big trouble. It seems to me that people over twenty-one get away with a whole lot more than they should."

"PDAs?" Christy asked. "What's that?"

"Public Displays of Affection," Cody whispered close to her ear. As if the temptation were too strong to resist, he caught her lobe between his teeth.

"Cody," she cried, "behave yourself."

"Hey, where are you going?" Cody demanded when Mandy started toward the barn. "I thought you were planning to stick around and chaperone the two of us."

"I'm going to the movies."

"In the barn?"

"Don't be cute with me, Cody Franklin. Just because you've been elected sheriff doesn't mean you can control *my* life."

"You're not the one I want to get cute with."

"Obviously. I figured you two would appreciate a little privacy. Billy Joe's driving me over to Melissa's, and I'm going to the movies with her. She got her license last week."

"I heard rumors along those lines," Cody said with a grin.

"Just don't go sending Bud or any of the other deputies out to tail us." Mandy wagged an accusing finger in Cody's direction. "I know you'd do it, too. Melissa's still a little nervous, and the last thing she needs is a sheriff's car following her into town."

"You think I'd radio for someone to follow her?" Cody sounded aghast that Mandy would even hint at something so dastardly.

"You'd do it if you thought you could." But she was smiling as she spoke.

Billy Joe, Russ's ranch foreman, stepped out from the barn, freshly shaved. His hair was wet and combed down against the sides of his head. "You ready?"

"Yup," Mandy said, walking toward his battered red pickup.

Taylor had explained that the foreman was interested in Melissa's widowed mother and had been seeing her for the past few months. Apparently Mandy and Melissa were working together to stage an evening alone for the two adults.

Eric wailed loudly, and after bidding Mandy farewell, Christy hurried inside the house and into the master bedroom. Eric was lying in the bassinet waiting for someone to answer his summons.

"What's the matter, big boy?" she asked, reaching for him. His damp bottom answered that question. "So you wet your diaper, did you?" she chided playfully, giving him her finger, which he gripped fiercely.

"I'll change him," Cody said from behind her.

Christy arched her brows in feigned shock. "This I've got to see."

"I'll have you know I've changed more than one diaper in my lifetime."

"That may be true, but it seems to me you took great delight in teasing Russ when he offered to change Eric."

"I've had more practice than Russ, that's all." Cody took a fresh diaper from the pile of folded ones on the dresser. "Both of my sisters have children, and being the generous uncle I am, I've helped out now and then. It's not nearly as difficult as Russ seems to think."

"All right, since you're so sure of yourself, go ahead and I'll see to our dinner." Carefully she handed Cody the baby, then walked to the kitchen.

Taylor had set a frozen pepperoni pizza on the kitchen counter. The only place in Cougar Point that served pizza was the bowling alley; Taylor could go without a lot of luxuries, but she needed her pizza. Every time she was in Miles City, she bought three or four pepperoni pizzas from a nationwide chain, brought them home and promptly froze them.

"I hope you're in the mood for pizza," Christy called, setting the gauge on the oven to the right temperature.

"You mean Taylor's willing to share one of hers? Without us having to ask?"

"I didn't even have to bribe her."

"I may volunteer to babysit more often," Cody said as he entered the kitchen, holding Eric against his shoulder. His large hand was pressed against the infant's tiny back.

Christy paused when she saw them, and her heart beat so fast, it actually hurt. Cody looked so natural with a baby in his arms. As natural as any father. Turning away in an effort to disguise her emotions, she clasped the counter with both hands and waited for the aching tenderness to pass.

She was engaged to an attorney in Seattle, a good friend she'd known for several years, and not once had she pictured him as a father. The fact that they'd likely have children someday had barely crossed her mind.

Yet here she was with Cody and her nephew, and the sight of this big, rugged man holding this precious child was enough to bring tears to her eyes.

"Christy, could you give me…" He hesitated when she didn't immediately respond. "Christy?"

She swallowed the lump in her throat, smeared the tears across her cheek and turned, smiling as brightly as she could. She doubted she'd be able to fool Cody, but she intended to try.

"What's wrong?" His question was filled with concern.

"Nothing…"

"If that's the case, then why are you crying?"

She didn't know how she could explain it, not without sounding as though she required long-term therapy. She was crazy in love with one man, and engaged to another. In a few hours she'd be leaving Cody behind. There were no guarantees, no pledges, no promises between them.

Nothing.

There couldn't be anything while she was engaged to James.

James. Two weeks away from him and she had trouble remembering what he looked like. Inconsequential details occurred to her—that he drank his tea with milk and hadn't worn a pair of jeans since he was thirteen years old. He was endearing, hardworking and brilliant.

And he loved her. At least he thought he did, the same way she'd once assumed she loved him.

The phone rang, startling Eric, who let out a loud wail. Cody whispered reassurances while patting the baby's back.

"I'll get that," Christy said, grateful for the intrusion. "It's probably Taylor calling to check up on us." She hurried into the hallway, wanting to catch the phone before it rang again and frightened Eric a second time.

"Hello," she sang out cheerfully. "This is Palmer's Pizza Parlor. May I take your order?" Taylor would get a kick out of that.

Silence followed.

"It appears I've dialed the wrong number," a male voice said stiffly.

"James? Oh, dear... I thought it was Taylor. This is Christy."

Cody heard Christy's laughter end two seconds after she answered the phone. He knew almost immediately that the man on the other end of the line was her fiancé.

Cody was instantly overwhelmed by confusion and an equally large dose of good old-fashioned jealousy. He was so resentful of Christy's engagement that a long painful moment passed before he could clear his head. He'd never been the jealous type, and now he was all but blinded by it.

He shouldn't have been surprised that James—he had trouble thinking about the other man without tightening his jaw—would call Christy. If Cody was the one engaged to her and she was a thousand miles away, he'd phone her, too. Frequently.

That realization, however, was no comfort. Before many more hours passed, Christy would be leaving Cougar Point. In another two days she'd be back with James. Her weeks with him in Montana would be little more than a fading memory.

Cody wasn't willing to kid himself any longer. There was no use trying to hide from it, or deny it or ignore it. He was in love with Christy Manning. He'd pledged a thousand times that he'd never allow this foolish emotion to take hold of his life again. So much for all the promises he'd made himself. So much for protecting his heart.

Dammit all, he was in love!

But Cody was realistic enough to put their relationship in the proper perspective. Or at least try. Christy was engaged to a hotshot Seattle attorney. He, on the other hand, was a backwoods sheriff. Christy might be infatuated with him now, but once she returned to the big city that could easily change. Believing these few days together meant more to her could be dangerous.

She was going to break the engagement. Or so she claimed. But now something was troubling her. Cody had sensed it when she was fussing with the pizza. When he'd first arrived, she'd been her usual warm, happy self. She'd joked with him as though she hadn't a care in the world.

Cody frowned. Since the afternoon of their picnic when they'd gotten caught in the downpour, Cody had noticed subtle changes in her. She seemed more spontaneous, more open with him.

He was willing to admit there'd been numerous intricate transformations in their relationship over the past ten days. They'd spent hours together, getting to know each other, growing to love each other.

And for most of that time, Cody had to struggle to keep his hands off her.

He found himself studying her at every opportunity, and whenever he did he liked what he saw. She captivated him. When they were alone together, he'd learned how dangerous it was to kiss her—and how difficult it was to stop. She'd press her soft body against his, and it was a test by fire of his limited control.

In the distance Cody heard the anxiety in her voice as her phone conversation with the other man continued. Not wanting to listen in, Cody opened the screen door and walked outside, carrying the baby. He sat on the top step and let his gaze wander across the acres of prime pastureland.

"See all those pesky cattle, Eric?" he whispered to the baby held securely against his shoulder. "It'll all belong to you someday. Take some advice, though, boy…" He was about to tell Russ's son not to get involved with women because all they did was cause a man grief.

But he stopped himself. Christy hadn't caused him grief or trouble. If anything, she'd brought him the truest joy he'd ever felt. He hadn't realized how lonely he was. Nor had he known how isolated his life had become until she'd walked into it, bold as could be.

Okay, he mused, sighing deeply. He was in love. It wasn't supposed to happen, but it had. Damned if he knew what to do next. For a man in his thirties he'd had precious little experience with it. The one other time he'd committed his heart to a woman, it had cost him dearly. He hadn't been willing to place himself at risk again. Not until he met Christy.

Fifteen minutes passed before Christy finally joined him. He heard her moving behind him in the kitchen and felt the swish of the screen door as it opened.

"That was James," she said as she sat down on the step beside him.

"I heard." He didn't mean to be, but he sounded flippant, uncaring.

"He…he's called two other times."

"That's none of my business," he informed her curtly.

"I know, but I want to be honest with you. Are you angry?"

"No."

"You sound angry."

"I'm not." And pigs fly, he told himself.

For a long moment Christy didn't say anything. She sat there looking like an angel, smelling like something out of a rose garden. How was a man supposed to resist her when she gazed at him with those large blue eyes of hers?

"I…almost told him about you. It was on the tip of my

tongue to try to explain. But James seemed so preoccupied. He was visiting my parents, and I spoke to them, too, and…" She shrugged. "It was impossible."

"Why's that?" He made a determined effort to take the starch out of his voice.

She hesitated before answering. "My mom and dad like James a lot."

"I'm sure he's perfect son-in-law material."

Christy ignored that comment, which was probably best. He knew he wasn't dealing with this situation well. In fact, he was making a real jackass of himself.

"Now…now that I've had these two weeks with you, I think I accepted his proposal more to please my parents than because I was in love with James."

"I see." Several questions popped into his mind. Christy was a kind person, affectionate and empathetic, someone who tried to please others. Her parents, James, *him*.

"They like Russ, too," she hurried to add.

Cody didn't know what that proved, and frankly he wasn't in the frame of mind to ask.

"Or at least they do now. At first—" She stopped abruptly, as if she'd already said too much.

Cody didn't doubt that the week to come, when she confronted James and her family, would be one of the most difficult of her life. If she went through with it, if she decided to break off the engagement, after all.

"I…can't bear for us to spend our last night together arguing," she whispered.

Cody forced himself to relax. He couldn't bear it, either. He lifted his free arm and placed it around her shoulders, drawing her closer to him and Eric. She turned and smiled shyly up at him. With unhurried ease he lowered his head until their mouths met. The kiss was long and slow and when he raised his head, Cody felt dizzy with yearning.

"Oh, Cody," she moaned, her fingers clutching his shirt collar, her eyes closed. "I hate to leave you."

He hated it, too, feared it more than he'd feared anything. He dreaded the moment she'd drive away from him.

Fear and dread. Fighting those emotions wasn't how he wanted to spend their last hours together.

"Are you sure you haven't forgotten anything?" Taylor asked for the tenth time. They stood beside Christy's car, Taylor in her housecoat, Christy in her traveling clothes—a comfortable pair of faded jeans and a long-sleeved T-shirt.

"I'm positive I've got everything." She'd checked the house twice, and even if she'd inadvertently left something behind, she'd be back. Soon, she hoped. As soon as she could clear up the situation with James. As soon as she was free.

Taylor hugged her, and Russ stepped forward, holding Eric. He placed his free arm around Christy and squeezed tight.

"Drive carefully," Taylor said, "and phone the minute you arrive in Seattle. You know I'll worry until I hear from you." Tears brimmed from her sister's eyes as she reached for Christy one last time. "I really hate to see you go."

"I'll phone," Christy promised. As for the part about hating to leave, that went without saying.

"Where's Cody?" Russ asked, frowning.

"He's got the day shift," Christy explained. Although she'd spent until the wee hours of the morning saying goodbye to the sheriff, she half expected Cody to come barreling down the driveway before she headed out.

"Be a good little baby," she whispered to Eric, kissing his brow. "Remember your aunt Christy." With no more reason to delay, she opened her car door and climbed inside.

As she was driving toward the road, Christy looked in the rearview mirror and caught sight of Taylor slipping her arm around her husband's waist. She rested her head on his broad chest and leaned against him, as though she needed his strength, his support.

The scene was a touching one, and Christy found herself blinking back tears.

She was still sniffling as she headed for the highway that would connect her with the interstate. It would be a straight shot to Seattle after that.

Christy planned to make the best time she could. The sooner she got home, the sooner she could set her life in order.

Reaching across the seat, she located the thermos of coffee Taylor had insisted she take with her. Holding it between her legs, she struggled to unscrew the cap. It was difficult to do with one hand. She'd just about given up when a flashing blue and red light was reflected in her rearview mirror.

Cody.

Christy eased to the side of the road, turned off the engine and threw open the door. It was impossible to hold her emotions at bay a moment longer.

Her gaze was blurred with tears, but it didn't matter. Cody had come to her.

By the time she'd climbed out of her car, he was out of his. Not waiting for an invitation, she rushed toward him, sobbing, so grateful he'd come.

He caught her, encircling her waist with his arms and lifting her from the ground. His lips found hers, their mouths connecting with such force that it threw her head back. Christy didn't mind; she was as needy as Cody. As hungry. As lost.

He continued to kiss her, saying with his body what he couldn't with words. That he loved her, needed her and was desperately afraid of losing her.

Christy understood and responded to each doubt.

"There's a side road about two miles back. Do you know where I mean?"

She nodded, remembered having driven past it minutes earlier.

"Meet me there?"

"Yes."

By the time she climbed back into her car, Christy was trembling from the inside out. Her stomach felt tight, and her heart was pounding. Cody made a U-turn and led the way. Christy followed willingly.

He pulled onto the dirt road, stirring up layers of fine dust, partially obliterating his vehicle. He drove past a wide curve, then he parked at the side. Christy watched as he reached for his radio. She got out of her car and waited for him.

"I told dispatch I wouldn't be available for the next fifteen minutes," he explained, his dark eyes holding hers. "I know it's not long enough to say what I want to say, but it's all the time I dare take."

Christy nodded.

He brushed his fingertips over her damp cheek. "You've been crying."

"I…couldn't get the thermos open."

"That's why?" he asked softly.

"No, of course it's not. I don't want to go. Oh, Cody,

it's so much harder to leave you than I th~~~ 30
be." She tried unsuccessfully to swallow a ~~~ bac

"Don't cry," Cody pleaded. He held her a~~~
chest and lowered his head. When he kissed he~~~
with desperation and urgency, his mouth slanting over
hers. She clung to him, giving as much as she took.

He kissed her neck, nuzzled it. Christy let her head
fall back, allowing him to do whatever he wished. She
was his for this moment, this hour, this day.

His warm mouth skimmed the length of her throat,
planting moist kisses along her shoulder blade…then
lower, much lower.

Slowly, as if he was calling upon all the self-control he
possessed, Cody raised his head. "Letting you go is the
hardest thing I've ever done," he whispered. He smoothed
the hair away from her face and kissed her again.

A well-modulated voice came over the radio of the patrol car, reminding them both who and what Cody was.
A man who'd pledged to serve and protect. As much as
he would've liked to stay with her, the time had come for
them to return to their separate lives.

"I'll follow you to the county line," he told her. He held
open her car door, looking very much like the dignified
sheriff he was. There was little evidence of the loving
interlude that had passed between them.

A nod was all Christy could manage. She slid into the
driver's seat. Her hand closed around the key. Cody held
on to her door, his eyes trained directly ahead.

"I guess this is goodbye," she said hoarsely. "At least
for now."

He nodded. "For now. You'll drive carefully?"

"Of course."

Again he nodded, closed her door and then stepped

.. He seemed about to say something else, but then langed his mind.

Christy waited for him to enter his patrol car before starting her engine. She sent him a smile and glanced in her rearview mirror as she entered the main road.

True to his word, Cody followed her for several miles. In the distance she read the sign that stated she was leaving Custer County. An immediate knot formed in her throat, making it difficult to swallow.

Her rearview mirror showed Cody's red and blue lights flashing. She pulled over and stopped. Cody eased the patrol car in behind her.

He was out of his vehicle before she had a chance to free her seat belt. Lowering her window, she looked at him expectantly.

"One last thing before you go." His voice was deep and gravelly. "I love you, Christy. Come back to me."

Eight

"James," Christy said quietly, "you know I consider you one of my dearest friends. I've always heard good friends make the best husbands…no," she mumbled, her hands tightening around the steering wheel. "That doesn't sound right. Think, Christy, think!"

She'd just crossed the Idaho-Washington border and was within six hours of Seattle and home. Every mile, every minute, led her closer to the confrontation with James and her parents.

For the past two days Christy had carefully rehearsed what she planned to say, outlining her speech, inordinately conscious of each word.

James would be devastated, her parents shocked.

When it came right down to it, Christy was more worried about confronting her parents than she was James, especially her father, whom she adored. Eric Manning always seemed to think he knew what was best for her; for the most part, Christy had agreed with him. And he'd decided James would be the perfect husband for his youngest daughter.

The hours sped past, far too quickly to suit Christy. As she approached the outskirts of Seattle she found that she was traveling well below the speed limit, which produced several heated stares from her fellow travelers.

Once she'd arrived at her apartment building and had unloaded her car, Christy paced her living room restlessly. She'd assumed that once she was surrounded by everything that was familiar, some of the uneasiness would leave her.

It didn't. In fact, she was more agitated now than ever.

Gathering her courage, she decided to call her family and deal with them first. She planned to ask if it was convenient for her to come over, hoping it would be. The she could quickly put an end to this madness.

Once she was alone with her parents, she'd tell them she intended to break her engagement. Her argument was prepared, her decision unshakable.

Her first choice would've been to do it over the phone, but that would be the cowardly way out. Her only option was to confront them together. Once that was finished she'd go and see James.

As she reached for her phone, her stomach tensed. She wasn't sure what to expect from her parents or James and tried not to dwell on how they'd react to her news. She closed her eyes and prayed someone would answer before she lost her courage and hung up the phone.

"Hello."

"Jason?" He was her second-oldest brother and the handsomest of the lot, or so he liked to claim. At thirty-two he was a "catch," only he enjoyed playing the field far too much to settle down with any one woman.

"Christy? When did you get back?"

"Just a few minutes ago." How odd she sounded. Christy prayed Jason wouldn't notice. "What are you doing there? Are Mom and Dad around?"

"I'm here 'cause I took the day off. Mom and Dad are

out but they'll be back any minute." He paused. "You don't know yet, do you?"

"Know what?" Jason loved playing games, dangling bits of information in front of her like bait, making her hungry for more.

"Never mind."

"Jason, I've been on the road for two days, and to be frank, I'm not up to any of your trick questions." Under normal circumstances Christy would have been amused and played along, but not now.

"Hey, sweetie, no trick questions with this one. All I can say is you have a real surprise waiting for you. Mom's slaved every day since you've been gone, so if I were you, I'd make my presence known soon."

"Thank you so much," Christy muttered sarcastically. "Talking to you is like looking through a telescope with the lens cap on."

"Always happy to oblige," Jason responded with a light chuckle. "Just drop by the house soon.... In fact, the sooner the better."

Christy intended on doing exactly that. "I'll be over in fifteen minutes. By the way, how's Mom?" Breaking her leg had kept Elizabeth Manning at home for several weeks, and Christy knew how terribly disappointed her mother had been about missing this important time with her eldest daughter and newborn grandson.

"Mom's doing great. Especially now..." He didn't finish the enigmatic statement, and Christy refused to fall into his hands by asking what he meant. "If you don't mind, I'll stick around for a while, too. I'd like to get a look at your face once you find out what's been going on around here. Mom's in seventh heaven. At the rate things are going, you're likely to end up in one of those celebrity magazines."

"Cute, Jason, very cute." Christy had no idea what he was talking about, but that was typical of her older brother. Over the last few years, his comments had taken on a biting edge. Christy didn't know what his problem was, but she wished he'd straighten out whatever was wrong.

In an attempt to delay the unavoidable, Christy played back the messages on her answering machine while she leafed through two weeks' worth of mail. Anyone who mattered wouldn't have phoned because they'd know she was out of town, but she couldn't help being curious.

There were several beeps, indicating that whoever had called had hung up before leaving a message. Probably salesmen.

Deciding it was a waste of time, Christy started for her front door when Taylor's voice, hesitant and unsure, came over the tinny speaker. "Christy, call me as soon as you get home. Something's come up that we need to discuss."

There was an uncharacteristic note in her sister's voice, an uncertainty that suggested something was terribly amiss.

Puzzled, Christy returned to the phone and placed a long-distance call to Cougar Point. Mandy answered, sounding as cheerful as ever.

"Taylor's not here," Russ's sister explained. "She drove into Miles City for Eric's first appointment with the pediatrician. Do you want me to have her call you once she gets back? I don't think it'll be too much longer. I know she was anxious to talk to you."

"No. I'm headed to my parents' house now. I'll phone again later." Hopefully by that time everything would be settled. She could contact Taylor and Russ and then talk to Cody. The mere thought of him made her go weak. Seemingly by accident they'd found each other and unexpectedly discovered what it meant to fall in love. Neither of them had been looking for this, neither of them fully understood why it had happened, but it was right. Right for Cody. Right for Christy.

After two long days on the road, she was physically exhausted and mentally depleted. She'd considered delaying this confrontation until she was well-rested and relaxed, but she knew she couldn't do that. The engagement to James hung over her head and she wouldn't find peace until all the obstacles were cleared out of the road that would lead her back to her sheriff.

Her parents' luxury vehicle was in the driveway when Christy drove up. Jason's car was in the street, and Christy parked her own behind his. Even before she'd turned off the engine, her father had opened the front door and was walking toward her, arms outstretched.

Eric Manning embraced his daughter, hugging her tight. From the time she was little Christy had always felt a special closeness to her parents. Most of her friends had rebelled in one way or another against their families, but never Christy. She'd never felt the need.

"When did you get back?" her father asked.

"Not even half an hour ago." She slipped her arm around his thickening waist and they walked toward the sprawling brick house. The lawn was a soft, lush green. Many a happy hour had been spent racing across this very same grass. Echoes of her childhood laughter seemed to mock her now.

Elizabeth Manning stood in the entryway, her left leg encased from her foot to just below her knee in a hot pink cast. She broke into a broad smile as Christy approached the front door.

"Sweetheart, it's so good to have you home."

"It's good to be home, and before you ask, yes, I brought tons of pictures of Eric."

"Oh, that's wonderful, I can't tell you how excited we are that Russ and Taylor named him after your father."

Christy stepped into the house. It was a large home built into a hill overlooking the freeway that cut a wide path through the heart of Seattle. The basement opened onto an enormous, landscaped yard with a profusion of flower beds and space for a vegetable garden, whose bounty spilled over to friends and neighbors every summer.

"How's the leg?"

"Better," Elizabeth said, dismissing her daughter's concern with a quick shake of her head. She was walking with a cane now, leaning heavily upon it. Christy knew her mother well enough to realize Elizabeth Manning would never want to burden her children with the fact that she was in pain. But her mother did look much healthier, Christy mused. The sparkle was back in her eyes, and a flush of excitement glowed from her cheeks. Christy couldn't remember how long it'd been since she'd seen her mother so happy. No doubt the birth of their third grandson was responsible.

"You're looking terrific," Christy said, kissing her mother's cheek.

"Actually, sweetie, we have you to thank for that," her father murmured, sharing an enigmatic smile with his wife.

"Me?" Apparently they were playing the same game as Jason.

"Eric, let's not discuss this in the entryway."

Her father chuckled, and Christy noted that his eyes seemed brighter, too. He certainly was in one of his better moods. Christy would like to think it was all due to her arrival and the fact that she'd brought pictures of their grandson. But somehow she doubted it, especially after having spoken to Jason.

Her second-oldest brother was sitting in the family room in front of the television when Christy walked in. He was wearing a Seattle Mariners baseball cap, which he had on much of the time.

"Welcome home, little sister," he greeted her. He stood and hugged her, then stepped back, wiggling his eyebrows.

"All right, you guys," Christy said, claiming the easy chair next to Jason. "What's going on around here?"

Her father's mouth started to quiver, as though he was having difficulty holding back his excitement. He shared another look with his wife of thirty-five years.

"If you'll recall, your mother's spirits were low after she fell and broke her leg. Missing out on this special time with Taylor and Russ depressed her."

"I didn't even realize how melancholy I'd become until Eric mentioned it," Elizabeth said. "Sometimes I swear he knows me better than I know myself."

Christy felt herself nod.

"Your father's the one who came up with the idea for an engagement party."

"An...engagement party," Christy echoed, coming halfway out of her chair, appalled and dismayed.

Her mother pressed her fingers to her lips, almost giddy with delight. "We knew you'd be pleased."

"I... I..." Christy was at a complete loss for words. Somehow she managed a smile and slumped back into the cushions of the overstuffed chair.

"You can't imagine what fun we've had," Elizabeth continued, her voice animated. "I'm afraid your father got carried away. He insisted we order the best of everything. We've rented the Eagles Hall, got the invitations mailed—engraved ones. Oh, sweetie, I can hardly wait for you to see them. We spent hour after hour with the caterers. I can't even *begin* to tell you what a fabulous time I—we—had planning every detail of this party. I can't help feeling proud of everything we accomplished in such a short time."

"It was just what your mother needed," Christy's father inserted smoothly, looking equally delighted. "Elizabeth's been like a kid again from the moment we decided to go through with this."

"I see." Christy went completely numb. It seemed impossible that no one was aware of it.

"I suppose we're a pair of old fools, but when Taylor married Russ in Reno, your father and I felt cheated out of a large family wedding. We've been looking forward to throwing one for years."

"When?" It was torture getting the word past the tightness that all but blocked her throat.

"That's the crazy part," Jason told her. "Mom and Dad put this entire thing together in two weeks."

Christy still didn't understand; not much of the conversation made sense. Her look must have conveyed her confusion.

"The party's tomorrow night," Elizabeth said, her face radiating her excitement.

"Tomorrow night?"

"I know it sounds crazy, and we took a chance booking it so close to the end of your vacation, but there were only a few dates available at the Eagles Hall, and it was either tomorrow night or three months from now."

"In fact, the only reason we were able to get the hall is because of a last-minute cancellation," Eric said. "I had no idea we'd need to book this sort of thing so far in advance."

"James?" No one seemed to notice she was having trouble speaking, which Christy supposed was a blessing of sorts.

"He knows, of course, but we decided to keep it a secret for you. A welcome-home surprise."

Christy nodded, hating the way she continued to sit in her parents' home, saying nothing when it felt as if the foundations of her world were crumbling at her feet. Her mother and father and Jason were all looking at her, waiting for some response, but for the life of her, Christy couldn't give them one.

Her eyes met with her brother's.

He winked broadly. "Mom and Dad are sparing no expense. If the wedding's half as elaborate as the engagement party, then your big day's going to be spectacular."

Eric Manning chuckled. "It isn't every father who has a daughter as special as Christy."

Christy forced a smile although she longed to stand up and beg them to put an end to this craziness. She didn't love James. She loved Cody. She couldn't possibly go through with an engagement to a man she didn't intend to marry.

She glanced from her mother to her father, both of them staring at her with bright, eager smiles, as though waiting for her to burst into a song of praise for their efforts.

"I… I…" The words froze on her lips.

"Honey, look," Elizabeth murmured devotedly to her husband. "Christy's speechless. Oh, sweetie, you don't need to say anything. Your father and I understand. If anyone should be giving thanks, it's me. I was so miserable after my fall. Planning this party was the best thing in the world for me. I've loved every minute of it. Keeping it a surprise has been so much fun."

There had to be a plausible excuse she could use to avoid this farce of an engagement party. "I don't have a dress." The words escaped her lips almost as quickly as they formed in her mind.

"Not to worry," Elizabeth said, her eyes glowing even brighter. "I thought of everything, if I do say so myself. I went shopping the other day and picked out a dress for you. If you don't like it, or it doesn't fit, we can exchange it first thing in the morning."

First thing in the morning. The words echoed in her ears. "I… I'm supposed to go back to work." That sounded reasonable to her. After two weeks away from the law firm, Christy was expected back. They needed her. They were short-staffed without her. She couldn't demand additional time off to exchange a party dress.

"No need to worry about that, either," Eric said. "James has that covered. He talked it over with the office manager, and she's given you two extra days off with pay."

"Tomorrow, of course, will be filled with all the last-minute details for the party," Elizabeth rattled on, rubbing her palms together.

"You didn't tell Taylor?" Her older sister would've said something to her; Christy was sure of it.

"Well, not right away. I mailed her a long letter and an invitation so it would arrive the day you were scheduled to leave Montana. I'm guessing she has it by now. I couldn't take the chance of mailing it any sooner for fear you'd find it, and I didn't want to say anything when we phoned in case she inadvertently let the cat out of the bag. I wanted to keep this a surprise."

"I see," Christy murmured.

"Your father and I don't expect Taylor to fly home for the party, not so soon after having the baby. She and Russ will come out for the wedding. Which is something else we need to discuss. Talk to James, sweetie—the sooner we have a date, the better. There's so much to do, and I so want this wedding to be carefully planned. I can't tell you how much I've learned in the past two weeks. Right after the party tomorrow night, we're going to sit down and discuss the wedding."

Christy nodded, simply because she lacked the courage to explain there would never be a wedding, at least not one in which James was the bridegroom.

"You are surprised, aren't you?" Jason demanded, looking exceptionally cocky, as though he was the person responsible for pulling this whole affair together.

Surprise was too mild a word for what Christy was experiencing. Even shock and dismay were too mild.

Horror and panic more aptly described her feelings.

James! She needed to talk to James. He'd help her. He'd understand, and then together they'd clear up this mess. Together they could confront her parents and make *them* understand.

She stood before she realized what she was doing. Everyone in the room seemed to be staring holes straight through her. Glancing around, she offered them each a weak smile.

Always dutiful. Always obedient. Never causing a concern or a problem. Christy was about to destroy her good-girl image.

But first she had to talk to James.

Two messages were waiting for Christy on her answering machine when she returned late that afternoon. The first was from Cody and the second from Taylor.

Christy didn't answer either.

Instead she sat in her living room, staring into space, weighed down by guilt, pressured beyond anything she'd ever experienced and entangled in circumstances beyond her control.

How long she stayed there Christy didn't know. Here she was safe. Here she was protected. Here she could hide.

That small sense of security, however, quickly disintegrated. Knowing there was nothing else she could do to stop the progression of events, she stood and walked into the kitchen. She paused in front of the phone, then abruptly picked it up before she had a change of heart.

Cody wasn't home, and she left an all-too-brief message. Her next call was to Taylor.

"Christy, what's going on?" Taylor burst out the instant she recognized her younger sister. "I got this crazy letter from Mom about a surprise engagement party for you. What's happening?"

"You mean about the party?" Christy asked. Her voice lacked any level of emotion. She had none left.

"Of course I mean the party," Taylor cried. "Do you mean to say you're going through with it?"

"I don't have any choice."

"Christy, you can't be serious! What about Cody? I thought you were in love with him. I may be out of line here, but I could've sworn you…" She inhaled deeply. "I'd better stop before I say something I shouldn't. Just answer me one question. Do you or do you not love Cody Franklin?"

Christy wiped the tears from her face and nodded wildly. "You know I do."

"Then it seems to me you're allowing Mom and Dad to dictate your life."

"You don't understand," Christy whimpered.

"What's there to understand?"

"Mom broke her leg—" She couldn't go on, wondering if she should even try to describe this hopeless mess. Even if she did it was doubtful Taylor would understand.

"I know about Mom's accident," Taylor returned impatiently.

"She was terribly depressed afterward. I saw it, we all did, but apparently it didn't go away like everyone expected it would. Then Dad came up with the brilliant idea of planning this engagement party."

"Oh, dear."

"Mom put everything she had into it, and now—"

"Christy, I know it's difficult, but you've got to remember Mom and Dad planned this party without consulting you."

That was true enough, but it didn't change the facts. "I can't humiliate them. I thought if I talked to James, told him about Cody, everything would work out, but then I discovered I couldn't do that, either. I wanted us to face Mom and Dad and make some kind of decision together about the party, but that's impossible now. Everything's so crazy.... I can't believe this is happening."

"Do you mean to say James doesn't know about Cody yet?"

Christy closed her eyes.

"Christy?"

"I...couldn't tell him." She stiffened, waiting for the backlash of anger that was sure to follow.

After a short silence, Taylor said, "You *couldn't* tell James about Cody?"

The trouble she had forming the words was painfully obvious. "You heard me."

There was another silence. "I see."

"How could you possibly *see?*" Christy demanded, keeping her voice level, when she wanted to scream at the accusation she heard in her sister's voice. "I went to him, fully intending to tell him everything."

"Then why didn't you?"

"For two months James has been preparing for the most important trial of his career."

"You mean to say you're worried about James's *career?* At a time like this?"

Christy ignored her sister's outburst. "A businessman from Kirkland... You must know Alfred Mulligan. He's the one who does all those crazy television ads. Anyway, he's been charged with cheating on his taxes. The whole case is extremely complicated, and you know as well as I do how messy this kind of thing can get when the federal government is involved." She waited for Taylor to agree with her.

"What's that got to do with anything?"

Christy hated the angry impatience she heard in her sister's voice. It was all too clear that Taylor was upset with her. Christy felt Taylor's disapproval as strongly as a slap. All her life she'd experienced love and approval, especially from her family, and it hurt more than she could bear to feel such overwhelming censure from her only sister.

"You don't understand," Christy tried again. "James has been working day and night for weeks to get ready for this trial. It was scheduled for the first of next month, but he learned this afternoon they've called the case early. He's making the opening statement tomorrow morning."

"I'm afraid I don't understand the relevance of all this."

"I don't expect you to. James has worked himself into

a frenzy. I've never seen him like this. So much hangs in the balance for him."

"That's fine, but I still don't—"

"He has a chance to win this case, but it's going to be difficult," Christy went on, cutting off her sister's protest. "James knows that. Everyone does, but if by some miracle he can pull this off, it could mean a partnership for him."

"Oh, Christy," Taylor said with a groan.

"If I broke off the engagement now, it could ruin everything for him."

"That's James's problem, not yours."

"Maybe it is his problem. I don't know anymore. I do know that I can't do this to him. Not on the eve of the most important trial of his career. Not when James has finally been given the chance to prove himself. If anything went wrong, I'd always blame myself."

The silence hummed as Taylor considered her words. "What about Cody?" she asked finally. "Have you given any thought to *his* feelings?"

"Yes." Christy had thought of little else. Never in her life had she asked more of a person than she was asking of Cody. Another woman had destroyed his trust, and there was nothing to assure Christy that he'd want anything to do with her after this.

As painful as it was, as difficult, she found she couldn't humiliate her parents and risk destroying James's chances with this case.

Even if it meant she lost Cody.

Nine

Something was wrong. Cody felt it instinctively, all the way to the marrow of his bones. Christy had left two separate messages on his answering machine, and every time he'd played them back, he'd felt an achy, restless sensation. It wasn't what she'd said, but how she'd said it. She sounded lighthearted and cheerful, but beneath the facade, Cody heard unmistakable confusion.

He'd tried to phone her back, but to no avail. Unable to sleep, he rose in the early morning hours and drove around the back roads outside town, trying to make sense of what was happening. Or not happening.

He couldn't find the answers, not when he didn't understand the questions.

His greatest fears were about to be realized. Once again he'd fallen in love, involved his life with a woman who couldn't be trusted.

Christy isn't Becca, his heart shouted, but Cody had virtually given up listening.

The sun had barely crested the hill as Cody sat in his Cherokee, looking at the valley below, pondering what he should do. If anything. Dammit all, he should never have let this go so far. Becca had taught him everything he needed to know about women and love.

Dawn burst over the hillside, with golden rays of sunlight splashed against the rugged landscape, and small patches of light on the horizon.

Cody released a jagged sigh, then started his car. As much as he'd like to turn his back on the entire situation and pretend the past two weeks with Christy hadn't happened, he knew the effort would be futile.

He glanced at his watch, knowing Russ and Taylor would be up and about. He needed to talk.

The light from the kitchen window glowed as Cody approached the ranch house. He pulled in to the yard, turned off the engine and waited until the door opened and Russ appeared on the back porch.

Climbing out of the car, Cody joined his friend.

"I thought that was you," Russ said, opening the door in mute invitation.

Cody removed his hat and set it on the peg while Russ walked over to the coffeepot and automatically poured him a mug.

"Taylor's feeding Eric," Russ said. "She'll be out in a few minutes."

Cody nodded and straddled a high-backed wooden chair.

Russ sat across from him. "Personally I don't think this thing with Christy is as bad as it sounds. Although, to be honest, if I was in your shoes, I don't know what I'd do."

Cody hadn't a clue what his friend was talking about but decided not to say anything, hoping Russ would explain without him having to ask.

"How're you holding up?"

"Fine." Cody was about to drop the charade and ask his friend what was going on when Taylor came in, wear-

ing a long pink housecoat. Her hair was mussed and fell
to the middle of her back. She offered Cody an apologetic smile, and once more he was left to interpret the
meaning. His gut was tightening, and he didn't know
how much longer he could go on pretending.

"Good morning, Cody," Taylor greeted him, helping
herself to a cup of coffee. It seemed to Cody that her
smile conveyed more concern than welcome.

It was all Cody could do not to leap to his feet and demand someone tell him what was happening.

"I suppose you're here to talk about Christy?" she
asked gently. If Russ hadn't said a word, Cody would've
guessed something was wrong just from the way Taylor
was looking at him—as if she wanted to put her arms
around him and weep.

"Christy's been on my mind," he answered brusquely.

"You realize she doesn't have any choice, don't you?"
Taylor added. Her eyes, so like Christy's, appealed to
him to be open-minded. "Russ and I've gone round and
round about this and—"

"Any choice about what?" Cody demanded. His
friends exchanged a surprised look.

"You mean Christy didn't get hold of you?"

"No."

"Then you don't know about the engagement party?"

"All I got was two messages in which she sounds like
Mary Sunshine. I *knew* she wasn't telling me something.
I sensed that right away."

It took a moment for the news to hit him. Engagement party? That meant she was still involved with… If
he hadn't already been sitting down, Cody would have
needed a chair fast. He'd heard of men who'd had their
feet kicked out from under them, but he'd never understood the expression until then.

"Oh, dear." Taylor reached for her coffee and it was clear that she was upset. Her hands trembled, and her eyes avoided meeting his.

Cody transferred his attention to Russ, who looked as uncomfortable as his wife. "What's going on?" Cody asked in a deceptively calm voice.

Once more, husband and wife exchanged glances as if silently deciding between themselves who would do the talking. Apparently Russ presented his wife with the unpleasant task, because she swallowed, then turned to Cody. "My sister's caught in a series of difficult circumstances."

"What the hell does that mean?"

"Apparently my mother took the two weeks while Christy was here in Montana to plan an elaborate engagement party. It seems her spirts needed a boost, and my father thought involving her in planning a party would help. Unfortunately he was right. Mom threw herself into the project and arranged the event of the year, starring Christy and James."

"Are you telling me she's going through with it?"

"She doesn't have much of a choice. The celebration's scheduled for this evening."

This second bit of information hit Cody with the same impact as the first. "You've got to be kidding!"

"I wish we were," Russ said, his expression annoyed. "My in-laws mean well, but Christy's trapped in this fiasco simply because there isn't time to cancel it now."

"What about James?" Cody asked, stiffening as he mentioned the other man's name. Every time he thought about the Seattle attorney, he struggled with anger and jealousy. James Wilkens had far more claim to Christy than he did. They both loved her, but it was James who'd given her an engagement ring. It was James her parents wanted her to marry.

"James is another problem," Taylor whispered.

Cody didn't understand. "You mean he's refusing to release her from the engagement?"

"He doesn't know Christy intends to break it off," Russ said without preamble.

Cody would've accepted just about anything more readily than he did this news. Christy had played him for a fool, used him the same way Becca had, for her own selfish purposes—whatever they might be.

"She's going to tell James everything," Taylor said heatedly in her sister's defense.

Cody didn't bother to comment, still reeling from this last news.

"When I talked to her, she'd just returned from seeing James. She'd gone to him with the best of intentions, wanting to tell him about you and break off the engagement before it went any further. She was hoping the two of them could discuss the engagement party and decide what could be done."

"She didn't say a word about me to James, did she?" At Taylor's wilted look, Cody decided that was all he needed to know. He stood, emptied the contents of his mug into the sink and set it on the counter so hard that it almost shattered.

"She couldn't tell him," Taylor cried. "If you love Christy the way you claim, you'll listen long enough to find out why."

Cody did love Christy, but he didn't know how much more battering his heart and his pride could take. He stood frozen, waiting for Taylor to continue.

"If she told James about you, she might put his entire career in jeopardy." For the next ten minutes Russ and Taylor took turns explaining the situation as best they could.

"Christy doesn't have any choice but to follow through with this farce of a party, don't you see?"

Taylor did an admirable job of presenting her sister's case; Cody would give her that.

She kept her pleading eyes focused on him. "If it'd been up to her, she would've ended the engagement five minutes after she got home."

Cody didn't respond, although it was apparent his friends were waiting for him to say something.

"You've got to appreciate the situation Christy's in," Taylor went on. "What would *you* have done had the circumstances been reversed?"

Cody closed his eyes, pondering the dilemma. What would he do?

He just didn't know.

"Oh, sweetheart!" Christy's mother exclaimed, stepping back to examine the effect of the full-length layered blue dress. "You look like an angel. Eric, come and see."

Eric Manning, wearing a white tuxedo with a pale blue cummerbund the same shade as Christy's dress, stepped gingerly into the living room. He eyed his younSSgest daughter and nodded approvingly. "You make an old man proud," he said with a warm smile.

"You've never looked lovelier," her mother added.

Christy managed a smile. She had no idea how she was going to make it through this party. She might be able to fool her parents, but surely someone would notice. Rich would. Of her three brothers, she'd always been closest to Rich. He'd take one look at her and immediately guess that something was wrong.

Not that it would make any difference. She'd stand before family and friends and pretend to be madly in love with James, pretend to be an eager bride-to-be. But the only thing Christy was eager for at the moment was to put this evening behind her.

"I'd like to propose a toast to the happy couple, my sister Christy and the love of her life, James Wilkens." Rich Manning raised his champagne glass to the couple.

Christy grinned at her brother and fought the urge to empty her champagne glass over his head. Of all the guests, she'd expected him to realize how miserable she was. Instead, he'd unwittingly made things even worse.

Smiling faces nodded appreciatively at her brother's words before the party-goers sipped the vintage champagne. The round of toasts had been going on for several minutes. Christy wasn't sure how much more of this she could endure.

Her father had proposed the first toast, followed by her uncles and all three of her brothers. Each seemed to add something to the list of blessings they wished for her and James.

Christy swallowed another sip of champagne as her fiancé stood at her side, tall and debonair. She could barely look at him without being overwhelmed with guilt. They'd spent two hours in each other's company, and neither had spoken more than a handful of sentences.

In retrospect Christy wondered how she could possibly have agreed to spend the rest of her life with James. He was wonderful, but it was increasingly obvious that they were painfully mismatched.

Hoping she wasn't being conspicuous, Christy scanned the gathering, wondering if it was possible for anyone to read her thoughts. Not that it would do any good.

"Would you like something to eat?" James asked, glancing toward the linen-draped tables where trays of hors d'oeuvres lay waiting.

Christy shook her head, positive she wouldn't be able to keep down a single bite. "Nothing for me, thanks. What about you?"

"I'm fine," James answered.

The music started, and a handful of couples were making their way to the gleaming wooden floor. "I've always been terrible at this sort of thing," James confessed, reaching for Christy's hand. "But I suppose it's expected of us."

Christy nodded, wanting nothing more than to escape. A path was cleared as James led her to the dance floor and slipped his arm around her waist, careful to maintain a respectable distance between them. The music was slow and melodious, a love ballad, whose words seemed to ridicule her more than anything that had preceded the dancing.

James smiled into Christy's eyes as they moved across the floor. Soon other couples joined them.

Her fiancé seemed to relax a little more now that they weren't the only two on the floor. For that matter so did Christy. "I'm sorry I haven't been myself this evening," James murmured regretfully.

Christy was ashamed to admit she hadn't noticed. Her whole attention had been focused on simply getting through this ordeal.

"The Mulligan case is going to take up a lot of my time over the next few weeks, and I can only hope you'll be patient with me."

Christy was horrified to realize she'd forgotten all about the trial and how important it was to him. "Oh, James, I'm so sorry. I didn't even ask how everything went this morning."

"Not as well as I'd hoped," he mumbled under his breath.

"I'm sorry," she said again. "But I understand you're

going to be busy. In fact, it might actually work out for the best. You see, I met—" She wasn't allowed to finish.

"I knew you'd be understanding," he said, cutting her off. He smiled gently and drew her toward him. "You always have been."

"You, too," she whispered sarcastically, but James didn't respond.

Closing her eyes, she tried to pretend it was Cody's arms around her. That was the only way she'd be able to continue this farce. Keeping his image in her mind gave her a sense of purpose, a means of enduring this disastrous night.

After a respectable number of dances, James escorted her off the floor. Until then Christy hadn't noticed how tired and defeated he looked. Several family members insisted on dances with her, and Christy found herself on the floor with a number of uncles, her brothers and longtime family friends.

James was doing his duty, as well, keeping the women from both families occupied. She did see that he managed to do so without dancing with any of them, and that made her smile, however briefly.

It wasn't until the end of the evening, when Christy decided she just might survive, that her aunt Lois, her mother's youngest sister, asked the impossible question. "When's the date for the wedding?"

The whole room went silent. The music ceased, and everyone turned to stare at Christy and James. They were sitting together in a long row of folding chairs against the wall. It was the first time they'd sat down that evening.

Christy felt like a cornered animal. The cracker in her mouth seemed to go down her throat whole.

"You don't have an engagement party without letting those you love know when you're planning the wedding," Aunt Lois said.

James glanced at Christy. "We haven't had a chance to discuss a date, have we, darling?"

"No," Christy muttered. It wouldn't look good to announce that she was counting the days until she could break the engagement. If she was going to discuss a wedding date with anyone, it would be with Cody. But he hadn't asked her, and after he learned about this evening, Christy doubted he'd ever want to see her again.

"Springtime is always lovely for a wedding." Aunt Lois stood directly in front of her, waving her arms, demanding the attention of Christy and everyone else. "George and I were married in May, and the flowers were gorgeous." Pressing her gloved hands together, she released a slow sigh of remembered happiness.

"But May's almost a year away," Elizabeth Manning objected loudly, walking across the dance floor to join this all-important discussion. "Why wait so long? I was thinking more along the lines of November."

"November?" Christy echoed.

"The leaves are always so pretty then. You know how I love orange, brown and yellow," she said, looking at her daughter.

Already Christy could see her mother's mind working, plotting and planning. She'd enjoyed making the arrangements for the engagement party so much that she couldn't wait to start on all the pomp and ceremony of a formal wedding.

"With your dark coloring, Christy, an autumn theme would be perfect."

"Personally I favor a December wedding," Eric Manning shouted. He'd obviously had more than his share of champagne.

"December?" Elizabeth shrieked, shaking her head. "Never."

"All right," Eric countered. "Let's ask Christy and James which date they prefer. This is, after all, their wedding."

"Ah." Christy couldn't think. Her mind froze along with her hands, which were raised halfway to her mouth, her fingers clutching a delicate artichoke canapé. In a panic she looked at James, her eyes wide in speechless appeal. If ever she needed rescuing, it was now.

"What do you say, sweetheart?" her mother asked.

By some miracle Christy managed to lower the cracker to her plate. "I... I haven't given the matter much thought."

"When George and I decided to marry, we couldn't do it fast enough," Aunt Lois informed the group.

"November," James said decisively. "Your aunt's right. There's no need to put off the wedding."

"We don't have to choose a date *now,* do we?" Christy asked. "Not when you're so busy with the Mulligan case."

His hand patted hers gently. "This trial will be over soon enough, and I've been selfish not to consider your feelings. Naturally you and your mother will want to start making all the necessary arrangements."

"November would be perfect." Elizabeth Manning opened her purse and withdrew a small appointment calendar. "Let's pick the date right now. How does the twelfth sound?"

Once more Christy found herself speechless. "Ah..."

"The twelfth sounds grand," James said triumphantly, and lightly touched his lips to Christy's cheek. "Isn't that right, darling?"

The whole world came to an abrupt halt, awaiting Christy's reply. The walls seemed to be falling in around her, until she could hardly breathe.

"Christy?" her mother probed, eyeing her curiously. "November 12 would be a beautiful day for a wedding, don't you agree?"

* * *

Cody slowly patrolled the deserted streets of Cougar Point, but his mind wasn't on the job. The crime wave of the century could be happening before his very eyes, and Cody doubted he would've noticed.

How could he? The only reason he'd agreed to take this shift was in an effort to forget that Christy was with James tonight.

While Cody dutifully served his constituents, Christy was sipping champagne with her attorney fiancé. No doubt his diamond was firmly placed on her ring finger and she was having the time of her life.

It hurt.

The pain was as real as anything he'd ever endured. Except that it hurt more. There wasn't a thing he could do to alter the chain of events that had led Christy into this predicament. Apparently there wasn't much she could do, either.

He tried to remind himself that the woman he loved would go to great lengths not to hurt others, even if it meant hurting herself. But Christy wasn't the only one suffering.

Cody felt like a casualty of circumstance. And there was nothing he could do....

It was late when he rolled into the station—after eleven. He got out of the patrol car and saw Russ's pickup truck parked out front. Frowning, he made his way inside.

Russ Palmer unfolded his long legs and stood. "About time you got here."

"Problems?"

Russ nodded. "A few. I thought it might be a good idea if we talked."

The anxiety that had been following him around all night grew more intense. "I'll meet you in ten minutes."

Since the bowling alley was the only restaurant in town that stayed open this late, Cody didn't need to mention where they'd meet.

Russ was already in the booth, holding a white ceramic mug, when Cody walked inside. Cody slid in across from him, wondering how his friend had come to pick the same booth he'd sat in with Christy. He'd been in love with her then and hadn't even known it.

"What's so all-fired important to bring you out this time of night?" Cody asked.

"Taylor."

That didn't explain a lot.

The cook brought out a second mug for Cody and returned to the kitchen. Russ stared after the other man.

"You don't mean Taylor, you mean Christy, right?"

Russ nodded glumly.

"What did she do now? Run off with Gypsies? Marry the garbageman?"

"Worse."

"I suppose this has to do with the engagement party."

Once more Russ nodded. "Apparently no one guessed her real feelings. It seems everyone was too concerned about how much liquor made it into the punch bowl to ask Christy how *she* felt about the whole thing."

"I should be grateful for that?"

"No," Russ answered. "She went through the evening like a real trooper. She loves her family, and she did this for their sake, but she didn't like it."

"She's not the only one."

"I can well imagine," Russ said with a sympathetic sigh. "I know how I'd feel in the circumstances."

"I'm not sure what to do anymore." Cody rubbed his face wearily. "Tell me what happened. I can deal with that better than not knowing."

Russ seemed uncertain where to begin.

"Just spit it out," Cody said, trying to persuade himself he should forget he'd ever met Christy Manning.

"She's sick. Started throwing up at the party. Taylor talked to her and said Christy's in pretty rough shape."

For all his effort to portray disinterest, Cody's heart raced at the news. "What's wrong?"

"It's not what you think."

"If she's feeling as bad as you say, then why didn't she contact me?"

"She's been trying to reach you for two days."

"I've been busy. What was I supposed to do? Phone her and suggest she enjoy her engagement party? I have some pride left, and frankly I'm holding on to it."

"She needs to talk to you. Call her."

Cody shrugged.

"If you've been avoiding her, don't. She doesn't deserve this. Not now."

"I've tried phoning," Cody confessed, as if admitting to a shortcoming in his character. "She's never there."

"You didn't leave a message?"

"No," he answered reluctantly. What was there to say in a message that would help their situation? As far as he could see, nothing.

"She's at her apartment now. Take my advice and put each other out of this misery. Talk to her."

Ten minutes later Cody unlocked his front door, turned on the light and walked into his living room. He scowled at the phone—but he didn't know who he was trying to kid. He practically lunged at it, he was so hungry for the sound of Christy's voice.

He dialed the Seattle number Russ had given him, and Christy answered even before the first ring had finished.

"Cody?" Her voice caught on his name before he had a chance to speak.

"Hello, Christy," he said in a voice that, to his own ears, sounded stiff and cold.

"Thank you for calling me."

Before he could respond, she asked, "Did Taylor tell you?"

"Tell me what?"

"What happened at the party."

"No." There was more? "Russ came into town and asked me to call you. He alluded to something but never said exactly what. Go ahead and tell me."

A slight hesitation followed. "I…it isn't easy."

"Dammit, Christy, what's going on now?" The possibilities that came to mind did little to put him at ease.

"I want to be honest with you," she said, her voice shaking. "I…" She paused, and Cody could hear her drag a deep breath through her lungs. "Something happened at the party tonight…something I never intended."

Cody wanted to come across as nonchalant, but he couldn't. He expelled his breath, trying to think of what she might have done that would make him stop loving her.

Nothing. She could do nothing. Even if she were to inform him that she'd given in to the pressure and married James that very night, it wouldn't be enough. He'd still love her. He'd always love her.

"November 12," she whispered.

"I beg your pardon?" She'd gone from guessing games to riddles.

"The wedding's set for November 12."

Ten

Christy rolled over and glanced at the illuminated dial of her clock radio. It was 10:00 a.m.

This was supposed to be her first day back at the office, but she'd had to phone in sick. A flu bug was what she'd told Marcia, the office manager, who was sympathetic enough to suggest Christy stay home. But it wasn't the flu that was making her ill.

It was something else entirely. Christy was heartsick, afraid she'd lost Cody forever. She felt trapped, doing what was right for everyone but herself.

Now she was wide awake, and the day stretched out before her. She could occupy herself with mindless game shows on television, but that would only use up an hour or two. Reading would help pass the time—if she could concentrate. She might even give some thought to phoning Cody.

No.

That was out of the question. Cody didn't want to talk to her, not anymore. She'd said everything she could to make him understand her predicament two nights earlier. The conversation had gone reasonably well until she'd told him she'd been forced to set a date for the wedding.

An unexpected sob tore through her throat, and fresh tears flooded her eyes. She'd done a lot of weeping over the past days. Damp, crumpled tissues lay scattered across her bedspread where she'd carelessly discarded them.

She loved Cody, and nothing she'd been able to say had convinced him of that. Cody, being a sheriff, saw life in terms of black and white. Either she'd agreed to the wedding date or she hadn't. Unfortunately Christy had sanctioned November 12, more or less, when pressured by James and her entire family. As soon as she confessed as much, her telephone conversation with Cody had ended abruptly.

She'd pleaded with him for understanding, tried to assure him she'd never willingly marry James, but it hadn't helped. They'd hung up with Cody promising to contact her after he'd had time to think.

Nearly thirty-four hours had passed. Surely he'd had adequate opportunity to come to some kind of decision.

The doorbell chimed, and sniffling, Christy reached for another tissue. She blew her nose before tossing aside her covers and climbing out of bed. She intended to send her visitor, whoever it was, away. She was in no mood for company.

With her luck, it was probably her mother wanting to discuss color schemes for the bridesmaids' dresses. If her car hadn't been parked directly in front of her door, she wouldn't even bother answering.

"Who is it?" she asked, squinting through the peephole and seeing no one.

"Cody Franklin."

"Cody...oh, Cody." Christy threw open the door. For one wild second she did nothing but stare into his wonderful face, convinced he'd been conjured up by her imagination. Before another second could pass, she launched herself into his arms.

Cody dropped his suitcase, clasping her around the waist with both arms. He hauled her to him with joyful abandon. Their mouths met in a kiss so fierce, it threatened to steal her breath. He held her as if he was starving for the taste of her, and meant to make up for every minute of every day they'd been apart.

Christy's arms encircled his neck, her mouth finding his. She kissed him over and over in an agony of need.

With a shudder Cody tore his mouth from hers and spread a wildfire of kisses over her face. His arms were around her waist, and her feet dangled several inches off the ground as his chest heaved with deep breaths.

Weeping for joy, Christy pressed her head against his shoulder, feeling completely at ease for the first time since she'd left Montana. She was in Cody's arms. Nothing could hurt her again.

"It might be a good idea if we went inside," he whispered.

Christy nodded. Slowly he released her, and she slid down.

"How'd you get here?" she asked, searching the parking lot for signs of his Cherokee.

"I flew," he explained as his hand stroked the tumbling curls away from her face. "I couldn't leave things between us the way they were. At least not without talking this out face-to-face. I took three days' vacation, hoping we could put an end to this craziness."

Christy was hoping for the same thing. She took his wrist and pulled him inside her small apartment. She closed the door, then turned to face him, her hands behind her.

From the moment she'd come home, she'd stood alone

against what seemed like overwhelming forces. Her mother needed her. James needed her. Everyone wanted a part of her until she felt as if she were being torn in two.

"How...how'd you know I was home?" she asked once her mind had cleared enough to process her thoughts.

"I phoned the law firm from the airport. They told me you were out with the flu."

Christy couldn't believe what she was hearing. Cody had phoned her at the office!

"You disapprove?" His eyes narrowed.

"No." But her heart was thumping loudly. It wasn't likely anyone had given his inquiry a second thought. Even if they had, she wouldn't be around to answer their questions.

"But the fact that I talked to someone who knew you *and* James upset you, didn't it?" He started to pace her living room. Four long strides covered the entire length of it. He buried one hand in his back pocket while the other massaged the muscles of his neck. "You're so afraid your precious James is going to find out about me."

"That's not true," she denied vehemently. Too late, Christy realized she probably was the most pathetic sight he'd ever seen.

Her eyes were red and swollen, and she wasn't even dressed. The five-year-old pajamas she was wearing were as sexy as dishcloths. Not that any of this seemed to bother Cody, who was apparently far more interested in arguing with her than ravishing her.

In her emotionally fragile condition Christy was much too weak to withstand a heated verbal exchange. She'd already heard from Taylor, who knew without a doubt what would be best. Russ, too. But they weren't listening to *her*. It was easy for them to dish out advice when they were a thousand miles from the situation.

She was the one on the front line, the one who'd have to face their parents. She seemed to be the only one who appreciated the long years of hard work that had led James to this point in his career. She couldn't, *wouldn't*, ruin his chances now.

If Cody Franklin expected her to buy their happiness at another's expense, then he didn't really know her at all.

He turned to face her. Boldly she met his eyes, staring down the hot accusation she saw in them.

Suddenly Christy felt his anger start to dissolve, replaced with doubt and pain. Defeated, he expelled a harsh breath. His shoulders sagged. "Forget I ever mentioned James. I didn't come here to fight about him."

"Why did you come?"

He didn't seem to have an answer, or if he did, he wasn't willing to supply it just yet. He looked away from her and plowed his fingers through his hair. "To talk some sense into you and end this confusion before we both go insane."

How Christy wished it was that simple.

"This isn't as complicated as you're making it," he said. "Either you're serious about loving me or you aren't. It should be a matter of setting the record straight, but—"

"I do love you."

"Then why are you wearing another man's ring?" he demanded. He stalked toward her and pulled her hand from behind her back. He frowned as he found her ring finger bare.

"I've only worn James's diamond once. The night of the engagement party," she said, surprised by how strained her voice sounded. "I took it off the minute I walked in the door and haven't put it on since."

Cody's large, callused hand curled over her fingers as he shut his eyes. The muscles in his jaw clenched.

Then, moving slowly, as though hypnotized, he lowered his mouth to hers.

Her lips trembled under his and Christy closed her eyes as hard as she could, wanting to shut out the realities that kept them apart. She longed to block out everything, except the man who was holding her so gently.

"We need to talk," he whispered.

"Isn't 'I love you' enough?" she asked. Although he struggled to hold her at bay, Christy spread nibbling kisses at the curve of his neck. She wanted him so much....

Cody released a ragged sigh and propelled himself away from her. He moved so fast and so unexpectedly that Christy nearly stumbled. Bewildered, she caught herself just in time.

By then Cody had put the full distance of the living room between them. "In case it's slipped your mind, I'd like to remind you that you're an engaged woman."

It seemed she was allowed to forget that when she was in Cody's arms. She blinked back her pain. Throwing this farce of an engagement at her now was cruel and unfair.

"If you flew all those miles to remind me of that, then you made a wasted trip." Humiliation tainted her cheeks and it was all she could do not to cover her face with both hands and turn away from him.

For several minutes neither of them spoke. She sensed that they both needed time to compose themselves. Cody continued pacing, while Christy stood rooted, leaning against the door, requiring its solidity to hold her upright. It was a shock to discover how badly she was trembling.

"I need to ask you to do something," Cody said crisply, as if whatever he was about to say didn't involve him.

"All right."

"Break the engagement to James." His dark eyes cut into her with sharp, unquestioning demand.

"Of course. You know I will as soon as I can—"

"I want you to do it now. Today."

Full of anguish and regret, Christy shut her eyes. This had tormented her from the moment she got home and talked to James. Surely Cody realized she didn't want to stay engaged to another man.

"Christy?"

"I...can't break it off. Not yet. You know that. James has been working for three months getting ready for this trial. He was as prepared as any attorney could be, and yet one thing after another has gone wrong for him. I can't add to his troubles by—"

"We have no business seeing each other," Cody interrupted. "We didn't when you were in Montana, and we have even less of an excuse now that you're home."

"But I love you."

Her words fell into an uncomfortable silence. Cody didn't answer for so long that she began to worry. His expression told her nothing.

"Love doesn't make everything right," he said, his eyes darkening with bitterness. "I wish it did, but the way we feel about each other doesn't alter one damn thing. You're promised to another man, and that's all there is to it."

"But... Cody—"

"Not only do you have his ring, you've set a wedding date."

"I explained all that," she whispered, feeling utterly defenseless.

"There's something you don't seem to understand," Cody said, frowning heavily. "I'm a man of honor, a man of my word..."

She nodded. "I couldn't love you as much as I do without knowing the kind of man you are."

"Then you must realize that I can't continue this. You must know how it makes me feel."

She stared at him, barely able to believe she'd been so stupid and selfish. Cody wasn't being possessive or jealous. It wasn't his pride that was injured or his ego. It was his sense of fairness. A matter of honesty.

He slowly shook his head. "For both our sakes, I wish I could be different. I'd like nothing better than to steal away with you for a few days, hold you, kiss you. More than anything else in this world I want to make love to you, but I can't allow that to happen."

Christy wanted all those things, too.

"The fact that you were committed to James bothered me when you were staying with Russ and Taylor. The fact that you didn't want to break the engagement over the phone wasn't unreasonable and I understood it."

Christy now wished she'd put an end to everything two weeks ago. If she had, her life would be so much simpler.

"It wasn't easy to keep my hands off you then, and it's a lot more difficult now." His voice was tight, and he didn't slacken his stride as he continued to pace. "I can't do this any longer. Either you break it off with James, right now, today, or it's over. I'll fly back to Montana and this will be the last time I see you."

Christy felt as if the entire ceiling had come crashing down on her head.

"The last time?" she repeated, struggling to keep her voice from rising.

"Christy, look at it from my point of view."

"I am. All I'm asking for…all I need is for you to be a little more patient. The trial will be over soon."

"I've been more than patient already."

"But it'll only be for a while. I swear to you," she said urgently, "I'll break it off with James at the first opportunity. But I can't do it now."

Once again her words fell into a void and she was left to wonder at his thoughts. "Cody...please," she whispered when she couldn't tolerate the silence anymore.

He pivoted sharply. "I know you. You're warm and loving, and you won't do anything that might hurt another person. You refuse to disappoint anyone—except yourself."

If he understood her so well, then surely he'd be patient just a little longer. She was about to say that when he added, "You've allowed your parents to manipulate you all your life."

"That's not true," she burst out, wanting to defend herself, angry that he'd even suggest it.

"They handpicked a husband for you, and you went along with it."

Her shoulders slumped, but her indignation had yet to cool.

"You didn't love James then and you don't love him now. Or so you claim."

"I love *you*," she cried. "How many times do I have to say it?"

"Yet when James offered you an engagement ring, you accepted his proposal."

"I... I..." Her outrage went limp for lack of an argument. Everything he said was true, but it had happened before she'd met Cody.

"You're so eager to take care of everyone else you're willing to sacrifice your own happiness."

"All I need is a few more days, just until this trial..." She didn't finish, since nothing she said was going to change his mind.

"Frankly I have a strong suspicion that you're going to wake up one fine morning married to dear old James and not realize how it happened."

"That's ridiculous." She folded her arms to ward off an unexpected chill. "I swear to you that will never happen."

"You swore to me you were going to break the engagement when you arrived back in Seattle, too. Remember?"

His eyes challenged her to deny it. She couldn't. He met her stare, but it was Christy who looked away first, Christy whose gaze flickered under the force of the truth.

"But how could I have known about the engagement party?" she asked weakly. Then, gaining conviction, she said, "You're not being fair. To even suggest I'd go ahead with the wedding is—" she searched for the right word "—ludicrous."

"Is it really?"

"Of course it is! You make me sound like some weak-willed… I can't imagine why you'd want anything to do with me if that's how you feel."

"I love you, Christy, and it's going to hurt like crazy to walk away from you. My request isn't unreasonable, although I know you don't agree with that."

She leaned against the door frame. "You can't ask me to make that kind of decision! Not right this minute. I need time…." In the back of her mind she was desperately praying the Mulligan case would be thrown out of court that afternoon and this whole regrettable affair could be laid to rest.

She might win the lottery, too, but she couldn't count on it.

"Is the decision that difficult?" Cody asked, frowning. "That on its own says something, whether you admit it or not."

Christy shut her eyes and took a deep breath. The man

she loved, her entire future, was about to walk out the door, and she knew of no way to stop him short of destroying another person's happiness.

Straightening, she glared at Cody across the room. "I don't know what's right anymore," she said defiantly. "How can I? All everyone does is make demands of me. First it's Mom and then James and now...you."

Then she started to cry. She couldn't help it. Her shoulders shook and her chest heaved as the sobs convulsed her and tears cascaded down her cheeks.

She heard Cody mutter a swear word. "Christy, please, I can't stand to see you cry," he whispered hoarsely.

He could break her heart, but he couldn't stand to see her cry. Christy found the thought almost laughable.

Cody moved across the room and took her in his arms. His hands stroked the hair away from her brow. With him she felt secure. With him she felt warm and protected. She hid her face in his shoulder as the emotion worked through her. He held her until she was able to draw in a deep, shaky breath. Christy could feel her control slipping back into place.

Still Cody held her, his hands caressing her back. For the longest time he said nothing. He continued to hold her close, and after several minutes Christy became aware of how intimate their position was.

She sighed longingly and tested her discovery by tenderly kissing his neck. A moment passed in which she waited for him to protest or ease himself away.

Experiencing a small sense of triumph when he didn't, she leisurely investigated the warm, tantalizing skin, making slow, moist circles over the hollow of his throat.

"Kiss me," she whispered. "Oh, please, Cody, just kiss me. I'll be all right if you do that."

He didn't immediately comply; in fact, he seemed inclined to ignore her, as if nothing would be proved, nothing would be solved by kissing.

He froze when she placed her hands on each side of his strong face, sliding her lips up his jawline and over his chin until their mouths were joined.

Cody pulled his mouth from hers. His whole body seemed to be shaking as he inhaled. He walked over to her sofa and sat on the edge, his elbows on his knees. "What are we going to do?" He shook his head in despair. "I'm not strong enough to walk away from you," he said starkly. "I thought I could."

"I won't let you go." She sat next to him, resting her forehead on his shoulder, and sighed. "I love you so much.... I'd give anything to marry you today."

Cody went stock-still. "What did you just say?"

Eleven

"I won't let you go, Cody. I can't," Christy repeated.

"Not that," he said, bolting to his feet. He started pacing again, and when she didn't immediately speak, he added, "It was after that."

She frowned. "I love you?"

"Not that, either. The part about marrying me today."

"I would." She didn't feel any hesitation in saying as much. Almost from the first day she'd met the sheriff of Custer County, she'd known she was going to love him all the days of her life.

"Will you marry me, Christy?" His expression was so open and sincere that she felt tears stinging her eyes.

"Oh, yes," she whispered. She'd probably be the only woman in the world engaged to two men at the same time, but that couldn't be helped.

"I mean now."

"Now?"

"I'd like us to be married this afternoon."

Her heart responded with a quick, wistful beat, but Christy didn't see how a wedding, that day, would be possible.

"Maybe it's different in Montana, but Washington

state has a three-day waiting period after we apply for the license."

A satisfied smile lifted the corners of his mouth. "Idaho doesn't."

"That may be, but Idaho's over 350 miles from here. If you're only going to be in Seattle three days, we'll end up spending two of them on the road."

"That's easily fixed. I'll rent a plane." He smiled a breathtaking smile that was so appealing, she thought she'd die a slow death if he didn't make love to her soon. "Am I going too fast for you?"

"No," she rushed to assure him, although her mind was abuzz. "It's just that I'm having trouble understanding. What about James?" She hated mentioning fiancé number one, but she had to be sure they were doing the right thing for the right reasons.

"What about him?"

"Will I…do I have to tell him about the wedding? I mean, it won't make much difference if he learns I've married you a couple of days from now or even next week. I'm only suggesting I delay telling him because of the trial."

Some of the happy excitement left Cody's eyes. "I'll leave that up to you. As far as James is concerned, I don't know what's right or wrong anymore. All I know is that I love you more than I thought it was possible to love any woman. It scares me to think I could lose you."

"There isn't the slightest chance of that."

His smile was sad. "I meant what I said earlier about being afraid you'd end up married to James. I've had nightmares about it, wondering if I'd get a call in the middle of the night. I actually dreamed that you phoned to explain how everything got out of your control and you'd married James before you could come up with a way to stop the ceremony."

"I would never allow such a thing."

He gave her a distrusting look, and although it injured her pride to admit it, Christy could understand Cody's concern.

"I feel a whole lot better making *sure* that couldn't happen." The warmth in his eyes removed the sting his words might have inflicted. "I learned a long time ago to cover all my bases. Marrying like this might not be the best thing, but we're making a commitment to each other, and heaven help me for being so weak, but I need that."

Heaven help *him!* Christy felt herself go soft. "Oh, Cody, I love you so much."

"Good," he said, his voice slightly husky, "because you're about to become my wife."

He smiled, completely disarming her. If Christy had a single argument, which she didn't, one of those devastating smiles would have settled it.

"How soon can you be ready?"

"An hour?"

"I'll check the phone book and make the arrangements while you dress." He took her hands and helped her to her feet, pausing long enough to plant a kiss on her unsuspecting lips.

In a daze Christy walked into her bedroom and searched through her closet for something special enough for her wedding. Smiling to herself, she walked to the door and leaned idly against it. "The whole thing's off. I don't have anything decent to wear," she said, teasing him.

Cody sat at her kitchen table, leafing through the impossibly thick yellow pages. He glanced up and chuckled. "Don't worry about it. Whatever you put on is going to come off so fast it'll make your head spin."

Christy chose a soft pink suit she'd purchased the year before at Easter. Carrying it into the bathroom, she closed the door. Quite by accident she caught her reflection in the mirror above the sink and gasped at the pitiful sight she made.

Leaning over the sink, she studied the woman who stared back at her. Her short dark hair was a mess, as if it hadn't been combed in weeks. Her eyes were another thing. Christy had always considered her distinctive blue eyes to be her best feature. Now they were red-rimmed and bloodshot as if she'd been on a two-day drunken spree. Her lips were red and swollen, although she attributed that to Cody's kisses. That man could kiss like nobody's business. She went weak all over again, remembering the feel and taste of his mouth on hers.

Bracing her hands against the sink, she was forced to admit that she was probably among the most pathetic creatures on earth. Yet Cody had looked at her as if she was gorgeous.

The man definitely loved her. That worked out well, since she definitely loved him.

Cody couldn't keep still. He couldn't seem to make himself stop pacing Christy's living room. Four steps, turn, four more steps, turn again.

He glanced at his watch. She was already five minutes past the hour she'd told him she'd need. What could be taking her so long? She'd locked herself in the bathroom, and he hadn't heard a peep since. His mind was beginning to play cruel tricks on him. Perhaps she'd changed her mind about going through with the wedding and, not wanting to hurt his feelings, she'd climbed out the bathroom window.

That thought revealed the shocking state of his mental condition more than anything he'd said or done in the past two hours. He'd flown into Seattle with one purpose. Either he'd settle this craziness between him and Christy or he'd end their relationship.

He hadn't counted on her enthusiasm. She'd been giddy with happiness when he'd arrived. Okay, he was the giddy one. He'd had no idea she was going to throw herself into his arms the moment she opened the door. Not that he'd minded... A slow smile relaxed his mouth. Everything had progressed naturally from there.

Cody had always considered himself a strong man. Not muscular or brawny, although he could hold his own and often had. His real strength, he felt, was his stubborn determination. He liked to think he had a will of iron.

Christy had proved him wrong in world-record time.

During the early-morning flight, he'd given himself a pep talk, outlining everything he intended to say. He'd planned to meet with her, explain his position and ask her as calmly and unemotionally as possible to make her decision.

It was either James or him.

If she chose the attorney, Cody was prepared to accept her choice serenely and walk out of her life.

Other than the rocky beginning of that conversation, everything had gone as he'd hoped. Never mind that Christy had managed to break down his resolve within five seconds. The instant she was in his arms, he could feel himself start to weaken.

No woman, not even Becca, had ever had as much control over him.

Now he and Christy would be flying into Coeur d'Alene, Idaho, and getting married. Smiling, Cody settled against the back of the sofa. He recalled when Russ and Taylor had come back to Cougar Point after serving as chaperones for the drill team, traveling with a busload of high school girls to Reno. They'd left town barely speaking to each other and arrived home a few days later married.

Cody could still remember how surprised everyone was. Most folks agreed Taylor was the best thing ever to happen to the opinionated Russ Palmer, but there'd been skeptics, too.

Understandably. Taylor was a city girl. Russ was a rancher. Taylor had only been in town three months.

But when folks in Cougar Point learned that Cody had married Christy after knowing her less than *one* month, there'd be even more raised eyebrows.

That didn't disturb Cody in the least. He loved Christy beyond a doubt, and next month when he stood before the citizens of Custer County to be sworn in as sheriff, she'd be at his side. It would be the proudest moment of his life, and he wanted her with him.

The bathroom door opened, and Christy stepped out. Cody turned around to inform her that she was twelve minutes late. His teasing comment wilted before ever making it to his lips.

She was stunningly beautiful, dressed in a pink linen suit. Her hair was perfect, her makeup flawlessly applied. Christy Manning was so beautiful, Cody couldn't help staring at her. It took more effort than he could believe just to close his mouth. He was too tongue-tied to utter a single word.

"Do I look all right?" she asked, gazing at him expectantly.

For the life of him, all Cody could do was nod.

Christy smiled and held out her hand. "Then let's get this show on the road."

The ceremony itself took place later that evening in a wedding chapel overlooking the crystal blue waters of

Lake Coeur d'Alene. Between the time they obtained the license, purchased a pair of gold bands and made the arrangements for the wedding itself, Cody half expected Christy to express some doubts.

She didn't. When she repeated her vows, Christy's strong, clear voice had sounded so confident and poised, he couldn't help marveling—and feeling both humbled and honored by her love.

The flight back to Seattle brought them into the airport shortly before midnight. In the space of one day Cody had traveled from Montana to Washington state, then had flown a two-seater Cessna from Seattle to Coeur d'Alene and back again. He should've been exhausted, but he wasn't. In fact, he felt more alive than he could ever remember being in his life. All he had to do was glance at Christy, who delighted in flashing him a sexy, slightly naughty smile, to feel the blood shoot through his veins.

They returned the Cessna to the hangar and headed toward his rental car. He held the door for her and pressed a light kiss on her lips when she climbed inside. She leaned against him, and it took all his restraint not to deepen the kiss right then and there.

He needed a moment to let his mind clear. "Where to, Mrs. Franklin?" he asked, sliding behind the wheel of the car.

She responded with a blank look.

"Choose any hotel you'd like." He wanted the best Seattle had to offer for Christy. A honeymoon suite. Champagne. Silk sheets. Room service.

"But I didn't pack anything," she protested.

Cody was about to comment that she wouldn't need any clothes, but he didn't get the chance.

"I have this white silk baby doll gown. Would you

mind if we went back to my apartment so I could put a few things together?"

"Your wish is my command, Mrs. Franklin."

Resting her head against his shoulder, Christy sighed audibly and murmured, "I like that in a man."

At the apartment complex, he went inside with Christy. His own suitcase was still there.

Christy hurried into the bedroom, then reappeared a moment later. She walked shyly up to him, then placed her hands on his chest. Cody gazed down at her as she slipped her arms around his neck and kissed him soundly.

Cody's response was immediate. He cradled the back of her head as he returned her kiss—and then some. Soon she was weak and pliant in his arms.

"What was that for?" he asked when he found his breath.

"Because I'm so happy to be your wife."

Cody locked his hands at the small of her back and glanced longingly toward her bedroom.

Christy reached up, kissed his cheek and deftly removed the Stetson from his head. Cody frowned when she tossed it Frisbee fashion across the room. It landed on a chintz-covered cushion as neatly as if he'd set it there himself.

Next her fingers were busy working loose the knot of his tie. "Christy?" Her name tumbled from his lips. "What are you doing?"

"Undressing my husband. I've decided I don't want to go to a hotel room, not when we're both here. Not when I can't wait another minute for us to act like a married couple."

"You're sure?" He didn't know why he was questioning her; he wanted her so much that he was trembling.

"Very sure." After discarding his tie, she began to unfasten his shirt buttons.

Cody's hands roved her back, his fingers seeking and not finding a zipper.

She peeled open his shirt and lightly ran her long nails down his bare chest. Shudders swirled down his spine as she nuzzled his neck, nibbling and sucking and licking her way to the throbbing hollow of his throat.

"Christy," he pleaded, his hands on her bottom. "Where's the zipper to your skirt?"

Smiling, she broke away long enough to remove the suit jacket and kick off her heels, which went flying in opposite directions. She twisted around and unfastened the button at her side, then slid the zipper open so the skirt could fall past her hips and pool at her feet. Stepping out of it, she reached behind her for the row of buttons that ran down the back of her silk blouse.

"I can do that," he said eagerly. His fingers fumbled awkwardly with the tiny buttons, but he managed. Her blouse and her lacy bra followed the path of his shirt, landing on the carpet somewhere between the sofa and television.

Unable to wait a second longer, Cody kissed her, his tongue surging into her mouth. The minute she leaned into him, Cody felt his body heat rise to the boiling point.

Slipping her arms around his neck, Christy let her head fall back, grazing his bare chest with her breasts.

He groaned, fighting the rising flames of his passion. She was slowly, surely, driving him out of his mind.

"Christy," he begged, not knowing exactly what he was pleading for. Not for her to stop, that much he knew. *More,* he decided. He needed more of her.

Tucking his arms behind her knees, he lifted her up

and carried her into the bedroom. The only light was the soft illumination from the single lamp in the living room.

Gently he placed her on the bed, and they hastily finished undressing each other. Cody looked down on her, nestled in the thick folds of a lavender comforter. She was so beautiful that for a moment he was lost to everything but the woman before him. He longed to tell her what he felt, and knew it would be impossible to put into words.

Lightly he ran his hands over her breasts and smiled....

Afterward he lay on his back with Christy beside him, her head on his shoulder, her arm draped over his chest. Cody sighed as she cuddled her body intimately against his.

Her eyes remained closed, her smile dreamy. "I guess I'm not a good girl anymore."

"Oh, yes, you are. Very good, indeed..."

"What are you doing now?" Cody murmured.

He was half asleep, Christy saw as she caught his earlobe between her teeth. "I'm making a citizen's arrest."

"Oh, yeah? What's the charge?"

"I'll trump something up later."

"Christy, hey, what are you wearing?"

"My new silk nightgown."

"I like you better with nothing on."

Ignoring his complaints, she straddled his hips and leaned forward to kiss his chin.

"Mmm, you smell good...flowers, I think."

"Remember, you're the one who emptied an entire bottle of bubble bath into my tub."

"You didn't object."

"How could I? You were doing your husbandly duty and pampering me...only..." She paused and drew in a soft breath as he closed his hands over her breasts. "I didn't realize it could be done in a tub."

"It?" he teased.

"Cody, I was supposed to be the one arresting you, remember?"

"Say it." He raised the silk gown high on her leg and began to caress her thighs with both hands.

"It embarrasses me to say it... Cody," she whimpered as his finger executed the sweetest of punishments.

"You *are* going to say it."

She couldn't utter a single word. She hadn't known her body was capable of giving her any more pleasure than it already had.

"I love it when you blush," he murmured.

Christy rested her head on his chest, listening to the steady, even beat of his heart. "Are we ever going to sleep?" she asked.

"Nope. The way I figure it we've got about forty-eight hours before my plane leaves, and at the rate we're going we can make love—"

"I'm too tired."

Christy felt him smile against her hair. "I am, too." he said. "We'll make up for lost time in the morning."

"In the morning," she echoed as her eyes slowly drifted closed.

A horrible racket woke Christy several hours later. She bolted upright and glanced at her clock radio. Just after 4:00 a.m.

Cody was already out of bed and reaching for his pants.

"Christy?"

The slurred voice belonged to none other than her

brother Rich. She'd given him an extra key to her apartment. He stopped in often, but had always phoned first.

"It's my brother. He has a key. Stay here. I'll get rid of him."

"Your brother?"

"Shh." She grabbed her robe, then kissed Cody before hurrying into the living room.

Rich stood by the door, looking like an errant schoolboy. "Hi," he said, raising his right hand.

"I don't suppose you know what time it is?"

"Late," he offered.

"How about early."

"How early?"

"Too early," she told him, praying he wouldn't notice the two sets of clothes spread from one end of the living room to the other. She marched across the room and gripped his elbow, turning him toward the door.

He gave her a hurt look. "You're sending me back into the cold?"

"Yes."

"I didn't drive here. I couldn't," he said. "I know you probably can't tell, but I've had a teeny bit too much to drink."

"I noticed."

"I was hoping you'd make me some coffee, listen to my woes and let me sleep on your couch."

"I have to be at work in a few hours." A slight exaggeration. Besides, when she didn't show up at the office, everyone would assume she was still home with the flu.

"Pamela cheated on me," Rich blurted. "I need some advice and I need it from a woman. Just hear me out, okay?"

Not knowing what else she could do, Christy moved into her kitchen and started making a pot of coffee. Rich pulled out a stool at her kitchen counter and plopped himself down. "Apparently she's been seeing him all along."

"Who?"

"Pamela."

"No, who's she been seeing?" This conversation was frustrating Christy.

"Hell if I know his name. Some jerk."

"It isn't like you were crazy about her."

"Maybe not, but I always thought she was crazy about me. What is it with women these days? Isn't anyone faithful anymore?" he said plaintively.

"Ah…"

Rich squinted into the darkened living room. "Hey, what's going on here?" Standing, he walked over to the chintz-covered chair and picked up Cody's Stetson. He glanced back at his sister.

"I can explain," she said in a weak voice.

Frowning, he returned to the kitchen and carefully placed the Stetson on her head. Several sizes too large, it rested well below her hairline in the middle of her forehead.

"Is there something you wanted to tell me?" he asked.

Twelve

"Who the hell are you?" Rich demanded.

Christy shoved the Stetson farther back on her head to find Cody walking out of the bedroom.

"It sounded like you might need a little help explaining things," her husband said casually.

Rich pointed at his sister and his mouth fell open. His eyes had narrowed, and disdain and disbelief marked his handsome features.

"It's not as bad as it looks," Christy said, ignoring his censure. Acting as nonchalant as she could, she poured him a cup of coffee.

Swiveling his gaze between Cody and Christy, Rich shook his head. "It looks pretty darn bad, little sister." He stared at the trail of clothing on the living-room carpet. His mouth twisted with disgust as he started toward the front door. "In fact, I don't think I've got the stomach to listen to you."

"You'll listen to her," Cody warned grimly, striding toward Rich. The two men stood no more than two feet apart, glaring at each other ferociously.

"And who's going to make me? You?" Rich's sarcasm

was sharp. "If that's what you think, I've got news for you, cowboy."

"Rich, shut up," Christy said. "The least you can do is hear what I have to say."

"I don't listen to—"

"Don't say it," Cody interrupted, his words so cold they almost froze in midair. "Because if you do, you'll live to regret it."

Rich mocked him with a smile. "Listen, Mr. Marlboro Man, I've taken about enough from—"

"Stop it, both of you!" Christy marched out from her kitchen. She stood between her husband and her brother, a hand on each man's chest, and glanced up at Rich. "I'd like to introduce you to my husband, Cody Franklin. Cody, this stupid oaf is my third-youngest brother, Rich."

"Your husband!"

"My husband," she echoed softly. She dropped her hands and slipped her arm around Cody's waist, leaning against him, needing his solid strength.

"I'll have you know," Cody muttered, "you interrupted my wedding night."

"Your husband," Rich repeated a second time, stalking across the room. He retrieved Christy's bra from the floor and twirled it around on one finger. "I don't suppose James knows about this?"

Christy snatched her underwear out of her brother's hand. "As a matter of fact, he doesn't."

"This is getting even more interesting." Sitting on the sofa, he picked up Cody's shirt and made a soft tsking sound with his tongue. "What about Mom and Dad?"

"They don't know, either," Cody said forcefully.

"Aha," Rich snickered, "the plot thickens."

"I'm so pleased you find this amusing." Christy moved hastily about the room, picking up pieces of discarded clothing, more embarrassed than she could ever remember being.

Cody poured himself a cup of coffee and joined Rich, sitting on the opposite end of the sofa. "I'm a good friend of Russ Palmer's," he said by way of explanation.

Rich nodded. "So my dear, sweet sister met you when she was in Montana visiting Taylor?"

"Cody's the one who drove her to the hospital," Christy added. She sat on the side of the sofa and curved her arm around Cody's broad shoulders.

"Then this was what you'd call a whirlwind courtship." Rich studied the two of them. "Exactly how long have you known each other?"

"Long enough," Cody answered, making it plain he didn't much care for this line of questioning.

"We didn't mean to fall in love so fast," Christy continued, wanting to untangle any doubts Rich had about her relationship with Cody. "It just happened."

"You might have mentioned it to James."

"I probably should've phoned and told him while I was still in Montana, but it seemed wrong to break the engagement over the phone, and then when I got home—"

"The surprise engagement party," Rich said, groaning loudly. "I can see that you were trapped. Mom put her heart and soul into that party. You couldn't back out without humiliating her. Not at the last minute like that."

"I wanted to tell James right away, but that didn't work out, either." The hopelessness of the entire situation nearly overwhelmed her. "The Mulligan trial was called early, and he's immersed himself in the most complicated case of his career. He's got to be emotionally and physically at his peak for that."

"Yeah, that's right," Rich commented. "I'd forgotten about that."

"The timing couldn't be worse. I can't tell James about Cody and me until he's through with the trial. And yet..."

Rich released a long, sympathetic sigh. "You do seem to have your problems, little sister."

Cody leaned against the back of the sofa. "You can imagine how I felt when I learned she'd been roped into that engagement party. To complicate matters, she set a date for the wedding."

Rich did a pitiful job of disguising a smile. "November 12, wasn't it?"

"That's not funny, Rich, so cut the comedy, will you?" Christy playfully punched his upper arm.

"You have to admit, it's kind of amusing."

Christy found very little of this amusing. She was deliriously pleased to be Cody's wife, but he was flying out of Seattle in another day, and she'd have to return to her job and live a complete lie with James and her parents. She wouldn't be able to keep up this charade for long.

"Perhaps this predicament is comical to someone else," Cody said grudgingly, "but trust me, it isn't if you're one of the parties involved."

Rich was quick to agree. "So the two of you decided to take matters into your own hands and get married."

Christy nodded. Her eyes met Cody's, and they exchanged a loving look. His fingers linked with hers. "It must sound crazy."

"Hey, it works for me," Rich said, "but I wouldn't be in your shoes for all the tea in China when you tell Mom and Dad what you did."

"Why not?" Cody asked with a dark frown.

"They were cheated out of one wedding when Taylor married Russ without a single family member present. I can only speculate what they'll say when they hear Christy did the same thing."

"They'll skin me alive," she muttered. In all the excitement, in all her enthusiasm, Christy had forgotten how much her mother was looking forward to planning her wedding—which would be far more elaborate than the engagement party. As they left the Eagles Hall that dreadful night, Elizabeth Manning had been filled with ideas and opinions and excitement.

"Your parents won't do any such thing," Cody insisted.

"Cody, you don't know them." Christy felt a return of the nausea that had overtaken her at the party. Elizabeth Manning might never forgive her, and she'd always done what her mother thought best. Until now.

"They won't say a word," he said softly, "because I won't let them."

"But you don't understand—"

"If your parents are looking for someone to blame, they can deal with me. I was the one who insisted you marry me now. You just went along with it."

"Because I'm crazy in love with you and because I want to be your wife more than I've ever wanted anything."

"Hey," Rich said, raising both hands, "if both of you want to stand in front of the firing squad, I'm not going to stop you."

A chill descended on the room. "I take it there was a reason for this unexpected visit," Cody said pointedly.

"I was having woman problems," Rich mumbled.

"I thought there was something bothering you the night of the party." Although Rich hadn't enlightened her with the details, Christy should've known something was amiss. Otherwise he would have noticed how upset she was that evening.

"I may be having a few problems," Rich continued. "But they're nothing compared to what you two are facing. Married to one man while engaged to another—that, little sister, takes the cake."

"How kind of you to point it out." Yawning, she covered her mouth with her hand. "I'll make you a bed on the sofa and you can spend the rest of the night there."

"And interrupt your honeymoon?"

"It's already been interrupted," Cody reminded him. "If there's any justice in this world, I'll be able to return the favor someday."

"No chance of that. I'm swearing off women. The whole lot of them," Rich said with an emphatic shake of his head.

"Oh?" Christy had heard that song before.

"It's true. They're fickle, money-hungry, materialistic—"

"Thank you very much," Christy said, standing.

"With a few exceptions." He eyed his sister and smiled in apology.

"Now where was it you said you wanted to go for dinner?" Cody asked, reaching for his suit jacket.

"What's the matter with eating here?" Christy asked, not wanting to leave the apartment. Everything had been idyllic, and she was almost light-headed with happiness. To walk outside these protected walls might well invite trouble, and she'd had enough of that to last her a lifetime.

"I thought you wanted to dine out?"

"Not really." At the time he'd made the suggestion, Christy hadn't been able to think of an excuse. Now her mind overflowed with them, only she doubted Cody would consider any of them sensible.

She checked her freezer and extracted a package of pork chops. "I could wrestle us up some grub in no time." She turned around and grinned. "Am I beginning to sound like a Montana woman?"

"No. You're beginning to sound like a cattle thief." He moved behind her, slid his arms around her waist and nuzzled the curve of her neck.

"I'm a good cook."

"I know."

"How could you? Every time I go to make something for us, you interrupt me with...you know."

"Are you still having trouble saying the words?"

"No..." She giggled softly. "You've cured me of that." Twisting around, she leaned against the refrigerator door with her hands primly linked in front of her. "I can talk about making love about as often as you want to do it."

"Then let's get out of here before you give me any ideas."

"I like giving you ideas."

Cody glanced at his watch. "It's well past dinnertime and I'm hungry."

She moistened her lips. "You want me to say some of the other words you taught me?"

"Christy...no."

"Come here." She beckoned him with her index finger. "I'll whisper a couple of humdingers in your ear."

Cody ignored her. "I'm not going to let you sidetrack me."

"Oh, but I enjoy sidetracking you."

"That's the problem," Cody said. "I like it, too." He cleared his throat and changing tactics, grabbed his hat. "As your husband, I command that we leave for dinner now."

"You command?" She couldn't help laughing.

"That's right," he said, his mouth quivering with a suppressed smile. "I've got to teach you that I'm wearing the pants in this family."

"If that's the case, then why are they so often unzipped?"

Cody actually blushed, and Christy smiled.

"Because I'm a needy husband," he said gruffly. "Are you complaining?"

"Oh, no." She sent him a saucy grin. "Because I happen to be a needy wife. In fact, I seem to be experiencing a need right now. Is it hot in here to you?"

"Christy?" Cody's voice contained a low note of warning.

"It seems very hot...much too hot for all these clothes." She jerked the light sweater over her head and let it fall to the floor. Next she lowered the straps of her bra. "There," she said with a deep sigh, offering Cody what she hoped was a tantalizing display of her assets. "That feels better."

Cody stood his ground for a couple of minutes. Then he removed his hat and sent it flying across the room.

Silently Christy rejoiced.

"What about those jeans? Aren't they making you hot, too?" Cody asked.

"Maybe they are. Only I can't seem to open the snap." He didn't seem to notice that she hadn't tried.

"I see." He stepped over to her and made short work of her bra, then cupped Christy's breasts, his hands firm and insistent.

Sighing, Christy closed her eyes, giving herself over to a host of delightful sensations. Cody used one hand to stroke her breast, his other hand busy at the opening of her jeans. The zipper purred, and Christy was filled with another small sense of triumph.

She shivered helplessly as Cody slid her jeans down her hips. Her bikini underwear followed and that was the last thing she noticed for some time. Other than Cody, of course...

* * *

Christy's gaze fell reluctantly on Cody's luggage, which lay open on her bed. The lump in her throat seemed to grow larger every minute, until she could hardly swallow. She'd decided earlier that she wasn't going to be emotional when he left. They'd talked everything out earlier, planned for their future as best they could.

"You called the office?" Cody asked, putting a clean shirt in the suitcase.

"Yes… I told them I still had the flu." Lying didn't come easy to Christy. She felt as though she'd dug herself into a deep pit.

"What did they say?"

"Marcia, she's the office manager, said it's a slow week and not to worry about it, but she did make a point of asking me if I'd be in on Friday, which seemed a little odd."

"What about James?"

"He was at the courthouse." Her eyes widened at the unexpectedness of the question.

"When's the last time you heard from him?"

"Ah…" She had to stop and think. "The day after the engagement party. We talked briefly, and he explained that he wouldn't be able to keep in touch while the trial's going on." Under normal circumstances she would've seen him at the office, even if it was only for a few minutes, every morning. The fact that he hadn't made an effort to contact her said a good deal about their relationship.

"I see." Cody was obviously surprised.

"He's very intense and single-minded."

"Do you think he'll get an acquittal?"

"I don't know," she said.

"Whatever happens, this can't go on much longer. You realize that, don't you?"

"It won't be more than a few days." In discussing the situation they'd agreed on a time limit. Even if the trial dragged on for more than a week, Christy had promised to return James's ring and tell her parents that she and Cody were married.

"I still think we should tell your parents now."

"Not yet," she pleaded. The way Christy figured it, she'd start dropping hints so the fact that she'd married Cody wouldn't come as such a shock. After Cody flew back to Montana, she intended to drop by the family home and casually point out that James hadn't called her once since the party. She was hoping her parents would conclude that perhaps he wouldn't be the best husband for her, after all.

"Christy, I'm worried." Cody stood in front of her, his face concerned. "I don't like leaving you, especially under these circumstances."

"You know I love you."

His mouth curved into a sensual smile. "Beyond a doubt."

"Good." She put her arms around his waist and hugged him close. His heart beat strongly and evenly, offering her reassurance. In time they'd look back on these bleak days and laugh, she told herself. Someday, but not now.

"I'll phone you twice a day," he promised in a husky whisper. "Morning and night."

"I'll need that."

"So will I."

A sigh of regret rumbled through his chest as he dropped his arms. "It's time to go."

Neither of them seemed inclined to talk on the ride to the airport. Once Cody had checked in at the airline counter, he hugged Christy and kissed her lightly. It was as if he dared not kiss her the way they both enjoyed for fear he wouldn't be able to walk away. She understood all too well.

"Take care of yourself," she whispered.

"You, too."

She nodded, barely conscious of the way she clung to him. "Of course. We'll talk tonight. And before we know it, we'll be together."

"Together for good," he added. "I've got to go."

She closed her eyes tightly to keep from crying.

Cody kissed her again, only this time his mouth was fierce and wild. He released her by degrees, his reluctance tearing at her heart. With everything in her, Christy longed to board the plane with him. How much easier it would be to leave with Cody and then call James and her parents. But Christy knew she couldn't abandon her responsibilities. Cody understood that, too; she was sure of it. Christy Manning Franklin had always done the right thing, even if it was sometimes for the wrong reasons.

The next morning Christy returned to work for the first time since she'd left for vacation. What a difference a few weeks could make. She wasn't the same woman anymore.

"Christy." James's voice rose as he hurried over to her desk. "You're back. I hope you're feeling better."

For all his brilliance, James had very little experience of life. That was even more obvious to Christy now, and it made her feel oddly protective of him. She smiled as he reached for her hand, squeezing her fingers. Kissing her, even in an empty office, would have been unthinkable. He'd never been openly affectionate, but he was tender and good, and Christy couldn't ignore her guilty conscience.

"I'm much better, thanks. How's the Mulligan case going?"

He frowned and briefly looked away before responding. "Not too well."

"How much longer do you think it's going to be?"

"I'm hoping to wrap everything up by the end of next week."

"That long?" She couldn't keep the disappointment out of her voice.

James frowned again. "I didn't realize how negatively this case was affecting you."

"It's just that…" She couldn't very well announce that she was looking for the right moment to tell him she was married to someone else.

"I know, darling." He said the last word softly, as though fearing someone might overhear him. "This is a difficult time for us both, but it'll soon be over, and we can get on with our lives."

Now that Christy had a chance to study him, she saw that he seemed exhausted. Deep lines were etched around his eyes and mouth. Clearly James wasn't sleeping well.

"The case is going worse than you expected, isn't it?"

James sighed. "It's difficult to hide something like this from the one you love. Yes, it's going much worse."

"Is there anything I can do?" Christy found herself asking.

"Nothing," he said, giving her a rare smile. "But your concern is greatly appreciated." He looked at his watch. "It's time I left for the courthouse. I won't be back for the rest of the day."

Christy nodded.

"I suppose we should meet for dinner. After all, it's been a long time since we've gone out. But—"

"Don't worry," Christy interrupted. "I understand." If

she was having trouble dealing with a short conversation as James was walking out the door, an entire evening in each other's company would've been unbearable.

"Have a good day," he said gently.

"You, too."

He nodded, but his expression was somber. It was all too apparent that he didn't think he'd be having anything resembling a satisfactory day.

At lunchtime Christy looked up to find Marcia standing at her desk. The office manager had been with the firm for over fifteen years and was one of the finest women Christy knew.

Christy smiled. "Do you need something, Marcia?" After a three-week absence, her desk was piled high with folders.

"Can you come into one of the conference rooms for a minute?"

"Sure."

Leading the way, Marcia paused in front of the wide oak doors and grinned sheepishly. "It's good to have you back from vacation, Christy. It made all of us appreciate how much your bright smile adds to our day." With that she opened the door.

Christy was greeted with a chorus of "Surprise" from her fellow workers. A large cake sat in the center of the table, surrounded by several gaily wrapped packages. She must have looked stunned, because Marcia placed one hand on her shoulder and explained. "It's a wedding shower for you and James."

Thirteen

A week had passed since Cody had come back to Cougar Point. By far the longest week of his life. He wanted Christy with him, hungered for her smile and the way her eyes darkened when she looked up at him in that suggestive way.

He loved Christy, and marrying her had helped him cope with the ridiculous set of circumstances in which they found themselves trapped.

He wasn't pleased that she was still engaged to James, but there seemed little he could do about it. If it had been up to him, he'd have settled it before flying out of Seattle, but Christy had been adamant that she was doing the right thing in waiting. Cody wasn't convinced, but the decision had been hers, and he didn't feel he could go against Christy's wishes.

So they were husband and wife. Cody *felt* married. It was as if he'd lived his entire life waiting for this woman. In the too-brief days they'd been together, Cody knew he'd changed. His life's purpose had been focused on his career, and in many ways it still was. Christy, however, added a new dimension to his personality.

She'd taught him to dream.

Unlike Russ, who'd always planned on marriage, Cody had given up hope of ever finding the right woman. It hadn't been a conscious decision; in fact, he wasn't fully aware of it until he met Christy.

He was getting downright philosophical, he mused. Christy gave his life a deeper meaning, and their marriage made everything else more...important, somehow.

Someone brighter than he was would have guessed what was happening the first time they'd kissed. He still recalled feeling lost and bewildered. When he learned she was engaged to marry James, Cody had been even more shaken than he dared to admit.

James. The other man's name brought a grim frown. Reluctantly Christy had shown him a picture of the attorney. He looked clean-cut, professional, intelligent. But he guessed that James Wilkens lacked passion. It was difficult to imagine James allowing a little thing like falling in love to overcome his inhibitions.

Throwing off his anxiety about Christy's engagement, he stood, moved into his kitchen and poured a cup of coffee. He was supposed to be packing, getting ready for his move to Miles City, but because of everything that had happened between Christy and him, he'd delayed until the last minute.

Almost everything in the living room was inside cardboard boxes, and Cody headed absently toward the bedroom, intent on getting as much accomplished that evening as he could.

He recognized his mistake immediately.

Christy had never slept on his bed, never even been in this room, but the fires she sparked to life within Cody were more evident there than anywhere else.

Feeling helpless, missing her so much, Cody sat on the end of the bed. He'd married himself one little hellcat. A smile tempted his mouth. She was a seductress in bed, and an angel out of it.

His need for her was insatiable. Half the time they were so impatient for each other that they hadn't bothered to use any birth control. They'd discussed that; if she were to get pregnant, Cody wouldn't mind. In many ways it would please him tremendously, although he admitted the timing would be all wrong for her. Christy had enough pressures on her already.

A week. They'd been apart for seven days, and it felt like an eternity. Dammit all, he wanted her with him.

Now. Not two days from now.

Not next week. *Now.*

His patience was wearing paper-thin. He picked up the phone and called the number he knew by heart. Christy answered on the second ring.

Her voice softened when she heard his. "Soon," she promised in a seductive whisper that nearly drove him crazy.

"How soon?" he demanded.

"A couple more days."

"Forgive me for saying this, but didn't you claim it would be 'a couple of days' a couple of days ago?" His voice was sharp despite his best efforts.

"Yes, but there are complications."

"Aren't there always?"

"Cody, please, don't be angry with me…"

"I called because I love you."

"I love you, too," she said, sounding a little bewildered. Cody realized he'd probably pushed too hard and backed off, spending the next few minutes telling his wife he loved her.

When he replaced the receiver, he was more frustrated than ever.

* * *

Cody was enjoying breakfast in the bowling alley early the following morning when Russ showed up. It wasn't unusual for Russ to eat in town, but rarer since he'd married Taylor.

The rancher slid into the booth across from Cody. "I thought I'd find you here."

"You looking for me?" he asked.

"You could say that." Russ turned over the ceramic mug and waited until the waitress came by and filled it for him. He reached for the menu. "You look like hell."

"Nice of you to say so," Cody muttered.

"I didn't come here to pick a fight."

Their friendship was too good for this kind of bickering. "I haven't been sleeping well," Cody admitted reluctantly, sipping his own coffee. Truth be known, he hadn't had a decent night's sleep since he'd flown home from Seattle.

"How's Christy holding up?"

"A lot better than I am." She always managed to sound cheerful, as if it was perfectly normal for a couple to be married three days and then separated for weeks.

"You sure about that?"

Russ's question caught Cody off guard. He narrowed his eyes, wondering if Russ knew something he didn't. Russ's attention seemed to be on the menu.

"I'm not sure of anything," Cody answered thoughtfully. "What makes you ask?"

Typically Russ shrugged. "Nothing in particular." He set aside the menu, declined to order breakfast when Mary delivered Cody's and sat there looking superior. "Go ahead and eat," he said, motioning toward the plate of sliced ham, eggs, hash browns and toast.

"I wasn't planning on letting my meal get cold," Cody

informed him frostily. His nerves were shot, and the last thing he needed was his best friend dropping obscure hints.

Cupping the mug with both hands, Russ leaned back in the booth. "Who else knows you and Christy are married?" he asked after a moment.

"Everyone except James and her parents." Christy's three older brothers were all aware of the fact that they'd eloped. Cody had spoken to the two oldest brothers, Paul and Jason, before he'd left Seattle. Rich had been the first to discover their secret, of course, and he'd quickly let the others in on it.

"Should I thank you for the fact that Mrs. Simmons stopped me in the street yesterday with a jar of her watermelon pickles?" Cody asked, eyeing Russ. "She says she heard the sheriff had taken himself a wife and wanted to give me a small gift."

"Ah... I might've mentioned something to Mrs. Simmons," Russ said, hiding a smile. Mrs. Simmons handed out homemade preserves at every opportunity. Each family in town ended up with at least one jar every year.

Russ took another drink of his coffee. "I guess you and everyone else in town figured out Taylor got pregnant on our honeymoon."

Cody was having trouble following this conversation. "What's that got to do with anything?"

"Nothing," he said with an enigmatic smile.

"Listen, Russ, if you know something I don't, spit it out, would you? I'm in no mood for games. Is something going on with Christy that I don't know?"

"Did she tell you about the wedding shower?"

Cody scowled. "No. When was this?"

"Last week. The girls in the office held it for her, threw it as a surprise."

"That was nice."

"It wasn't for you and Christy," Russ barked. "What's with you, man? The shower was for Christy and James."

Cody rubbed his face. She hadn't said a word, not a single word about any wedding shower. And now that he knew, Cody thought that, maybe, just maybe, Christy did sound a little less cheerful than usual. He was fast losing his perspective.

"I bet she hasn't told you something else, either."

Cody resented having his brother-in-law tell him things Christy hadn't even mentioned. "You mean there's more?" he asked darkly. "Did her mother take her shopping and spring for a five-thousand-dollar wedding dress?"

"Nothing quite so drastic," Russ said with a hint of a smile. "I overheard Taylor on the phone last night. She was talking to Christy."

"What did Christy say?"

"I don't know. I only heard half the conversation."

Cody had talked to Christy, too. He'd hung up with a restless feeling he couldn't identify, but he'd attributed it to the fact that she was still in Seattle when he wanted her in Montana.

"And?"

"And when I asked Taylor, she seemed reluctant to say much. But I heard her discuss symptoms."

"Symptoms?"

"I tried to tell you earlier," Russ informed him with a look that questioned Cody's intelligence, "but you got so damn defensive, I shut up." Russ shook his head. "Taylor got pregnant in Reno. Think about it, Cody. Taylor and Christy are two of *five* children. Doesn't it seem obvious to you that the Manning women are a fertile lot?"

"Christy's not pregnant," Cody said with a confidence he wasn't feeling. He felt his head start to spin.

"You're sure of that?"

"She'd say something if she even suspected. I'd bet on it."

"Of course. She tells you everything."

"I'd like to think she'd confide in me," Cody said, growing more uncertain.

"If she didn't tell you about the wedding shower, you can damn well wager she wouldn't mention that she's hanging her head over a toilet every morning."

Cody felt as if he'd been kicked in the stomach. Christy was pregnant and too concerned about protecting her parents and James to risk telling him.

Hell, she *couldn't* tell him. He hadn't made it easy for her, had he? Missing her the way he did, Cody was irritable and impatient while Christy carried the brunt of the load.

Hastily he slid out of the booth and put on his hat. He'd been looking for an excuse to put an end to this nonsense, and now he had one.

"Where you going?" Russ demanded, reaching across the table for Cody's untouched breakfast plate. He leaned forward and retrieved the salt and pepper shakers.

"Seattle."

Chuckling, Russ nodded. "That's what I thought."

"Enjoy your breakfast," Cody muttered sarcastically.

"Thanks," he responded between bites, "I will."

Christy had been feeling blue all day. Cody wasn't home when she'd tried to call, and that depressed her even more. Nothing made sense. Nothing. She felt weepy and excited. Confused and elated. Engaged to one man. Married to another. She might be pregnant. It might be the beginning of an ulcer. She didn't know which.

She couldn't sleep, although she desperately needed to.

Her appetite was nil. After going through the bother of fixing herself spaghetti and a salad for dinner, her meal sat uneaten on her kitchen table.

Feeling wretched, she sank down in front of the television and turned on the movie channel, silently chastising herself for not writing thank-you notes to her friends from the office. Sending notes of appreciation for gifts she intended to return seemed a ridiculous thing to do.

A 1940s war movie with an incredibly young John Wayne and Maureen O'Hara was on, and she was soon caught up in the fast-paced action. How minor her troubles seemed compared to those on the screen.

Damp tissues crowded her end table. She was sniffling ingloriously when her doorbell chimed.

Whoever was on the other side was certainly impatient. The doorbell rang a second time before she was halfway across the carpet. "Hold your horses," she said peevishly. She wasn't interested in company.

Christy quickly changed her mind.

"Cody," she whispered when she saw her husband. "Oh, Cody." Without another word she broke into tears and flew into his arms.

Seconds later, his mouth was on hers in that urgent, hungry way that was so familiar between them. Cody directed her into the living room, then closed the door with his foot, all the while kissing her.

Christy's hands roamed his face when he released her. She giggled and locked her arms around his neck, holding on to him for everything she was worth.

"Oh… Christy, I missed you," he breathed. His hands

caressed her face. Then he was kissing her again and again as if he'd never get enough of the taste of her.

"I've been so miserable without you," Christy admitted, feeling weepy and jubilant at the same time.

"Me, too, love." He looked at her for a long moment, frowning, then smiling, then frowning again.

"What is it?" Christy asked, reacting to his confusion but not understanding it. She sensed a wonder in him, too, as if he couldn't quite believe they were married.

Christy believed it. Their love was the only thing that had gotten her through the trauma of the past week.

"Are you pregnant?" he asked without preamble, running his splayed fingers through her hair. His hold on her tightened, but Christy doubted he was aware of it.

Involuntarily her eyes widened at his question. "I… I don't know yet."

"You've been ill?"

"Yes… How'd you know that?" Usually she'd been sick in the mornings, but often in the afternoons, too. If she was looking for a pattern, there wasn't one. She was confused and anxious, and not knowing where to turn, she'd called her sister. "Taylor?" Christy had never dreamed that her older sister would say anything to Cody. She'd counted on Taylor to be discreet.

"No," Cody admitted, scowling. "I had breakfast with Russ this morning. Rather Russ ate *my* breakfast while he cheerfully pointed out that Taylor got pregnant while they were still in Reno and—"

Christy interrupted him. "You came because of that?"

"No." Cody dropped his hands and stepped away. "Well, not completely. I did come in part because I was afraid…no, afraid's the wrong word. I was concerned for you. I came for another reason, too."

He was so sincere, so forthright. "Yes?"

His eyes darkened. "You didn't tell me about the wedding shower."

Christy's gaze fell. "I couldn't."

"I realize that now, and I realize a whole lot more. This has to be the end of it, Christy." His eyes burned into hers. "As your husband—the man that loves you—I can't let you continue this charade any longer."

Spontaneous tears filled her eyes as she nodded. "I don't think I can pull it off another day. I...thought I was doing what was best for everyone involved, but I see now that I was only prolonging the agony—mostly my own. You were right, so right. There'll never be a good time to tell Mom and Dad. I did us both a terrible disservice by refusing to acknowledge that."

Cody's lips brushed her forehead. "Don't be so hard on yourself."

"There's no one else to blame. It's just that it's really difficult for me to disappoint my parents. I love them both so much, and they're so fond of James."

"But they don't have the right to pick your husband for you."

"I know." She exhaled softly. "I would've liked to have spared James this, but he has to know. I... I did him a disservice by not telling him the afternoon I came home. James isn't as emotionally fragile as I've made him out to be."

Cody's eyes flared briefly before he spoke. "How soon can we get you in to see a doctor?"

"A doctor?" she asked. "Why?" Sure, she'd been overprotective of James and reluctant about telling her parents the truth, but that didn't mean she needed medical help.

"If you're pregnant—"

"Oh, that," she said, relieved. "Taylor recommended

I buy one of those home pregnancy test kits, which I did this afternoon. Only I decided I could deal with *not* knowing better than I could handle knowing. Does that sound crazy?"

Cody chuckled. "No. But do you mind satisfying my curiosity? I, for one, am anxious to find out if I'm going to become a father."

"You definitely are," she said, loving the way Cody's face brightened at her words. "The only question is whether or not it's going to be nine months from now."

Cody's arms were around her, his eyes filled with a tenderness that made her knees grow weak. "The test takes about twenty minutes," she said, sliding her hands up the front of his shirt.

"Twenty minutes," Cody repeated.

She moistened her lips, thrilled when her husband's narrowed gaze followed the seductive movement of her tongue.

"Are you suggesting what I think you're suggesting?" he whispered.

Christy nodded.

"But if you're pregnant, will it hurt the baby?" His voice was hoarse, and a dark flame seemed to leap to life in his eyes.

"Not according to Taylor."

"You're sure?"

"Positive. Besides, it'll do this baby's mother a whole lot of good."

Christy lay contentedly in his arms, her long, sleek body nestled intimately with his. If they spent the next ten years exactly like this, Cody wouldn't have a single complaint. He loved this woman. He loved everything about her.

"Are you disappointed?" she asked softly, rolling over so she could look at him when he answered.

He kissed her, his mouth clinging to hers, his hands caressing her. "You've got to be kidding."

They'd been on fire for each other from the moment he'd arrived. Their hands had trembled as they'd hurriedly undressed each other, their mouths eager, filled with promises and pleas.

Raising herself on one elbow, Christy smiled dreamily down on him and lovingly traced her fingers over the hard angles of his face as though memorizing every feature. To Cody's way of thinking, that was unnecessary. He never planned to leave her again.

"I wasn't talking about the lovemaking," she said. "I was referring to the pregnancy test."

His arm curved around her trim waist. "No. When the time's right, we'll start our family and not because we were in too much of a hurry to—"

"May I remind you how much of a hurry we were in a few minutes ago?"

"No, you may not." He clasped her around the waist and they both dissolved into laughter.

A woman he could love *and* laugh with—how did he get so lucky?

"It might be a good idea if I went over to my parents' house alone," Christy said. She looked up at him beseechingly. "Please, Cody?"

"I won't hear of it, Christy," he answered in a voice that brooked no dissent. "We're in this together."

"But..."

"You phoned James?"

"You know I did. He'll arrive at my parents' within the hour." James had sounded surprised to hear from her, and even more perplexed when she explained she needed to speak with him urgently. He'd offered to come to her apartment, but when she'd suggested they meet at her family home in an hour, he'd agreed.

"How did Rich find out we're telling your parents?" Cody asked, frowning.

Her scoundrel of a brother had been visiting their parents when Christy called and in fact had answered the phone. There must have been something in her voice that conveyed her intent, because Rich had made it clear he planned to stay around for the fireworks display. That comment reminded Christy that the coming scene was bound to evoke plenty of emotion. Christy wished Cody would wait for the worst to pass before he presented himself as their latest son-in-law.

"Don't even think of arguing with me," he said. "We're doing this together."

"All right," she murmured, holding in a sigh. "The way I figure it, we'll have forty-five minutes to explain everything to my parents before James arrives."

"Good." Cody nodded.

"Are you ready?" she asked, and her voice trembled despite every effort to maintain an optimistic facade. Her heart felt frozen with fear. Although she'd wanted to handle this on her own, she was grateful Cody had chosen to go with her.

They spoke infrequently on the drive to her parents' home. When they did, it was to murmur words of encouragement, or reinforce how much they loved each other.

As they pulled in to the driveway, another car came in after them. "Oh, no," Christy breathed.

"What's wrong?"

"It's James." Christy climbed out of the car, not waiting for Cody. She turned to face her fiancé. "You're early," she said, struggling to keep the annoyance out of her voice.

"I called your parents, and they suggested I come now." James's gaze narrowed as Cody came to stand behind her and rested his hand on her shoulder.

It was clear that James took offense at the familiar way Cody touched her. His eyes went cold as he demanded, "Who is this?"

Fourteen

Christy felt Cody's hand tighten involuntarily. The two men glared at each other like hostile dogs who'd inadvertently strayed into each other's territory. She supposed it wasn't a complimentary analogy, but it seemed fitting.

"James, this is Cody Franklin," she said, hating the unexpected way her voice squeaked.

"So the gang's all here," Rich shouted, coming out the front door, ready to greet the two men. "I suppose you're wondering why I've called this meeting." He laughed, obviously in a playful mood.

Christy glared at him, wondering what he was doing.

"Do you mind waiting a few minutes?" Rich asked. "Jason and Paul are on their way."

"As a matter of fact, I do mind," Christy snapped. She gripped Rich hard by the elbow and forced him back into the house. "Please introduce Cody to Mom and Dad," she said.

Rich's mouth fell open. "Me? No way, little sister. I happen to value my neck."

"I'll take care of everything," Cody said, slapping Rich on the back. "You have nothing to fear but fear itself."

"James," Christy said reproachfully, turning to face

the attorney, "it would have helped matters if you'd come when I suggested, but since you're here now, we'll settle this in the kitchen."

She walked into the house and passed her mother, who was watching her curiously.

"We'll talk in the kitchen," Christy reminded James when he hesitated in front of Elizabeth Manning and shrugged.

"Christy?" her father called. "What's going on here?"

"I'll explain everything in a few minutes, but first I have to clear something up with James."

"Actually, I'll be more than happy to explain," Cody said, stepping forward. He offered Eric Manning his hand, and they exchanged a brief handshake as Cody introduced himself.

"Exactly what's going on?" James wanted to know as they entered the kitchen.

Christy stopped at the huge round oak table. She pulled out a chair and sat down, then gestured for James to do the same.

He complied, but with some hesitation. "You never answered my question. Who is that man?"

"Cody Franklin."

"That doesn't explain much."

"No, it doesn't," she agreed readily. With a sigh, she wondered where she should even begin. "He's from Montana."

"Ah, that accounts for the cowboy hat."

"We met when I went to spend time with Taylor. Cody's the new sheriff of Custer County."

James nodded, urging her to go on. She'd explained the easy part; everything else was hard.

Unable to stay seated, Christy surged to her feet and frowned as she organized her thoughts. "Sometimes, not often I think, but sometimes when two strangers meet something happens…something special." She paused and looked at James, hoping, praying she'd see a glimmer of understanding. She didn't.

"You're talking about fairy tales," he said, and laughed as though she'd made a poor joke. "Are you going to break into song next?"

Christy ignored the question. "A special magic, a chemistry that flows between the two of them," she went on. "There was magic when Taylor met Russ. At first they both resisted it and—"

"Yes, yes," James interrupted, "but what have your sister and her husband got to do with anything?"

"Cody and I experienced that same…chemistry," she announced, astonished this genius attorney could be so obtuse. "Neither of us was expecting to fall in love."

"You didn't," James said flatly, dismissing her claim.

"But I did."

"You can't be in love with Franklin. It isn't possible when you're in love with me."

"James, please, let me explain—"

He interrupted with an upraised hand. "Christy, darling, what you experienced for this man is a simple case of homesickness. It's perfectly understandable, and forgivable. We were only engaged a day or two, and after working so hard for all those weeks, it only makes sense that you'd look to another man for companionship."

"James," she said, taking both of his hands in her own, "that's not the case. I wish it was that simple, but it isn't."

"Nonsense." James hadn't been touted as a brilliant attorney without reason. With infuriating ease, he twisted everything she said around to suit his own purposes.

"I love Cody." She said it forcefully enough, she prayed, for James to accept it as truth.

"As I already said, that isn't possible." He stood, placing his hands on her shoulders, his look indulgent. "You love me, remember? Otherwise you wouldn't have agreed to become my wife."

"I agreed to your proposal because I *like* you. And because it pleased my mother and father," she cried.

"Christy." He said her name softly, as if she were a petulant child. "I'm sure you're mistaken."

"I'm not." Her hands on his forearms, she stared directly into his eyes. "I love Cody Franklin so much I married him."

It hurt Christy to watch the transformation come over his face. She hated the pain she saw. The disbelief. The humiliation.

"It's true," she said before he could question her.

Anger flickered in his eyes. He jerked his arms free from her and dropped them to his sides.

"When?"

"Does it matter?"

"No, I guess not." His eyes drifted briefly shut. That said more than any words he could have spoken.

She took a moment to open the clasp of her purse and take out the diamond ring he'd given her. When she handed it back to him, James stared at the velvet box as if he'd never seen it before. "Keep it."

"No, I can't."

He removed it from her hand and turned away long enough to shove it into his coat pocket. When he looked at her again, he was able to mask the pain, but she knew him well enough to realize how deeply she'd hurt him. Causing him such intense suffering was the most difficult thing she'd ever had to do. James didn't deserve to be treated this way.

"I intended to tell you the minute I got home from

Montana," she said in her own defense, the words coming so fast they nearly blended together.

"The engagement party," he supplied for her. "You tried to tell me then, didn't you?" He didn't wait for her to answer. "I sensed something was wrong and trapped you into setting a wedding date." He scowled. "On a subconscious level I ignored the obvious, immersed myself in my work, hoping whatever had happened with you would pass. I know I made it difficult to talk to me. But am I that unreasonable that you couldn't have told me the truth?"

"That wasn't it." Christy felt it was important to correct that impression. "I just didn't feel I could. You were so heavily involved in the Mulligan case and I didn't want to—"

"I'm still involved."

"I know. But the worst of it's over, and I couldn't go on pretending. I'm sorry, James, sorrier than you'll ever realize."

He snickered, but didn't openly contradict her.

"I'm terribly fond of you and I'd give anything to—"

"Fond." He spit out the word as if it were an obscenity.

His vehemence was a shock. James wasn't a passionate man. Rarely had Christy seen him reveal any emotion, in or out of a courtroom.

Once more she tried to explain. "I don't expect you to understand how difficult this was for me. That would be asking too much of you." She knew she sounded shaken, but she couldn't help that. "If there was any possible way I could've done this without hurting you, I would have."

He didn't respond.

"You're a wonderful man, James, and someday a woman will come into your life—the right woman. And you'll know what I mean."

"You were the right woman. Or so I believed."

"I'm sorry. So very sorry."

He shook his head as if he didn't quite believe her. His hand was buried in his pocket, and Christy guessed he'd made a tight fist around the diamond.

"I only wish you the best," she whispered.

He breathed deeply, then nodded, although Christy had the impression he didn't agree with her. She was about to say something more when a thunderous shout came from the direction of the living room.

"Your father?" James asked.

Christy nodded. "Cody must have told him."

James's gaze continued to hold hers. "You'll be all right?"

"Of course."

He seemed to accept that. "Can I kiss you, one last time?"

In response she opened her arms to him, her eyes brimming with unshed tears. James reached for her, his touch gentle. He held her close for just a moment, then pressed his mouth to hers.

He broke away, and his finger touched her cheek, his eyes clouded. "Be happy, Christy."

"I will."

With that he turned and walked out of the kitchen. Christy stood by the window and watched him move down the walkway, then climb inside his car. For what seemed an eternity, James sat in the driver's seat with his hands gripping the steering wheel as he stared straight ahead.

Christy couldn't delay the confrontation with her family any longer. Squaring her shoulders, she walked into the living room to find her brothers, Paul, Jason and

Rich, perched on bar stools as though viewing a stage performance.

"Christy," her mother sobbed, dabbing a tissue under her nose, "tell us it isn't true."

She moved next to Cody and sat on the arm of the chintz-covered chair. She slipped her hand into his. "Cody and I were married last week."

"Married!" Her father stormed to his feet as if she'd desecrated the Constitution of the United States.

Confused, Christy's eyes went to Cody's.

"I hadn't gotten around to telling them that part yet," he told her.

"Married," her mother repeated. "It can't be true. Christy would never do anything so… We have a wedding to plan. You couldn't possibly have gone off and gotten married without telling your own mother and father. It isn't like you to do something so underhanded."

"I thought they knew," she whispered, bewildered. "I heard Dad shout, and I thought… I assumed."

"All I said," Cody explained, "was that you wanted a little privacy with James so you could return his engagement ring."

"Oh." She swallowed and closed her eyes for a moment. "Well, Mom and Dad," she said brightly, looking at them once more, "I see you've met your new son-in-law."

"Welcome to the family," Paul said, holding up a soft drink can in tribute. "From what Rich said, you're a friend of Russ's."

Cody nodded.

"But you couldn't possibly be married," her mother whimpered, turning to Eric as though he could explain everything.

"Trust me, Mom, we're married."

"They're married," Rich said, saluting them with his

own can of soda. "I should know. I was at their wedding night."

"Hear, hear," Jason cried, wearing the ever-present baseball cap. "Wait a minute. At their *wedding* night?"

"I don't find any of this humorous or in good taste," Eric roared. "Your sister's turned down the best man in three states for some...some small-town lawman. Bad enough that Taylor had to marry a country boy, but Christy, too? Never!"

"Dad," Christy reminded him softly, "the deed is done."

"But, Christy," Elizabeth wailed, "I bought the material for the bridesmaids' dresses and we've put down a deposit on the hall for the reception, and—"

"I didn't mean to cheat you out of a wedding, Mom. I really didn't."

"What will we say to our friends?" Her mother appeared to be in a state of shock. She'd gone deathly pale, and her shoulders jerked as she tried to gain control of her emotions.

"If you're worried about what to tell your friends," Paul said, sounding knowledgeable, "I'd suggest the truth."

"Stay out of this," Eric shouted, dismissing his eldest son with a shake of his head. "We're in one hell of a mess here."

"How's that?" Cody asked.

"Christy's married to you is how," Eric informed him none too gently. "My daughter doesn't belong in the country. She was born and raised in the city. We've already got Taylor living out in the sticks. I won't allow Christy to be out there slopping hogs or whatever you do in that backwoods community."

"Dad!" Christy was outraged. "It's *my* decision. And

Cougar Point isn't any backwoods community. Besides, we won't be living there."

"You're moving to Washington state?" Elizabeth asked Cody, her eyes wide and hopeful.

"Sorry, no."

Her mother drooped against the back of the sofa and reached for a fresh tissue. She wadded it up and pressed it over her eyes as if to block out this horrible scene.

"Cody's the sheriff," Christy said, wanting to impress both of her parents with the fact that he was a responsible citizen. "We'll be living in Miles City once he's installed."

"A sheriff should please them," Jason said under his breath, speaking to his two brothers.

"I think they prefer an attorney over a sheriff," Rich concluded when neither parent responded to Christy's announcement.

"I recognize that this is all rather abrupt," Cody said in a reasonable voice. "I don't blame you for being shocked. I can't even blame you for being concerned. You wouldn't have raised a daughter as wonderful as Christy if you weren't the kind of people who'd care about her happiness."

"That's good," Paul whispered to Jason. "He's going to win them over with flattery."

"Will you three shut up," Eric yelled, infuriated with his sons and not bothering to disguise it.

"Dad, please try to understand," Christy tried again. "I fell in love with Cody."

"Falling in love is one thing, but marrying him on the sly is another."

"While she was engaged to James, I might add." Rich apparently didn't know when to keep his mouth closed.

Both Eric and Cody sent daggers his way. Guarding his face with his hands, Rich pretended to ward off their attack.

"I can only say I love you both," Christy said. "I'd never intentionally do anything to hurt you. In fact, most of my life I've done everything I can to please you, right down to becoming engaged to James."

"I can't believe I'm hearing this," Eric said to his wife. "We raised her the best we knew how, and now this."

"Darling, we thought you loved James," her mother pleaded.

"I thought I did, too, until I met Cody." Her hand clasped Cody's, and she smiled down at him. "I know I made mistakes, lots of them."

"*We* made mistakes," Cody corrected, his gaze holding hers.

"No one's making a list," her father mumbled, "but if I were—"

"Nothing on this earth will ever convince me I made a mistake marrying Cody." Her father obviously wasn't willing to accept what they'd done. As Christy suspected, her family would need time to come to terms with her marriage and the fact that she'd be leaving the Seattle area.

"I gave my week's notice when I returned from vacation," Christy said. It had been one of the low points of her life, telling Marcia she was quitting her job in order to prepare for her wedding. The lie had all but choked her.

"You're leaving your job?"

"She couldn't very well continue working with James," Eric muttered to his wife. "And from the sounds of it, she intends to live in Montana."

"Poor James," Elizabeth said with a regretful sigh. "He would've made such a good husband."

"I'll make Christy a good husband, too," Cody promised. "I love your daughter."

An awkward silence followed Cody's words. "My daughter doesn't belong in Montana, and she deserves a decent wedding with her family around her. Christy's not the type of girl a man takes to a justice of the peace."

"We were married by a minister." Christy knew even before she spoke that there was little she could say to appease her father. He wasn't accustomed to having his authority challenged. Not even by a sheriff.

"It might be best if we gave your parents a chance to get used to the idea," Cody suggested.

Christy agreed, but leaving her family home was one of the most difficult tasks of her life.

Paul, Jason and Rich followed them outside.

"They'll come around," Paul said to Cody as they exchanged handshakes. Paul was tall and silver-blond, the only one in the family who'd inherited that coloring.

"Just give 'em a year or three," Rich said with less than diplomatic cheer. "Grandkids will be sure to win 'em over. There *will* be children, won't there?" He was eyeing Christy as if a good stare would tell him if she was in the family way.

"Don't worry about a thing," Jason said, throwing his arm over Cody's broad shoulders. "Mom and Dad will accept your marriage before you know it."

"They've got two days," Cody said darkly.

"Two days?" Christy echoed, a little stunned, although she shouldn't have been. Cody's life was in Miles City, and he'd recently taken three days of his vacation to spend with her. He couldn't afford to take off any more, not during this important period of transition.

"Is that too soon for you?" he asked, his eyes revealing his concern. "I figured that would give us enough time to get your things packed and shipped."

She nodded, slipping her arms around his waist. Her life was linked to Cody's now, and there was no turning back.

They hadn't gone through airport security yet, but Christy delayed, glancing around the terminal building, certain if she stayed there long enough her parents would rush in and throw their arms around her, telling her how much they loved her and how they wished her and Cody well.

Only they hadn't come.

"Honey," Cody said patiently. "They aren't coming. We have to go."

"I know, but I'd hoped. I…thought they'd at least want to say goodbye."

Christy hadn't heard from them in the two hectic days they'd spent packing up her apartment. She'd tried not to let it affect her, but she'd always been close to her parents, and being shunned this way hurt more than anything they could have said.

"Give them time," Cody said—he'd been saying that a lot—and it seemed as if her pain belonged to him, too.

Christy offered him a brave smile and nodded.

They joined the security line, then hurried to their departure area, arriving just as their flight was called. Christy realized there was nothing left to do but board the plane that would take her away from everything that was familiar and bring her to a whole new life.

"You're not sorry, are you?" Cody asked once they were seated and about to take off.

"No." Beyond a doubt Christy knew she was meant to be with Cody. She would've preferred to have her parents' blessing. But if she had to do without it, then she'd learn to accept that.

Cody was her love. And now he was her life.

Since Paul, Jason and Rich all worked days and hadn't been able to come to the airport to say their goodbyes, the three of them had taken Christy and Cody to dinner the night before.

Everyone had made an effort to have a good time, and they all had.

Only something vital had been missing. No one said anything. No one had to.

Eric and Elizabeth Manning weren't there. And what was missing was their love. Their blessing. Their approval.

Christy didn't know when she'd see her parents again.

"Oh, Cody," Christy whispered, stepping back to study her husband in his full dress uniform. "You look… wonderful."

They'd been in Miles City, Montana, a week. In that time they'd moved into their first home, unpacked their belongings and gone about making a place for themselves in the community.

"When will Russ and Taylor get here?"

"Oh," she said, still a little awed by how handsome Cody looked. "I forgot to tell you Taylor phoned. They're going to meet us at the courthouse for the installation."

"Good." He straightened the sleeves of his crisp uniform jacket. "Well, I'm ready."

"I'm not," Christy told him. "In case you haven't noticed, I'm not dressed yet."

Cody wiggled his eyebrows suggestively. "All the better to seduce you, my dear."

Christy giggled. "I do believe you've seduced me in

every room of this house, Sheriff Franklin. More than once."

"There's time—"

"There most certainly is not." She scurried past him. She wasn't quick enough, and with little effort, Cody caught her in his arms.

"Cody," she warned him. "We...can't. You don't want to be late for your own installation. And I don't want to arrive at the ceremony looking like a disheveled mess."

Cody hesitated. "Well..."

She entwined her arms around his neck and kissed him soundly.

"Shameless hussy," he said with a grin as he unwound her arms. "Get dressed before I change my mind."

"Yes, sir." Mockingly she saluted him.

A half hour later they entered the courthouse. Judge Carter would be doing the honors, and the room was filled to capacity. Christy was escorted to the front row of reserved seats. Many of the citizens of Cougar Point were in the audience.

The ceremony was about to begin when Taylor, carrying Eric, and Russ slipped into the chairs to her right. That left two empty seats on her left. Christy was so busy greeting her sister that she didn't notice the vacant chairs had been filled. She turned to smile and introduce herself to her seatmates, and to her astonishment saw her parents.

"Mom. Dad." Without warning, tears flooded her eyes. She looked at Cody, who was standing at the podium with Judge Carter. When she nodded toward her family, Cody's face brightened.

"Are you willing to forgive your father for being a stubborn old cuss?" Eric asked in a low voice.

Christy nodded, shaken by the intensity of her relief.

She hugged him and then her mother, who was as teary-eyed as Christy.

When the ceremony was over, Cody joined them. Christy's husband and father faced each other. Eric Manning offered his hand first, and the two exchanged a hearty shake.

Judge Carter came forward to introduce himself a few minutes after that, and soon they were all talking at once.

A small reception followed, and Cody held Christy's hand as he led the way.

"Thank you," she whispered.

He shook his head. "Honey, as much as I'd like to take credit for bringing your parents out here, I can't."

"Not that," she said, smiling up at him from the very depths of her soul. "Thank you for loving me."

"That," he said softly, "was the easiest thing I've ever done."

"Eric Manning," Christy could hear her father say over the din of raised voices. "I'm the sheriff's father-in-law. We're proud of the boy. Glad to have him in the family."

"Not as glad as he is to be part of it," Cody murmured, smiling at his wife.

* * * * *

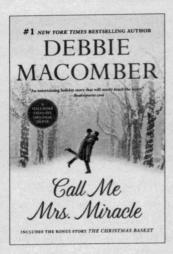

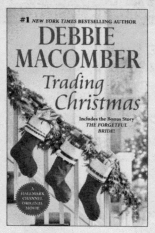

Turn your love of reading into rewards you'll love with

Harlequin My Rewards

**Join for FREE today at
www.HarlequinMyRewards.com**

Earn **FREE BOOKS** of your choice.

Experience **EXCLUSIVE OFFERS** and contests.

Enjoy **BOOK RECOMMENDATIONS**
selected just for you.

PLUS! Sign up now
and get **500** points
right away!

Earn
FREE
REWARDS
HarlequinMyRewards.com
Join
Today!

MYR16R

REQUEST YOUR FREE BOOKS!

2 FREE NOVELS
FROM THE ROMANCE COLLECTION
PLUS 2 FREE GIFTS!

YES! Please send me 2 FREE novels from the Romance Collection and my 2 FREE gifts (gifts are worth about $10). After receiving them, if I don't wish to receive any more books, I can return the shipping statement marked "cancel." If I don't cancel, I will receive 4 brand-new novels every month and be billed just $6.49 per book in the U.S. or $6.99 per book in Canada. That's a savings of at least 19% off the cover price. It's quite a bargain! Shipping and handling is just 50¢ per book in the U.S. and 75¢ per book in Canada.* I understand that accepting the 2 free books and gifts places me under no obligation to buy anything. I can always return a shipment and cancel at any time. Even if I never buy another book, the two free books and gifts are mine to keep forever.

194/394 MDN GH4D

Name	(PLEASE PRINT)	
Address		Apt. #
City	State/Prov.	Zip/Postal Code

Signature (if under 18, a parent or guardian must sign)

Mail to the **Reader Service:**
IN U.S.A.: P.O. Box 1867, Buffalo, NY 14240-1867
IN CANADA: P.O. Box 609, Fort Erie, Ontario L2A 5X3

Want to try two free books from another line?
Call 1-800-873-8635 or visit www.ReaderService.com.

* Terms and prices subject to change without notice. Prices do not include applicable taxes. Sales tax applicable in N.Y. Canadian residents will be charged applicable taxes. Offer not valid in Quebec. This offer is limited to one order per household. Not valid for current subscribers to the Romance Collection or the Romance/Suspense collection. All orders subject to credit approval. Credit or debit balances in a customer's account(s) may be offset by any other outstanding balance owed by or to the customer. Please allow 4 to 6 weeks for delivery. Offer available while quantities last.

Your Privacy—The Reader Service is committed to protecting your privacy. Our Privacy Policy is available online at www.ReaderService.com or upon request from the Reader Service.

We make a portion of our mailing list available to reputable third parties that offer products we believe may interest you. If you prefer that we not exchange your name with third parties, or if you wish to clarify or modify your communication preferences, please visit us at www.ReaderService.com/consumerschoice or write to us at Reader Service Preference Service, P.O. Box 9062, Buffalo, NY 14240-9062. Include your complete name and address.

ROM15

DEBBIE MACOMBER

(limited quantities available)

TOTAL AMOUNT	$ _____
POSTAGE & HANDLING	$ _____
($1.00 for 1 book, 50¢ for each additional)	
APPLICABLE TAXES*	$ _____
TOTAL PAYABLE	$ _____

(check or money order—please do not send cash)

To order, complete this form and send it, along with a check or money order for the total above, payable to MIRA Books, to: **In the U.S.:** 3010 Walden Avenue, P.O. Box 9077, Buffalo, NY 14269-9077; **In Canada:** P.O. Box 636, Fort Erie, Ontario, L2A 5X3.

Name: _____

Address: _____ City: _____

State/Prov.: _____ Zip/Postal Code: _____

Account Number (if applicable): _____

075 CSAS

*New York residents remit applicable sales taxes.
*Canadian residents remit applicable GST and provincial taxes.

MIRA®

MDM1015BL

www.MIRABooks.com